TO CARVE A FAE HEART

THE FAIR ISLE TRILOGY BOOK ONE

TESSONJA ODETTE

1

Every young woman dreams of marrying a royal. A king, a prince, it doesn't matter, so long as he's richer than sin and handsome enough to fake a smile at. What else could a girl ask for?

Well, a working brain, for starters. And I do suggest all young women have one of those. That way, she'd know marrying a royal would be The. Worst. Thing.

You see, here in Eisleigh, all young women are eligible to be married off to a king. There's just one problem.

He'll probably eat you before you make it to your wedding bed.

And I'd rather not get torn to shreds by razor sharp fangs, thank you very much.

So you might be wondering why, after such a declaration, a sensible young woman like me would be traipsing through the woods toward the faewall in the middle of the night. I'll tell you why. To bribe my way to freedom.

Some might call it superstition to leave gifts for the

fae. If fae weren't real, I'd agree. Unfortunately for the residents of Eisleigh, they are real. Dangerously, terrifyingly, blood curdlingly real. And I'm not about to offend them tonight.

I hear a rustling nearby. The snap of a twig to my left. The crinkling of falling leaves. I whirl to find nothing but the silhouette of an owl launching from a branch overhead to soar into the night sky. With a shaking breath, I pull my heavy wool cloak tighter around me and refocus on the path ahead. Even with the moonlight speckling the forest floor, I can barely make out the well-worn trail between the trees.

Yet I manage, trying my best not to trip on twining roots and rocks and all sorts of earthly assassins bent on making me regret coming here alone. It's usually Mother who comes to the faewall with me. Or Amelie, my sister. Tonight though, it's just me. I'm too old to need the protection of my mother, and Amelie—well, I'm usually the one protecting *her* even though she's two years older than I am. Besides, she has better things to do tonight.

You're welcome, Amelie. I hope you're enjoying your date. Hopefully my hard work can keep us both from certain doom! In all honesty, I can't blame her for not being with me tonight. For all she knows, this might be her last night of freedom.

Once the trees begin to thin, I catch a glimpse of the faewall up ahead. The wall is always an unsettling sight, no matter how many times I've seen it. It's composed of massive standing stones, twice my height and three times as wide, set a dozen or so feet apart. Between the stones, all you can see is dense mist towering high into the sky, showing nothing of the fae lands beyond. The wall spans from one end of the Fair Isle to the other, dividing it in half to separate the human lands of Eisleigh from the fae lands of Faerwyvae.

A shiver crawls up my spine as I approach the wall. There's no mistaking the danger radiating from between each pair of stones and the mist beckoning behind them. Each *between* is an entrance to Faerwyvae, the place humans never go on purpose and never return from when they do.

My heart quickens, and I pat the sheathed dagger that hangs from the belt around my waist, feeling the comfort of its weight against my hip. With slow, creeping steps, I make my way to one of the stones, then unshoulder my bag. From within, I remove a plate and saucer—both marked with my family surname and the name of my village on the bottom—and set them on the ground at the base of the stone. Then I take out a heel of fresh brown bread and a canteen of goat's milk, placing the bread on the plate and pouring the milk into the bowl.

My movements are routine and reverent, following the tradition Mother taught me every year to commemorate the anniversary of the Hundred Year Reaping. It's meant to curry favor with the fae in a way that will ensure my sister and I won't be chosen for the next Reaping. Since the Hundred Year Reaping comes at dawn tomorrow, I could use that favor now more than ever.

I stare at my offering, then look at similar ones farther down the wall. At the next stone over, I see a patterned scarf with a sparkling, moonlit brooch perched upon it. Farther down, I'm almost certain I see the silhouette of an entire deer corpse.

I return my attention to my offering of bread and

milk. It's always been bread and milk, ever since I was a girl. Mother says anything fancier could draw the attention of the Reaping, while anything less could be seen as an insult fit for punishment. It seems the only way to guarantee my sister and I won't become the brides of monstrous fae is to remain respectfully unmemorable.

Why the fae give a lamb's ass about silly human offerings in the first place is beyond me. We couldn't possibly give them anything they don't already have in the fae lands. Besides, do fae even eat? Aside from human brains and the tears of young maidens?

I take one last glimpse at my offering, hoping it's enough to keep me and my sister safe, then turn around.

A new wall blocks my path.

A towering, brooding wall of shadow and teeth. I gasp and launch a step back. My vision clears and focuses, revealing the figure of a man, taller than me by two heads. He's dressed in dark, nondescript clothing beneath an equally dark cloak that makes it impossible to get an impression of anything but his face. That accounts for the shadows I saw at first glance. As for the teeth, I must have been mistaken, because there are none to be seen beneath his self-righteous smirk. My eyes trail from his mouth to his upturned nose and angled eyes.

A fae. Great.

It isn't unusual for fae to be seen on this side of the wall, but there are only two reasons one would be here at all. First, to cause trouble. This is most often performed by lesser fae—goblins, sprites, trolls. Second, to clean up said trouble. This is usually done by the fae ambassadors, sent by the high fae who like to pretend their kind mean us no harm. So which one is he? Trouble? Or charm?

It doesn't matter, I suppose. Even the most refined-seeming fae can tear out your heart before you see it coming.

I steady my breathing and put on a brave face, reminding myself to blink as I hold his gaze. If I forget to blink, he could maintain eye contact long enough to glamour me. Or, more accurately, he could maintain eye contact long enough to suppress the proper functioning of my amygdala.

This fae is just like any other creature, I remind myself. A dangerous creature, yes, but a creature bound by the laws of science. Science, I can understand. Science, I can confront.

Despite my mantra, I know I'm in the presence of danger. I'm vulnerable, small, wildly aware of my state of undress. My cloak suddenly seems too frail a thing to hide the fact that I'm wearing a thin cotton nightdress tucked into trousers. Why couldn't I have put on a proper top? Then again, I wasn't expecting to find anyone here, much less a fae. A towering, beautiful, horrible fae.

Luckily, his eyes don't stray to my clothing as he extends his hand toward the stones and the offerings at their bases. "Seeking favor, human? Hoping you'll be chosen to win the hand of King Aspen?" His voice is low and deep, dripping honey.

I suppress a laugh. Does he honestly believe any of us would *want* to be chosen as a bride of the fae? It's called the Reaping for a reason. Otherwise, we'd call it the Hundred Year Whimsy. Now, how do I answer that question without getting my face ripped off? "I ask only that my offering is received fairly and that my relationship with your kind maintains its good and distant standing."

His lips twitch, but I can't tell if he's on the verge of smiling or scowling. "Your gift comes too late. The Chosen have already been selected."

The blood leaves my face. The two Chosen have already been confirmed? But the announcement isn't made until dawn. "Is that why you're here? To finalize the names?"

"I just returned from doing so."

So he must be an ambassador after all. *But if he just came from finalizing the names...then that means...*

I can hardly finish the thought. No other village but my own is near this part of the faewall. I can only hope he came from farther south. With a deep breath, I say, "Might you tell me their names?"

He takes a step forward, a dangerous glint in his dark eyes. "For a price."

Of course. I should have known better than to step into that predictable trap. No peace of mind is worth making a bargain with a fae. "On second thought, I'll wait until dawn. I'll just be on my way then." I step to the side to skirt around him, but he's faster.

Again, his wall of a body is blocking me. "It will be an easy bargain. Give me your name and I'll give you theirs."

"Ha, I'm sure!" I regret the outburst as soon as it's made. Mother did say my mouth would be the death of me. But he's ridiculous if he thinks I'll fall for that! I know what he'd ask after I gave him my name. *Is that your true name you've given me?* Such an innocent question—if you're daft. But anyone who knows fae knows affirming he has my true name is all it takes to put me under his complete control. It would go beyond the power of a simple glamour, giving him the ability to make me do unspeakable things. A glamour, at least, ends by cutting eye contact. But giving one's name? Rumor has it only death can sever that level of control.

I gather my poise and put together a more polite reply. "Clever wording, but no, I will not give you my name."

He smiles wide. My eyes move to his mouth, looking for sharp teeth. In the dark, I barely get more than a flash of white between his full lips. "How about you *tell* me your name then. In return, I will tell you theirs."

My eyes flick back to his, and I turn his words over a few times in my head. I don't think he's left room for a trap. Breathe. Blink. Breathe. Blink. "Fine. I will tell you my name. It's Evelyn."

"Evelyn..."

I plaster a pleasant smile on my face. I'm sure it doesn't reach my eyes. "First names will do. Now it's your turn."

He glares, but his lips are curled with amusement. "You aren't afraid of me, are you?"

How could he ask me that? Surely, he can hear how loudly my heart is pounding in my chest. "Why would I be afraid?"

He lunges forward, lips peeling back with a snarl. Instead of lurching away, I stand my ground, dagger in hand as his fingers reach my neck. I raise my blade. He freezes, his nose an inch from the iron tip.

We hold our positions. His fingers are wrapped around my throat, the pressure uncomfortable, but not tight enough to constrict my breathing. My chest heaves. If he squeezes even the slightest bit more, I'll plunge my dagger into his eye socket. It wouldn't be easy. I've never killed a fae before, or anyone for that matter. But, as a more than capable surgeon's apprentice, I have a steady hand and am no stranger to cutting a blade into flesh. I know just how much pressure is needed to slice through every kind of tissue, know how deep and how hard I would need to thrust to reach vital organs.

His finger flinches at the base of my collarbone. I prepare to strike.

In the blink of an eye, he's taken a step back and his head is thrown back in bellowing laughter.

I keep my dagger raised, chest heaving with rage. "What's so funny?"

"I love being surprised. You're scared after all. Scared but unflinchingly prepared. You'd have killed me."

I swallow hard, resisting the urge to rub my neck as I glare back at him. "And you?"

He sobers from his laughter, but his smile remains wide. "I wasn't going to kill you. I simply wanted to see what you'd do. You're wise to carry iron around here."

"Thanks," I say through my teeth. "I'll be going now. Let me pass this time."

He turns to the side, extending a hand toward the forest in a perfect impersonation of a gentleman. I brush past him, the hilt of my blade still clenched in my fist.

"What about our bargain?" he calls after me. "Don't you want to know the names of the two Chosen?"

I pause, hesitating before I turn to face him. "Go on."

He doesn't move toward me, just holds my gaze for endless moments.

Breathe. Blink. Breathe. Blink.

Finally, he utters the words I'm waiting to hear. "Theresa and Maryanne Holstrom."

The Holstrom girls. From Sableton. *My* village. I should feel terror for them, anguish for their families. We grew up together, after all. But all I feel is relief. Sweet, overwhelming, glorious relief. I can't fight the smile that tugs at my lips, and I tip my head back and close my eyes. "Thank you," I whisper, although I don't know who I'm thanking. The fae? The stars? The Great Mother above?

I hear an amused laugh not too far away and remember the presence of the fae male. My eyes fly open and dart his way. But he's gone.

I whirl around, expecting him to be waiting menacingly behind me, but it seems the forest is empty. Good riddance. I return the way I came, no longer jumping at the sounds of snapping twigs or rustling leaves. Nothing can shake my joy right now. Nothing.

For the first time in my eighteen years of life, I can consider myself safe.

2

My bed trembles beneath me as if the very earth is shaking. And yet, I can't be bothered by it. Not when there's such delicious sleep to be had.

"Evie. Evie! Get up!"

The voice startles me fully awake, and I open my eyes to find Amelie's face an inch from mine. I groan and roll away from her. The bed returns to shaking, in earnest this time. Amelie is on her feet, bouncing from one side of my mattress to the other.

"Evie, how can you sleep? You haven't heard the news yet!"

The news. She must mean the announcement of the Chosen. How long did I sleep? Finally, I roll onto my back and look up at my sister. Her copper hair is backlit by the morning sun coming in through my window. Her green eyes are bright beneath her long, feathery, black lashes. She's dressed in one of her finest daytime dresses, a cream, lowcut gown with a mauve floral pattern. Of course, she's outfitted in a fancy dress. That's how she celebrates.

Amelie plops down on the bed next to me and takes me by the shoulders. She's grinning so wide, I can see all her neat, perfect teeth. "It's the Holstrom girls! It isn't us!"

I realize I should act surprised. There's no reason to tell her about my encounter last night, which would be the only excuse I'd have for knowing the news she's bursting at the seams to share. I sit, trying to look eager. "Oh? The Holstroms?"

Amelie's smile turns into a frown as my blanket slides from my shoulders. I follow her gaze and realize I'm still wearing my cloak. She pulls back the rest of the blanket, revealing the dirty hem of my trousers and mud-splattered boots.

"Really, Evie? You didn't even bother to remove your shoes before bed?"

I stretch and shift my legs to hang over the side of the mattress, then begin working at the laces of my boots. "I was tired. You know, from securing our great victory?"

Amelie floats to my dressing table and stares at her reflection in the mirror that hangs above it, prodding at her brows and cheeks. "That explains why I didn't see you at the plaza. When Mother and I left to hear the announcement, your boots weren't by the front door. We figured you'd already left."

I kick off one of my boots and begin unlacing the next, still puzzling over how deeply I slept last night. I don't think I've ever slept so well in my life. Relief will do that to a girl, I suppose. "Did I miss anything? Aside from the announcement itself, I mean?"

Amelie whirls toward me, grinning. "You should have

seen the look on Mrs. Holstrom's face when Theresa and Maryanne's names were called. She almost fainted!"

A pinch of guilt tugs my chest. Would our mother have fainted if she'd heard our names? But the sinking feeling evaporates before it can take hold. I'm still too grateful it wasn't us. "Fainted? That must have been a sight."

"*Almost* fainted. She did cry. A lot. The girls have already been taken beyond the wall. You should have seen the coach that came for them! Gold and pearl with dark, lustrous wood."

I stand and cross the cold floor to my window. "They've already been taken to Faerwyvae? What time is it?"

"It's almost noon." I meet Amelie's gaze and she frowns at my hair. She pats the chair at my dressing table. "Come. You look like a dead bird."

I should be offended, but I'm used to my sister finding fault in my appearance. She's always been the pretty one, the silly one, and the one most beloved by all the folk in our village. There's a reason she was out with a man last night while I was alone in the woods. She likes company and men and friends. I like practicality. And sleep.

I take a seat and Amelie stands behind me, immediately worrying at the knot in my hair that once was a braid. In the mirror, the contrast between us is stark. My sister is all copper hair, bright green eyes, pale peachy skin, and a smile that remains even when she's frowning —which she's doing now at my hair.

I, on the other hand, am a more subdued version of the girl behind me. My hair is a dark auburn that only looks remotely copper in direct sunlight, my eyes are a dull blue instead of green, my skin is far too bland to be considered peachy, and too dark to be considered fair. Then there's my smile. Let's just say the women in the village call it a *perpetual pout* when they're trying to be honest about my looks without being insulting. I do appreciate how sultry my perpetual pout makes me sound, but I know the truth of it. I look like I'm angry. All the time.

Once Amelie has finished undoing my braid, she sets to brushing out my tangles, a task that earns me a deeper frown from my sister. I smile. No matter how futile, she never gives up trying to make me presentable. "How was your date last night?"

I catch her eye-roll in the mirror. "It can hardly be called a date. It was nothing more than batting my lashes at Bertrand from across the parlor while stuck in awful chatter with his boring sisters for three hours straight." She pauses, then smiles. "We did kiss behind the stables before I left though. I thought we were going to be caught when his driver came looking for us. Thank the Great Mother Bertrand's fingers are like sausages, or he'd surely have had me out of my corset by then."

"Will you be seeing him again? Now that you know you're a free woman?"

"Why would I? I'm seeing Magnus tonight."

I furrow my brow. "Magnus?"

"Magnus Merriweather." She pauses her brushing, eyes going wide as she meets mine in the mirror. "I haven't told you, have I? That's the best part! After the announcement, Magnus invited me to dinner. Through his cousin, Annabel, of course. But I saw the way he looked at me from across the plaza. He and Theresa

Holstrom were practically engaged. Now that she's...well, you know...he has to marry me!"

"Has to?"

"Well, Theresa was obviously his first choice, but I've always known I was a close second."

"And you're happy about that?"

Amelie's smile grows radiant as she returns to brushing my hair. "Magnus is the most handsome man in Sableton. Maybe all of Eisleigh, though I haven't traveled the Isle much, as you well know. But I can't imagine a man more dignified than he. And now he's stuck with me. I couldn't feel luckier, Evie."

I try my best to suppress my laugh. Despite Amelie being what I very much define as a *silly person*, I never go out of my way to make fun of her. She may be two years older, but she's more fragile than I am, like a tiny violet in a patch of weeds. That fragility was almost the death of her once. I'll never forget what it felt like to think I was going to lose her, and I've been fiercely protective of her ever since.

"We're both free women now," Amelie says, shaking me from my thoughts as she pins my fully brushed hair into a low chignon the way I like. She's given up trying to get me to wear my hair down like hers. "How are you going to celebrate?"

My eyes fall on the stack of books on my dressing table. All are either human anatomy or medical guides, to aid my studies as a surgeon's apprentice. Hidden beneath the stack of books is a letter. A letter I've read and reread a dozen times or more since receiving it last month. I've been waiting to respond to it until this very day—the day I can declare my absolute freedom.

I feel my cheeks flush before the words are out of my mouth. Not with shame. With excitement. "I'm going to mainland Bretton. To medical school. I'm going to become a *real* surgeon."

Amelie's eyes go wide as if I've just told her I plan on exchanging my head for a new one. "The mainland? You're leaving the isle?"

My heart drops at the hurt in her tone. It was always my plan to leave the Fair Isle after the Reaping. I would have left already if it would have been allowed. According to the treaty, all young women who would come of age during the Reaping are forbidden to marry or leave the isle three years prior. You can only imagine the influx of weddings and moves to the mainland that took place three years ago. I was livid Mother wouldn't comply with my wishes and leave with us immediately. Amelie was furious she was forbidden to marry at age seventeen. But mother was fixed on staying in Eisleigh, convinced our offerings would keep us safe. *I understand the fae,* she would say. *We will not be driven from our home or forced into rash behavior. We'll work with them. You'll be safe, I promise.*

Mother was right. We're free from the Reaping once and for all. Now I can do what I've always wanted to do. "I'll still visit you and Mother."

Amelie forces a smile, but I can tell she's hurt. "When will you go?"

"I've been invited to join the fall quarter at Bennings University of Medical Arts. It begins at the end of the month."

My sister sighs, pinning the last strand of hair in place. She steps back, admiring her work, then places a hand on my shoulder. "You'll see me get married at least, right?"

I feel my throat grow tight as I stand to face her. "Of course I will."

Amelie pulls me into a hug with her slender arms. My head barely reaches her shoulder. "It won't be the same without you."

I blink back tears. "Nothing will be the same without you."

She releases me but keeps her hands on my shoulders. "Have you told Mother?"

"Told me what?"

I whirl to find Mother standing in the doorway.

"Evie is leaving us for medical school on the mainland," Amelie says with a pout, then floats away from me, past Mother, to my door. "Meanwhile, I have a man to steal. Good day." With that, she disappears into the hall, leaving me to face Mother alone.

3

"Is this true, Evelyn?" Mother asks, her voice soft. "You're moving to the mainland?"

I feel my shoulders collapse and have to turn away to avoid her tear-glazed eyes. "It shouldn't be a surprise." My voice comes out more defensive than I intend, but I'm not sure what to say. I wasn't ready for this conversation yet. *Thanks, Amelie.*

I grab a pile of clothes from my table and move behind my dressing screen. Again, I'm surprised to find my trousers so dirty and recall the night before. The wall. The offering. The fae male. I shake the memories from my mind and peel off the pants and nightdress and toss them to the floor. I don a fresh pair of wide-legged trousers, then retrieve my stiff corset from the floor. With a grimace, I wrap it around my waist. A moment later, I hear Mother's footsteps approach from behind, followed by the gentle pull of the laces. She knows better than to lace it as tight as Amelie's. Mother dislikes corsets almost as much as I do. However, she's convinced it's the burden we must bear for propriety's sake. At least until they fall out of fashion.

With my corset done, Mother returns to the other side of the screen, and I put on a cream satin blouse with round pearl-like buttons, followed by a short-waisted coat in a deep gray. I still can't meet Mother's eyes when I step out from behind my dressing screen, but I can feel her scrutiny at my trousers. I'm likely the only woman in my village who prefers trousers to dresses, and Mother hasn't decided her stance on them when it comes to propriety.

Not that propriety is Mother's only concern. She has her own curious ways, like her trailing scarves, colorful hair ornaments, and mismatched shawls. She's an odd mix of both me and Amelie, as if we were split from two sides of her personality, each taking an equal half. On one hand, Mother is whimsical, fair, and pretty like Amelie, with the same copper hair and green eyes. She knows how to fit into society and earn the acceptance of her peers. On the other hand, Mother has always been a bit of a secret rebel. She came to the Fair Isle from the mainland after she parted ways with my father. Yes, she *willingly* parted ways with a decent man, leaving the more traditional structure of the mainland for the less judgmental people of the isle. That's how she explains it, anyway. I've never known the residents of Sableton to be anything other than petty gossips with empty heads and rigid ways.

But the people here respect her, lone mother of two, witch of Sableton. Of course, she prefers the term healer. I prefer the term charlatan.

"When did you even apply to university?"

Finally, I meet her eyes. "I sent my application in the summer and received the reply a few weeks ago. They've invited me to join the next class. Ma, this is huge for me." I'm hoping the excitement in my tone will lift the corners of her mouth, but it doesn't.

"Why didn't you tell me?"

"Because I knew you'd be upset. Besides, I didn't want to say anything until we were safe from the Reaping."

"After all the work I've done to make sure I won't lose you, I'm going to lose you anyway."

I take a step toward her. "You did all that work to keep us *free*. That means giving me the freedom to choose."

Her eyes are pleading as she closes the distance between us and puts her hand on my cheek. "Couldn't you be happy here? Continue your path as a surgeon's apprentice for Mr. Meeks?"

With a groan, I skirt around her and head for my door. I hear Mother's footsteps fall behind me as I enter the hall and descend the stairs. "I don't want to be an apprentice forever. I want to be a full surgeon. Do you think Sableton has room for another one? No. Mr. Meeks will be surgeon here until he dies, and his son will be surgeon after him."

"Well, that's not a bad idea, Evelyn," Mother says as I reach the platform at the bottom of the stairs. "You could take the Meeks' example and do the same with me. You could learn my craft. You could help me run the apothecary."

Irritation courses through me. She's never stopped trying to convince me to *learn her craft*. I round on her.

"Ma, we've had this discussion a million times. I don't want to brew silly potions and make up stories from tea leaves. I don't want to lay my hands on people until their made-up ailments dissolve from their imaginations."

Mother's face falls, and I know my words were too cutting. "Is that what you think I do all day? Fool around and take people's money for nothing? How do you explain the things I know? The miracles people experience after working with me?"

I release a sigh and continue down the hall, past the parlor and the door that leads to the public shop that is Mother's apothecary. "I didn't mean it like that. It's just... there's a rational explanation for everything. I'm sure what you do *helps* people. Just not in the way I want to help people."

"But you have so much potential. I can feel it in you."

I enter the kitchen, where I take a seat at the thick wooden table, reaching for what remains of this morning's loaf of bread. "Mr. Meeks says I have potential too. Real potential. He says I have a steady hand and the right disposition for surgery. When I graduate from university, I'll have the skills I need to make a difference in the world. I can do more than just make people feel better. I can *save lives*."

"Someday you'll realize you have the power to save lives already inside you."

A wave of anger sends heat to my cheeks. "You mean, like you?"

Tense silence grows between us, and a flash of guilt crosses Mother's face. "You'll never forgive me for what happened with your sister, will you? It kills me that your sister suffered for my mistake, but I promise you, I would have taken her to Mr. Meeks before things got too far."

Again, I know my words were too harsh, but it's the truth. Amelie nearly died four years ago, not because of some mistake, but because of Mother's entire belief system. Mother may help people in her own way, but she doesn't save lives. Pretending she can only hurts the people who actually need medical intervention.

I avert my gaze to avoid the hurt look on her face, instead taking in the jars of herbs lining the shelves spanning each wall, strands of drying plants hanging from the ceiling, tinctures and potions brewing on the countertops in glass jars. The sight makes my muscles tense. It's chaotic and messy and none of it is *me*. I crave the order and neatness of a sterile surgery room, not the messy kitchen behind an apothecary. I let out a heavy sigh. "Ma, you know I forgive you. Amelie forgives you. But the fact remains that Sableton isn't where I belong. Eisleigh isn't where I belong."

"You'll never be happy on the mainland. There's no magic there, no—"

"I don't believe in magic. You know this."

Mother's lips flicker into a sad smile, and her tone becomes wistful. "You used to believe in magic. You used to help me make draughts and potions. You used to sit at my side all day and read the tea leaves of the shop patrons. Don't you remember what it was like back then? Amelie would play the piano and sing while you and I would lay our hands on the sick and cleanse their energy. You were so powerful then."

I shake my head. "I was a child. A little girl who

confused her imagination for magic and thought she gave offerings to the fae because they were friends with the humans. I know better now."

"If you don't believe in magic, how do you explain the fae?"

"The fae aren't magic. They're creatures like any other. Everything they do can be explained with science."

"Science doesn't explain everything," Mother says. "Sometimes you have to follow your heart."

With gritted teeth, I force a smile. "Lucky for me, both science and my heart are telling me to go to the mainland. That's my choice. You won't change my mind."

We hold each other's gaze, and I try my best to maintain my composure, even as Mother's eyes fill with tears. The bell rings from inside the shop. A male voice calls out, a patron entering the apothecary, but Mother makes no move to greet him. She looks like she wants to say more to me, to find the right words that will convince me to stay with her. *Nothing will convince me. Nothing.*

Finally, Mother averts her gaze and peeks out the window that looks into the shop. "Mr. Anderson is here for his tincture," she whispers.

I take the opportunity to shove a piece of bread in my mouth, but after the argument with my mother, its taste is bitter.

Mother leaves the table and heads to the doorway. She pauses beneath the arch, back facing me. Her voice comes out with more sorrow than I expect. "Don't lose all faith in magic, Evie. Keep at least a flicker of it alive in your heart and know no matter how far you go, you can always come back home."

She disappears into the shop, and I hear her cheerful

voice greet Mr. Anderson. I should feel victorious after winning the argument with Mother. I should feel excited about medical school.

But all I feel is empty, the haunting tone of Mother's words still echoing through my head.

The tang of blood mixed with the sharp aroma of alcohol fills the air of the surgery room. I refuse to tremble as I hazard a glance at the mangled limb of the patient and what used to be a hand. All that remains are strands of tissue, muscle, and bone in unnatural angles dangling from the forearm. Hank Osterman groans on the operating table, writhing beneath my hands as I keep a firm grip on his shoulders.

"Chloroform, Miss Fairfield," Mr. Meeks says, his voice calm yet firm.

I rush to obey, soaking a cotton cloth in chloroform, then placing it inside the metal inhalation cone. "It's going to be all right, Mr. Osterman." I try to mimic Mr. Meeks' calming tone as I cover the patient's nose and mouth with the cone. After a few breaths, his groans subside and his body grows slack.

"Tourniquet," Mr. Meeks says.

I fix the strap above Mr. Osterman's elbow, then turn

the screw that tightens the slack. The flow of blood begins to lessen.

"Bone saw."

I reach for the saw. My stomach dives as Mr. Meeks takes it from me. I'd hoped he would let me operate the bone saw this time. With hardly a blink, I swallow my disappointment and keep my eyes trained on Mr. Meeks' every move. His motions are smooth and deliberate. In no time, the lower arm is completely detached. I dispose of the mangled remains, then hand over clamps, needle, and thread, watching Mr. Meeks' deft fingers as he ties off arteries and stitches the skin together over the wound. Like always, I'm at a loss for words, awed with the power a surgeon like Mr. Meeks has. The power to save lives.

Sweat is dripping from my brow by the time the operation is over.

Mr. Meeks looks at me for the first time since the surgery began. His gray eyes crinkle at the corners as he smiles. "You did well, Miss Fairfield. I'm glad you were able to get here so quickly. It would have been quite the challenge without you, dear girl."

His praise lifts my shoulders, and I grin with pride. Never mind his tone erred on the side of patronizing. I like to tell myself he simply thinks of me too much like a daughter to forgo with the cosseting. "I'm glad I could be here too. Every chance I can learn the trade is a chance I'm eager to have."

"Yes, well, my son is on holiday on the mainland, as you know. Since he couldn't be here today, I'm pleased I was graced with the next best. Now, my dear, do clean up if you will. Mr. Osterman will be awake soon and I'd rather he didn't have to see this mess."

I deflate as Mr. Meeks shuffles out of the room. He didn't mean to insult me, I'm sure, but sometimes the old man can be quite daft, regardless of his genius status amongst the people of Sableton. I know he's fond of me as his apprentice, but he never hesitates to make it clear his son is his successor, not me. His special little fop of a son, who I'm sure hasn't spent half the time in the surgery room as I have. He clearly cares more about taking one holiday after the next than helping his dear old father.

Great Mother above, help the injured residents of Sableton once Mr. Meeks retires and leaves the village in the hands of his idiot son.

I shake out my wrists, realizing my nails have dug into my palms. *Never mind that. Never mind. It's not my concern anyway,* I remind myself as I grit my teeth and haul the tray of bloodied tools to the stove. *I'm going to medical school. I'm leaving Sableton behind for good.*

Once the tools have been cleaned, boiled, and dried, I untie my bloodstained apron, adding it to the basket of soiled laundry. I heft the basket and start toward the door when I hear a moan from behind me.

"Mr. Meeks!" I shout into the hall, then rush to the operating table where Mr. Osterman is beginning to stir. His eyelids flutter as he lets out another pained groan. Without so much as a tremble, I reach for the bottle of laudanum, extract a dropperful, then place the dropper between his lips. "This will help." He grimaces but doesn't fight me as I drop the liquid—thirty drops, with precision—into his mouth. I call for Mr. Meeks again. Even though I have everything under control, there's one thing I can't do alone, and that's help Mr. Osterman to the parlor. His towering weight would crush me, even if I could get him to walk mostly on his own.

The patient's groans subside, and his muscles begin to relax. "The fae did this," he mutters drowsily, one word rolling into the next. His lids are still fluttering over his eyes. "She tricked me. She made me put my hand...in a bear trap."

I freeze. A fae is responsible for this? Hank Osterman is one of the best hunters in Sableton. What kind of evil creature could trick him into doing such a thing? And why?

He lifts his head. It wobbles, giving him a glance at what remains of his arm before he rests it back on the table. He bares his teeth in an angry snarl. "I thought she was a woman. She *looked* like a woman."

His tone chills me, leaving me without a reply.

"Ah, Mr. Osterman, you're awake," Mr. Meeks says as he approaches the table, his surgeon's calm never faltering. "Come, let's get you to the parlor to wait for your wife."

"My wife," Mr. Osterman echoes.

"Yes, she's bringing the carriage. Come now." Mr. Meeks puts his hand behind the patient's head, helping ease him into a sitting position.

Mr. Osterman steadies himself with his good arm, and the amputated limb twitches, as if trying to copy the movement of the other. A wince of pain shoots across his face, and he closes his eyes.

I reach for the bottle next to me. "More laudanum."

Mr. Meeks shakes his head. "No, he's had enough for now. We'll send him home with a bottle for his wife to administer. Now, come Hank. On your feet."

Mr. Osterman doesn't obey. Instead, he opens his eyes and glances again at the severed arm. For endless moments he just stares at it. Then his shoulders heave, head falling into his remaining hand. Sobs tear out of him.

All I can do is stare with wide eyes as Hank Osterman —undoubtedly one of the strongest, burliest men in my village—is completely undone.

And the fae are to blame.

My heart sinks. I think about the Holstrom girls, gone nearly a week now. What's it been like living in Faer-wyvae, in that horrible, monstrous place? Are they being tormented by the same heartless creatures that did this to Mr. Osterman? The thought ties my stomach in knots. Now that the giddy relief over Amelie's and my safety has worn off, it's much easier to feel bad for the Holstrom girls.

As the minutes tick by, Mr. Osterman's sobs don't seem to be letting up, no matter how much Mr. Meeks tries to console him. Finally, Mr. Meeks takes a step away and turns to me with a whisper. "Poor man. I wish we could have done more for him."

I keep my voice low. "He said a fae was responsible. Do you think he was glamoured?"

Mr. Meeks looks back at his sobbing patient, expression grave. "He may have been, although I'd be surprised if that were true. He was wearing rowan berries around the arm we removed. I think it may be a matter of simple fae trickery."

"Rowan berries?" I'm shocked. Not by Mr. Osterman wearing them, but by Mr. Meeks' belief in them. He's always sharing his scientific theories with me, explaining the fae through logic. I never took the wearing of rowan berries to be anything more than superstition. A false magic.

"Rowan berries have proven to be effective at preventing a glamour," he explains. "It hasn't been studied thoroughly, but those of us in the scientific community believe rowan berries release a chemical upon skin contact that somehow helps preserve the function of our amygdala in the presence of the fae. That way, one need not rely solely on severing eye contact to prevent a glamour."

Awe washes over me as my lips pull into a grin. Logic never ceases to have that effect. "That actually makes sense."

Mr. Meeks pats me on the head. "Such an apt pupil. Now, run along, Miss Fairfield. Mr. Osterman wouldn't want a young lady to witness him in such a state." He tilts his head back at the sobbing man.

My grin slips from my lips. I want to remind him I'm more than just some *young lady*. I'm a surgeon's apprentice and soon-to-be medical professional. However, Mr. Meeks has always been the one person I can't bring myself to argue with. His mentorship has been my ticket to freedom. If I spoke to him the way I speak to most people, I never would have gotten the apprenticeship, much less kept it for the last two years. Instead, I nod and wish him a good evening.

As I'm about to pass through the door, Mr. Meeks says, "Oh, and don't forget the laundry, dear."

I grit my teeth, finding the basket I'd dropped earlier when Mr. Osterman woke. With an irritated sigh, I take it to the laundry room.

The September air is mild when I leave Mr. Meeks' house, the sun beginning to set. At the end of the drive, a carriage comes my way. It must be Mrs. Osterman. I refuse to look inside as I pass it, not wanting to witness the woman's worry. She must be terrified for her poor husband.

I take my time back to Ettings Street, where most of the shops are located. Once there, I stop at the post. We already got our letters this morning, but I'm eager to see if anything has arrived for us since. It's silly of me to expect anything from the university so soon. It's only been four days since I sent my acceptance letter. But that doesn't stop me from checking twice a day. A girl can't be sensible in *all* things, you know.

I leave the post empty handed, then continue my walk. At the other end of Ettings is Mother's shop, Fairfield Apothecary, which is also our home. It's nestled between the baker and the dressmaker. You can imagine Amelie's delight to be so near a dressmaker. As for me...I prefer the bakery.

My stomach growls at the thought. Surgery always works up an appetite for me. After all the gruesome parts are well past done, of course.

I can think of nothing but warm soup and buttered bread as the bakery comes into view. Then something unusual snags my attention—a figure walking toward me with sure, calculated steps. It's then I realize how quiet Ettings Street is. The few villagers passing between shops seem frozen as they watch the figure make his way along the sidewalk.

He's fae.

My mind brings forth visions of the fae I met at the

wall, and I try to find what I remember of his features in the male coming my way. But this fae is undoubtedly shorter, stouter. He wears thick-rimmed spectacles, which I didn't know fae wore, and a long, burgundy and bronze jacket that reaches his ankles. Beneath the jacket, he wears a pair of cream trousers, a russet waistcoat, and a bronze cravat in a floral pattern. The only similarity between him and the fae from the wall is the smug smile.

I don't meet his eyes as he passes by, but a shiver runs down my spine once he's behind me. I can guess where he's heading. He's clearly a fae ambassador and likely on his way to smooth things over with the Ostermans.

A fae drawing human blood could be seen as an act of war—*should* be seen as an act of war. Yet, I already know that's not how things will go. The ambassador has probably already spoken with the mayor, delivering sleek words and sorry excuses for the troublesome fae's unwitting behavior. Then he'll go to the Ostermans, offer to pay for the surgery we performed and make financial amends for loss of limb and income. The council will let it slide. Again. Just another accident. A misunderstanding.

I'm so angry, I could explode. It's then I notice the street has remained quiet. The villagers are still loitering outside the shops, staring at where the fae ambassador went. I whirl around, but he's out of sight. It makes me wonder if something else happened. Maybe the mayor *didn't* cave for once.

Whatever the case, the mood on Ettings Street has me rattled. I quicken my pace, forgetting the bakery as I make a straight line for home. That's when I realize the villagers aren't staring after the fae ambassador. They're watching *me*.

Nausea wrenches my gut as my mind begins to spin. There's a reasonable explanation for this. Maybe they're only staring because I had the nerve to walk past the fae while everyone else stood frozen in fear.

I want to be right. I have to be right.

As I reach the door to the apothecary, I'm surprised to find it in the process of opening. I'm more surprised when Harriet, the baker from next door, is revealed coming from behind it. Her face is pale, and when her eyes find me, her lips pull into a sympathetic frown. She reaches a hand and places it on my shoulder. "I brought you some bread, dearie."

"Bread," I echo, brows knitting together as I try to puzzle together her words with her expression. It isn't unusual for Harriet to bring us bread. We buy some from her almost daily. So why is she saying it like an apology?

Harriet nods. "I had plenty left over after I brought some to the Holstroms."

I stare at her, unable to make sense of her seemingly disconnected statements. "What's this all about?"

Her eyes widen and her mouth falls open, but she doesn't say anything.

Terror seizes my chest. "What's going on?"

She squeezes my shoulder. "You should talk to your mother."

I don't wait to see Harriet the rest of the way out the door before I rush into the shop. The front is empty, so I barrel into the kitchen, then to the parlor. That's where I find them.

Amelie is lying on the couch, her head in Mother's

lap. Her cheeks are flushed and streaked with tears as she sobs uncontrollably into a white kerchief. Something sparkles from the finger of the hand she's dabbing her tears with. A ring.

I meet Mother's eyes and find her staring blankly ahead, face devoid of all color.

"Ma, what happened?"

She slowly turns to meet my gaze, but her expression remains empty. "The Holstrom girls are dead. You and Amelie are being sent to Faerwyvae in their place."

5

Mother's words make no sense. They are neither rational nor reasonable. And they do nothing to stop my mind from spinning. There's no way she can mean what I think she means. My voice comes out shaky. "Ma, what are you talking about?"

She looks from me to Amelie, then strokes my sister's hair. Amelie lets out a louder sob.

"Let's speak in the kitchen." Mother gently scoots Amelie's head off her lap, leaving her to nestle deeper into the couch.

I follow her to the kitchen. "Please tell me what's happening. I feel like I'm losing my mind."

Her eyes are glazed as she takes two mugs and a jar of herbs, then sets them on the kitchen table. "The fae ambassador just left after coming here to tell me all of this. I've hardly had time to process it myself."

My eyes widen. The fae I saw a moment ago...he came from *here*? No wonder everyone was staring at me.

Mother spoons some herbs into the mugs, then places

the kettle on the stove. She returns to face me. "He explained the Holstrom girls were...executed last night."

"Executed! Why?"

"All the ambassador would say is that the girls were found guilty of treason by King Aspen."

I put my hands on my hips. "We're supposed to believe sweet little Theresa and Maryanne Holstrom committed treason against a fae king? That's insane. What exactly was their treasonous crime?"

She sighs. "You know how the fae are."

Cruel. Irrational. Evil. "You mean they offended him. Wore the wrong color on the wrong day of the week. Forgot to say some silly rhyme before eating fae food. Is that it?"

Mother doesn't answer. It's not like I expect her to know the truth anyway. The ambassadors never come with the truth. They come with excuses.

I grind my teeth. "Why are we being sent to Faerwyvae? They got their Chosen for the Reaping. It's not our fault the king executed them already."

She shakes her head. "The ambassador says the marriages hadn't taken place yet. The treaty states at least one marriage must take place between a Chosen and a fae every hundred years to secure the pact."

"What does the treaty say about the fae executing their fiancées? Drawing human blood is an act of war."

Her voice comes out soft. "So is treason." The emptiness in her tone is so resigned. So final. So hopeless.

I fight back tears, focusing instead on the flicker of indignation burning inside me. "You're just going to let this happen? You're going to let them take us?"

When she meets my eyes, her expression hardens,

turning to anger. Not at me, I realize, but at the situation. "I don't know what else to do. I thought I did everything to keep the two of you safe. I thought you'd *always* be safe."

Anger is growing inside me too, and my words come out bitter. "You mean you never saw this in your cards? In your tea leaves? In all the times you took us to the wall with our offerings, promising us you *understood* the fae?"

"Evie, I—"

"Where is your precious magic now, Mother? Are your tinctures going to save us? Your potions and draughts? Do you have any mystical talismans to hang around our necks to ensure we don't lose our heads?" My words are laced with sarcasm, and I watch as she wilts beneath them.

As her expression falters, so does my heart. I shouldn't have said any of that; my anger isn't meant for her. Yet, I'm too full of fury to apologize. If I take it back now, the rage will rot inside me, eating me alive.

The kettle whistles from the stove, saving me from the tension growing between us.

"We were going to get married by the sea," says a wistful voice.

With a jump, I whirl around to find Amelie hovering in the doorway to the kitchen, eyes unfocused. I go to her, placing a hand on her arm.

She meets my eyes, then holds up a frail hand, the one bearing the ring. It's a ruby on a circlet of gold. "Magnus asked me to marry him this afternoon. Now I'll...I'll never..."

Mother pushes a mug of tea into Amelie's hands as a fresh sob escapes my sister's throat. "Drink."

Amelie does as told, then wanders back to the parlor. The sight of her uneven steps chills me to the bone.

Mother sighs, closing the lid to her jar of herbs with more force than necessary. "I should bring this to the Holstroms. It will help with their nerves. You may not believe in my craft, Evie, but I know Mrs. Holstrom will appreciate it."

I want to tell her laudanum would be far more effective than whatever herbal infusion she's created, but I hold my tongue. I've said enough already. And if I'm not ready to apologize...

I hold out my hand for the jar. "I'll take it to them."

Mother cocks her head, then seems to understand the olive branch I'm offering. "Very well. But don't stay long. The ambassador will be back at midnight..." Her words dry up, ending with a choked sound.

Midnight. Amelie and I will be taken to Faerwyvae at midnight.

The house suddenly seems too small for my swarm of thoughts, for the anger and confusion and shock swirling inside. I take the jar from Mother, then rush outside faster than I can blink.

I make my way to the Holstrom farm, which is on the northern edge of Sableton. The sky is almost dark by the time I arrive, but there's enough light to stop me when I reach their gate. For there in front of the farm lies a scene far more gruesome than anything I've witnessed during surgery.

The grounds in front of their stables and pens are littered with dismembered bodies. Animal bodies. Pigs, sheep, goats. Blood splatters the dirt, entrails stream between corpses. I take a step back, bile rising in my throat. This could be none other than the work of fae.

"Disgusting," says a voice at my side. I hadn't noticed Maddie Coleman arrive. She holds a basket full of coffee, chocolate, and other exotic food items. Her parents own the biggest merchant ships in Eisleigh, and her uncle is the mayor—which she thinks makes her Queen of Sableton. She wrinkles her nose at the scene before us but doesn't seem nearly as disturbed as I am. When she turns to me, her eyes fall on the jar of herbs in my hand. "What a quaint gift."

I watch as she sways side to side, as if trying to accentuate the oversized gift basket in her arms.

"Mother sent me," I say flatly.

"Mine sent me as well, although I doubt the Holstroms need it. Visitors have been coming all day." She returns to face the yard. "And yet, they still haven't managed to clean this unsightly mess. How are we supposed to make it to the front door without soiling our dresses?" Her eyes trail from the gore to my trousers, prompting a smirk. "Or should I say, dress?"

I glare at her. "They're probably too busy grieving their daughters to clean right now."

She turns her nose to the air, her blond curls at the sides of her head bobbing with the movement. "They deserve it. Their daughters committed treason, after all."

My mouth falls open, and I imagine punching Maddie Coleman in her perfect pink nose. "How can you say such a thing? You really think the Holstroms deserved the execution of their daughters? And for their entire farm to be destroyed?"

She rolls her eyes. "King Aspen gifted the Holstroms

with enchanted farm animals, a blessing that would have led to riches for generations to come. And what does he get in return? Two treasonous girls."

"First off, the farm animals weren't enchanted, they were simply well-bred. Second, Theresa and Maryanne couldn't have done anything to deserve execution. You know that, right?"

She shrugs. "Perhaps the Holstroms wanted the war to return. Uncle says some residents of Eisleigh are in favor of another war to win the Fair Isle from the fae."

I'm surprised by this. Could some of our villagers actually want another war? Could the Holstroms be among those who do? I shake the idea from my head. There's no way the Holstroms would put their daughters' lives in danger in favor of war. Both the fae and the humans nearly perished during the last one a thousand years ago. The treaty was the only reason the bloodshed was able to end.

"I was supposed to be next in line, you know," Maddie says, eyes narrowed at me. "Marie and I were supposed to be chosen next if the Holstrom girls didn't work out. I was to marry King Aspen, and Marie was to marry Prince Cobalt. But *you* were chosen instead."

It takes me a moment to register what she's implying. "Wait...you *wanted* to be chosen for the Reaping? To be married off to a fae?"

"A fae *king*."

"A fae king with horns."

Maddie rolls her eyes. "He's called the *Stag King*. It's more likely he has antlers."

I flourish my free hand. "Wow, what a difference that makes."

"It does make a difference. And for someone who's always telling everyone how clever and sensible she is, you should get your facts straight before spouting off about them."

Heat rises to my cheeks. Since when does Maddie Coleman get the upper hand in an argument with *me*? "When did you become such a diehard fae lover? Last time I saw you in the presence of a fae, you ran screaming. You probably wet your knickers too."

"That was a goblin, not a king," she says. "Besides, I'd take horns, antlers, or fangs if it makes me a queen, not to mention the wealth and riches my family would be blessed with."

My eyes bulge with the restraint it takes to keep from laughing in her face. "Well, it turns out when the Great Mother was handing out working brains, she passed you over entirely. Regardless, I have the perfect solution for us both. If you want so badly to marry the Stag King, by all means, take my place."

Her mouth falls open, cheeks burning crimson as she processes my insult. Then with a scowl, she snaps her mouth shut and averts her gaze. "I can't."

"Why not? Your uncle is the mayor. He's in charge, isn't he?"

"My uncle is in charge of Sableton, but he has no control over the fae."

"What does that have to do with anything? The names have already been selected. If you were chosen as backup, then why are Amelie and I involved at all?"

Her lips press into a tight line, as if it pains her to say the next words. "You were chosen by the fae. It was a choice that overrode all previous selections."

My mind goes blank. "Why? Amelie and I have done nothing to attract the attention of the fae."

"You weren't selected as a pair, stupid," Maddie says. "*You* were selected. Personally. Your sister is only involved because of you."

I'm too shocked; I can't even bristle at her insult this time. "I was...selected?"

"The fae ambassador requested you by name. *First* name."

By name. My entire body goes cold.

I can do nothing but gape, words stripped from my lips as I make sense of Maddie's statement. I was chosen by name. Me. That can mean only one thing. I'm being punished.

I think back to my visit at the faewall and the cloaked fae ambassador. He's the only reason the fae would know me by first name and the only fae with motive to punish me. Images of my blade hovering in front of his face, ready to strike, flood my memory. But he attacked me first! Or was it my sharp tongue that sparked his ire?

It could have been anything, honestly. I frowned too much, spoke too much, spoke too little. Offended him with a misinterpreted gesture, said the wrong word in the wrong tone. Who knows what makes the fae react in anger? Why did they execute the Holstrom girls? Why did they slaughter their animals? Why did they trick Hank Osterman into sticking his hand in a bear trap?

There's no purpose trying to figure it out. The fae are

unpredictable. Dangerous. And I'm about to be the bride of one.

The fight is leached from my bones. I can't even feel my rage anymore. Only hollowness remains.

I shove my mother's jar on top of Maddie's basket without a word, then turn away from the farm. Maddie calls after me, but I don't answer; I can't even make out what she's saying through the sound of blood rushing through my ears.

This is all my fault.

THE DARK OF NIGHT HAS FULLY SETTLED IN BY THE TIME I make it back to Ettings Street. My eyes are unfocused as I wander the sidewalk toward the apothecary, only narrowing when I notice a hulking shape in front of the shop. A carriage.

I stop, mind reeling as I process what time it might be. Surely it isn't midnight yet! But the carriage parked in front of my home is undoubtedly fae. I can't make out the color in the dark, but vines of gold twine up the edges, glinting in the moonlight. The horses at the front of the carriage are thin, dark, unearthly creatures.

With a shudder, I run to the door of the shop and dart inside. I find Mother in the parlor. Her hands are on her hips as she scowls at a figure standing in the middle of the room. He's stout and barely taller than Mother, with neatly trimmed brown hair, pointed ears decorated with gold jewelry, and brown slanted eyes behind horn-rimmed glasses. His jacket is pristine lines of burgundy and bronze with elaborate golden clasps shaped like leaves down the front. It's the fae I saw in the village earlier.

Mother whirls toward me with a sigh. She returns to face the fae, irritation tensing her posture. "I told you she'd be back," she snaps.

The ambassador shrugs. "You must understand my suspicion."

"No, I must not," Mother argues. "The girls aren't to be taken until midnight. They still have three hours until then."

"I am simply here to assure they comply. Don't mind me. I won't be a bother."

"No, you won't be," Mother says, "since you'll be waiting in your carriage."

The ambassador looks shocked, his hand moving to his chest as if she suggested he wait in a gutter. I'm equally surprised. Mother has never spoken about the fae with anything but reverence and curiosity, or at the worst of times, with amused frustration. It shows how hopeless our situation really is.

When the ambassador makes no move to leave, she takes a step toward him. "There's nothing in the treaty that states you are allowed in my house while my children pack for their imprisonment. Now go. They'll be out the door at midnight."

He sniffs, then turns on his heel.

I listen for the sound of the front door opening and shutting, then let out a heavy breath. "Three hours until midnight?"

Mother nods, her expression unreadable. She looks angry and hopeless all at once, but there's something else there I can't place. "I'll be in the kitchen," she whispers, then brushes past me out of the parlor.

I consider following her but don't. I'm not ready to face her after the hurtful things I said earlier. Especially since I know whatever I say to her next will be the last she'll hear from me again.

My throat feels tight as I make my way up the stairs toward my room. As I reach the top landing, I hear whimpering coming from the door straight ahead. Amelie's room. I tiptoe forward and peek through the crack between the door and the frame. Amelie is in the middle of her floor, surrounded by her favorite dresses. An over-stuffed bag lies at her feet, more dresses spilling from it. I'm about to enter her room when I stop myself. How can I try to comfort her when I know I'm to blame? Does she already know? Does Mother know?

Tears spring to my eyes at the sight of my sister, but I force myself to leave, quietly crossing the hall to my bedroom. Once inside, I sit at the edge of my bed. Part of me wants to cry, to fall into a fit of sobs on my floor like Amelie. The other part of me won't let me cry, knowing I must be strong for the both of us.

My eyes rove my room, taking in everything I'm leaving behind. I expect to feel nostalgic, but I don't; I was already planning on leaving here anyway. My room isn't full of trinkets and luxuries like Amelie's is. My wardrobe isn't brimming with gowns and beaded slippers. The thing I treasure most of all lies on my dressing table—the invitation to university.

Longing tugs at my heart. My mind races to think of some way out of this. *Any* way out of this. I imagine sneaking out the back door, leaving before the ambassador returns to escort us to the carriage. How far could I get by midnight if I left now? I could take the money I've saved for university, use it to take me south where I can catch a ship to the mainland.

Excitement sparks within me, a smile nearly pulling at my lips. Then it all comes crashing down. I think of Amelie. What would happen to her if I ran away? Would they still take her? Punish her with a fate worse than being a fae's bride? No, I can't leave her, especially when I'm to blame for this mess. Could I convince her to come with me?

My sensible side takes over, and I know running away is neither logical nor possible. A marriage must take place for the treaty to be upheld. Our village has already lost two girls to the Reaping without securing the pact. What will happen if we break the treaty too? The council could select another set of Chosen. The fae could request another girl to be punished.

Or it could start a war. A war that brought near-annihilation a thousand years ago. A war I'd be responsible for.

I close my eyes, shutting the door to all my thoughts of escaping this. My dream of moving to the mainland is over. I won't be going to university nor will I become a great surgeon. I won't be anything but a bride. If the fae let me live that long.

Anger returns to me in a rush, making my hands clench into fists. I stand and stride over to my wardrobe, flinging the doors open with more force than necessary. From the bottom of the wardrobe, I extricate a bag. Beneath it lies a wooden case. I take that too and bring both to my bed. I open the case, revealing an array of tools—bone saw, tourniquet, scalpel, trephine, forceps, tenaculum, knives. My surgery kit, a gift from Mr. Meeks on my eighteenth birthday. A gift I never got to use.

Most significantly, the tools are carbon steel—an alloy I know contains iron. Whether an iron alloy has any effect on the fae, I don't know. But I'm willing to find out.

I close the box and place it at the bottom of the bag. Then I return to my wardrobe and pull out my cloak. From my dressing table, I retrieve my nightdress, an extra pair of trousers and a blouse, as well as my belt and dagger. I stuff the clothing in my bag and secure the belt around my waist. The dagger at my hip and the blades inside my bag have cooled some of my rage. I feel safe now. In control.

I may have to marry a monster. I may never get to leave Faerwyvae again. But I won't go down without a fight. The treaty may force me to marry, but as far as I know, it says nothing about letting a fae touch me or letting one come anywhere near me. In fact, I doubt it says anything about my husband needing to be alive for the treaty to remain valid.

I'll go to Faerwyvae. I'll do my part. I'll sacrifice myself for the safety of Eisleigh. But if any of the fae try to hurt me or my sister, I'll be ready. My future husband can try all he likes to touch me, but he'll find no luck with an iron blade between us.

I grin, but it's short lived as my thoughts return to Amelie. There will be times when my blade will only be able to protect one of us, times when we'll have to leave each other's sides. How will I keep her safe?

The door creaks open behind me, and I turn to find Mother in the doorway. We lock eyes, staring wordlessly, until she joins me at my bed. She places a stoppered jar on top of the clothing in my bag. "Tincture of iron, St. John's Wart, and daisy. Take half a dropperful daily."

She wants me to ingest...an iron supplement?

Everyone in Eisleigh knows iron is our greatest defense against the fae, something humans discovered during the war. Most people think it's magic that makes iron so harmful to the fae, but Mr. Meeks explains they have a severe allergy to the metal, preventing their blood from clotting and their wounds from healing. He says their olfactory system is highly attuned to it, allowing them to avoid it through scent. I think of the slaughtered animals at the Holstrom farm, of Hank Osterman's mangled arm. While I'm not sure having adequate levels of iron in my blood will keep me from getting killed by a fae, at least I'll less likely get eaten by one.

My mouth falls open, realizing Mother has never seemed more brilliant than she does now. Before I can thank her, she takes my hand and presses a pouch into my palm. "Salt all your food. Even a pinch will counteract any harmful magic. Turn your clothes inside out. And wear this at all times." She takes a long strand of odd-looking red beads and places them around my neck.

I run my fingers along the necklace. Dried rowan berries. I remember what Mr. Meeks said about them, how they help preserve proper brain function through skin contact. Mother has been selling them in her shop for years, something I'd always scoffed at before hearing Mr. Meeks' explanation today. For once, her craft has aligned with logic.

Yesterday's magic is today's science, Mr. Meeks likes to say.

Perhaps my mother deserves more credit. She may be giving people false hope with her silly magic, but only rarely do her treatments cause real harm. I'll never believe in her craft, but sometimes her treatments are rooted in science. She just doesn't know it.

More than that, she deserves credit for being my mother. For loving me with all my sharp words and harsh edges, hardly ever giving me more than a word of reproach when I cross the line. If she can love me with all my flaws, I can love her with all of hers. And I do. So much, I feel like my heart is being torn in two.

"Ma." The word comes out in a sob as I wrap my arms around her neck and breathe in her scent. Her arms go around me, and she rubs my back like I'm a child again. For a while, I let myself be a child, let Mother comfort me and stroke my hair. I take it all in—every word, every whisper, every angle of her face and shade of red in her hair—and lock it into my memory.

That's the only place I'll ever see her again.

7

Three hours later, Amelie and I sit in the carriage across from the bespectacled fae ambassador, riding through the night toward the fae lands.

My eyes feel raw and red, my throat like sandpaper each time I swallow. At least my tears have dried. I refuse to show weakness in front of the fae male across from me.

Amelie, on the other hand, continues to whimper and cry. Her cheeks are red and coated in a sheen of fresh tears. We sit close, her arm entwined with mine, my wrist held in her vise-like grip. Her free hand tugs at the seam of her inside-out dress, then fiddles with the strand of rowan berries she wears. I can only imagine her distress at being forced to be dressed so unfashionably, regardless of circumstance.

Once Amelie falls asleep, head on my shoulder, the carriage goes silent. I force myself to stay awake as the hours pass, constantly checking on the presence of my dagger hidden beneath my cloak. The ambassador doesn't utter a word as he alternates between staring out the window of the carriage and leaning back for a nap.

It isn't until sunlight is beating my eyelids that I realize I've fallen asleep. I jerk upright, my hand flying to my dagger. Still there. The movement has woken Amelie, who lifts her head from my shoulder and sniffles. Her hand returns to squeezing my wrist.

Now that the sun has risen, warm light beams inside the carriage, drawing my curiosity. I lean forward just enough to see out the window. There I find sunlight diffused through a canopy of leaves in reds and golds and coppery brown, blinking like stars as they sway on the wind. The trees are birch and oak and others I can't identify. September may be beautiful in Sableton, but this is beyond any fall landscape I've ever seen. My breath catches in my throat, but I suppress my wonder, forcing my gaze away from the window as I settle back into my seat.

"We've entered Autumn, as you can tell," the ambassador says. He has a lazy, high-pitched way of speaking. It reminds me of the few nobles I've met, or snobs like Maddie Coleman.

His words puzzle me, and my intellectual needs override my desire to remain aloof. "When you say we've entered autumn, what exactly do you mean?"

"The Autumn Court, obviously," he says. "Your new home."

It never occurred to me to care to learn about King Aspen or the court he rules, but it does explain the unearthly beauty of our surroundings. Yet, his words, *your new home,* have left a sour taste in my mouth that no intellectual stimulus can erase.

His eyes move from me to Amelie. "There's no reason to be scared, you know. Honestly, it's silly the way you cower like that."

I shoot him a glare. "Silly? You think we're *silly*? Was it silly for the Holstrom girls to be executed?"

He lets out a trill of laughter. "Oh, that. Yes, I can see why that would frighten you. But you need not worry. That is, unless you're plotting treason. You don't seem the type though."

"Did Theresa and Maryanne seem the type?"

His brows furrow. "Now that I think about it, no, they didn't. Hmm." His smile returns as if we haven't been speaking about death and treason at all.

But I'm not done with the subject. "Why did they die?"

He shrugs. "We already told the human council. They performed an act of treason."

"Cut the lies," I say. "What's the real reason? What exactly did they do to earn a death sentence?"

"First off, fae can't lie. Second, that is a classified matter. If you'd like to ask the king when you meet him, perhaps he'll tell you. For now, just know their crime was grave indeed."

I roll my eyes. "Is that the same excuse you gave for poor Hank Osterman? I'm sure you were sent to tidy up that mess as well. Or did they send the ambassador in the black cloak instead?"

"Ambassador in a black cloak? Hank Osterman? I assure you, I know neither of these people. Care to enlighten me?"

I narrow my eyes at him. "I'm sure you know about Mr. Osterman. He lost his arm because of one of you. A fae tricked him into sticking his hand in a bear trap. What clever words were used to excuse that act?"

The ambassador pulls his head back in surprise. "You mean the Butcher of Stone Ninety-Four?"

"The what?"

"The Butcher of Stone Ninety-Four," the ambassador says, like it's supposed to be obvious. "That man is a menace. He comes hunting near the wall and enters Faerwyvae between stone ninety-four and stone ninety-five on the Spring axis. He enters only as far as he can get away with and leaves traps, hoping to catch the kind of fae he can sell for parts. Is that the man you speak of?"

"No, of course not! Hank Osterman would never—"

"He was injured just yesterday, right? Caught in his own bear trap? Fae trap, more like."

I hesitate. Mr. Osterman hadn't said if it was his own trap or not, but it's possible. "Yes, and one of your lesser fae—"

He hisses a sharp intake of breath. "Ah, we don't use that term. That's a human convention. Lesser fae and high fae are labels we in Faerwyvae take offense to. We prefer unseelie and seelie."

I glower. "One of your *whatever* fae tricked him into mangling his hand. He had to have his entire lower arm amputated."

The ambassador cackles. "Oh, Lorelei. What a scamp."

Heat rises to my cheeks. "A scamp. That's what you call a creature that tricks a man into losing his arm?"

"It's not like he didn't have it coming. She isn't the first fae the Butcher of Stone Ninety-Four has terrorized. He caught Lorelei's lover too. Probably sold her wings to a merchant and dumped her body in a ditch. Don't even get me started on the unicorns. I don't know how much longer I would have been able to cover for his treachery. Lorelei's little stunt likely saved us from war."

I'm at a loss for words. The ambassador must be mistaken. The fae may be adamant that they can't lie, but I'm sure it has more to do with cultural custom than physical ability. Besides, even if he were incapable of lying, it wouldn't mean he's telling the truth. He must not *know* the truth. Because the Hank Osterman I know would never hunt unicorns or kill fae. Would he?

"The lesson is, don't set traps and you'll be fine," the ambassador says.

"A simple matter then."

"Exactly!" he says with an approving nod.

I frown. Another stretch of silence falls over the carriage until a new question comes to mind. "Which are you? Seelie or unseelie?"

"Obviously, I'm seelie. I'm dressed in regal clothes and riding in a carriage, aren't I?"

"Is that all the difference amounts to?"

"Do you know nothing of Faerwyvae? Are you not taught our ways growing up, like we are taught about yours?"

We are, but I don't say so out loud. For the things we are taught about the fae are hardly flattering.

He huffs. "I'm an ambassador, not a nursery maid. Regardless, I'll educate you. All fae once were unseelie, which you so callously deem lesser fae. Back when the isle was ours alone and no human had set foot here, we were different. We were...creatures, you might say. Spirits. Animals. We were so alive back then." His voice sounds wistful. "Or so I'm told, at least. I'm hardly old enough to have been born that long ago. In any case, we didn't start to change until your kind came to the isle."

I find myself leaning forward, genuinely curious to hear what he has to say. I've been told about the war between the humans and fae, the repercussions, the treaty, but never anything about what the Fair Isle was like before.

He continues. "We were curious about these newcomers, and they were equally curious about us. There were mishaps and misunderstandings, of course, but for the most part, we were friendly with the humans. Then the humans started leaving us gifts, sharing their food. You taught us words, made us clothes. That's when we began to change."

"How did you change?"

"We began to feel like you, look like you, hurt like you. It was a curse. And a blessing. We experienced things we never had before. Love. Hate. Rage. Passion. Sorrow. Some of us welcomed these changes, exploring the vast array of new experiences. The others retreated from human settlements, vowing never to eat human food or wear human clothes again. That was the beginning of the divide between seelie and unseelie. The unseelie considered seelie fae unnatural, an abomination of what we were meant to be. They wanted the isle back, for the humans to be eradicated. The seelie, meanwhile, weren't willing to give their new identities away and wanted to protect their friends, the humans. And...well, you know the rest."

I'm not sure I do, but I can't find the words to admit it.

"Which one is my husband?" Amelie's voice startles

me. It's the first time she's spoken since we left home. "Seelie or Unseelie?"

"Well, at present both King Aspen and Prince Cobalt are politically seelie," the ambassador says. "However, King Aspen tends to shift unseelie from time to time, both physically and politically. He has a temper, you know."

Amelie blanches, her hand clutching her rowan berries. "Which am I to marry?"

"That depends. Marriages from previous Reapings were made according to age. By the way, not all got to marry kings and princes, you know. You're lucky. The last Reaping from a hundred years ago paired the girls with minor cousins of the Summer Court Queen. Now, which of you is Evelyn Fairfield?"

"I am."

"Pleased to meet you, Miss Evelyn Fairfield," he says with a bow of his dark head. "My name is Foxglove. Forgive me for not introducing myself until now. I wanted to make sure the two of you had a good and proper sulk. Young human females seem fond of doing such. I take it you are the eldest?"

Amelie springs forward in her seat, an appalled look on her face. "Evie? Eldest! That's absurd."

I pat her knee and say to Foxglove, "Amelie is eldest."

Amelie leans back in her seat, arms crossed over her chest. "Why would you assume me to be the younger?"

Foxglove scratches the side of his head, then adjusts his spectacles. "I'm not sure. I do suppose you are taller, now that you are sitting upright and no longer have the tears of a small child in your eyes."

Amelie's mouth falls open. "Tears of a child? How

rude! And another thing. Never mind how tall I am. Even if I wasn't taller, I'd still be older. Height is hardly an indication."

I suppress a grin. It's nice to see Amelie acting like herself again.

"I was certain height was an indication of human age, but I was obviously mistaken," Foxglove says.

"Does your kind keep growing forever, then?" I ask, imagining monstrous, mountainous fae strolling through the trees, heads above the treetops.

"Only for several hundred years. King Aspen has reached his full height by now, I'm sure, being the thousand years that he is."

Amelie lets out a gasp. "A thousand years? He's positively ancient!"

Foxglove nods. "He was born nearly the day the war ended. The tide turned upon his birth, and I say that with some irony, as his mother is Queen of the Sea Court. She was unseelie through and through, as was her husband, King Herne of the Autumn Court. King Herne died during the war, however, leaving Melusine as regent. Somehow, against all odds, King Aspen was born in seelie form, taking his deceased father's place as heir to the Autumn Court. This, in turn, changed his mother's heart and brought the majority vote to side with the seelie. The Council of Eleven Courts forged peace with the humans through the treaty."

"You haven't answered my question," Amelie says with a pout. "Who are we each to marry?"

"As the eldest, you will marry King Aspen while Evelyn will marry his younger brother, Prince Cobalt."

Amelie's eyes go wide. "I have to marry the Stag King?"

"You do!" Foxglove says. "You're so lucky. The Stag King is quite yummy to look at. Plus, he has a huge...*kingdom*, as rumor would have it." He waggles his brows, his grin wide enough to show his slightly pointed teeth.

Fangs. I knew it—*wait*. Did he just make an innuendo? "Huge kingdom?"

He winks. "So I've heard. Prince Cobalt, on the other hand, has remained much more of a mystery. If he's taken many lovers, neither he nor they brag about it. Quite a shame. You'll have to let me know about his...kingdom yourself."

A blush of heat rises to my cheeks. I most certainly will not be reporting anything about Prince Cobalt's *kingdom*, for I plan on never laying eyes on it. I give a subtle pat to my dagger, taking comfort that it remains a presence at my side, then avert my gaze to the window, watching golden leaves fall.

8

The journey through Autumn isn't easy, neither on my body nor my mind. Every muscle aches, both from sitting so long and from tensing due to nerves. Amelie and I were allowed two short breaks during our travels, and these were only to relieve our humanly urges, something I never care to relive again. Nothing could be more frightening than trying to squat behind a tree in the forest of the fae. I could swear every leaf, vine, and branch had eyes, watching me, mocking me. My only hope now is that our new home has a proper toilet.

Then again, whenever I think of our *new home*, my mind becomes frazzled, my muscles tense yet again, and I feel like my lungs will collapse in my chest. What awaits us at the end of this carriage ride?

Warm light of the setting sun blazes through the window of the carriage, bathing the inside in a red-orange glow. I lean forward, looking out the window. It seems the trees have cleared, and we are no longer in the dense forest. The sky is every shade of gold, pink, and orange, but the quality of color is unlike anything I've ever seen before. It glimmers and glows, enhanced by the red leaves of the trees covering the distant hillsides.

I lean back and Foxglove takes my place at the window. "Ah, we're almost to the palace," he says.

My heart begins to race. As much as I want the ride to be over, I'm not ready to enter the home of the king and my husband-to-be. The thought alone churns my stomach, making bile rise in my throat.

A moment later, the carriage begins to slow, and I feel the weight shift, as if we're making an ascent. Amelie grips my hand, chest heaving as she clutches her necklace. Her fingers tremble within mine. Or are mine the ones trembling? With a deep breath, I close my eyes, steadying my nerves and smothering my panic in a blanket of calm. The calm of a surgeon.

The carriage stops. "We're here," Foxglove says.

I force myself to open my eyes. *Breathe. Hold yourself together.*

Foxglove pushes open the carriage door and exits. Amelie's grip grows tighter, and neither of us makes any move to leave our seats. After a few moments, Foxglove peers back inside. "Come on. Did you not hear? You're home!"

Another deep breath. My free hand pats my dagger. As if moving through water, I slowly leave the seat and make my way to the door. Amelie trails behind me, her fingers laced in mine. Foxglove offers me his hand as I step from the carriage to the marble path beneath it. More light from the setting sun greets me outside, overwhelming my senses.

Foxglove extends his free hand, indicating the other side of the carriage. "Welcome to Bircharbor Palace."

I step away from the carriage and turn until massive golden spires come into view. My breath catches in my throat, and for one blessed moment, I forget my anxiety. The palace is more beautiful than any structure I've ever seen, with walls of red-orange carnelian, yellow citrine, and golden-brown tiger's eye. There's nothing behind the palace but blushing sky, no forest, tree, or shrub. It's as if the palace stands at the end of the world. A cool breeze brushes my face, slightly warmer than the autumn weather back home, and I catch the hint of salt on the air.

I'm nearly swept beneath the weight of my awe, but I dampen it, reminding myself this is not a beautiful palace but a prison. A place of death. I'm not standing before an architectural miracle but at the maw of a vicious beast.

I steal a glance at Amelie, who seems to be struck with the wonder I felt a moment ago. Her head tilts to the side as she studies the palace. The look on her face is the same she gets when considering a new gown.

"Come," Foxglove says and rounds the carriage.

We follow, but I freeze when we reach the horse-creatures that had been pulling the carriage. This is my first opportunity to see them up close and beneath proper light since our travels began. Last night, I had only the impression of something beastly and strange, but the sight before me is more chilling than I'd imagined.

The creatures have sleek, equine bodies covered in smooth black fur, and flowing manes of onyx hair. Their necks are longer and slimmer than a regular horse, curving sinuously, the legs more graceful and less jointed. Their teeth are bared, showing sharp razors of opalescent white. Their glowing yellow eyes seem to bore into us.

Foxglove rolls his eyes impatiently when he sees we've stopped following him. "Puca. Harmless, really, especially when you have them under control."

"And...you have them under control?" Amelie asks in her quavering voice.

Foxglove laughs. "They serve King Aspen. Puca are great for aiding transportation. Not nearly as fast as a kelpie, but let's not speak of them."

It's unnerving that he didn't answer the question, considering he supposedly can't lie.

"Impressed with the puca, are we?" A feminine voice draws my attention away from the creatures to the woman approaching us. She's petite with brown skin and olive-green eyes, her face dusted with gold on her eyelids, lips, and over her cheekbones. Her hair is in wild, black curls, tangled with tiny sticks, leaves, and branches. She wears a gauzy gown in a deep bronze. It covers less skin than a nightdress and leaves little to the imagination, despite the fact that the thin fabric reaches past her ankles.

"Darling! It's so good to see you." Foxglove reaches out to her and they embrace, exchanging kisses on the cheek.

When she pulls away, the small woman eyes Amelie and me. She lifts an eyebrow, as if uninspired by what she's found. "Are these the girls?"

"Yes, they are," Foxglove says. "Meet Amelie and Evelyn Fairfield."

The woman puts her hands on her hips. "Hey."

I hesitate, waiting for her to introduce herself. "And you are?"

"I'm to be your...what's it called?" She looks to Foxglove. "A slave? Servant?"

He laughs. "I think in the human world it's called a lady's maid, Lorelei."

"Yes. That." She doesn't look pleased.

Her name sparks recognition, and it takes me a moment to place it. "Wait, you're Lorelei? *The* Lorelei?"

She grins. "My reputation precedes me."

"For getting Hank Osterman's arm mutilated by a bear trap."

She lifts her chin with pride, as if I'd complimented her. "That was me."

A flush deepens in my cheeks, which Foxglove seems to notice. He steps toward me, hands fluttering in the air as if they can pull the tension from it. "Lorelei is serving you as punishment for her crime against the Butcher of Stone Ninety-Four, or whatever human name you call him. See? Amends are made."

My eyes narrow at Lorelei, who seems to be relishing in my anger.

"Come now, Lorelei," Foxglove says. "You're supposed to make them feel welcome."

She plasters an exaggerated smile on her lips, then says in the most honey-sweet, high-pitched voice, "Oh, by all means. Welcome."

Foxglove claps his hands, then turns toward the palace. "That's better. Come along everyone."

I give Amelie's fingers a reassuring squeeze as we follow Foxglove and Lorelei toward the palace. We make our way down the marble path away from the carriage, then up massive, citrine steps. The enormous double doors are open wide, and two guards outfitted in bronze armor engraved with maple leaves stand on either side, golden spears in hand. I'm surprised to find one of the guards appears female, her features slightly more feminine than her counterpart, with a long brown braid of hair plaited down her back. I don't think I've ever seen a female guard in Eisleigh. Then again, I've hardly had the opportunity to meet any royal guards before this, considering Eisleigh's king resides on the mainland.

Inside the palace, I feel equally as overwhelmed as when I first saw the outside. Everything from the floor to the walls is constructed of stone in golds, reds, browns, and yellows. Golden arches and spiraling staircases steal my attention, then the smaller details like paintings, tapestries, and vases assault my senses.

Foxglove leads us through hall after hall, stair after stair. Orb-like lights hover above sconces along the walls, some strange sort of fae lighting. Oil, perhaps? They look nothing like the oil lamps back home. I make a mental note to investigate later before I remind myself I don't care about any of this. Returning my attention to our path ahead, I attempt to keep track of all the turns and twists. While it's impossible to gather my bearings completely, I get the sense we're winding deeper and higher into the palace.

By the time we come to a stop, I'm nearly out of breath. I try to keep my panting to a minimum while Foxglove approaches a set of double doors and pushes them open. He waves us forward, and Amelie and I step inside.

We enter a room in the same warm hues as the rest of

the palace. An enormous bed lines the far wall, a wardrobe spans half the length of another wall, and a desk, dressing table, and dressing screen stand in a corner. In the middle of the room is a magnificent citrine tub. Wafts of steam curl up from the water inside.

"First things first," Foxglove says. "The two of you need to bathe before you meet your future husbands. You may either take turns or share the bath."

I didn't expect such a luxury to await me. In fact, I'm not sure what I expected, but it was supposed to be more terrifying than this.

"I will tell the king and prince you are here and arrange a meeting," Foxglove says. "Is there anything else you will require in the meantime? Lorelei can help you undress and wash—"

"No," I say. "We would like to bathe alone."

Lorelei shrugs. "Suit yourself."

"She'll be on the other side of the door if you need anything." Foxglove gives a bow of his head, then hurries to add, "Please don't plot murder or anything."

I frown at his back as he and Lorelei leave, closing the doors behind them.

Amelie finally lets go of my hand and looks around the room with mournful eyes. "This is really happening, isn't it?"

I sigh, wishing I'd wake up from this beautiful nightmare. But it isn't going anywhere, and it's only just begun. "Unfortunately, it really is."

9

The warmth of the bath soothes my muscles and calms my frazzled nerves. I know it's nothing more than a false sense of security, but the comfort lulls me into a feeling of safety. I wish I could stay in the bath all night.

Amelie sits across from me in the tub, playing with a sprig of rosemary. Other herbs and marigold blooms float on the water's surface, filling my senses with an intoxicating aroma. An aroma that reminds me of home. Of the apothecary kitchen. Of Mother.

"At least they've given us this room together," Amelie says, her frown flickering into a weak smile.

I don't want to crush her hope by telling her we'll likely be separated once our marriages take place, so I do nothing but nod.

"And this bath is nice," she says. "How do you think they keep the water warm?"

I don't have an answer to that and have been trying my best to tamp down any fascination with the palace or the fae. But I can't deny I am stimulated with all the questions brimming in the back of my mind. We must have been in the tub for an hour by now, and the water is still as warm as when we entered it. There's no drain, no visible plumbing, no heating element.

"It's magic, isn't it?" Amelie asks.

I shake my head. "You know I don't believe in magic."

"Even after all of this?" she says, waving her hand to indicate the room around us. "How else are those orbs of light staying lit? How else was a palace this big constructed?" She lifts her rowan berry necklace from her neck, the length of it trailing behind her to keep from soaking in the tub. "How else do magic talismans work against the fae?"

"It isn't magic. There's a perfectly logical—"

"—explanation for all of it," she finishes with me. "I know, but you don't have the slightest idea what that explanation could be, do you?"

"Actually, I know exactly how rowan works against the fae. You see—"

She splashes me, leaving me sputtering and blinking water from my eyes. When Amelie's face comes back into view, she's grinning mischievously.

I splash her back. "How dare you interrupt my scientific explications!"

She squeals, then launches more water at me. We fall into fits of laughter, and for a moment, it's like we're little girls again, sharing the tub while Mother scrubs our backs. The thought sobers me, and I'm again reminded of our situation.

Amelie seems to feel the same, her smile slipping back into a frown. Finally, she stands and reaches for one of the blanket-like towels on the floor. "I'm going to explore the wardrobe."

"Of course you are." Classic Amelie behavior. Solve all problems with clothes. The bath doesn't feel nearly as friendly now that I'm alone, so I follow suit. I step out of the tub and grab the towel, releasing a sigh as its warmth envelops me.

Amelie gasps, making me jump. My eyes locate my pile of discarded clothing. I'm ready to dive for my dagger buried beneath them when she gasps again, then turns toward me with a wide smile. She holds a shimmering pink dress up to herself, swishing the hem of the fabric back and forth. "Evie, can you even believe your eyes?"

I let out a sigh of relief and join her at the wardrobe to examine the gown. Its fabric is thin and gauzy, like Lorelei's, but the skirt is constructed of numerous layers, making it look like petals of a flower. Dresses may not be my favorite, but I must admit it's pretty.

She puts it back and pulls out another, this one in a seafoam green. Again, she holds it up to her body. "Each is more stunning than the last. Have you ever seen anything like this? What are you going to wear?"

I look back at my pile of clothes. "I'll probably wear my trousers."

Amelie's mouth falls open aghast. "No. How could you when you have all this at your disposal?"

A feeling of unease ties my stomach in knots. I feel oddly betrayed by Amelie's excitement over the dresses. Aren't we supposed to be angry about all of this? Still, I can't bring myself to dampen her sudden joy.

She replaces the seafoam dress, then takes out another, purple this time. The skirt is made of shimmering silk decorated with tiny, amethyst jewels. The top is made from a similar silk in shades of purple, constructed of tiny, overlapping pieces of the cloth, making it look like scales. "Oh, I am definitely wearing this one."

"What if these are supposed to be formal dresses?"

She shrugs, letting the towel fall to the floor as she puts the dress over her head. "Who cares? If I'm going to get eaten by a fae king, at least I'll look good before I die."

I'm stuck between a gasp and a laugh, then that sense of unease returns. Again, I feel betrayed by how well Amelie seems to be adapting. How could she feel so lighthearted after spending the best part of our ride here sulking and crying? She's out of her wits. *I'm* being the sensible one. Aren't I?

A knock sounds on the other side of the door, and Amelie suppresses a shriek. She hurries to pull the dress the rest of the way down, succeeding just as Lorelei steps inside.

"Brought your things," the fae says, four bags in hand. Three are Amelie's, while one is mine. As she crosses the room, I realize for the first time that her gait is less than graceful. There's something crooked about the way she walks, her steps not dainty like Foxglove's.

She reaches the dressing table and hefts the bags on top of it. When she turns to face us, she catches us staring. Amelie tugs at her gown while I pull the towel tighter around me. "What?" she says, pulling her head back. "Did you not want your things?"

I lift my chin. "In the human world, a knock doesn't forewarn one entering. You usually await permission to enter first. Especially when one is known to be bathing."

A corner of her mouth lifts but her eyes narrow at me. "Well, aren't we fussy. I may be your lady's maid, but the first thing you need to get right is this: you aren't in the human world anymore. You're lucky you got a knock at all."

I glower. "I didn't ask you to be my lady's maid. In fact, tell the king we don't need one. Let him punish you elsewhere for your crimes."

Lorelei crosses her arms and strides up to me. I fight the urge to lean back as she holds my gaze with her furious olive eyes. "For one thing, I don't tell the king anything. He tells me. I am his subject as you are now too. For another, I shouldn't be punished at all. What I did to the Butcher was a favor to my people."

I remember what Foxglove said about the traps on the Faerwyvae side of the wall, about Mr. Osterman selling fae parts. "You see, that's where you're mistaken. Hank Osterman would never do what your kind are saying he did."

She bares her teeth. "Has it ever occurred to you that being human doesn't make you an authority on everyone of your kind? The man you call Hank killed my lover in front of my eyes. I watched him do it. How? My leg was stuck in one of his iron traps. I watched as he took Malan and cut the wings from her back with an iron blade, sliced out her emerald heart, then stuffed her body in a bag. I screamed the entire time. The only reason I'm alive is because I got lucky."

I blanch, taking an inadvertent step away from her. *No, she's wrong. This can't be true.*

She continues. "When he released me from the trap, I put myself under a glamour. It took all the strength I had not to give in to the pain from my wound. I could have let myself die, could have joined Malan in the otherlife, but I didn't. Instead, I thought of those I could help if I made the Butcher pay. So I glamoured myself as a beautiful human woman. I crawled away from him, and he saw it as a seduction, a tease. He followed me, reaching to touch me, to put his hands in all the forbidden places he craved. I finally pulled myself in front of another of his traps. He watched a beautiful woman open for him. And he did all the rest."

I feel like I'm going to be sick, her impossible words and my own logic battling for supremacy inside me. "It's still cruel," is all I can say. "You glamoured him—"

"No," she snaps. "I glamoured *me* alone."

I throw my hands in the air. "What's the difference?"

"Do you know nothing about our magic? Placing a glamour on a human controls them, lowers their inhibitions, allows us to suggest actions they readily accept."

This I know about, and there's a rational explanation to it. Mr. Meeks theorizes that the fae emit a certain hormone during prolonged eye contact—an automatic function for the fae. That hormone, unfortunately, is what suppresses our amygdala, compromising our response to danger, opening our minds to suggestion. That's why blinking is so effective at preventing a glamour. It keeps the fae from secreting whatever hormone is responsible for attacking our brains.

"Trust me, I know all about a fae glamour," I say, hazarding a glance at Amelie, who blanches. "I've seen it happen before."

"Then you'll know that's not what I did to the Butcher," Lorelei says.

"What exactly did you do to him, then?"

"Like I said, I glamoured *myself*, changing my appearance to look like a human instead. He saw a helpless woman before him. He could have done anything—ignored her to find the fae he'd captured, asked her what she was doing alone in the woods—but his vile urges were stronger."

I shake my head, unable to reconcile the man she's describing with the hunter from my village. He's lived in Sableton my entire life. He has a wife! Could it be I never knew him at all? That no one really knows him?

I remember what he said after he woke from surgery. *I thought she was a woman. She looked like a woman.*

Equally disturbing is Lorelei's assertion that she can glamour herself, change her appearance at will. I refuse to believe that's possible. Again, there must be a scientific explanation. Another undiscovered hormone the fae emit that wreaks havoc on our nervous systems, altering our perceptions, our interpretation of visual stimuli.

"Sorrow not," Lorelei says, a bitter edge in her voice as she lifts the hem of her dress. "He may have lost an arm, but iron through the leg is a lot to heal from for a fae."

I can't help but look at the flesh she's exposed. One of her legs is perfect, slim, and brown, while the other is scarred and misshapen, wrapped in thin vines like a makeshift cast.

She continues. "He, on the other hand, still has his wife while Malan will never again be amongst the living."

I shudder, my chest heaving. I want nothing more than to change the subject. For her to leave. To unsee the battered flesh of her leg.

"Can I wear this?" Amelie's voice comes out small.

She strokes the skirt of the purple gown she's already wearing.

Lorelei swings her head toward my sister. Some of the fire seems to drain from her eyes, her shoulders slumping forward. "Yes. In fact, wear the nicest dress you can find in there."

I point to my bag on the dressing table. "I was going to wear—"

"Wear. A. Dress," Lorelei says, eyes locking back on me. "A fae dress. You are about to meet King Aspen and Prince Cobalt. This is not the time to argue about it or cling to your silly human ways."

Amelie squeals in delight and tosses the seafoam dress at me. I catch it with a resigned sigh.

"I take it neither of you need or want my help," Lorelei says, her tone still icy. "Meet me in the hall when you're dressed."

I feel empty after she leaves. Partially from guilt, but I'm used to my sharp tongue getting me into tight corners with others. What's more unsettling is the upside-down world I've been thrust into. One where fae find me ignorant and the people I've trusted my entire life are seen as monsters.

For the love of iron, is any of this real?

10

"Must I wear these?" Amelie asks.

I peer from behind the dressing screen to see my sister stroking the rowan berries around her neck. Her nose wrinkles, a frown tugging her lips as she stares into the full-length mirror next to the dressing table.

"Yes," I say, then pull back behind the screen. I'm wearing the seafoam dress after turning it inside out and back again several times. The fae dresses don't have visible seams and look appropriate worn either way. Not that I thought Mother's *wear your clothes inside out* suggestion would help anyway. I can think of no logic to such a superstition. But it was worth a try.

She lets out a heavy sigh. "But it doesn't match the dress."

"Neither does getting glamoured."

"That makes no sense, Evie. Besides, it's not like I'll do anything that will put me in a position to get glamoured. I know how to blink. I'm not stupid."

"I know you're not." She wasn't stupid when she fell under a glamour four years ago either, but I don't say so. Instead, I retrieve my dagger from the pile of clothes I've hidden it in, then strap the belt around my thigh. It's snug, but the gray leggings I found should keep it from chafing too badly. Luckily, the seafoam dress has several layers to the skirt, making the belt and dagger invisible to prying eyes. "Rowan works against the fae. We need to keep wearing the necklaces Mother made us. Make sure at least part of it is touching your skin at all times."

"Oh, *now* you believe in Mother's craft."

I roll my eyes, then check the fit of the dress. It feels fine. Unlike the dresses we wear at home, these ones are loose and flowing, easy to put on without much assistance. Best of all, no corsets.

I meet Amelie at the mirror, and she grins at my reflection. "You look beautiful, Evie!"

As much as I hate to admit it, the dress suits me, complementing the copper tones in my dark hair. I quickly look away, then approach the dressing table to rifle through my bag. "Did mother give you a pouch of salt and a tincture?"

Amelie drags her gaze away from the mirror with some difficulty, then stands at my side. "Yes, yes. Do we bring them both with us?"

"Bring the salt," I say, tying the pouch to my waist. Salt is another one of Mother's prescriptions I can believe in. While I don't believe it wards off magical enchant-ment—because, obviously, enchantment isn't real—I do believe it helps protect our digestive tracts from harm. Mr. Meeks once told me he theorized salt could coun-teract the harmful effects of fae food by neutralizing any acids and helping us digest unfamiliar components. "But take the tincture now. Half a dropperful like Mother said. Remember?"

She nods, then finds the pouch and bottle in one of her bags. Once she's finished tying her own pouch to her waist, we face each other.

"Ready?" I ask.

She blanches a little, then nods.

Lorelei waits for us outside our door. We find her leaning against the opposite wall with her arms crossed. "Finally," she mutters, then takes off down the hall.

As we follow, I try to memorize every turn we make, to familiarize myself with the halls and doors, but I keep finding myself drawn to Lorelei's now-unmistakable limp.

I avert my gaze back to our surroundings, to the staircase up ahead. We climb it, and I feel a cool breeze, again carrying the smell of salt. As we reach the top of the staircase, an enormous room comes into view. Open air greets us at the other side of the room from a wide expanse cut from the wall, lined with a white rail, and interspersed with citrine columns. The air is cool without being unpleasant, and the night is dark beyond it.

At the center of the room is a long table with two ornate chairs on each end. One chair is taller than the other, its legs and back in the shape of twining branches, or—more accurately—antlers. The chair on the other side is similar in design but with a shorter back. The table is laden with plates of food, thick yellow candles, and numerous cups and bottles. Along the length of the table are about a dozen much simpler chairs.

The room is empty, save for Foxglove, standing near

the open expanse. Lorelei waves for us to follow as she crosses the room toward him.

He turns with a wide grin, adjusts his spectacles, then assesses Amelie and me. "Ah, much better. The king and prince will arrive shortly."

The smell of salt is stronger now, and I hear a rhythmic crashing. Curiosity draws me forward, and I look over the rail. Vertigo seizes me as the world seems to fall away, plummeting down into a black expanse below. I grab the rail, steadying myself, and blink a few times to clear my vision. Once stabilized, I see the palace is built at the edge of a sea cliff. The ocean sends waves lapping up and down the shore. As my eyes adjust to the moonlit dark, I notice something else about the shore. Dark holes pock the ground, like chasms. Some of the water reaches them, disappearing into their depths before the water recedes and gathers into another wave.

"King Herne built Bircharbor Palace at the edge of the sea," Foxglove explains, "to be near his wife, Queen Melusine."

"The Queen of the Sea Court," I say, remembering his story from earlier. "Didn't you say the king died in the war?"

"He did." His tone is mournful. "King Aspen could take up residence elsewhere in Autumn, especially considering Queen Melusine rarely visits land much these days. Yet he remains here. It is a lovely palace."

I lean over the rail again, watching the waves crash upon the shore. "What are those holes in the ground?"

"Ah, you'll have to look again when it's day. The beach gives way to coral and those are coral caves. Queen Melusine constructed them. Some think they lead to her underwater palace, but it's nothing more than a menace of a maze, if you ask me. Anyone who's ever tried to map the caves drowns by high tide. Even the sea fae who've tried never succeeded. Only Queen Melusine seems to know how to navigate them, and she prefers to keep her secrets to herself."

"The lesson being, don't go swimming," Lorelei says.

"Very true," Foxglove says with a grave nod. "Better avoided altogether. At low tide, you'll fall into a cave before you make it out to deep enough water for a swim. Even then, you'll find yourself trapped on the other side of the caves and get dashed into the coral. At high tide, you're lucky if the current doesn't suck you into the caves or worse."

"Or, again, dash you into the coral," Lorelei adds.

"Lesson understood," I mutter.

"I don't like swimming," Amelie says, wrinkling her nose at the sight of the dark ocean.

"Neither do I," Foxglove says. "The salt dries out my hair, and I can't get it looking right for days. I prefer to lie down for a seaside tan in the Summer Court, where the waves are less obnoxious."

A smile twitches at the corners of my lips. Despite my best efforts, Foxglove is growing on me.

"Are these our new guests?" A new voice rings out behind us, male, and dare I say...joyful?

The four of us whirl around to face the newcomer. Foxglove and Lorelei fall into easy bows while Amelie and I sink into clumsy curtsies half a minute too late. I wait until Foxglove and Lorelei rise before I do the same. Amelie's pinkie winds its way around my own.

Foxglove takes a step forward. "May I present to you Amelie and Evelyn Fairfield."

The fae male grins, taking confident steps toward us. His face is somehow both boyish and ancient at once, with dimpled cheeks, high cheekbones, and glittering blue eyes. His hair is straight and a deep shade of blue so dark it's almost black, loose strands falling over his forehead and brushing the tips of his pointed ears. He wears blue-black trousers and a jacket with an indigo waistcoat patterned with gold stitching and a blue cravat.

He bows, then looks from me to Amelie. "Pleased to make your acquaintance. I'm Prince Cobalt."

I can't take my eyes off him, much less speak. In all my terrified imaginings, I never thought a fae could look so regal, so kind, so...attractive. And he's—oh for the love of iron, he's Prince Cobalt. My husband-to-be. I can't tell if the thought terrifies me or excites me. Shame reigns supreme when I consider it could be the latter. I remind myself he's fae and recall everything I've heard about Faerwyvae. I can't afford to be flustered by a pair of blue eyes.

I open my mouth to relay a greeting, but Amelie beats me to it. "It's a pleasure." Her tone is formal, which I'm grateful for. By the look in her eyes, I can tell she's as enchanted as I am by his appearance. Still, she's keeping her composure, which means she has her head on her shoulders. Good.

A dark shadow looms behind the prince. Cobalt turns, bowing his head.

Again, Foxglove and Lorelei sink into bows. This time Amelie and I are quicker to catch on. When we rise from our curtsies, the Autumn King's eyes are on me.

I know he's the Autumn King, because never have I seen the season so perfectly embodied in a living being. Not only does he have an elaborate rack of dark brown antlers, but he wears bronze satin from head to toe. The jacket and trousers are a deeper shade of russet, but the waistcoat is closer to the red-bronze of fall treetops and is patterned in gold-stitched maple leaves. He has the same slim build as Cobalt but towers a head taller than the younger fae, not including the height of his antlers. Like his brother, the king has blue-black hair, but his is longer, curling at the nape of his neck. Aspen's eyes, however, are brown. Unlike Cobalt's, they don't glitter when he smiles, they narrow, and his smile is more smug than warm.

His gaze burns into me. "Evelyn," he says.

I hate how he says my name with such informality. Such scorn. I hate how the corner of his mouth turns up when he says it, like my name is a joke coming from his lips. Most of all, I hate the chill that runs down my spine when I hear it, sparking something familiar.

A dangerous echo.

I've heard that voice before. Seen that smirk.

In fact, I've told him my name.

11

I don't know how King Aspen could be the same fae I met at the wall, but I know it's him. Even with antlers and fashionable clothing, there's no mistaking his expression, his voice. He's the fae whose ire I've sparked. *He* brought me here.

Rage ignites within me, so hot it feels like it will boil over. I want to shout at him, to demand an explanation for why he sought fit to punish me. I almost do, when I remember I never confessed my guilt to my sister. She has no idea I even met a fae at the wall, much less drew enough attention to get us into this mess. I grit my teeth and meet his gaze with a glare.

"Pardon, Your Majesty, but *this* one is your bride-to-be, not she," Foxglove says, misreading the exchange between me and the king. He pushes my sister forward a step. "This is Amelie Fairfield, the eldest daughter of Maven Fairfield of Sableton Village."

King Aspen shifts his gaze to her, and Amelie forces

an uncertain smile. His smirk disappears, and something crosses his face, but I can't read his expression. He almost seems taken aback. With a grunt of either acceptance or displeasure, he turns around. "Let's eat."

"You heard him," Foxglove whispers, waving for us to follow the king to the table.

As I move to obey, Prince Cobalt offers me a gentle smile and falls into step at my side. "That leaves you and me," he says. "To marry, I mean."

I don't say anything in reply.

As we reach the dining table, Cobalt steps in front of me and pulls out a chair. I hesitate before accepting the seat. He leans forward and pushes the chair in as I sit, bringing his face next to mine. He pauses with his lips by my ear and whispers, "I'm sorry for what happened to the girls before you, but I hope you can forgive me for saying...I like you better."

I'm surprised by this and turn toward him in time to see a blush creep up his cheeks. He catches my eyes and flashes me a smile, then makes his way to the seat at the end opposite his brother.

When I face forward, I meet Amelie's frown across the table. She turns her scowl to King Aspen, then loudly drags the chair away from the table. She sits, then pulls the chair forward in a few exaggerated scoots until she's nestled close to the table. The king pays her no heed, his eyes fixed firmly on his dinner plate.

"You can sit," he barks. I realize then that Foxglove and Lorelei had retreated to the edges of the room. "Both of you."

The two jump forward like timid pups eager to obey

their master, then take seats at the table. Foxglove sits next to me, while Lorelei sits next to Amelie. I try not to meet Lorelei's eyes across the table.

Several figures enter the dining room—servants, from the look of their stoic expressions and reserved bearing. Most resemble the average, youthful human in stature and physical features, save the telltale ethereal beauty and pointed ears. Some, however, have additional attributes like upturned snout-like noses, whiskers, and even the odd tail. A few smaller fae are present with leathery skin and aged, wrinkled faces, limbs that appear more tree branch than arm or leg. Regardless of appearance, all are dressed in resplendent silks in russets, golds, reds, and browns.

One of the youthful fae, a male, approaches me and fills my goblet with a deep red liquid. Another, female as far as I can tell, with long, white whiskers framing a pink button nose, stands on my opposite side, heaping portions of food onto my plate from the many dishes on the table. The first servant moves on once my glass is full, but the second is still adding more food to my plate.

I manage to find my voice. "That's enough, thank you."

The fae steps away, and I look across the table at my sister. She wears an odd expression, somewhere between suspicion and longing, as she studies the items on her plate. With a lick of her lips, she reaches for a pastry.

I scoot forward and aim a kick at her shin. She scowls as my foot meets its mark, then meets my eyes with a questioning glare. I lift the bag of salt from my waist, widening my eyes in silent warning. *Salt your food.*

She gives me a nod of understanding, then retrieves her pouch. We each sprinkle our plates with a dusting of the pink crystals.

"What is this?" asks a dry, mocking voice. My eyes flash to the head of the table where King Aspen sits. His eyes rove from Amelie to me.

I'm at a loss for words as I seek an explanation that won't get me killed. Thankfully, Foxglove lifts his hand. "I believe it's a human folk remedy," he says. "They believe salt wards against evil."

"Salt." The king lets out a bark of cold laughter. His eyes lock on me. "You know we already use salt when cooking, right? And the salt sprays in from the ocean daily. If salt could do fae harm, we'd already be dead."

I'm still too furious to trust myself to speak. All I'd do is argue anyway. Besides, we don't salt our food to harm the fae, we do it to protect our digestive tracts. Instead of saying any of this, I deepen my glare, eyes still locked on the king, then dump another heaping pinch of salt on my plate.

He leans back in his chair with a dismissive snort.

"I think it's smart." Prince Cobalt's voice comes from the other side of the table, his gentle tone in contrast to his brother's. He smiles at Aspen, but his eyes are glowing with mischief beneath a raised brow. "They aren't the only ones with precautions in mind."

I look back at Aspen and realize a small tree-like fae is perched at his side, fork in mouth. The fae then reaches for Aspen's goblet and takes a sip. The king holds Cobalt's gaze for a few moments while the servant takes another bite of food from Aspen's plate.

Foxglove leans in close to me and whispers, "The king always has his food and drink tested before he eats."

The odd exchange makes much more sense now, but the tension between the two royals remains intact.

"You're right, brother," Aspen says in his cold, drawling voice. "One can't be too careful." The servant takes one more bite, then offers a bow. Aspen waves him away, then picks up his fork. "Eat."

Everyone except Amelie and I rush for their forks, but we follow suit shortly after. I push the food around my plate, trying to investigate what I've been served. It appears entirely recognizable, from the fillet of fish to the roasted potatoes and apple tart. The aromas are familiar as well, making my mouth water. I know I should eat. I *want* to eat. If only my stomach would agree. It's been in knots ever since I laid eyes on King Aspen, felt that anger rise inside me. How can I eat now?

I look at Amelie, who has already taken several bites from her plate. She meets my eyes, grinning while she chews. I force a grin, then with equal effort, bring a bite of food to my lips.

AFTER A MOSTLY SILENT DINNER, KING ASPEN AND PRINCE Cobalt leave the dining room with curt farewells, and Foxglove and Lorelei guide us back to our room. Again, I try to memorize all the twists and turns, try to orient myself between the dining room and our bedroom. As far as I can tell, our bedroom is two floors down from where we ate.

Foxglove leaves us at our door, but Lorelei lingers in

the doorway, leaning lazily against the frame. "Do you need me to stay?"

"That's not necessary," I say, trying to keep my voice neutral. I'm still not sure how to act around her after our argument.

She pushes off the door frame and lets out a yawn. "Fine. I'll be sleeping next door. Call if you need anything." With that, she closes the door and leaves me and Amelie alone.

Amelie rushes to the bed and flops belly down into the middle of it. It bounces, then sinks a little beneath her. "I'm so tired." Her face is pressed into a pillow, making her voice come out muffled.

I feel the same, in mind and body. Like Amelie, I want nothing more than to sink into the luxurious bed. But the pressure of the dagger belt around my thigh is too irritating to ignore. I grab my nightdress from my bag and take it behind the dressing screen. Once changed, I meet Amelie at the bed, slipping my sheathed dagger behind one of the pillows.

She lifts her face, blinking up at me. "Do you think the wardrobe has special nightdresses?"

I can't help but laugh. "I'm sure it does." Amelie scrambles out of bed and rushes to the wardrobe, while I turn down the covers and crawl beneath them.

After a time, Amelie twirls across the floor, a sheer, silky nightdress rustling around her ankles. She crawls into bed next to me. "This place has the best clothes."

"At least the fae realm has one thing going for it."

"It's really not as awful as I thought," she says. "I was certain I'd be fearing for my life by now. You know, monsters and goblins and harpies and such. But so far, no one has tried to so much as nibble me."

"That's because we haven't been left alone with our mates yet."

She's silent for a while, and I'm worried I've scared her. Then she scoots closer. "I don't like mine, Evie. He's so dour."

"No kidding."

"You clearly don't like him, either. I saw the way you glared at him. I was starting to think I'd missed something."

My muscles tense. Should I tell her? I'm not sure why I'm so afraid to confess my meeting with King Aspen at the wall. It's not like my good-natured sister would blame me forever. Besides, she's already adapting so well. But for some reason, I can't bring myself to talk about it. It feels...shameful. I don't even want to remember the way he said my name today, as if he has any right—

"Yours isn't so bad, though." Her voice shatters my thoughts. "He's a gentleman, at least. Perhaps you could come to like him."

"Perhaps I could wake up with horse hooves."

She giggles. "Do you think they throw balls in the palace?"

"Balls, human heads. Only time will tell."

"Really, Evie, you're so strange sometimes."

I don't reply. Instead, I close my eyes and try to breathe away the tension coursing through me. After a while, I hear Amelie's even breathing. Of course she falls asleep first. Of course she feels safe in this place of beautiful luxury. Of course I'm the only one aware of our fragile mortality in a place like this.

I toss and turn for what feels like hours, unable to relax, much less sleep. Finally, I give up. I grab a lightweight cloak from the wardrobe, wrap it around my shoulders, then slip out the bedroom door, leaving Amelie sleeping peacefully alone.

12

I make my way back through the palace halls, trying to see if I can find my way to the dining room. Not for any particular desire to return there; it's more to lock down my sense of direction in the palace. If I can at least navigate between two places inside the palace, I'll feel like I'm in control of *something* again, no matter how small.

The halls are eerily quiet and eerily as dark, the orbs of light hovering above their sconces now diminished to a subtle glow. No one crosses my path, which I'm grateful for, despite getting lost numerous times. I eventually find myself in front of a familiar staircase and climb. When I reach the top, the dark, empty dining room opens before me.

My chest swells with pride. But now what? Do I just go back to my bedroom, see if I can reach it faster than I reached this place?

The sound of crashing waves calls to me, its rhythm

softer than it had been earlier. And there's something else. Voices. Or music.

I tiptoe across the floor to the open expanse, placing my hands on the rail like I did before. The ocean is black beneath the moon, small waves gently rolling into the base of the cliff beneath the palace. Gone are the black chasms of the coral caves, as the tide has come in and hidden them beneath its watery depths. It chills me how much the shoreline can change in a matter of hours.

Music falls on my ears again, and I search the night for the source. There are large rocks near the cliff at the end of the shore, and I'm almost positive I see figures perched on top of them. Are they singing? There's a feminine trill in the air, both beautiful and terrifying.

Nearer movement draws my attention away from the rocks and back to the shore. There I see the forms of what appear to be women, skin white and glistening beneath the moon. Their bodies are naked, sinuous with their slow movements as they circle each other on the beach, laughing as the waves roll around their ankles. The way they move has me entranced, filling me with calm.

They're dancing.

"Selkies."

I whirl to find King Aspen behind me, expression hidden in shadow. My first instinct is to pat my dagger, until I remember tucking it behind my pillow. I clutch my rowan berry necklace and press myself as close to the rail as I can.

Aspen steps forward into the moonlight, then stands next to me at the rail. He's changed from his suit into a simple pair of dark trousers and a loose linen shirt. The shirt is open at the neck, revealing the golden skin of his upper chest. His expression is different than it was earlier, softer, eyes on the scene below us. "They come here to dance at night sometimes, leaving their sealskins on the rocks while they take the forms of human women."

As much as I don't want to speak to him, my curiosity again gets the better of me. "Are they the ones singing?"

"No, those would be the sirens upon the rocks."

I squint into the night, trying to make out more than vague silhouettes of the creatures.

Silence stretches between me and the king, and with it comes a growing tension. He's so close I can see the rise and fall of his chest from the corner of my eye. His hand rests on the rail, fingers glittering with red jewels, just inches from my own.

"How do you like it here?" His voice is irritatingly gentle.

That's all it takes to bring forth my anger. I round on him. "You mean, how do I like this prison you've brought me to?"

His brows furrow for the merest moment, then his eyes go steely, lips twitching into a smirk. "I take it you aren't impressed."

"Why are you punishing me?"

"Is that what I'm doing?"

"Answer my question," I say through my teeth.

"Ask a better one."

I cross my arms over my chest. "You're the fae from the wall, I know you are. What did I do to make you so angry that night? Why did you bring me here?"

He shrugs. "I'm sure you know what happened to the

previous Chosen. Two girls needed to be brought in their place."

I let out a bitter laugh. "You think I don't know? Two other names had already been selected as backup by the council. You chose me by name."

He nods, unashamed. "Yes."

"Why? What did I do to deserve this? To be torn from my mother and my home? To drag my sister away from her fiancé?"

"You held an iron blade to me." He says it less like an accusation and more like an observation.

"You attacked me first! I was defending myself."

"Are we done?"

"No, we're not done. I want to know what happened to the girls before me. Why did you have the Holstrom sisters executed?"

Aspen's expression darkens. When he speaks, his tone is edged with razors. "You haven't once addressed me as Your Majesty since we began this conversation, nor did you bow."

I lift a shoulder in a shrug. "What are you going to do about it? Execute me, like you do everyone else who slights you? I'm sure you killed the Holstroms for far less, so what's the point of toeing the line?"

"You seem to have your opinion set about me and my involvement with the Holstroms. Why bother asking me at all?"

I open my mouth, but all I can think to say is, *this is just the way I am.* I must have truth. Order. Logic. My life is supposed to make sense. But what do the fae care about logic and order? This place is backwards, upside down, and dizzyingly frustrating. In this strange court, the fae are righteous and the villagers I've trusted my whole life are butchers, yet the ruler wears human clothes, serves human food, and expects to be treated according to human custom. It's enough to make my blood boil.

Instead of saying any of this, I turn to my only available weapon. My words. "I want to know what kind of monster I'm being forced to live with."

He shakes his head, a sneer curling his lip. "I thought you were smarter when I met you at the wall. I thought you had the sense to fear me."

I know I should back down now. I should bow. I should apologize. But I don't. "And I thought you'd have the sense to recall what else you learned about me. I'm prepared, remember? Just try and tear your fangs into me. We'll see if you like the taste of iron."

He holds my gaze, and I'm sure he's going to lash out at any moment. *I'm dead. I'm thoroughly dead.*

Then a wicked grin shatters his glower, and he throws his head back in laughter. When he returns his attention to me, his eyes are crinkled with amusement. It's not a comforting sight. "Fangs? What...do you think I want to *eat* you?"

He laughs again, and a blush creeps up my cheeks as I wait for him to sober. "Nothing I said was that funny."

"Fangs," he repeats. "Let me guess. You ingest iron of some sort? I can smell it on you."

The mention of him smelling anything about me makes my cheeks blaze. Still, I maintain my composure. "So what if I do?"

"I don't eat humans. I'm not that kind of fae." Despite his reassuring words, his tone is menacing.

"But there are types of fae who do eat humans?"

"Plenty."

I hope he can't see me blanch. "Regardless, I'm not harmless, you know."

"Yes, but I don't see that blade of yours. Even so, I could do worse at a distance."

My breath hitches as I imagine what kind of glamour he wants to force me under. "I'm prepared for that too."

He lifts his hand and I flinch away, but his fingers fall on the strand of rowan berries. The hair lifts on the back of my neck as he gives them a light tug. "Rowan," he says. "A lot of good that will do."

I lift my chin, breathing deeply to keep the trembling at bay. "It will keep you from glamouring me." For the love of iron, I hope it will. I blink several times for good measure.

"I don't need to glamour you to make you do what I want. If I wanted, I could make you fear me. Crave me. Love me."

His words are like a dangerous hiss, making my chest feel tight, like my lungs are shrinking into nothing. "I doubt that." I cringe at the uncertainty in my voice.

"All I'd have to do is glamour myself. I did it at the wall when we met. You never saw my antlers or anything other than my cloak and my face. You had no idea who I was."

My eyes flick to his antlers, taking in their size, their sharp tines. I swallow hard. "Yet I still charged you with a dagger."

He takes a step forward, closing the distance between us until I can feel the heat of his body. My eyes are locked on his chest as I press myself closer to the railing. There's no farther I can go without launching myself over the edge. "Look at me."

I don't know why I obey, but I do. Whether it's madness, stupidity, or something else, I want to look at him. I want to see what he can become. My eyes find his —a rich dark brown I can barely make out in the moonlight. A curl of blue-black hair falls into them, and I have a terrifying urge to sweep it away from his forehead. My breaths are growing ragged, shallow, the smell of his skin and clothes invading my senses, a spicy herbal aroma like rosemary and cinnamon as well as something earthy like fresh leaves. I try to hold my breath and avert my gaze, but that only shifts my attention to the curve of his lips.

He's beautiful, the most breathtaking creature I've ever seen. My mind reels to comprehend this, and I feel myself losing control, like my feet could fall out from under me at any moment.

A sound comes from somewhere nearby, and I blink a few times. Belatedly, I realized the sound was of someone clearing their throat.

Aspen's gaze lingers on me before he takes a step away and turns toward the figure standing on the other side of the room. It's Cobalt.

"I thought I heard voices," he says. "Wanted to make sure everything was well."

"All is well," Aspen says with a note of irritation in his voice. "I was showing our guest the selkies."

I lean to the side to widen the distance between me and the king. "And I was just leaving."

"Come," Cobalt says with a warm smile, "I'll walk you to your room."

I take a few steps away from the king; it's a miracle I

can walk at all with the tremors of rage rushing through me. I pause. Without looking at Aspen, I whisper, "Don't do that to me ever again."

I can hear the grin in his voice. "Why? Did you like it too much?"

"I hated it. And if you ever so much as try a stunt like that again, I'll murder you in your sleep." I cross the room toward Cobalt, my lie ringing in my ears. I hate what he did. I hate that Lorelei was right, that the fae really can affect us by glamouring themselves. He may not have changed his appearance, but he altered my perception of him, made me see desire instead of danger. I hate that he has that kind of power over me. But during the glamour? I didn't hate it at all. I loved it. Loved staring at his lips, his eyes. Loved the pull between us, the smell of his skin, the heat of his body.

Rowan berries did nothing to prevent it. Blinking did nothing to stop it. Logic was nowhere to protect me.

That frightens me more than anything.

13

Cobalt and I walk side by side in tense silence. The farther we get from the dining room, the easier I breathe. I let the prince lead the way, not even bothering to pay attention to the journey this time. He slows his pace once we enter a familiar-looking hallway and stops outside a closed door. My room, I realize. I'm about to reach for the handle when Cobalt puts his hand on my arm. I flinch from his touch.

He draws his hand back, then faces me. "You shouldn't be alone with my brother."

I open my mouth, a spark of indignation heating my core. He may be my husband-to-be, but that doesn't mean he owns me or my actions.

He lowers his voice. "He's dangerous."

My anger cools, realizing he isn't chastising me. He's... scared for me. "Can you tell me what happened to the Holstrom girls?"

The prince looks at the floor, shuffling from foot to foot. "I shouldn't have said anything. He's my brother."

"Please tell me. I just want to know what's going on here."

Cobalt meets my eyes, lips pressed tight. "Honestly, I don't know what happened that night," he finally says. "All I know is that the Holstrom girls were alone with my brother when they..."

"When they what?"

"When they were killed."

The blood leaves my face. "You mean he murdered them? Then was their charge of treason a lie?"

"I don't know," he says in a rush. "Aspen claims they performed an act of treason in his presence, and he doled out justice immediately."

"Is there no formal justice system in Faerwyvae?"

"There is. Normally, criminals are imprisoned until they can stand trial before the Council of Eleven Courts. But if any ruler of the Eleven Courts sees fit to execute swift punishment, they may do so. It's rare though." He lowers his voice further. "And even though it was his right to do so, I think it was wrong. His actions nearly caused us to break the treaty. Luckily, the council was able to convince him to try another set of girls."

I hate the way he says that, *try another set of girls*, like we're nothing more than a pair of trousers for the king to wear or discard. "No one knows the supposed reason the Holstroms were charged with treason?"

Cobalt shakes his head. "There are rumors that the girls tried to kill him, but there's no proof, and Aspen won't share the entire story."

Probably because he can't lie. If the girls really did try to kill him, then it had to have been in self-defense. But even that is hard to believe. Theresa and Maryanne have always been the most timid, dutiful daughters in all of Sableton.

"Promise me you'll be careful," Cobalt says, brow furrowed.

His concern makes me uneasy, both the depth of it and the affability with which it's bestowed upon me. We've hardly spoken since we met, yet somehow he seeks to protect me. To care. Perhaps not all fae are as monstrous as I thought.

Still, his gaze makes me uncomfortable, his nearness reminding me too much of what it was like to be enraptured by his brother's glamour. "I'll be careful," I say, moving to my door.

He offers me a bow, and I return it with a curtsy. I watch him stroll down the hallway and out of sight before I slip into my room. As I close my door, I'm almost certain I see a dark figure looming at the other end of the hall.

MY SLEEP IS FITFUL, BUT I DO FINALLY MANAGE TO CATCH A few hours of rest. When I wake, it's to the subtle sound of birdsong, an oddly harmonious blend of gull cries, raven caws, and songbird melodies coming from every direction around the palace. The lilting tunes are both familiar and strange, reminding me of the siren song last night.

That, of course, brings more unpleasant memories— the king, his closeness, my loss of control, his brother's warning.

I can tell it's morning by how the sunlight blazes

upon my eyelids, but I don't want to open them to confirm it. Perhaps if I keep them closed, the day will never proceed, and I won't have to leave this room. I smother my face in my pillow, then reach my hand beneath it until my fingertips touch my dagger. Safe. I'm safe. I'm in control.

I feel the weight of the bed shift next to me, followed by a peaceful sigh. "This is the most luxurious bed I've ever had the pleasure to lie in," comes Amelie's voice.

"How many beds besides your own have you lain in?" I tease, my words muffled in my pillow.

"Not nearly enough." Her tone is wistful. "I should have taken Magnus to bed, or at least behind the stables after he proposed. Can you believe Bertrand is the last man to have his hand down the front of my corset? What an unpleasant fact!"

I'm surprised she's able to speak of such matters so lightheartedly. It wasn't more than a day ago that she was sobbing uncontrollably over leaving home. Finally, I roll toward my sister and open my eyes. I flick her on her shoulder. "I thought you liked Bertrand!"

"Well, I did. But that was before Magnus."

"And now?" I ask. "Would you marry Bertrand if it meant we could go back to the way things were? Before we were sent here, I mean."

Her eyes unfocus, smile slipping from her lips, but she doesn't reply. She rolls onto her back, staring at the ceiling. I follow suit, noticing for the first time the canopy of red and gold leaves painted there in hyper-realistic detail.

Another sigh escapes Amelie's lips. "Do you think we could come to be happy here?"

I turn my head to face her, shocked at her words. "Happy? *Here*?"

She blushes, then rushes on to say, "I mean, I don't think I'll ever love the Stag King. He's too mean. But...do you think this arrangement could come to be worth it? This beautiful palace, these amazing luxuries. They're all ours!"

I hate to dampen her optimism, but I must be the voice of reason. She'll only get her heart broken if I don't. "Ami, we've been here less than a day. Just because they fed us, put us in a luxurious bedroom, and gave us an endless supply of gowns doesn't mean we're safe. The fae are dangerous."

"I know."

I sit up. "Do you, though? Do you have any idea what they're capable of, what they could do to us?"

She gives me a pointed look. "I know more than anyone what they're capable of, Evie. But what if all fae aren't...well, you know. Evil?"

"If you're thinking the fae here are worthy of your trust, you should reconsider. Have you forgotten what they did to the Holstrom sisters?"

She rolls her eyes. "No, of course I haven't."

I open my mouth to say more, to tell her what Cobalt hinted at last night, but I stop myself. I want her to be smart, not terrified. Instead, I say, "You need to be careful with King Aspen."

"Yet another thing I already know."

"*Really* careful."

She stands from the bed and faces me with her arms crossed. "Why must I be careful while you get to go on acting the same way you always do?"

"What's that supposed to mean?"

"I saw the way you looked at King Aspen. You could have melted iron with that scowl, and he noticed too. But did you lose your head? No."

"True, but King Aspen isn't my husband-to-be. He's yours."

"More of a reason for you to be careful, not me. Surely, he'd prefer his fiancée to remain alive."

"He didn't seem to mind murdering his last one."

"Murder!" She gasps, eyes growing wide. Finally, I've triggered her fear. "Do you really think..."

"I'm not trying to scare you. I just want you to be careful. In fact..." I say, then get up from the bed. Once I reach the dressing table, I begin to rifle through my bag. From the bottom, I retrieve my surgery kit. Amelie joins me, peering over my shoulder. I grab one of the smaller knives and face my sister. "I want you to keep this on you at all times."

She furrows her brow, looking at the knife as if it's some vile object. "I don't know how to use it."

"Take it anyway. I don't have a sheath for it, so wrap it in silk and tie it to your waist or around your thigh."

She presses her lips tight. I imagine she's considering how she can follow my instructions without them interfering with her clothing choices. Reluctantly, she takes the knife. "Are you going to carry one too?"

I go to the bed and pull my belt and dagger out from behind the pillow, then begin strapping it around my thigh. "I've been wearing this since we left home. Now, let's get dressed before Lorelei comes to wake us. We don't need her to see what we're hiding."

Amelie watches me as I finish strapping the belt. A

mischievous grin plays on her lips. "Will you be wearing a dress then?"

I pause, realizing a dress will provide the only easy way to reach the dagger while hiding it from view. "I suppose."

She squeals, then runs to the wardrobe. "I'll pick one for you."

We finish dressing just before Lorelei knocks, once again barging through the doors before we can tell her to enter. This time, Foxglove follows in her wake.

"Good morning, good morning," he says. "And don't we look lovely."

Amelie and I are dressed in another set of fae gowns. My sister wears the shimmering pink one she was looking at yesterday, while I wear a pale blue dress with flowing, bell-like sleeves and two strands of pearls criss-crossing over the low-cut back. The skirt is loose with multi-layered ripples of floral-patterned fabric, hiding my dagger. My sister has her knife wrapped in pink silk and stashed in a tangle of gauzy sashes she wears around her waist.

"I was just about to do Evie's hair," Amelie says. Hers has already been brushed into long copper waves.

Foxglove nods. "Proceed. I can share what's on the agenda for today while you do so."

Lorelei steps forward, looking annoyed like always. "Need me for anything?"

Amelie hesitates before flashing her a smile. "Sure. You can hand me the hairpins."

"How nice," the fae mutters, then joins us at the mirror.

I pull up a chair and sit while Amelie attacks my hair with a brush.

Foxglove stands behind us. "King Aspen has finalized the date for your weddings. Normally, the hosting court of the Chosen is given one month to secure a wedding alliance to validate the treaty. But because of the mishap with the Holstrom sisters, our schedule got a bit thrown off. Worry not, we have it all sorted out. The human wedding ceremony will be exactly one month from now. The mate ceremony, however, will take place much sooner. It's scheduled ten days from now and will happen on the topmost balcony at sunset."

"The mate ceremony?" I echo.

"Yes. It's a fae celebration for paired couples. We don't call the resulting pair husband and wife; we call them mates. While it isn't nearly as binding as a human wedding, it is the closest thing we have here in Faerwyvae and is required by the treaty. It's usually reserved for noble pairings and alliances, situations where a bit of fanfare is needed. Afterward, you and your mates may perform...um...*the ritual*."

I swallow hard, wondering if he's referring to consummation. "What exactly does *the ritual* mean?"

He hesitates before answering. "That's a private matter, one you will discuss with your mate. It's a very ancient and sacred ritual, one that is not discussed with such informality as we are speaking with now."

"Are you talking about sex?" Amelie doesn't so much as blush, just looks at Foxglove questioningly.

"Sex?" He puzzles over the word, then his eyes go wide with understanding. "Oh, you mean mating. Ha! No. Mating is not so sacred here in Faerwyvae. Honestly, your human ceremony puts much more emphasis on the sanctity of the mating act than we do. I mean, it is expected that you and your mate will...well, mate, but—for the love of oak and ivy, you're doing it all wrong. I can't stand by and watch this."

Foxglove steps forward, shoving Amelie out of the way and taking my hair in his hands. With deft moves, he undoes the few pins my sister already had arranged, then coils several strands of my hair at the base of my neck. He pins them in place, then pulls a few loose strands to frame my face.

"Now you," he says to Amelie, snapping his fingers for her to replace me in the chair.

I'm surprised when she rushes to obey. She never wears her hair up, preferring a longer style that showcases her natural color and texture. But when he finishes and steps aside, my sister is glowing, jaw hanging on its hinge. "I was offended at first, but my goodness, Foxglove! I've never done nearly such a beautiful job as that!"

"Obviously," he says, assessing his work with smug admiration. "I am a flower fae. I know a thing or two about beauty."

Even Lorelei looks impressed. "You're putting me out of a job. Perhaps you should be their lady's maid."

Foxglove scoffs. "I think not. Anyhow, let's not get off track. I haven't finished explaining the agenda."

I blush, remembering our mating conversation.

The ambassador continues. "With the mate ceremonies just ten days away, the king has decided you shouldn't be complete strangers by then. You will spend this time getting to know King Aspen and Prince Cobalt when they are free to entertain you. Which brings us to today's agenda. Amelie, the king will meet with you this afternoon in his study. Evelyn, during this time, Prince Cobalt will take you on a walk outside the palace."

My pulse quickens. Amelie and I are going to be separated. My sister will be alone with the Stag King. "Can't we get to know our fiancés within a group setting? The four of us? Perhaps you and Lorelei as well? I mean, it's hardly proper for us to be alone with..." I trail off at Foxglove's raised brow. Right. Human propriety doesn't mean much in Faerwyvae.

He laughs. "Oh, don't be frightened, my dear. Remember our chat yesterday? Don't set traps. Don't plot treason. Don't go swimming. Simple!"

I cross my arms, searching for the right argument.

Amelie sighs, then bounces the side of her hip lightly into mine. "I'll be fine, Evie."

I face her, hoping I can convey all the warning I can with my eyes. She tugs her rowan berry necklace, then brushes her fingers over the sashes at her waist. The sashes that hide the knife I gave her.

It isn't much, and it might not be enough. But in the end, it's all we can do.

14

N o hidden blade can comfort me as I find myself trekking through the woods a few hours later, marching up a steep incline behind Cobalt. All worry of Amelie has been swept from my mind, now that my main concern is trying to breathe properly.

Is he trying to kill me? He is. He must be.

Cobalt casts a glance behind him, winking when he meets my eyes. "Almost there, I promise."

I grind my teeth in reply, silently cursing Foxglove for describing my outing with Cobalt as a *walk outside the palace*. This isn't a walk. It's a hike. There's a distinct difference.

Cobalt, unwinded and unhindered by sweat and mortal lung capacities, leads the way higher and higher while I pant behind him, struggling to keep up with his long stride. He pauses and offers me his hand a few times, which I refuse. It only makes me want to hide my exertion better.

Thankfully, the incline begins to even out, the trees

thinning until there's nothing but a vast field strewn with
red leaves, like a blood-red sea. The field ends in a sharp
edge that opens to nothing but blue sky. Cobalt sprints
forward, then stops abruptly at the cliff's edge. When I
make no move to run after him, he waves at me to hurry,
face split into a wide grin. "Come on! You've got to see
this."

I let out an irritated sigh, then slowly make my way
forward. A delightful breeze brushes over my skin,
drying the sweat from my brow. I pause several feet
behind him, again that question nagging at me. *Is he
trying to kill me? Did Cobalt bring me here just to push me off
the edge of a cliff?*

My eyes shift from the prince's back to the view
before us. All prior thoughts go still. A chill runs down
my spine, but it isn't from fear. It's awe that has me in its
grip. Below stretches red-orange hills rolling to the left
and right, with endless ocean straight ahead. Bircharbor
Palace is a tiny silhouette in the distance, perched at the
edge of its cliff. Gulls soar high overhead in the clear blue
sky, sunlight glinting off their feathers.

"Beautiful, isn't it?" Cobalt asks.

There's no point denying the truth. "It is."

"I've impressed you!" His smile is infectious, and I
find myself averting my gaze to hide the tiny spark of joy
fighting for dominance over my face. Cobalt doesn't seem
to notice my struggle and turns away from the view to
walk to the middle of the leaf-strewn field. There he
plops down in the grass and begins unpacking the goods
from the basket he brought.

I follow but hover a few steps away from where he
sits.

He pats the grass next to him. "Come. I packed us a meal."

I stay where I am, eying the spread of cheese, nuts, and unfamiliar fruits he's laid out.

When he sees I haven't moved, he pauses and meets my eyes with another disarming grin. "I'm not going to hurt you, Evelyn. You're safe with me."

He can't lie, I remind myself. "Promise me."

"I promise I won't hurt you."

I let the vow hang between us for a few moments. While I don't believe a fae promise is a thing of magic like most people think it is, I know the fae put much stock into the word. A promise is a thing of deep reverence to them, like their inability to lie. It's something I can use like a shield.

With a deep breath, I take a seat opposite him, on the other side of the food-laden cloth. The earth is warm beneath me, the noonday sun beaming down upon us. My stomach rumbles at the sight of the meal, so I pick up a piece of cheese.

Cobalt takes a piece of fruit shaped like a pear, but with tiny red spikes all around it. He bites into it, spikes and all. "They aren't sharp," he says through the mouthful.

"Fae fruit, I'm guessing?"

He nods. "You have to try some. It's unlike anything you've ever had before."

I stare at the fruit with suspicion. "I'm not sure if that's a good thing."

"It is, trust me. Besides," he says, taking another bite, "you brought your salt, right? If you're worried, sprinkle some on every bite you take."

As much as I'd like to avoid all things fae and potentially dangerous, the fruit does look appetizing, especially the way the golden juice runs between Cobalt's fingers when he takes a bite. After the grueling hike, I could use something refreshing. I grab my pouch of salt, then choose a piece of fruit—one shaped like an apple but with an opalescent golden skin.

"Good choice. We call that an autumn equinox apple. You're going to love it."

He's right. Even with the salt, the flavor is overwhelmingly delicious. It's sweet and bright with a crisp, juicy texture. I close my eyes to enjoy the sensations.

"So...tell me about yourself," he says, popping a blood-red berry in his mouth. "What was life like for you before you came here?"

I salt my apple again and take another bite while I consider what to say. I'm hesitant to speak about anything personal, but I suppose it wouldn't hurt to share some. Right?

"Well, let's see. I grew up living in an apothecary run by my mother. For the past two years, I've been working as a surgeon's apprentice. And before I was forced to come here, I had plans to attend medical school on the mainland."

"Surgeon, wow. So, you cut up human bodies?" Cobalt asks as he grabs an apple like mine.

"I suppose you could say that, although it's more complicated. It's a healing practice. Surgery is often the difference between life and death for humans. Is there nothing like that here?"

He shrugs. "We aren't easy to kill. If there's ever a time

we're wounded badly enough to require intervention, it usually means there's no coming back from it."

I take another bite of salted apple, pondering over what kind of wound would be bad enough to kill a fae. I've heard stories about the fae's impressive abilities to rapidly heal from injury, their supposed immortality. As far as I've been told, their main weaknesses are iron and ash. But can they heal from a wound inflicted by either material or is it always fatal? And what about a wound from an ordinary wood or metal? I know what kind of wounds can kill a man, but does the same apply to the fae?

"I'm sorry," he says quietly, shattering my morbid thoughts. "About you being forced to be here. I can tell you were passionate about your plans for school."

I nod but say nothing in reply. His words make me wonder if he knows why I was brought here—knows about my first meeting with his brother at the wall. If he does, he's doing a good job not bringing it up. Whatever the case, I'm done talking about myself. "Now it's your turn. Tell me about your adolescence."

He reclines on the bed of leaves, elbows supporting his weight. "Hmm. I am much older than you by several hundred years, so it'll take me a moment to think back that far."

"Several hundred years, you say? And to think you don't look a day over three-hundred and seventy-two."

"Ah, perfect. I was beginning to think my blues were showing. That's what humans get, right? Different colored hair with age?"

"Something like that." I take my last bite of apple and exchange the core for one of the pear-like fruits.

"Ha, thought so. Now, let's see. I was born the second son of Queen Melusine. She returned to the sea not long after I was born, which basically meant Aspen had to raise me, although he was barely more than an adolescent himself at the time."

"Your brother raised you? Does that mean the two of you are close?"

He ponders that for a moment. "I've lived with him my entire life, but I wouldn't say we've ever been close. I love him and I'm sure he loves me, but it isn't always smooth sailing between us. He frustrates me at times, and I know he resents me."

"Why would he resent you?"

His expression turns apologetic. "It's no secret many of the council would prefer to see me on the throne."

Part of me wonders if that wouldn't be a good idea. So far, Cobalt seems far more civilized than his brother. "How do you feel about that?"

"I just want what's best for Faerwyvae."

"Isn't that what every good king should want?"

He shifts, looking flustered.

My stomach drops, realizing my words are bordering on treason. There I go with that mouth of mine again. Time to change the subject. "Tell me more about your childhood. Who's your father? Foxglove said King Herne died before your brother was born, so I take it you don't share his paternity."

He shrugs. "I never met my father. He was one of Mother's many undersea consorts and never bothered coming to land to meet me. It's the unseelie way." There's a note of sorrow in his voice, and I can't help but feel a squeeze of sympathy for him.

"I don't remember my father," I say. "He parted ways with my mother when my sister and I were small. When Mother moved us to Eisleigh, he stayed behind. We've never heard from him since."

"I'm sorry. At least you had your mother, though. You must miss her terribly."

My throat tightens. I do miss her, and I can't fight my regret over the sharp words I said to her the night I left. She knows how much I love her, doesn't she?

"What's wrong?" Cobalt's brow is furrowed as he studies my face from his reclined position.

I don't want to tell him what's really on my mind. If I talk about my mother, I won't be able to trust myself not to cry. Instead, I voice another valid worry. "I just hope Amelie is faring well with your brother."

"You mean at her interrogation?"

I bristle at the word. "Why do you call it that?"

He frowns. "You know he's only spending time with her to make sure she doesn't plan on killing him, right?"

"Amelie? Kill King Aspen?" I may have given her a knife for protection, but if anyone were to kill the king, it would be me. Of course, I don't say so out loud.

"He thinks everyone is trying to kill him," Cobalt says, a note of irritation in his voice. "You've seen how paranoid he is, how he has his food tested before he eats it."

"Why is he like that? Does anyone have reason to kill him?" Aside from him being an insufferable prick, that is.

His eyes unfocus as he considers this. "He has many enemies—basically every fae on the Council of Eleven Courts. But I can't imagine they would target him with the kinds of underhanded assassination attempts my brother fears. If anything, they'd demand his removal from the throne."

"Why does the council hate him so much?"

"Well, to be honest, he's the most unstable ruler in Faerwyvae, always switching from seelie to unseelie and back again for no reason at all. I think he does it on purpose, just to stir chaos."

I remember what Foxglove told me during the carriage ride, about fae politics and the history of the original unseelie fae. "What do you mean he switches from seelie to unseelie? Do you mean politically or physically?"

"Politically. We all shift into our physical unseelie forms from time to time. But when it comes to politics, the rulers are supposed to take a firm stance on what each side represents. The unseelie ultimately want control over the isle. They were responsible for the war a thousand years ago and are the main supporters of going back to war and ridding the isle of humans. The seelie, on the other hand, are determined to keep war from ever reaching the isle again. They keep the unseelie in check and smooth things over with the humans when tensions arise."

"So, you're saying your brother constantly changes his mind about whether he supports war?"

"Yes, but it's more than that. I doubt he even cares about the politics at all, otherwise he wouldn't play the games he does. You see, in order to pass any new motions, the council needs a majority vote. Ever since the war ended, the council has remained mostly seelie. Occasionally, a ruler will change sides, especially when a court is inherited by a new ruler. But every time this happens, my brother switches sides too, to whatever opposes the newest change."

I furrow my brow. "Why would he do that?"

"To be difficult. There could be no other reason. If he was doing it to keep Faerwyvae from going to war, it would make sense. But he even shifts sides when an unseelie votes seelie."

"You think that's why the council dislikes him?"

"I know they do. The seelie hate him because his constant shifting keeps the council from getting anywhere near unanimously seelie, which in turn prevents them from bringing in new measures to further the seelie cause. If the council were to shift heavily seelie, they'd be able to make bigger and better changes. Changes that would do more than the treaty does now. Changes that could make human-fae relations even stronger."

"And the unseelie hate him for the same reason."

"Exactly. If the council were to shift heavily unseelie, the same would happen. Drastic changes but with an opposite result. However, the unseelie probably hate him more than the seelie do, on principle alone. It was his birth that ended the war. My mother turned seelie just as the council was ready to pass a motion that would rid the isle of humans."

I shudder at that. "Why did your mother turn seelie when Aspen was born?"

"I can't promise any of this is true," Cobalt says, "but the stories tell how Aspen was born in his seelie form and how my unseelie mother couldn't figure out how to care for him. She tried to nurse him with seawater, but he wouldn't take it. In a matter of hours, he was near death.

Mother was so distraught about the possibility of losing the child that she became desperate. In a final attempt at saving her baby's life, she snuck past the war camps to the nearest human settlement and located a nursing mother, begging her to nurse Aspen. The woman agreed on one condition—that my mother make a bargain. End the war and the woman would nurse Aspen to full health. She'd even teach my mother how to care for the boy herself, if she'd agree to take on a seelie form."

"She made the bargain, I'm guessing?"

He nods. "She donned human clothing for the first time ever and learned to nurse her son. This changed her. Not only was she forced to make good on the bargain, but she found she wanted to rid the isle of war, to make the land safe for her newborn son. As Queen of the Sea Court and Regent of the Autumn Court, her vote on the council was substantial. When she turned seelie during that final council meeting, the war was over. The seelie vote won and they were able to forge the treaty we follow today."

"Considering the name of the fae council," I say, "Faerwyvae must have eleven courts. Aside from Autumn and Sea, what others are there?"

"There are three other seasonal courts in addition to Autumn," Cobalt says. "Spring, Summer, Winter. Then there are three elemental courts in addition to Sea; Wind, Fire, Earthen. The final three are celestial courts; Solar, Lunar, and Star. Sea, Winter, and Lunar have remained firmly unseelie the past few hundred years, with a couple others varying from time to time, based on the political climate. But no one has shifted sides as much as my brother."

I let his words sink in, awed over all the new information. Growing up, I only ever heard about the human side of the war, not the fae side. We were taught how the fae presented us with a treaty and that both our kind and theirs worked to finalize the terms. There are still a few things I never understood, however. "Do you know why the Hundred Year Reaping exists?"

"It's a demonstration of peace," he says. "When the war ended, the fae agreed to show our goodwill by exiling the King of the Fire Court. He was the first fae to engage the humans in organized violence and was determined to eradicate them. We bound him in iron and shipped him off to what you humans call mainland Bretton. Being so far from the Fair Isle and the magic here is certain death. And since we banished one of our kings to die, humans were required to make a similar sacrifice, especially considering they spilled the first blood that sparked the unrest to begin with."

More information I never knew. Was any of it true? Were the humans the ones to spill first blood? I always imagined it was the fae, creeping into human villages in the night, stealing children and slaughtering travelers. More proof this world is upside down from everything I knew. "So, my people chose human girls to be their sacrifice?"

He nods. "Likely to atone for that first blood they spilled. It's said the Fire King took a human lover. Back then, human-fae pairings were forbidden. Humans were afraid any children born from such a union would become witches or demons. So when the Fire King's lover admitted to being pregnant with the child of a fae, they executed her. In retribution, he burned her village to the ground. That's what sparked the war. The Reaping is meant to repair that which was torn between the humans and fae, to maintain a balance of give and take between them. Two human girls are sent to a different court every hundred years, and at least one marriage alliance takes place. In exchange, the family is blessed with a gift from the court the girls are sent to."

"Is that why the two girls are almost always related? So the fae only have to gift one family?"

He shrugs. "Perhaps. Although I'd like to think it's so neither girl will be lonely."

This last part almost makes me laugh. I can't imagine the fae caring much about the emotions of their Chosen. I'm pondering everything else Cobalt said, eyes unfocused, when I remember the pear-like fruit in my hand. I've still yet to taste it. With a sprinkle of salt, I bite into it, finding the red spikes are soft and oddly flavorful after all, like ripe strawberries. But the flesh inside is even better, crisp, tart, and honey sweet. I take another bite and a wave of euphoric lightness floats to my head.

I only have a moment to realize something before my thoughts slip away into a chaotic jumble.

I never salted the second bite.

15

I stare at the fruit, panic rising inside me. It only lasts a moment, however, before I find myself laughing, giddy over...something. Everything?

"Oh no." Cobalt sits upright, expression shifting between amusement and worry. "Did you take a bite of honey pyrus without salting it?"

The panic returns in a flash. "Yes. Is that bad?" My stomach churns, but not a moment later, my laughter is back. Cobalt is the one making me laugh. He's so funny. His face is funny. Everything is...*wow so pretty*. "Honey pyrus," I say slowly, my tongue feeling thick and heavy.

Cobalt's face is spinning as he inches closer to me. He's laughing now too, and it sounds like a thousand tiny bells. "Hey, I think it's best you lie down for a bit."

"Did you just say your words backwards?"

"Sure. Here, just lie back. The leaves will feel really nice. In fact, I'll join you. Honey pyrus no longer makes me feel as euphoric as you feel right now, but it does make me sleepy." He lays down next to me and pulls me down with him.

Or perhaps I fall down next to him. Either way, the ground is pulling me down and I'm sinking into an endless sea of vibrant red leaves. I could drown in it and I wouldn't mind. The sky is a swirling vortex of color overhead, clouds passing in shapes that make me laugh louder than I think I've ever laughed before. The panic continues to swell now and then, but I chase it away each time.

No, I'm not chasing panic.

I'm chasing a butterfly.

A ladybug.

No, a sprite.

A sprite with glowing yellow wings is leading me to more honey pyrus, which I'm desperate for. It's all I can think about. I just need more of that delicious fruit. Down the hill we go, and I'm laughing with every step, even when it leads me to tumble over roots and rocks. On and on we go, deeper into the woods. This is the most fun I think I've ever had. Why was I afraid earlier?

Afraid. Was I afraid? Should I be afraid?

The panic returns, and I come to a halt, looking wildly around me. I'm no longer on the leafy field next to Cobalt. I'm in the middle of a dense forest of oak and maple, and there's no one else in sight. Wasn't I chasing a sprite? I remember my craving for more honey pyrus, but it no longer has me in its grip. It's fear I feel now. And a pounding headache.

My legs feel suddenly weak beneath me, and I wince, my muscles screaming from exertion. Did I run all the way down the hill from the cliff? How long have I been out here alone? And...where exactly is *here*?

I look up at the canopy of orange leaves, finding daylight in the blue sky overhead. That's something, at least. I turn in a circle, trying to see if the ground hints at the beginning of an incline, but the forest is too dense. In fact, I don't remember going through a forest like this when Cobalt and I were on our way to the cliff. Our path from the palace took us through endless rows of slim white birches.

Panic rises further, sending my heart racing. *Calm down,* I tell myself. *Panic won't get you anywhere.* I take a step and nearly twist my ankle on a rock. In doing so, I catch sight of my tattered hem. It's torn in numerous places and pierced with twigs. I look at both arms, which are equally battered, tiny red scratches and blossoming bruises covering my flesh. What the blazing iron happened?

I remember the euphoric flavor of the honey pyrus, but the memory tastes sickly sweet, bringing bile to my throat. Before I know it, I'm doubled over and heaving out the contents of my stomach. Tears spring to my eyes, and I let out a moan of distress. I've hardly been more than tipsy from the occasional glass of wine, so this is a far cry from anything I've ever experienced before.

I curse myself for being so stupid as to try fae fruit in the first place, salt or no.

My hand flies to my side, finding my salt pouch gone. I likely left it at the picnic. Another thought crosses my mind, and I reach for my thigh, sighing with relief when I feel the hilt of my dagger.

I close my eyes, summoning a sense of calm. Control.

With a deep breath, I lift my soiled hem and take one careful step and then another, avoiding ill-meaning rocks this time. I turn my head this way and that, seeking some sign of a worn path to no avail. Then I turn my eyes to the sky, trying to make out where the sun is. The sun set over the horizon behind the palace last night. If I can follow the trajectory of the sun, I might be able to find the palace. Maybe. It's the only logical step I can think of.

Here goes nothing.

HOURS PASS AND THERE'S STILL NO SIGN OF A TRAIL, MUCH less the palace or Cobalt or the cliff we picnicked on. I've yet to cross paths with any living being, save for birds and insects and the occasional rodent. This, at first, I was grateful for. Now I'm starting to wish I'd come across a fae. Surely, Cobalt will have sent someone to find me by now, right? Perhaps I should have stayed where I was.

"Help," I call out. "Can anyone hear me?"

Silence.

My heart feels like it will burst from anxiety and my feet are covered in blisters within the dirt-caked slippers I wear. I can't go much farther.

"Please." I try again, letting my voice carry throughout the quiet forest. "I'm lost and need help. I'm...fiancée of Prince Cobalt of the Autumn Court."

More silence.

This is the day I die after all. Not because of some vile fae, but because I'm an idiot who got tipsy on fae fruit and decided to run alone through the woods after what was probably an imaginary sprite. My throat feels tight and tears prick my eyes. I can't cry. I can't fall apart right now.

Control. Where is my control?

A sound comes from behind me. I whirl to find a dark shape in the distance. My breath catches, and I realize it's a black horse, similar to the ones I saw at the head of our carriage yesterday. What had Foxglove called them? Puca? It comes closer, slowly, and I fight the urge to flee.

"Did you come to help me?" I ask, trying to keep my voice steady.

"Come with me." The voice is somehow audible yet ethereal, as if carried not by vocal cords but the wind. The horse comes closer, and I see it's somewhat larger than the carriage-pulling puca. This one is more muscular too, with a long mane that blows in a wind I don't feel and eyes that gleam red instead of gold. It's beautiful.

I shudder. There's something sinister in this creature's beauty, reminding me of King Aspen's striking glamour. "Will you take me to the Autumn Court palace?"

"I will," says the ethereal voice. "I'll take you to Bircharbor Palace. Climb on my back."

I take an automatic step away as it approaches and lowers its head. Everything in me is screaming at me to run, but what other choice do I have? I'm lost with no guarantee I'll come across another fae before I get eaten alive by something worse. Besides, my mind is still too foggy from the honey pyrus to construct a tighter bargain. This one will have to do.

I grit my teeth and haul myself onto the creature's back. As soon as I'm righted upon it, it takes off. I reach for its mane, wrapping the thick strands of black around my hands to keep from falling off.

As the puca gallops through the forest, deftly avoiding branches and tree trunks as if by magic, I notice the forest begins to thin. It looks familiar as oaks and maples give way to stands of birch, and I'm almost positive it's the same way Cobalt and I came earlier. There's no sign of the prince or the cliff, but we can't be too far from the palace now.

My breathing begins to slow. Relief crawls over me bit by bit, and before long the ride becomes something close to enjoyable.

The sun is beginning its descent in the sky by the time the puca slows to a canter. The trees thin to a well-worn path, and a welcome sight comes into view—the palace. I sigh with relief, fully aware of the irony that I could feel so happy to return to what yesterday felt like a prison. Anything beats being alone in that eerie forest again.

"I brought you to the palace," says the puca. "Yes?"

"Yes, thank you."

As soon as the words are out of my mouth, the puca picks up pace again, charging forward. I feel like he's going to ram us both straight into the palace walls. I try to release his mane, hoping I can tumble from his back before we crash. To my horror, my hands are somehow stuck in place. It's not me holding the mane after all, but the mane holding onto me.

Before we slam into the palace wall, the creature veers sharply to the right. The golds of the palace speed past my vision and are replaced with the reds and pinks of the sunset behind it. The puca gallops ahead with no sign of slowing before we reach the end of the cliff.

I scream as the ocean comes into view below us, my stomach dropping as he leaps off the edge. We crash not too far down, the puca gaining purchase with little effort on a small outcropping of the cliff wall. It leaps and crashes again, jolting me with every landing. In a matter of seconds, we've descended the face of the cliff and are speeding along the narrow sliver of beach. Straight for the ocean.

I struggle to release the mane again, trying to reach my thigh, my dagger, but the strands of hair pull tighter and tighter. The tide is high, which means we plunge into the water before I can take a breath. There's no sign of the coral caves, no sign of anything but deep, dark water and the blinding sunset above.

The puca is equally as agile in the water as he was on land, and it isn't long before we clear the small inlet and move into the open ocean.

That's when the puca plunges beneath the waves.

I gasp for breath before the water closes over my head, but it isn't enough. My lungs are already screaming as the creature dives deeper and deeper into the ocean. I struggle, pulling at the puca's mane, but my hands have lost all feeling.

This is the end, I realize. I can hold my breath no longer.

Water floods my mouth a wave of tiny bubbles crashes into me, obscuring my vision. The last thing I feel is a pair of hands encircling my waist.

16

When I wake, everything hurts. My eyes, my lungs, my throat. Every muscle feels like it's on fire. My eyelids flutter open, and I try to sit but can manage no more than lifting my head before a searing pain behind my eyes has me sinking back into the pillows beneath me.

"Evie!" The voice belongs to Amelie, though I don't dare open my eyes to find her. The pain in my head is too great.

"I'll help her sit," says another voice, which takes me a moment to recognize as belonging to Lorelei. An arm moves to my upper back, lifting me, and I feel a mountain of pillows fill the space behind me until I'm propped up slightly. "Drink this."

The rim of a cup touches my lips, and I don't bother to fight the warm liquid. I'd drink fae wine or the juice of a honey pyrus, if it meant quenching my razor-sharp thirst. The liquid tastes like a mild tea, like something Mother would have made me when I was sick. Its soothing effect is immediate, easing the pain in my throat and sending a wave of relaxation over me. Finally, I open my eyes.

Squinting into the semi-darkness of what appears to be my bedroom at the palace, I find Lorelei and Amelie hovering before me, concerned expressions on both their faces as they sit next to me on the bed.

"What happened?" My voice comes out like a croak, renewing the pain in my throat and lungs.

"Oh, thank the Great Mother above." Amelie brings a hand to her heart, shoulders drawing down with relief. "You are coherent."

My brow furrows at her words. She said it like she expected otherwise. "How long have I been asleep?"

Amelie and Lorelei exchange a glance. "What has it been? Three days?" Amelie asks.

Lorelei nods, then faces me. "You've been coming in and out of consciousness, but mostly sleeping."

"Three days?" I jolt forward, but the motion sends my head reeling again. Squeezing my eyes shut, I lie back until the pain recedes.

"Drink more," Lorelei prods.

I do as told, relishing the sweet, familiar herbs that remind me so much of home. When I open my eyes again, Amelie is grinning.

"Foxglove was sent to the village for a remedy," she says. "He brought you something from Mother's shop. Isn't that wonderful?"

I want to argue that he should have returned with antibiotics, but I can't help but admit how much comfort the tea is bringing me. "He...saw Mother? Did he say how she is?"

"I sent him with a letter, told her we're being treated well, aside from your unfortunate incident with the kelpie. She sent one back, expressing her love and wishes for you to return to full health. Would you like me to read it to you?"

"Yes—wait. The kelpie? Is that what the creature was?"

Amelie nods. "Cobalt told me all about it. You should have seen him! He looked quite the hero as he carried you in his arms through the castle, dripping water in his wake. His skin was blue too, it was so odd."

"He'd shifted into his unseelie form," Lorelei explains, "when he rescued you. He's a nix."

"He...rescued me?" I shudder, remembering the deadly ride on the puca—or kelpie, I should say—and how it drove us into the ocean and pulled me underwater. I remember the burning, searing pain as water entered my lungs, followed by the hands of someone pulling me by the waist. That's the last thing I remember. "Why did the kelpie try to kill me?"

"Apparently, dragging lost travelers to their deaths is their specialty, according to Prince Cobalt," Amelie says. "He had to sever the creature's mane with a shard of coral to release you from its grip."

"But how did Cobalt find me? We were separated during our picnic."

Amelie scoots closer, hands an animated flurry, as she explains. "He said he went looking for you when he realized you were missing. There was no sign of you, and he had no idea where you'd gone, but when he caught scent of the kelpie, he knew exactly what had happened. He followed the trail and dove in after you when he saw the kelpie drag you into the ocean." She puts her hand to her heart and sighs. "He's so romantic."

"Romantic? No. This entire situation—" I swallow my words as another wave of pain radiates through my skull. With a deep breath, I wait for the sharp ache to pass, and force my body to relax back into the pillows. I grind my teeth, hating how helpless I feel, how helpless I've been for three days. *Three days.* Anything could have happened in that time.

Amelie grabs my hand. "What's wrong? You look distressed."

I press my lips together, eyes flashing toward Lorelei.

As if the fae can sense my sudden tension, she stands from the bed. "I should go tell the king you've woken."

"Thank you, Lorelei," I say.

Once the door closes behind her, my eyes find Amelie again. I let out a deep sigh. "Tell me what's happened while I've been out."

She cocks her head. "What do you mean?"

"I mean, what have you been doing? Have you continued carrying your knife? And your rowan necklace?"

She rolls her eyes and pats the sash at her waist, then lifts the strand of rowan berries from beneath the bodice of her dress. "Yes, Evie, I've remained well protected. Not only that, but I managed to keep you protected as well. See? I trimmed my necklace in half to replace the one you lost. Yours didn't survive your little dunk in the ocean."

My hands fly to my throat, and I find the familiar feel of rowan berries. The new necklace is noticeably shorter than mine had been, and only now do I realize Amelie's is half as long as well. I must admit, I'm impressed by her consideration. I would have expected her to abandon the necklace altogether without me reminding her to wear it every day. "Thank you, Ami. Now, what else? Have you been alone with the king?"

"If you must know, I've seen the king for an hour each of the last three days."

I try to sit straighter at that, eager for everything she can tell me. "What have you done together? Did he...do anything to you?"

She stares at me with a pointed look and puts her hands on her hips.

"Ami, I need to know if you've been safe with him. If he tried to hurt you—"

"Then what? What would you do about it?"

I open my mouth, but no words come.

"Look, I know you care about me and you're afraid for the both of us. But you need to trust me to take care of myself sometimes. I'm not the same fragile girl I was four years ago."

I tense. Four years ago. When I almost lost her. It began with a fae glamour and nearly ended with my mother's folly. If it hadn't been for Mr. Meeks, Amelie would have died. I shudder, breathing the memories away. It's not something either of us like to talk about.

Still, she has a point. Amelie was never to blame for what happened to her back then. It could just as easily have happened to me. And this time, it did. This time, I'm the one who almost died. And if appearance is proof of circumstance, Amelie really does seem well. Her cheeks are rosy, her eyes are bright and alive. Perhaps I'm not giving my sister the credit she deserves.

I let out a heavy sigh. "I'm sorry, Ami. You're right. I've been treating you like you can't take care of yourself while I'm the one who keeps getting into these messes."

"These messes? Have there been multiple?"

I blush, again reminding myself she knows neither about me meeting Aspen at the faewall, nor about our tense conversation in the dining room the night we arrived. "So, at the risk of sounding like an overprotective little sister, what *can* you tell me about the past few days? No, better yet, what would you *like* to tell me? What wonderful things did I miss?"

Her smile returns, and she sits closer to me, folding her legs under her. "As you know, the king insists I spend time with him daily. He's not as bad as you think he is, Evie, although he's incredibly dull. Pleasant to look at, but no personality. He mostly sits at his desk in his study working while I talk and drink wine and eat the most decadent confections."

It's hard to reconcile my experience of the king with Amelie's. I can't imagine he and myself sitting alone in the same room without it ending with my knife at his throat. Never would I picture him as dull. Hostile, arrogant, and impossible maybe, but never dull. Then again, my sister is much more agreeable than I am. "What else?"

She lowers her voice. "Well, there's this handsome servant. I saw him yesterday when I asked Aspen to have some wine brought in for me during our daily chat. My goodness, Evie! I had no idea fae could be so beautiful."

I want to shake my head but know the movement will jar my skull. Instead, I settle for a smirk. "Leave it to you to find romance in captivity."

"It isn't hard. Have you even taken the time to look at

the males here? I can hardly remember what Magnus looks like anymore."

"Wasn't it just three days ago you were lamenting over not having taken Magnus to bed?"

"I can still lament such a thing while making room in my new bed. Metaphorically speaking, of course. *You've* been taking all the room in my bed the last three nights."

I laugh, but sober quickly. Again, it's my turn to cut through Amelie's optimism with my brutal realism. I lower my voice. "You do know your bed is already spoken for, right?"

She shrugs.

"Ami, I'm serious."

"Oh really? I thought you were serious when you apologized for treating me like a helpless child."

I press my lips together. "You're right. I'm sorry. Again."

"My bed. My business."

I reach toward her and lay a feeble punch on her arm. "Not while I'm in it. Dirty harlot."

She giggles and punches me back. "Haggard prude." Before I can muster the energy to lay another blow, a knock sounds on the door. I expect it to be Lorelei returning, which means she'll barge in any moment. When the door remains closed, Amelie springs from the bed to see who's there.

"Your Highness," Amelie says. My heart races as Cobalt enters and approaches the bed. I find myself suddenly self-conscious, knowing I couldn't possibly be pleasant to look at after surviving a near-drowning and sleeping for three days. I do my best to summon an air of confidence and meet his smile with my own. "You'll forgive me for not standing to curtsy, I hope. I don't think my aching head would allow it."

"Only if you'll forgive me for not better protecting you on our picnic." There's remorse in his eyes, hesitation in his voice. He looks like he's worried I might be angry with him.

It gives me pause, and I choose my words with careful consideration as I navigate the best way to assuage his guilt. "Of course, I forgive you. Besides, if the rumors are to be believed, you did valiantly rescue me."

"Barely. If I had taken any longer...well, I don't even want to think about what could have happened."

I blush beneath his gaze and turn away, looking instead at Amelie. She, however, isn't looking at me at all. Instead she's swooning over Cobalt. When she finally meets my eyes, she arches a brow. I can almost hear her thoughts. *See? So romantic.*

Cobalt shakes his head as if to clear his thoughts. "Anyhow, I'd hoped you'd be well enough to join us for dinner, but you still seem out of sorts."

I cringe at the thought of leaving the bed. "I'll have to decline tonight, Your Highness. But I thank you for the invitation. And for your concern."

He turns to Amelie. "You'll join us, though, won't you? I'm sure my brother would appreciate your presence."

She beams at him. "Of course I will."

My eyes bore into Amelie, and I want to tell her she can't leave me. It takes all my willpower to remain quiet. *I have to trust her to protect herself. Especially when I'm in no position to leave my bed.*

"Very good," Cobalt says. "Dinner should be ready by now. I'll meet you and the others in the dining room.

Would you be so kind to give me a minute more to speak with your sister?"

She looks from him to me, then back again, finally understanding his request for privacy. Again, it's a struggle not to tell her to stay. "Oh, yes! Yes. Of course." With a curtsy for him and a smile for me, she leaves the room.

As soon as Cobalt and I are alone, he sits at the edge of the bed. He seems suddenly shy, as if he's too embarrassed to meet my eyes, his gaze instead fixed on my hand. "I came to see you a few times."

His words spark a memory, his face looking down at me, my hand in his. Other similar memories flash through my mind, of the other faces who'd come to see me. Amelie, Foxglove, Lorelei, and—strangely—King Aspen. "I briefly remember, but I apologize if we exchanged any words. I remember nothing else."

He shakes his head. "We didn't speak. The most you produced was an incomprehensible mumble until now."

Heat rises to my cheeks. "How humiliating."

"Humiliated was how I felt when I woke up at our picnic and found you missing. I couldn't believe I'd fallen asleep." Finally, he meets my eyes and reaches a tentative hand toward mine until he covers my fingers in his.

I flinch at the touch but don't pull away. "Your hands are cold."

He grimaces. "Part of being a nix," he says. "That's a kind of sea fae. Do you dislike it? The cold, I mean. Or my touch?"

His vulnerability tugs at my lips, pulling them into a smile. "No, I don't dislike it."

He grins, keeping his hand in place. "I really am sorry for not protecting you better."

I want to argue that I don't need protecting, but the point would be moot. I've already proven the opposite to be true, as much as that fact irritates me to no end. "It's not your job to protect me. I should have protected myself better."

His brows knit together. "As your fiancé, it *is* my job. But it isn't just duty that makes me want to protect you." He averts his gaze, expression shy again.

I'm at a loss for words. Could Cobalt have actual feelings for me? I knew he was kind when I first met him. At the picnic, I realized he was easy to be around. But could our relationship mean more to him than a forced arrangement? Could he...*like* me?

Cobalt meets my eyes again, and I know no one has ever looked at me the way he's looking at me now. He's looking at me the way men usually look at Amelie. Like I'm worth looking at. Like I'm interesting. Fascinating. Pretty. "When I saw the kelpie take you underwater, I thought I was going to lose you forever."

My heart races beneath the weight of his stare. He inches forward, and I wonder if he's about to kiss me. My breath catches in my throat. Do I...want him to kiss me?

His eyes study my face, then stray down my neck, hovering over the skin exposed above my nightdress. There's a hunger in his eyes, something I'd be delighted to see in any other circumstance, but right now I'm painfully aware of how awful I must smell, how crazy my hair must be. Cobalt doesn't seem anything but pleased to be near me, but there's no way I'm going to experience my first kiss with my future husband from my almost deathbed. At least let me bathe first.

I pull my hand from beneath his and drag the blankets higher over my torso, wishing I could cover my face and the flush of heat I know is clear on my cheeks. "You should enjoy your dinner, Your Highness, and I should get some more rest."

He opens his mouth as if he wants to say something but resigns with a nod. "You're right. I shouldn't keep you up."

The disappointment in his voice makes my heart sink, and I have the overwhelming urge to see his smile return. "Will I see you tomorrow?"

I'm rewarded with his beautiful grin. "Of course."

When he departs, I'm left staring at the ceiling, puzzling over my thoughts and feelings. Cobalt was going to kiss me, I'm sure of it. And if I'd felt more confident, I would have let him.

I turn on my side and cover my head with my blankets. Amelie's question from just a few days ago rings through my head. *Do you think we could come to be happy here?*

I'm starting to wonder if that question wasn't so stupid after all.

17

The next morning, I only feel half as terrible as I did the night before. Bright light streams through the windows, telling me I've slept late into the morning. Not only did I sleep late, but I slept deep too. The last thing I remember was my almost-kiss with Cobalt. I don't even remember Amelie coming to bed after dinner, or her getting up this morning.

Wait. Did she even come to bed?

My curiosity over her whereabouts is a welcome distraction from the other thoughts on the periphery of my mind—Cobalt's eyes as he drank me in, moments from closing the distance between us. And, of course, my subsequent reaction. It isn't long before those memories take over all other thought, making my heart race. At the time, pulling away from the potential kiss made sense. I was tired, dirty, weak—humiliatingly human. Now, after a full night's sleep, my reaction feels mortifying. He'd tried to kiss me. *Kiss* me. There was a strong part of me that wanted it. Yet, I rejected him.

Now I can only face the facts. I was scared. And not for the reasons I'm used to fearing about the fae. I was afraid because I'm not like Amelie, with her rotating list of endless suitors and lovers. The few courtships I had back home in Sableton were nothing to give up medical school for. Yet, none of those men had ever looked at me the way Cobalt did.

What would it have been like if I'd let him kiss me last night?

I let out something between a laugh and a frustrated moan as I smother my face in my pillow. A moment later, the sound of the door opening grabs my attention, sending me bolting upright. To my relief, there's no pain shooting through my skull at the motion.

"Good morning," Lorelei says in her bored tone. "Your sister said you might be up by now and would likely enjoy a bath."

"I would, thank you." I swing my legs over the side of the bed and place my feet on the cold marble floor. "Where is my sister, anyhow?"

She's taken aback for a moment, likely surprised I've accepted her help for once. "She was at breakfast. Now I believe she's walking the palace grounds."

I swallow the anxiety that bubbles up inside me. "Alone?"

"Well, Foxglove and I were at breakfast with her, but she didn't say if she was enjoying company on her walk or not."

I want to demand her reasoning for allowing Amelie to go anywhere alone but stop myself. Lorelei is our lady's maid, not our guard. And Amelie can take care of herself. At least, I promised I'd pretend to feel that way.

"King Aspen and Prince Cobalt will be at dinner tonight," Lorelei says. "They request the presence of both of you. That is, if you are feeling up to it."

"I am." Even if I hadn't been feeling better today, I'd still force myself to go. I've let Amelie out of my sight long enough.

"Very well. I'll put the order in for your bath."

After she leaves, I walk around the room, testing my legs after being dormant for so long. I move from the bed to the dressing table where I find my tattered gown—or what remains of it. To my relief, my dagger lays on the table next to it, belt intact. At least that wasn't lost during the struggle, although it didn't do me any good when I needed it. I set it behind the dressing screen so I can put it back on when I get dressed. When I return from behind the screen, wafts of steam draw my attention to the tub, which is suddenly full of swirling, fragrant water. I approach it, puzzling over how or when this happened. I've still yet to discover any source for the water to come through, not to mention the herbs and flowers floating on the surface.

Whatever the case, the bath is too tempting to linger outside it, and moments later I'm sinking into its comforting depths, forcing my questions and hypotheses to recede from my mind. I let out a heavy sigh, closing my eyes and feeling my muscles relax in response to the luxurious heat.

It's a struggle to pry my eyes open again when I hear the knock on the door. A moment later, Amelie bounds into the room and Lorelei follows closely behind. The two are laughing, as if sharing a joke, and I feel a squeeze in my chest. Since when did they become such fast friends?

"Lorelei, dear," Amelie says, "will you pick out a dress for my sister to wear today? She must look her best for dinner tonight. Oh, and see that Foxglove comes to do our hair."

"Of course," the fae says, then goes to the wardrobe.

Amelie comes to me and perches on the side of the tub. "You look much better today, Evie. How are you feeling?"

"I'm feeling well. How are you? Your cheeks are flushed."

She sighs, not meeting my eyes. "It's a beautiful day outside. I should have waited for you to wake before walking the grounds, but I just couldn't bear it. I'm sorry."

There's something about her tone and the way she averts her gaze that gives me pause. She's hiding something. "Who did you walk with in my stead?"

The pink in her cheeks deepens. "Oh, the palace is abundant with good company, if you know where to look. The residents and staff are most friendly, as you will soon learn once you're ready to move out and about again."

The residents and staff. Perhaps...a certain servant she mentioned last night? I catch a glimpse of Lorelei still digging through the wardrobe, back facing us. I lower my voice. "I didn't hear you come in last night."

"Ah, well I didn't want to wake you. I was quite discreet when I came to bed after dinner."

Her words weave double meanings in my mind, and I wonder if what I'm reading between the lines is truly there or simply my imagination. "How was last night's dinner, by the way?"

"Oh, very pleasant. I wish you would have been there. The food was divine, and the wine was even better." Her eyes take on a distant look, one that tells me more than her words can. I've seen this look before, many times. Amelie is in love.

The question is, with whom?

I WATCH MY SISTER LIKE A HAWK AS WE ARRIVE AT DINNER later that night. We're dressed in flowing fae gowns—I in coral and Amelie in sky blue—with our hair expertly piled on the top of our heads, thanks to Foxglove. We meet the two royals in the dining room. Aspen and Cobalt sit at opposite ends of the long table, while Amelie and I sit across from each other. Like the first night, Foxglove and Lorelei sit with us, although this time they don't wait for Aspen to invite them. The mood feels much lighter than it had the first time we were here.

Well, I should say the mood of everyone *around me* seems lighter. I'm once again a ball of tightly wound nerves. It doesn't help that I can hear the rhythmic crashing of the ocean far below the palace, the sound coming through the open expanse at the other side of the room. A shudder crawls up my spine.

Amelie whispers something in Lorelei's ear, prompting a giggle from the fae. I feel that squeeze in my chest again. It's not that I dislike the friendship that seems to have bloomed between them. It's more that I hate feeling left out. My sister has always been my best friend. And I've always been her confidante.

Amelie catches my stare, then reaches across the

table and puts her hand over mine. She turns her smile to Aspen. "Doesn't my sister look so much better, Your Majesty? She's like a rose come back to life after a winter frost, isn't she?"

Aspen doesn't so much as look up from his plate as servants pile it with one food item after the other. A second servant—the same wood-like fae from before—takes a dainty bite out of each piece that lands on the plate. "She looks the same as ever." His voice is flat, disinterested, with none of the seething danger I've heard when his words were meant only for me. Perhaps Amelie's perception of Aspen isn't too far off. Maybe for her, he really is as dull and harmless as she said.

Amelie laughs as if he's made some silly joke. She turns her smile to Cobalt next. "What do you think, Your Highness?"

With some trepidation, I lift my eyes to meet the prince's. It's the first time I've dared look at him since arriving to dinner. I've been too afraid to read what his expression might say. Too afraid I'll see none of the warmth I saw last night.

His lips pull into a shy smile and his eyes lock on mine before he answers. "She looks positively radiant. As much as I missed her presence at dinner last night, I'm glad she got some more rest." His eyes move from me to my sister. "It's just as you said. She's like a rose come back to life. I couldn't have put it any more eloquently myself."

My sister beams at him. "You're too kind, Your Highness. Now, how about some wine?"

I sit upright in my chair, eyes locking on the approaching servant. Is this the one Amelie was gushing over last night? The fae male steps forward and fills her glass. He's tall and slim with boyish good looks, pale golden eyes, and brown, tousled hair that brushes past his pointed ears to his shoulders. I watch the way Amelie smiles up at him, the way her gaze lingers on his when he bows to her. Is he the one? The one she's in love with?

"Evie, you must try this wine." My eyes flash to Amelie as she takes a sip. I didn't even catch if she salted it first. "I can't get enough these days."

The handsome servant lifts the decanter questioningly. I shake my head, but Amelie insists. The servant circles the table to fill my cup. I expect Amelie's gaze to follow his every move, but her eyes are on me, all innocence. Why is she being so difficult to read?

Once my cup is full, the servant returns to the far wall, and I lean toward my sister, lowering my voice. "Did you bring salt? I lost mine at the picnic."

She lifts her chin, a haughty grin on her face. She pushes a silk pouch across the table toward me. "Of course I did, silly."

I retrieve the bag of salt and sprinkle a dash in the wine, then over my plate. When I return it to my sister, she does the same. "Now try the wine already!"

Amelie watches eagerly as I take a sip. The flavor is sweet with just the right hint of bitterness, and the texture is as smooth as velvet. I can't help but close my eyes as I savor it.

"See?" Amelie winks. "Isn't it divine? It's one of the many pleasures I've enjoyed since coming here."

I narrow my eyes at her over the rim of my glass. "What other pleasures have you enjoyed, dear sister?"

"Oh, food, dresses, delightful conversation." Her eyes fall on each of us sitting at the table, ending with King

Aspen, who has finally taken a bite from his fully tested plate. "And, of course, my time spent getting to know the king. He's been quite the gracious host, Evie."

Aspen looks up from his plate, as if only just remembering our presence. He grunts as he finishes chewing. "Now that you mention it," he says to my sister, "I'd like to request your presence tonight in my study after dinner."

Amelie smiles and bows her head. "Of course, Your Majesty. Will there be more wine? And chocolate?"

"Whatever you like," he says flatly.

She turns her grin to me, eyes sparkling. "See? Isn't he just a dear?"

I furrow my brow, trying to decipher my sister's tone. She's emphasizing her words, exaggerating her contentment. Is she trying to tell me...could Aspen be the one she's in love with?

I can't decide whether that's better or worse than her being in love with some random servant. On one hand, being in love with the man she's forced to marry is ideal. It means she has a chance at happiness, as opposed to risking her life while trying to hide an affair. On the other hand, I don't trust Aspen. He killed his last fiancée. And his brother's too.

"No, sweetie, he's a stag." Foxglove's words startle me from my thoughts.

Amelie lets out an easy laugh while I cock my head at him.

He rolls his eyes as if I'm daft. "She said, 'isn't he just a dear?' But he isn't a deer. He's a stag."

I blink, then realize the joke too late. My eyes meet Aspen's and find an amused smirk on his lips. When he looks at me, he wears the same smug expression I've seen before. The same irritating pride. The same stunning beauty. The kind only a blade can keep at bay. I pat the dagger strapped to my thigh. *Control. I'm in control.*

The king burns me with his stare a few moments longer, then returns his gaze to his food, bored again, as if I'd imagined the silent exchange. But I hadn't imagined it. He'd stared. Taunted me with his eyes.

Perhaps the Stag King isn't as dull as he's been pretending to be in front of my sister.

But why pretend at all?

What are you hiding, Aspen?

18

After dinner, Amelie and I walk arm in arm through the dark yet elegant halls toward Aspen's study. The king left dinner while the rest of us were still enjoying dessert. Now that every course has been served, it's time for Amelie to join her betrothed for their daily chat.

"You didn't have to come with me, you know," Amelie says. "Lorelei could have walked me here."

She's right, but there was no way I'd let her out of my sight until the last possible moment. Even though it meant I had to turn down Cobalt's company back to my room. "I know. It's just...after three days of unconsciousness, I missed you."

"How could you miss me if you weren't even awake?"

I shrug, then watch her out of the corner of my eye. A dainty smile pulls at my sister's lips while her free hand contentedly lifts and swishes the hem of her blue skirts, as if she's moments from spinning into a twirling dance.

"Are you actually looking forward to spending time with Aspen?"

"He isn't as awful as you make him out to be, Evie." I'm surprised at the defensiveness in her tone. "You shouldn't be so quick to judge. You'd like him if you gave him a chance."

I slow our steps and gently turn Amelie to face me. "I didn't mean it like that, I swear. I'm merely curious how you feel. Do you like him then?"

She smiles. "He's boring, but he's not bad."

Not bad. That doesn't sound like something one would say about a lover. Unless she's trying to hide that she's in love with him. But what would be the point? Surely, she'd know I'd be happy for her if I knew there was love involved. Wouldn't she? "Ami, tell me honestly. Are you in love with Aspen?"

The smile still plays at her lips, but she turns away from me and continues her slow steps down the hall. Again, she swishes the hem of her dress and spins in a circle. "Wouldn't it be for the best if we loved the men we were to marry? If we could find happiness in the best possible way?" Her voice is light, whimsical. Heavy with the adoration she's trying to suppress.

I catch up to her, tugging on the sleeve of her gown until she stops and faces me again. "Yes, I agree with you. And I know you're hiding your true feelings from me." She opens her mouth, but I continue before she can deny it. "I understand why. You feel like I've been judging you, underestimating you. Criticizing this place that you've already come to love. I need you to know that, while I may not trust Faerwyvae, or the king, or the creatures here, I trust you. Whatever brings you love and joy, I support it. You know that right?"

Tears well in my sister's eyes, and her face crumples. She reaches for me, pulling me into a tight embrace. "That means so much to me, Evie. You have no idea how much."

The longer we remain locked in the hug, the more ease I feel. The tension melts out of me, the warmth of my sister's arms like a blanket.

When we finally pull away, Amelie grins. "Everything is going to work out perfectly for both of us, I promise. You'll see." Her tone seems conspiratorial, but perhaps I'm imagining it. Before I can analyze further, she links her arm with mine and pulls me down the hall, a spring in her step. "Then when we're married, we'll have to compare notes. See whose *kingdom* really is bigger."

A burst of laughter escapes my lips, and we take turns hushing each other as we make our way down the quiet hall. We're still giggling when we reach a closed door flanked by guards. My heart sinks as Amelie pauses before it. This must be Aspen's study.

"Time for me to go," she says as she faces me. "I'm glad we talked."

I reach for her hand and squeeze it. "Me too."

As if he could sense our presence, the door sweeps open, revealing Aspen. He barely looks at us before he turns away and takes a seat behind a large, ornate desk, leaving the door open between us. "Come in," he says.

Amelie gives my hand a final squeeze, then enters the room. I watch as she takes a seat in a throne-like chair opposite his desk, next to a table laden with plates of chocolate and a decanter of wine. She squeals with delight as she pops a truffle into her mouth.

I'm about to remind her to salt the chocolates when Aspen's drawling voice startles me. "You may go. Unless you'd prefer to stay, of course."

I meet his eyes, finding that dangerous glint, that half-smirk. A blush creeps up my cheeks as I realize the absurdity of me hovering in his doorway, an uninvited onlooker on his private time with his betrothed. I tear my eyes away from his to light on my sister. She gives me a reassuring smile.

I barely turn away before I hear the door close behind me.

WHEN I RETURN TO MY ROOM, I CAN'T FIGURE OUT WHAT to do with myself. I pace the length of the room, trying to occupy myself from thoughts of Amelie and Aspen. As much as I meant what I said to Amelie about supporting her, I can't shake my suspicion of the king. I can't fight the way my skin crawls when I think about the two of them as lovers. There's something so wrong about the pairing, although I can't say exactly what or why. Is it just because I know Aspen is dangerous? Or is it something else? Some fact I'm forgetting?

My door opens and I jump, startled from my thoughts. Lorelei enters and gives me a half-hearted curtsy. "I came to see if you needed help dressing for bed. I assume you don't, but—"

"Yes," I say, surprising myself. I'm eager not to be

alone with my thoughts right now. Not to mention, I may be able to probe the fae for information.

Lorelei looks equally as surprised. "Very well. I'll find you a nightdress."

She goes to the wardrobe while I take my place behind the dressing screen. I quickly remove the belted dagger from my thigh and slip off my gown. I'm in the middle of hiding the dagger beneath the discarded dress when Lorelei approaches.

She pauses, studying me, then raises a brow at the heap of dress at my feet. "You don't need to hide it. Everyone knows you carry it. Same with your sister."

The blood leaves my face. "Oh?"

She hands me a nightdress in a blush-pink lace. "I mean, did you think we can't smell the iron on you? Besides, you weren't hiding much when Prince Cobalt carried you in from the ocean. The dagger around your thigh is no longer a secret, if it ever was before."

I pull the nightdress over my head to avoid meeting her gaze. "And you say everyone knows? That we carry blades among your kind?"

"Sure. Yet, the king doesn't seem to hold it against you. Which is surprising, considering his history."

"You mean his temper?"

"No, I mean the threats to his life."

I furrow my brow. "Do you really believe the last girls tried to kill him unprovoked?"

She shrugs, arms crossed. "I believe humans can be dangerous. I can say that from personal experience." The bite in her tone reminds me of the confrontation we had over Mr. Osterman. Lorelei may have become friendly with my sister, but there's still a chasm between us. The fae turns away. "Will that be all?"

She doesn't wait for me to answer before she begins to head toward the door, each step slightly uneven from her limp.

"Wait," I say as she reaches the door.

She pauses, then turns to face me.

I hesitate before rushing to ask, "Can I look at your leg?" She narrows her eyes at me, and I rush to add, "I'm a surgeon's apprentice. Well, I *was*, at least. I can't help but want to check on your leg and make sure it's healing well."

Lorelei doesn't move. "It's healing."

"I know, but...can I check on it? Please?"

Her expression softens, and she lets out a sigh. "Fine. What do I do?"

"Go ahead and lie on the bed." As she does so, I retrieve my surgery kit.

"What is that?" Lorelei sits upright, eyes on the kit as I make my way toward her.

"It's my surgery tools, although I doubt I'll need them. It just helps me feel more professional to have it by my side."

Her eyes go wide. "Don't you dare use them on me. I can smell the iron from here."

"I won't then." I push the kit away from me, and Lorelei settles back on the bed. A question I've had hovers in my mind, and I try to find a tactful way to ask it without making her suspicious. "My tools are carbon steel, an iron alloy. Is such a metal harmful to fae?"

"Normally only pure iron is lethal to us, especially if it maintains contact with our flesh for too long, but any iron injury weakens us until we fully heal, making even weaker human metals unbearable to touch." She lifts her head and eyes me with a scowl. "Don't get any ideas."

I kneel at the side of the bed next to her and adopt my most soothing bedside manner. "I won't hurt you."

Lorelei lets out a resigned grumble as she lifts the hem of her silky bronze dress to reveal the injured leg. My stomach churns to see her battered flesh again, to see the pink, puckered skin where iron teeth had torn it to shreds. I inspect every inch of the leg, looking for signs of infection. Although, I'm not entirely sure what to look for, aside from what I'm used to seeing in humans; I have no idea what to expect from fae infection.

Next, I gently prod the skin in places, asking Lorelei to tell me if anything feels tender. There are a few painful areas, but for the most part, her leg appears to be on the mend. Her bones seem to be set correctly. I'm almost certain I detect stitches in places, although they look nothing like the stitches I've seen. Hers are fine and delicate, weaving the skin together with little evidence of intervention.

"Who tended your wounds?" I ask.

She turns her head to face me. "I did some on my own. As a wood nymph, I was able to speak to the vines and roots to brace my leg and hold my torn flesh together so I could make it to Bircharbor. Gildmar did the rest."

"Who's Gildmar?"

"She's an Earthen fae employed by the Autumn Court for healing. She cleansed my wounds with herbs and stitched the deepest ones with spider silk."

"It looks like she did well. I'm going to check your range of motion now." I lift her leg, easing her to bend slightly at the knee. "Does it hurt when you walk or put weight on the leg?"

"A little." Her words are still laced with a bitter edge. "Other things hurt more. Things no one can ever heal."

My stomach sinks. I rotate her ankle slightly one way then the other. "What was she like?"

She furrows her brow. "Who? Gildmar?"

"No. Your lover. The one you lost."

Her eyes turn to the ceiling, a blank expression on her face. The weight of her leg seems to grow heavier, as if the question drained all the strength from her. I think she might ignore me, until she finally says, "Malan was beautiful. A pixie from the Spring Court with wings as pink and fine as cherry blossom petals. Her hair was the same color, a silvery-pink that always smelled of roses." She sighs. "Malan was the best part of me. She kept me kind. Made me laugh. I loved her."

My throat feels tight as tears prick my eyes.

Lorelei lifts her head to meet my gaze. "Are you finished?"

Her tone isn't unkind but snaps me out of my daze. I realize I'd released her leg, my hands frozen and resting lightly on her shin. With a shake of my head to clear it, I rise to my feet. "Yes. I feel confident you will heal well. I see no sign of infection and your range of motion is what I'd expect at this point of recovery."

Lorelei stands, shifting her weight from one foot to the other. "You know, it actually feels much better." She lifts her gown, examining her leg. "It looks better too. What is it a surgeon does, anyway?"

I'm torn between laughing and maintaining my professional manner. She must have thought my actions were more than simple inspection. How can I explain I didn't do a thing to help her? That whatever ease she feels is nothing more than a placebo? "A surgeon usually operates on tissues and organs with tools like the ones I have in my kit."

She takes a few steps, then flashes me a smile—something I've rarely seen from her. "Well, whatever you did, it worked. It hardly hurts."

"Perhaps the stretching and motion exercises helped," I say, not wanting to lose her gratitude by telling her the truth. "See if you can continue gentle stretches daily to improve your overall flexibility."

"Sure. Uh, thank you for this." She wrings her hands, as if suddenly uncertain around me, then bites her lip. "I suppose I should apologize, shouldn't I?"

I tilt my head. "For what?"

She sighs. "I'm not sorry for what I did to the Butcher —to your friend. But I know it must have hurt you to see him in pain. That I'm sorry for. And for saying you were a self-righteous harpy with a mouth bigger than her brain."

"You never said that."

She waves a dismissive hand. "Not to you, of course."

My lips tug into a smile. First Foxglove, now Lorelei is beginning to seem charming too. "I'm sorry as well. I misjudged you. It's just...I haven't had the best experiences with the fae."

"I doubt either of our kind have had many positive interactions since the war."

I nod. "You're right. It's funny, though. I grew up with a sort of terrified reverence for your kind, instilled by my mother. I was fascinated with what little I knew about Faerwyvae, with the idea of magic, but then...

something happened. It changed everything I thought I knew."

My throat feels tight as the memory seizes me. Perhaps it's my worry over Amelie being alone with Aspen, but I can't shake the images that flood my mind— my sister's face, eyes alight with mischief as we ran through the woods toward the faewall. It was a perfect summer night, aside from the presence of Maddie Coleman. It was her dare that brought us to the faewall that night four years ago and sent the three of us circling one of the stones to prove we were brave enough to cross the wall. We'd maintained contact with the stone the entire time, holding our breath as we circled it to the fae side, then burst into fits of laughter when we returned safely to the human side seconds later. Our laughter died when we turned to run back home and saw the fae that stood before us.

Lorelei wrings her hands again, and her voice comes out soft. "You can tell me about it. If you want to, that is."

I consider shaking my head, telling her it's nothing, but I stop myself. After the vulnerability she shared with me tonight, perhaps I can return the honesty. I take a deep breath. "Four years ago Amelie and I met a goblin, tiny and horrid with sharp fangs and wrinkled, sagging skin. There was no mistaking it was there to cause mischief. We were frozen, terrified and fascinated at the unusual sight. It seemed it was equally fascinated with us. Amelie, in particular. Its beady eyes locked on hers, and she stared right back. After a while, she forgot to blink."

I remember my horror when Amelie's face went slack, recall the glint in the goblin's eyes when he realized he had her under his control. That's when Maddie Coleman ran screaming, leaving Amelie and me alone with the creature.

"The goblin ordered Amelie to come toward him, and she did. He ordered her to put her hand out, and she did. She paid me no heed as I tugged at her arms, pulled at the sleeve of her coat. All she could do was walk toward the creature, hand outstretched toward his vicious mouth, a placid smile on her face all the while. When he lunged forward to sink his teeth into her palm, I threw a rock, hitting him between the eyes. That's when Amelie was able to return to herself. We ran, but he chased us, nipping at our heels and shouting after us, saying if he didn't get a taste, he'd make our insides rot."

"You got free, though," Lorelei says.

"Yes. I don't remember when we could no longer hear him following, when his teeth and claws ceased to graze our heels. By the time we got home, the backs of our dresses were torn to shreds, our voices incoherent as we told Mother what had happened. She could hardly make sense of what we were saying. We just kept repeating that a fae had attacked and cursed us. All she could do was give comfort, tell us we were safe. Then later that night, Amelie collapsed, writhing in pain. She began vomiting, grasping her belly. She was certain the goblin's curse was coming to take her, insides rotting just like he said. Mother tried to break the curse using tinctures and counter-charms. We stayed up all night while she chanted over my sister, trying to purge the curse from her."

"Your mother is like you then?" Lorelei asks.

I shake my head. "No. My mother's craft is nothing like surgery, and surgery was what Amelie needed. It turns out, she wasn't plagued by a curse after all but a very serious medical condition. We only discovered this because I was stupid enough to try to return to the wall the next morning. I wanted to seek out the goblin, beg him to lift the curse from my sister. If that didn't work, I was prepared to offer myself in her stead. I couldn't bear to see my sister in pain and would rather die than lose her."

"What happened? Did you find the goblin?"

"No. Luckily, I was intercepted by Mr. Meeks, Sableton's surgeon. He saw me in distress heading toward the woods and made me tell him what was happening. Once I told him about Amelie, he insisted on seeing her. He raced home, got his surgery kit, then came to our house. That's when I learned the power of modern medicine and got to witness true healing. Amelie was never cursed. She was glamoured, yes, but what happened after was nothing more than a coincidence. My sister had developed appendicitis. If Mr. Meeks hadn't intervened, her appendix would have ruptured, and Amelie would have died."

Lorelei's eyes are wide. "I have no idea what an appendix is, but it sounds terrible."

Her statement shatters my somber mood, and I find myself laughing. She laughs with me, although it's clear from her expression that she isn't sure what we're laughing about. Once I begin to sober, I let out a heavy sigh. "Thank you for listening, Lorelei. That's not a story I like to tell, but oddly enough, it feels good to have told someone."

She smiles. "I think that's what a lady's maid is for, right?"

"Listening to me ramble on about my adolescence goes above and beyond the duties of a lady's maid." If I were ready to admit it, I'd say it falls into the realm of friendship.

"I never thought I'd hear that high praise from you," she says. "Is there anything else you need from me tonight?"

"No, go ahead and retire. I'll wait for Amelie to return."

"Very well." She offers a curtsy—one deeper than any she'd given me before—then leaves the room.

Once I'm alone, my eyes begin to grow heavy, muscles pulling with fatigue as if I really had performed a surgery. Or perhaps it's from the story I told. With slow steps, I retrieve my dagger from behind the dressing screen and stuff it beneath my pillow before crawling under the covers.

I'm determined to stay awake until Amelie returns. Then again, what if my suspicions are correct, and she's been sleeping elsewhere? Will she stay the night with Aspen?

The question makes my blood boil, but it quickly fades as sleep overtakes me.

In the night, I dream.

A dark figure looms over me, teeth sharp and glinting with moonlight as a snarl pulls at his lips. He lowers his face until it's hovering mere inches from mine. His chest heaves with anger.

It isn't a dream.

I reach for my dagger, hilt in hand and blade at the figure's throat. He pays me no heed as Aspen's voice growls, words rumbling with rage, "Where is your sister?"

19

H is words echo through my mind. *Where is your sister?*

The question takes me by surprise, making my dagger hilt tremble in my fingers. Aspen's warm, wine-scented breath on my face brings me back to myself, reminding me of his proximity. As my eyes adjust to the moonlit dark, his shadowy features take shape in front of me. I press the blade to his throat, letting its edge break the skin. "Get. Off. Me."

He jolts back, wincing from the searing iron as I spring from the bed, keeping the dagger between us as I back up a few paces. It only deters Aspen a moment. He bounds toward me, and I retreat until I find my back pressed against a wall. Nothing but my dagger separates us as he closes the distance, the tip of my blade pressed to his sternum. With one thrust, I could have it buried in his chest.

Aspen doesn't seem to care. "Where is your sister?" he repeats.

I push his chest with my free hand, trying to force him back. It does nothing but shift the cloth of his shirt. "Why are you asking me? She was with you, you fool. Don't act like I didn't leave her in your study."

His chest heaves with rage. "She isn't there anymore. Where did she go?"

I narrow my eyes at him. "What, did she disappear into thin air?"

"No," he growls. "I left for only a few minutes. When I returned, she was gone."

"Gone? How is that—" My eyes widen, and I thrust the dagger tip forward. He winces and springs back a few inches. This time I'm the one closing the distance, forcing his retreat as anger heats my blood. My voice comes out with a snarl that could almost match his. "What did you do to her?"

"What did *I* do? Me?" His fingers lock around my wrist before I can prick him with my blade again. "I did nothing."

"Nothing?" I slam his chest again with my free hand. "Why else would she run away at the first chance? You did something to her. What did you do?"

"So, you admit she ran away."

My mouth hangs open. I struggle to free myself from his grip, but his fingers don't budge, suspending my wrist and dagger in midair. "Running away is the only logical conclusion based on what you've told me," I say through my teeth as I continue to struggle in vain.

"Where did she go?"

"I don't know."

"You're lying. You're in on it too. What are you planning? Aside from trying to kill me with this pathetic blade?" He turns my wrist, forcing my fingers to open. The dagger clatters to the floor, and he kicks it away.

I hold my ground, crossing my arms over my chest. "If I was trying to kill you, I would have slashed my blade through your throat when I had the chance. Besides, if one of us is lying, it's you."

He fixes me with a seething glare. "I can't lie."

"Then I suppose we're at an impasse, because I'm not lying either. What will you do next? Execute me for treason?"

Aspen holds me with a glower for what feels like an eternity. Finally, his breathing begins to steady, the heaving of his chest subsiding. He takes a step away but doesn't tear his eyes from mine. With a snap of his fingers, a warm light illuminates above the sconces in my room, bringing him into clear view. I try not to wonder at how the light could have responded to him like that, and instead take in his appearance. His hair is disheveled, and a thin, red line runs across his throat. It looks like dried blood, the superficial wound I gave him likely already healed beneath it. "You don't know where your sister is?"

"No. Like I said, last time I saw her, she was with you."

"She was there," he says, voice still much like a growl. "We spoke for a time until she requested more wine. I ordered some to be brought up, but the idiot servant brought honey pyrus wine. You, of all people, should know why that could have been disastrous. Still, she seemed as content as ever when I left to exchange it. When I returned, she was gone."

Wine. A servant. Could it be? What if I'd gotten our earlier conversation wrong? What if Amelie wasn't in love with Aspen after all? Would she do something so foolish as to run away with a handsome servant? Then again, perhaps it was a matter of Aspen catching a lingering glance between the two, igniting his jealousy. This entire confrontation could be a ruse to cover something far more devious. "Who brought the wine? Was it the same servant you used during your earlier visits with Amelie?"

"What does that have to do with anything?"

"Answer the question."

He runs his hands through the blue-black hair between his antlers. "I don't know. I have a lot of servants."

I squint at him, trying to decipher if there's deception beneath his words. I proceed with caution. "Did something else happen? When the servant brought wine? Did you...see something you didn't like?"

He tips his head back. "What is that supposed to mean?"

Footsteps sound in the hall outside my room. Aspen whirls around as several guards march in. One approaches Aspen. "Your Majesty," she says as she gives him a hurried bow, "someone was seen running toward the coral caves."

"When?" barks Aspen.

"Just now."

The caves. I'm too stunned to comprehend what this could mean. Was Amelie running away? *Truly* running away? She would have to be terrified out of her wits to do something as reckless as that. To leave me behind. My rage returns hotter than ever. "What did you do to her?"

Aspen ignores me. "Send guards after her."

The guard nods. "I've already dispatched some, Your

Majesty, but the tide is already coming in. She won't make it long in there, nor will the guards."

He gives the fae a withering look, and his voice comes out cold. "Send guards to search every cave. I want the water up to their chins before a single one tries to return. And after that, I want guards stationed on the beach. If you don't find her alive, I want her body retrieved when it washes ashore."

The guard salutes and leaves my room, while I bristle at the carelessness of his words. "You're a monster."

He rounds on me. "I'm not the fool who ran into the caves. And if I find out you have anything to do with this, I'll throw you in the ocean after her." With that, he storms out of my room. I race after him, but before I reach my door, he shouts at the other guards who had remained in the hall. "Don't let her leave her room."

I halt as the fae guards bar my path. One reaches forward to slam my door shut. I'm left gaping, heart racing. What in the blazing iron is happening? All I can think of is my sister, running for the caves. Running from terror. From Aspen.

I channel my rage into beating my door with my fist, begging the guards to let me out. It doesn't matter that the action is fruitless. I must do something—*anything*— with my body to keep myself angry. Because if I'm not angry, I'll be anxious. Terrified. I'll lose my mind.

Hours pass, the light of dawn breaking through my windows, yet I continue to shout and throw my weight at the door. My voice is raw, shoulders and hands throbbing, by the time the handle begins to turn. I'm so shocked, I barely have time to move out of the way before the door swings open. Cobalt's eyes lock on mine, and before I realize what's happening, he pulls me into his arms. I hardly register the fact that I'm crying into his chest, my entire body racked with sobs.

He brushes a hand along my back, smoothing my hair. "Let's get you out of here," he whispers.

"Here's her cloak," says a voice behind me. Lorelei. She drapes the heavy fabric over my shoulders, and I pull it tight around me. That's when I remember I'm in nothing more than my nightdress. Cobalt rests his hand on my lower back and guides me out of the room. When we reach the hall, the guards are nowhere to be seen.

"I sent them on a false errand," he says. "I can't believe my brother locked you in your room when your sister is missing. That was cruel, and I'm sorry."

"He was only being cautious," Lorelei says from the other side of me, "but I agree. It wasn't the right thing to do in this situation."

I'm lost in a daze as we move through the halls of the palace. "Where are we going?"

"I don't know," Cobalt admits. "I just wanted to get you out of your room. I knew you'd be worried sick. I can take you to my room, if that makes you feel more comfortable."

Someone rounds a corner at the end of the hall, then begins racing toward us. As the figure closes the distance, I realize it's Foxglove. "They found someone," he says breathlessly.

The words make me alert, clearing the fog from my brain. "Where? Is it my sister? Is she all right?"

Foxglove wrings his hands. "They're bringing her from the caves now."

"Take me to the shore," I demand.

"My brother has the lower part of the palace heavily guarded," Cobalt says.

I face him. "I need to see her."

He holds my gaze. "You might not like what you see."

I don't want to consider what he means by that. Instead, I grit my teeth. "I don't care."

"The dining room," Lorelei says. She takes off down the hall, and I follow. Up the stairs we climb until we reach our destination. I rush to the other side of the dining room to the rail at the edge of the open expanse. There, beneath the dim light of the rising sun, I see the narrow sliver of beach, crawling with guards. The rest is hidden by the tide, revealing only the slightest hint of a cave as the crashing waves recede.

I hardly blink as I watch every movement of every guard, seeking any sign of my sister.

Foxglove gasps, then points toward the beach. "The cave. Look."

I watch as the rolling waves pull away from the shore, revealing movement at the mouth of the only visible cave. A guard pulls himself from the opening just as another wave crashes into him. He holds his ground until the water pulls away, then he reaches into the opening. His arms wrap around something that he hoists forward, a blur of white and blue. Another figure emerges from the entrance, pushing the bulk of their burden to the shore. Once the two guards are free from the cave, several more follow, all dripping seawater.

The first two guards reach for the bundle they'd pulled ashore. One lifts a set of pale arms. The other hoists up her legs. A third spreads a thin, blue fabric— what remains of a tattered dress—over her body like a shroud, covering even her face. What I can see of her hair looks nothing more than a mass of dark tangles, heavy with water and kelp. Still, I know it's her.

It's my sister.

She's dead.

My scream splits the air.

20

My feet fly beneath me as I tear across the dining room floor and down the stairs. I follow twists and turns, descending more stairs, taking any path that seems to lead me farther down in the palace. Shouts of caution follow me, but I ignore them. Ignore Cobalt as he takes hold of my arm and tries to make me stop.

I shake my arm from his grasp. "Let me go!"

He obeys but sticks close to my side as I take off running again. "My brother won't let you down there. As soon as he sees you, he'll lock you in your room again."

"I have to see her. I have to see my sister."

"There's nothing to see, Evelyn."

A fiery rage boils my veins, and I round on him. "Nothing to see? That was her body they pulled from the caves! How is that *nothing to see*?"

He opens and closes his mouth a few times. "It's just... why would you want to see that up close? You know she's...dead, right?"

His words drain the fight from me. The blood leaves my face, sending a wave of dizziness through my skull. I collapse to my knees, head hanging as tears obscure my vision. It's not that I didn't already know, but hearing him say it shatters all that remains of my feeble hope. "No. This can't be. She can't be gone."

Cobalt crouches next to me and places a hand on my shoulder. "I'm so sorry, Evelyn."

"Did he do it?" My voice comes out small. "Did Aspen have her killed when she was found? Or did she drown?"

He shakes his head. "I don't know. He's capable of anything, and if he finds you here, he'll have you sent back to your room. Or worse."

I wipe the tears from my cheeks and force myself to my feet, willing my mind to push emotion aside and find logic instead. I steady my expression beneath my surgeon's calm. "I still need to see her." At the horrified look on Cobalt's face, I add, "It's a human thing. We identify our dead."

"You know my brother won't let you see her right now. In fact, we need to get you higher in the palace before he—"

Footsteps sound down the hall, and before I can so much as think, Aspen rounds the corner, followed by a retinue of guards. He freezes when he sees me and Cobalt. "What is she doing here?"

With a deep breath, I square my shoulders and face him. "Where is she? My sister? What did you do with her body?"

A flash of surprise crosses his face. "You know about the body?"

"I saw her."

He takes a few steps toward me. "Did you, now?"

"I have a right to identify her body. Take me to her."

"You said you already saw her. Does that not qualify as identifying her?"

I stumble to find my reply. "It's—no, I—"

He turns to his guards, motions at a pair to his left. "Take her back to her room and make sure she stays inside this time. The Council of Eleven Courts will be here any moment."

The two guards surge forward, but I don't balk or argue or run. I simply burn Aspen with a hateful glare, then turn on my heel and begin walking in the opposite direction. I pay the guards no heed when they catch up.

"Don't touch her," Cobalt barks, when one tries to grab hold of me. "You may follow my brother's orders and accompany us, but I'll be walking her back to her room." Cobalt puts a hand on my lower back, his touch a steady guide as we make our way through the halls.

Only when I'm alone in my room do I let myself fall apart.

A DAY PASSES, THEN A NIGHT. I DON'T SLEEP AND I DON'T receive any visitors. I refuse the trays of food the guards push inside my door, letting the uneaten plates pile up on the floor. When morning breaks, my well of tears is fully dry and my sensible side tugs me back to reality.

My sister is gone. Dead. And there's nothing I can do to bring her back.

I'm tired.

I need to eat.

With shuffling feet, I cross the floor from the bed to the door, where the leftover food remains untouched. On my way, I find my dagger, lying useless on the floor where it landed after Aspen kicked it away. I retrieve it, then investigate the plates of food, finding a roll of bread as the only appetizing feature. I bite into it, not even caring that I haven't salted it. Luckily, the bread appears harmless, as it does nothing more than slightly quell the aching hunger in my stomach.

A knock sounds on my door, making me jump. Lorelei peeks inside, then enters, closing the door behind her. She meets my eyes with a look of apology. "Are you all right?"

I puzzle over the question before I answer. "I guess so," I lie. In truth, I'm not even close to all right. But she probably knows that.

"You are requested at breakfast," she says.

I set down the bread roll. "Just like that, my appetite is gone."

"I'm so sorry. I know the king is the last person you want to see right now, but his temper has calmed regarding you. By now he must realize you had nothing to do with your sister's disappearance."

"Yes, but how do I know *he* had nothing to do with it?" I mutter.

"He couldn't have wanted things to turn out the way they did," Lorelei says. "After every Reaping, the hosting court of the Chosen is put under deep scrutiny. The month leading up to the wedding that secures the treaty is a precarious time. Whatever happens between the hosting court and the Chosen is the difference between peace and war. You must see these mishaps have done nothing to benefit the king. They only make the council question his competence as a ruler. He could lose his throne if they find him unfit. Do you think he wants that?"

"Perhaps that's for the best."

Lorelei bites her lip before replying. "You know, he isn't so bad as you think he is."

I let out a bitter laugh. "Amelie said the same thing. And she's now dead."

"Fair enough," she says with a sigh. "I can't sway your opinion, especially when your loss is so raw. I, more than anyone, can understand that. But you must go to breakfast. Follow his summons. For now."

I meet her eyes. "What do you mean by that?"

She shrugs. "The council left at first light. That means they came to some conclusion about the treaty. For all you know, what happened with your sister could have broken it. Aspen could have been forced to step down. You might even be sent home."

Sent home. Relief washes over me, then terror. How can I return home without Amelie? How can I face my mother and tell her what happened? Something else tickles at my mind. "Wait. If the treaty is broken, wouldn't that mean war?"

She nods solemnly. "Yes."

I'm struck with a sudden resolve to know the truth. If there is to be war, I don't want to linger here any longer than necessary. Beyond that...I don't even want to think about it. "Fine, I'll go."

∾

Once I'm bathed and dressed, Lorelei leads me to breakfast. I'm surprised to find it held in a smaller dining room, one I've never been to before. Whatever the reasoning for the change, I'm grateful for it. I don't think I could look at that open expanse in the formal dining room without remembering my sister's body. Not today.

Aspen hardly glances my way as I enter and take a seat at the small table, while Cobalt offers me a sad smile. The two brothers are already eating, and a plate of food has been laid out for me next to a bowl of salt. Once I salt my food, I push the items around the plate, but can't seem to bring any to my lips.

"I'm sorry about your sister."

I'm shocked to hear the words uttered from Aspen's end of the table. I look at him, but his eyes are on his food. My mouth feels too dry to respond.

"I shouldn't have locked you in your room either," he says. His words are strained, like it pains him greatly to admit his fault.

"No, you shouldn't have," I say. My voice comes out weak, but my anger is helping clear my mind from its daze. "Are you going to let me see her body?"

He takes his time chewing his food before answering. "No."

"Then your apology is wasted on me."

Silence falls over the table again, my scorn hanging over our heads like a shroud. I can feel Aspen's anger rolling in waves, but I try to pretend I don't notice.

Cobalt leans toward me, his voice low. "You should eat. The guards say you haven't touched the food that was brought to you."

I open my mouth to reply, but Aspen's voice halts my

words. "Maybe she'd prefer wine," he says. With a snap of his fingers, a servant steps forward, decanter in hand.

My eyes jolt to the face of the servant, expecting to find the handsome male, but this one is unfamiliar to me.

"In fact," Aspen says, "all servants who have served me or any of my guests wine since the Fairfield girls arrived, please step forward."

The servants exchange hesitant glances. Then, one by one, several step forward from their places along the walls. I eye them all, then meet Aspen's penetrating gaze.

"Do any of these servants spark recognition?" he asks.

I'm about to say no, when I think I see the handsome one I remember from the other day. He shifts anxiously from foot to foot. "I don't understand," I say. "Why are you asking me this?"

Aspen narrows his eyes, fingertips steepled together as he leans back in his chair. "You seemed to suspect one of these servants after your sister went missing. Since you never explained yourself, I've come to suspect them too. Why did you ask me about a wine servant? About seeing something I didn't like?"

My mind goes blank as I seek an explanation. What can I say that won't condemn me or any innocent person? I have no idea if my suspicions are valid in the first place. Besides, it's *him* I'm more wary of.

I take a breath to calm myself, then meet his gaze. Two can play at this game. "You mistake me, Your Majesty. It wasn't your servants I suspected, but you."

A flicker of surprise crosses his face before he steels his expression. "Explain."

"Well, you see, I only brought it up because I thought perhaps you were a jealous male. There are many handsome fae here in the palace, but none could match the beauty of my sister. It made me wonder if you disliked the way they looked at her."

"You specified a wine servant. Why?"

I lift my shoulder in a casual shrug. "They seem to me more beautiful than the rest, that's all. If I were a jealous male, I might feel inadequate around them, king or no. And clearly," I wave my hand toward the servants around us, "they have you riled up indeed."

His knuckles go white as his fingers curl into fists. Perhaps I went too far. "Guards," he growls. Fae guards enter the room from the hall, bronze armor glistening in the light of the morning sun. "Take these servants to the dungeon. Execute them."

The guards surge forward to obey, and I leap to my feet. "What? Why?"

Cobalt stands as well. "This is absurd, brother. What did they do wrong?"

He says nothing as the servants are taken hold by the guards.

The horror on the servants' faces makes my stomach churn, heart racing as I watch their arms wrenched behind their backs as the guards shove them forward. I don't know why I should care. These fae are nothing to me. Yet, for some reason, I *do* care. The servants are likely innocent and are only being condemned because of something I said.

Before I have time to consider my actions, I'm rounding the table to approach the king. I place my hands on the tabletop as I lean toward him, lowering my voice to a furious whisper. "I'll admit, I suspected Amelie was in love with someone. I hoped it was you, but part of me wondered if she had feelings for someone else. Now that she's gone, we may never know. However, the truth remains that I was never worried one of these men would do her harm, but that *you* would. If you execute them all, it proves you have something to hide."

His lips return to their twisted smirk. "You want me to show them mercy, do you?"

"Yes," I say through my teeth.

He holds my gaze a moment longer. "Did you hear that?" His voice echoes through the room, stopping the guards in their tracks, freezing their attempts to funnel their prisoners into the hall. "Miss Fairfield requests mercy."

Silence answers. No one moves.

He returns his eyes to meet mine. "Fine. I'll heed your advice. I'll show them mercy. Considering you'll soon be their queen, I'll allow this choice to be yours."

His words send a wave of confusion through me. Their *queen*? Me?

He addresses the guards. "Take them to the dungeon for questioning only. At sunset tonight, release them and allow them to return to their stations."

Sighs of relief escape the prisoners, and the guards leave with them. The tension eases out of the room, yet I remain in place next to Aspen. Finally, I discover my words. "What did you mean about me becoming their queen?"

He smiles a devious grin, making my stomach drop. I know what he's going to say. "You're going to be my wife."

21

"No!" Cobalt and I shout at once.

Aspen seems unperturbed by our outbursts and returns to his meal, fork in hand. After taking a few bites, he says, "It's what the council thinks is best for the treaty to remain valid. A marriage must still take place."

"Then Evelyn can marry *me*," Cobalt says. "There's nothing in the treaty that says who the marriage should be made to, only that it is made to a fae of the hosting court."

Aspen fixes his brother with an indignant stare. "Yet, I am king, so I decide who she marries."

Cobalt's shoulders heave, and I expect him to shout. Instead, he lets out a growl of frustration and storms from the room.

"You get your way yet again." My voice is quiet, filled with iron. "Another potential bride. Another waiting victim. Another way to punish me."

He throws his fork down, letting it clatter on his plate.

"If I wanted to punish you, I *wouldn't* marry you. Is that what you want? For the treaty to become invalidated? For war to rage over the isle? For every person you love to die?"

"You could allow me to marry Cobalt instead. The treaty would remain valid."

"I could," he says, face smug, "but I won't."

My fingers curl into fists, nails digging into my palms. "You have no claim to me just because you're king. I am not a thing to be owned."

He closes his eyes and rubs his temples with a groan, as if I'm the impossible one. His words come out strained through his clenched teeth. "I'm starting to believe war wouldn't be the worst idea. All I do is maintain the safety of the isle, yet I'm repaid with treason at every turn."

"Treason? You're out of your mind! No one is committing treason against you. If you had any sense at all, you'd see the real terror to the isle is you."

He rolls his eyes. "I don't care what you think of me. The choice is yours. Either you marry me, or the Fair Isle reverts to war. I'm getting tired of caring one way or another. What's it going to be?"

Fury roars through me, making my limbs tremble with rage. "I hate you."

His face twists into something between a glower and a menacing smile. "So much that you can't fathom marrying me for the sake of your people?"

I lean toward him. "So much that I will carve out your heart if you try to take me to your bed. I'll marry you. I'll sign the contract. But don't think for a moment we'll be anything more than cold allies."

His expression doesn't falter as he brings his face closer to mine. "So you accept my proposal?"

I hate the way my eyes are drawn to his mouth, the way he drags his tongue over his bottom lip, as if he's savoring the anger radiating off my skin. I want to shout at him, to slap the smug look off his face as his eyes rove over me, claiming me.

But I'll never be his.

With some effort, I push away from the table, away from him. Even when I turn away, I can still feel his eyes burning into me.

THE COOLNESS OF THE HALL OUTSIDE THE DINING ROOM IS A welcome comfort. I didn't realize until now how warm I'd become. Sweat drips down my neck and beads at my forehead. I quicken my pace, not quite knowing where I'm going. My only thought is to widen the distance between me and Aspen, to forget his words, to shake his face from my mind.

I don't even see the pair of arms that reach for me from the shadows of the hall. With a squeal, I leap back and draw my dagger, only to realize it's Cobalt.

"I didn't mean to startle you," he says, palms forward in surrender as his eyes dart from me to the dagger.

"It's all right," I say, releasing a heavy sigh and returning my blade to its sheath beneath my skirts. "What are you doing here, anyway?"

"I came out here to cool my rage, then decided to wait for you. We need to speak in private."

I nod, and he takes my hand. We move quickly down

the hall until he pulls me into a room and closes the door. The room is small, curtains drawn shut, revealing mostly shadows and a few sparse furnishings.

"It's an unused parlor," Cobalt explains. "Used to be my mother's. Don't sit on anything. It hasn't been dusted in years."

I make no move to contradict his request, and we remain by the door. "What did you want to talk to me about?"

He takes my hands in his. When he meets my eyes, his expression falls. "I'm so sorry about all of this. I can't imagine how you must feel right now."

After my confrontation with Aspen, I only feel numb. "I don't think I've had enough time to process it all. I don't know how to feel or what to do."

"I still can't believe he'd do this. I know exactly why he's doing it too. He can't stand the idea of looking weak next to me, of the advantage it would give me if I were the one to secure the treaty with a marriage instead of him." He gives my hands a squeeze, expression pained. "He can't take you from me."

"Apparently, he can do whatever he wants." My voice is cold, bitter.

His hands move to my shoulders, bringing me closer to him. I can feel the coolness of his palms through the fabric of my dress. He lowers his voice. "Not if we act first."

"What do you mean? What could we possibly do?"

"We could leave together," he says, tone pitched with a blossoming excitement. "Perform the mate ceremony, then get married in secret. Our marriage would keep the treaty intact."

"But your brother," I argue. "He would never let us live after such a betrayal."

"We could fight him. We'd find no shortage of allies who would stand against him. I already told you how the council feels. They don't want him on the throne if he keeps acting this way."

For a moment, I let the fantasy take hold, let the idea weave images through my mind. I imagine me and Cobalt running away together, imagine us rising against Aspen, watching the council pull the throne out from beneath him. I think of a court ruled by Cobalt, gentle, kind, and fair. I think of the peace his steadfast nature would bring his people and mine. It's a beautiful fantasy, but I know it's just that. A fantasy. Cobalt may be able to gather allies, but is that enough to beat Aspen without getting himself killed in the process? And what about me? There's no fight left in my bones. Not after what happened to Amelie. Not after the hateful words spoken between me and Aspen.

"No," I say, my voice barely above a whisper. Slowly, I reach my hands to cover his, then pull them away from my shoulders. I give his hands a gentle squeeze, enjoying the coolness of his fingers, before I release them and take a step back. "I can't put you in danger."

"I don't care about the danger. I care about protecting you."

I offer him a sad smile, then pat the dagger at my thigh. "I'm not vulnerable."

"But I care about you."

My throat tightens. "If we care about each other at all, the best thing we can do is protect each other from Aspen's wrath. You may not care about the risk, but I do. I won't be able to live with myself if Aspen tries to hurt you. In fact," I take another step away from him until my back is against the door, "this is the last time we can meet like this. I won't do anything that rouses Aspen's suspicion against you. You saw what he nearly did to the servants."

He looks down at his feet, shoulders slumped. When he lifts his head, his expression sends shards of glass into my heart. "This is really what you want?"

I nod, then reach behind me for the handle.

"My feelings won't change." His voice breaks on the last word. "I'll do what I can to protect you, even if you become his wife."

"Thank you," I say, then open the door. I'm about to step into the hall when Cobalt stops me with a word.

"Wait."

Our eyes lock, and he closes the distance between us, hands framing my face. His lips find mine and press them into a firm kiss. It happens so fast, I can hardly comprehend it, much less enjoy it. I'm too stunned to move. If I were Amelie, I'd put my arms around his waist, pull him close to me, part my lips to allow the kiss to deepen.

But I'm not Amelie.

Thoughts of my sister drain me of all potential passion, making my shoulders go rigid. Cobalt must be able to tell, because he gently pulls away. "I'm sorry," he says. "I just had to do that once."

"I—I'm glad you did." *It might be the last kiss I'll ever have,* I think to myself.

"Also...there's something you should know. It's about the mate ceremony."

The worry in his eyes sends a chill down my spine. "What is it?"

"Aspen still plans to go through with the mate ceremony as previously scheduled, which will be in four days' time. Afterward, you'll be expected to participate in a fae ritual. You must refuse."

I remember what Foxglove had said about the mysterious ritual before we got sidetracked by talk of mating. It occurs to me I've yet to get a clear answer on what it involves. I furrow my brow. "Why?"

"Because it would mean giving my brother your true name."

My true name. *That's* what the fae sacred ritual is all about? My blood goes cold.

I've seen what a regular glamour nearly did to Amelie, but that's nothing compared to what a fae can do when he's been told he has your true name. Mr. Meeks says the hormone the fae release during prolonged eye contact is an unintentional function of their biology. Yet it's hypothesized that fae custom is the only thing preventing them from secreting the hormone purposefully and in greater quantity. The *true name* itself has no meaning. There's no secret name to utter, no chant to perform. It is but a statement that you are on a level of deepest intimacy, which to the fae, means they can do whatever they wish to you.

If Aspen had my true name, I'd be under his control with no free will of my own. My stomach churns at the thought.

"Promise me you won't do it."

"Trust me, I'll do whatever I can to avoid it." Even if it means my death, I don't add. Before he can say anything else to make me linger, I open the door and step into the hall. As I return to my room, all I can think about is Cobalt's crushed expression when I turned him down. I had no other choice. We'd never be able to survive Aspen's wrath.

I have to protect him. Protect Eisleigh.

I have to marry a monster.

22

I count the days until the mate ceremony with numb awareness, stumbling in a daze, going through the motions. It feels like wading through mud, each day a struggle to get through. Most of the time, I try to turn off my emotions, following logic instead. Eat. Breathe. Do as I'm told.

Four.

I tolerate dress fittings with Lorelei, give half-hearted answers to Foxglove's questions about requested foods for the celebratory feast that follows the ceremony. He takes me through the steps of some strange dance I'm supposed to perform with the king. I learn it, memorize it, but I feel like I'm hardly there.

Three.

Foxglove says something about ribbons and masks. I nod, but the ribbons remind me too much of Amelie. She always loved pretty ribbons. I turn away from him to stare out the window for a while. That night I dream about seawater filling my lungs, of my sister calling my name as waves drag her into the coral caves.

Two.

When I wake, I force my pain to subside, put on my mask of calm. Try not to think of Amelie. More dress fittings. More masks and ribbons. Another round of practice for the dance.

One.

When the day arrives, I stand before my mirror, staring at the stranger in front of me. She wears my face, lips covered in a deep burgundy rouge, cheeks powdered a rosy blush. A russet-gold dusts my eyelids and lines my lower lashes, along with some rich browns and yellows. The makeup distracts from the dark circles I know lie beneath, and helps cover the ghostly pallor I've adopted as of late.

My eyes rove over my dress, a flowing gown of pale blue spider silk dotted with white pearls. The skirt is layered with a sheer fabric stitched with silk leaves in the same pale blue and flutters with every move I make. The colors on my face and dress bring to mind autumn leaves falling through a clear midday sky. To someone else, this would be a dream dress. To me, it's a nightmare.

It reminds me too much of a wedding gown.

Even though I know the mate ceremony isn't an actual wedding, it still makes my stomach churn. The way Foxglove explained it, the mate ceremony is a way for Aspen and me to present ourselves as a couple—*mates*. The first step in securing the alliance. The final step is our wedding ceremony. That will occur in just over two weeks.

I shudder.

"You look beautiful," Foxglove says, fixing a loose strand of auburn hair into place.

"He's right," Lorelei says. "There's no doubt you're the Queen of the Autumn Court."

Her words send a chill down my spine. Queen. I still haven't gotten used to the idea that I'm going to be a queen after we're married.

"Now for the final touches." Foxglove reaches for an elaborate mask from my dressing table and steps behind me to secure it over my eyes. It only covers the top portion of my face above my nose, but the embellishments adorning the top make the mask appear much larger than it is, creating a halo of robin feathers and golden leaves overhead. The mask itself is made of bronze, carved with elegant swirling patterns and decorated with pearls.

Next, Foxglove grabs a handful of long ribbons, motioning for me to raise my arms. He explained the ribbon part of the ceremony to me, but I'd only been half listening. Something about a ribbon representing each element, and how we'll have to untie them from each other. Foxglove ties the first—a red ribbon—around my hips, then a yellow one around my waist, a green one around my chest, and a blue one around my head and the mask. The bow of the final ribbon hangs slightly into my line of vision as it dangles from my brow.

"There," Foxglove says, admiring his work. He looks pleased, but I feel like a gaudy present as I look at my reflection.

"It's time," says a voice from the other side of my room. I find Cobalt hovering in my doorway. He wears a simple blue mask, lips pressed into a tight line. A pang of sadness tugs at my heart as I meet his gaze, but I quickly release it. I can't let myself consider regrets. No what-ifs. "Are you ready?" he asks.

"I suppose so," I say, trying to keep my voice neutral. I'm determined neither to fake joy nor reveal distress. I shall be calm. Composed.

Cobalt enters my room and meets me at the mirror. "I'll walk you," he says, extending his arm.

I hesitate, wondering if it's smart to walk with him. Then again, if Aspen didn't come to take me himself, perhaps he doesn't care. Without a second thought, I place my hand at his elbow and we leave my room. The halls are quiet and nearly empty, with most servants and guards congregating higher in the palace near the topmost balcony where the ceremony will take place.

Foxglove and Lorelei follow behind me and Cobalt as we make our way through the halls and up the stairs. We pass the landing that leads to the formal dining room, then climb another set of stairs even higher. Too soon, the sound of voices falls upon my ears. We come to the bottom of a final staircase that ends in bright sky overhead.

"I'll leave you here," Cobalt says, then leans in closer. With a shiver, I think he might steal a kiss, but his words whisper in my ear, "You remember what I told you? About the fae ritual?"

How could I forget? "Yes."

"You won't do it, right?"

I raise a brow. "Do I look crazy to you?"

"Well, you are about to become my brother's mate."

"Fair enough."

A shadow falls overhead, bringing my attention to the

top of the stairs. I find a silhouette stark against the clear blue sky, a tall, lean frame with antlers. Even with Aspen's features obscured in shadow, I know he's glowering. But is it at me or his brother?

Cobalt all but leaps away from me, then proceeds up the stairs. As he reaches the top stair next to his brother, the two face each other. I can feel the tension between them until Cobalt turns ahead and continues out of sight.

Aspen faces me and extends his hand, like darkness itself beckoning me to join him.

"Go on," Foxglove says with a gentle touch on my shoulder.

With trembling steps, I make my way up the stairs, trying my best to keep my head held high. I'm momentarily blinded as I cross the threshold from the dim staircase to the open air of the balcony above. When my eyes adjust, I take in the wide platform opening before me. Its floor is of smooth citrine and the perimeter is lined with a golden rail. Two throne-like chairs perch on a raised dais at the far end, with a bronze silk rug leading to them from where I stand. On each side of this rug are nearly a dozen unfamiliar fae. Since the balcony is set at the pinnacle of one of the palace's highest towers, nothing but open sky surrounds us, giving way to views of distant hills colored in all shades of red, gold, and brown. The sound of crashing waves and crying gulls echo from far below.

It's the first time I've been here, and I must admit it's beautiful. For a moment, it's enough to make me forget the fae male before me.

All it takes is a breath for the moment to shatter. I can feel Aspen's eyes burning into me, hand still outstretched.

My eyes flash toward him, taking in his elegant bronze suit beneath a red and gold cape lined with leaves and raven feathers. A crown of gold shaped like maple leaves and dotted with rubies sits between his twining antlers, slightly obscured behind the feathers of his mask. His mask matches mine, and the same four ribbons are tied around his body. Part of me wants to laugh at how comical the ribbons look in contrast to his regal bearing and elegant state of dress. But this is no time for laughter.

I swallow hard, then accept his hand, allowing him to steady me as I take the final stair to stand at his side. "You look beautiful." His words are so quiet, I have to question whether I heard him right.

"Meaningless flattery," I mutter through my teeth.

He lets out a low grumble and leads me forward. I try to remember what Foxglove told me during our preparations. *First, walk to the other end of the balcony, hand-in-hand with the king.*

We take a step, and the sound of harp begins to float in the air. Our next step prompts the beat of a low drum. I seek out the source of the music, finding a fae at the bottom of the dais, strumming an enormous harp. The fae has a feminine, human-like upper body and a long, fish-like tail. She must be a siren. Next to her sits a stout, heavyset fae with leathery skin and long, green hair who beats a wooden drum. The music picks up with every step we take, rumbling beneath my feet as we walk down the aisle between the fae.

My attention moves to these unfamiliar figures dressed in elaborate gowns and eccentric suits. These must be the ambassadors Foxglove told me about during our preparations. He said an ambassador from each court would be present for the ceremony today. Each fae wears a mask, although none are as embellished as mine and Aspen's. As we pass, they stare down at me with their piercing eyes. I do my best to keep my gaze trained straight ahead. My composure remains intact until we reach the other end of the balcony and I find a face I recognize. A *human* face. Sableton's vicar nods to me as we pass him, looking quite out of place in his somber black robes and unmasked face. I'm surprised by his presence, even though Foxglove did say a human would be here today to bring word of our actions back to Eisleigh's council. It just never occurred to me it would be someone I know.

Once we reach the base of the dais and the two thrones, we pause, then again face our audience. The music trails off into silence. My breaths grow shallow as I recall what's supposed to come next. Every pair of eyes is upon us, and I suddenly regret not paying more attention to the previous days' preparations. This ceremony may mean nothing to me, but that doesn't mean I want to look like an idiot in front of these strangers, not to mention Sableton's vicar. I blink a few times, clearing the fog from my mind. Aspen still clutches my hand, and I feel my palm growing sweaty in his.

"Are you ready?" he whispers.

"No."

I can see his smirk from the corner of my eye. Without another word, he lifts our hands, and the music begins again. The beat is deeper, heavier, the harp slow and sensuous. Dread fills me.

That's right. It's time for the stupid dance.

The fae shift to form a semi-circle around us. Aspen

releases my hand and takes a step back. I mirror his steps, recalling all the times I practiced with Foxglove these last few days. We step in again, our hands touching, then break away once more. This time when we come back together, Aspen reaches for the red ribbon around my hips. It's a struggle not to flinch from his touch as he pulls one end of the bow. "The earth in you is the earth in me," he says, and the ribbon falls away from me.

We step away. Return. This time I must do the same with him. "The earth in you is the earth in me," I mutter, yanking on the ribbon until it comes from around his hips.

We step to the side, hands touching, then face each other again. He takes hold of the yellow ribbon at my waist. "The fire in you is the fire in me."

My turn again. The music pounds in rhythm with my heart, and somehow I manage to keep the beat with my motions. I take his yellow ribbon and echo his words.

We turn, backs facing each other. Step to the side. Face forward. Aspen takes the blue ribbon from my brow. "The air in you is the air in me."

Turn. Step. Turn. Echo. My breaths go heavy as we near the end of the dance. Step forward, step back. To the side, turn. Side. Turn.

We face each other, and Aspen pulls the green ribbon at my chest. "The water in you is the water in me."

Repeat. "The water in you is the water in me." My words come out breathless. From the exertion of the dance? From nerves? From the terror of what comes next?

He lifts his right arm out to the side, ribbons clutched in his fist. I do the same. With his other arm, he puts his hand at my lower back, pulling me close. My arm trembles as I mirror the motions. We circle and sway, circle and sway. Foxglove steps forward to take the ribbons from Aspen. Lorelei takes mine. Next, they move behind us and remove our masks. The freedom from the mask makes me feel surprisingly naked, and I wish I could shove it back on.

We pause. The music, however, continues. I feel the drumbeat in my bones, feel the harp rushing through my blood. It's dizzying, terrifying, invigorating. We release each other and press our palms together, bodies remaining close. Lorelei and Foxglove stand on each side of us, tying the ribbons around our joined hands. I lift my head and meet Aspen's eyes for the first time since we began the dance, meet his penetrating gaze with a glare. I know what happens next.

Before I can prepare myself, Aspen leans in and presses his lips to mine. A raging fire roars through my blood. I want to push him away, but with our hands bound, I can do nothing but squeeze my eyes shut and remind myself it will all be over soon. Besides, the ridiculous fae custom states we are to kiss until the ribbons are untied from our hands. It feels like an eternity that Aspen and I stand there, lips pressed limply together. I wonder how much longer it will be before Foxglove and Lorelei get on with it and free us already.

Aspen's lips flinch against mine, and for a moment I think he's going to pull away from the kiss early. But instead of pulling away, he moves closer, lips parting slightly to sink the kiss deeper. It ignites my rage, but I find myself leaning into the feel of his lips, the press of his torso against my breasts. The music seems to wrap around us, weaving our kiss into its song. Aspen's lips part again, and I find myself doing the same. His tongue brushes against mine. Something roars inside me, and I can't tell if my anger has reached new heights or burned into something else entirely.

Before I can ponder it further, the kiss ends and Aspen stands upright, a confused look in his eyes. Did he feel the rage coursing from my lips to his? Or is it that *something else* that has him so bemused?

It takes a few moments to realize our hands have been freed. I let go of him and take a step away, burning him with a glare. That kiss was far more than I signed up for. Not that I signed up for any of this.

He tears his eyes from mine and takes my hand again, raising our fists in the air.

Our audience erupts with cheers.

23

With the ceremony over, we adjourn to the dining room for a celebratory feast. I'm about to take my usual seat at the middle of the table when Foxglove sidles up next to me. "Not anymore, sweet one," he whispers, then ushers me down to the end of the table, opposite of where Aspen sits. It's the secondary place of honor. Cobalt's usual seat.

"What about the prince?" I whisper.

"You're the king's mate now," he says, "and soon-to-be queen. Your place is here."

The king's mate. I grit my teeth, trying not to think about that infuriating kiss. As if he can sense my thoughts, Aspen lifts his eyes and meets mine from the other end of the table, a crooked smile quirking his lips. I avert my gaze and take my seat.

The guests quickly fill up the remainder of open chairs. Cobalt sits to the right of his brother at the other end, while Foxglove and Lorelei sit on either side of my end. I'm relieved to have them here, especially surrounded by so many strangers. The remaining guests are the fae ambassadors as well as Sableton's vicar. I'm surprised to see the latter take the seat opposite Cobalt, next to Aspen.

I look over the table, finding it laden with aromatic fruit, plates of oysters, bowls of violets, and towering tiered trays of chocolates. Several decanters of wine in every shade of red are set out. Everything is rich and decadent, evocative of sensuality. Even the room has been decorated to match the mood; deep red tapestries cover the walls, the floor is strewn with plush velvet pillows, and dark red lilies fill every vase.

My eyes rove to the fae ambassadors. They chat animatedly as they settle in, reaching for foods to fill their plates, holding their glasses for the servants to fill with wine. I can't see much of their faces, since only Aspen and I have taken off our masks, but they all appear quite civilized. I see a few whiskers, snouts and swishing tails, a few mouths with pointed teeth, but nothing I haven't already seen here at the palace.

I lean toward Foxglove. "Are all the fae ambassadors seelie?"

He nods approvingly. "You are correct in your observations. The ambassadors from every court, regardless of political affiliation, are seelie. This is because they must interact with humans on occasion, and we learned long ago that unseelie make terrible ambassadors to the human lands."

It makes me wonder what it would be like if I were in a room with unseelie fae instead. Are the unseelie kings and queens goblins and trolls? Vicious beasts like the kelpie? Whatever the case, the ambassadors are an interesting sight. Their gowns are bright and elaborate, like costumes in a play. The more masculine suits are composed of varied colors and fabrics, some with padded shoulders, others with trailing, glittering coattails.

A painful thought comes to mind. *Amelie would have loved to see this.* My throat tightens, lungs constricting as I try to keep the tears at bay.

To distract myself from my grief, I return my attention to the ambassadors and challenge myself to discern which fae belongs to which court. It takes a moment to recall all eleven courts Cobalt had named during our picnic, but I'm pretty sure I have them committed to memory.

I see a fae female with blue skin and a mask of seaweed and coral—an obvious Sea Court fae. A male with dark brown skin, a leafy-green suit, and moss for hair seems a candidate for Earthen. An androgynous fae next to him seems composed entirely of shimmering particles of glitter, making me think Star Court, while the next fae over must be Lunar, with her black dress speckled with glimmering opals and moon-white skin. Or did I get the two swapped? The pixie in a ruffled pink dress with wings the color of a robin's egg could be Spring. Or perhaps Wind? No, Wind must be the fae with the streaming hair that constantly moves as if in flight. And the two fae with golden skin and bright hair are equally convincing as both Fire and Solar.

I'm lost in my game of logic, certain the fae female in the revealing, paper thin gown in shades of green, orange, and blue is Summer Court, when the sound of my name startles me. Silence falls over the room. I find Aspen's eyes at the other end of the table, lips pulled into his mocking grin as he raises a wine glass. All eyes lock on me, staring expectantly. Even the vicar watches from his seat next to Aspen. I feel my face flush with heat. What in the name of iron did I miss?

"He's raising a glass to you," Foxglove whispers under his breath, "as his mate."

With a trembling hand, I reach for my glass and lift it. "Thank you." My voice comes out flat and uncertain.

Most of the ambassadors smile with approval, while the rest squint at me, as if puzzling over a foreign object, but all reach for their glasses. Sound returns to the dining room, and before long, I'm once again forgotten in favor of the meal.

"Did he get the human gesture right?" Foxglove asks. "A *toast*, I think it's called? Silly name and quite deceptive."

"Yes, why? Was he trying to impress the vicar?"

"No," Foxglove says. "It was meant for you—"

"More wine?" A servant steps between us, decanter in hand.

I'm about to say no—I haven't had a single sip—when I recognize the server. I can't see him fully beneath the slim gold mask he wears, but I'm sure it's the handsome one I suspected Amelie might have been fond of. The thought sends another squeeze of pain to my chest. After a moment of hesitation, I say, "Please."

As he leans forward to fill my cup, he whispers, "Thank you. For asking the king to show us mercy."

"You're welcome. I'm glad he followed through with his promise to release you."

"Of course he did." He says it as if he's unable to comprehend my doubt.

Oh, to be fae and never have to question another's promise. I, on the other hand, never believed Aspen was going to release the servants after questioning, much less let them return to their previous posts. That's how much I trust *his* promises. Before I can say a word more, the fae flashes me a smile and moves down the table to serve the others.

"Are you going to eat anything?" Lorelei asks, raising a brow above her dainty green mask. I feel like it's all she's done the past few days—remind me to eat. She pushes a bowl of salt toward me.

With a sigh, I salt my food and wine, and pretend to enjoy my dinner.

APPARENTLY, A CELEBRATORY FEAST IN FAERWYVAE consists of seven courses, four of which are wine. By the time we reach the end, the dining room is filled with laughter and chatter and all sorts of menacing sounds that make my head throb. All I want is quiet and to be alone.

I lean toward Foxglove. "Can I leave now?"

He's leaning back in his chair with his feet propped on the table, head thrown back in laughter at something Lorelei said. His spectacles rest on his forehead while his mask sits askew over his eyes. Lorelei sits on the table facing him and can barely finish her story, wine sloshing from the rim of her cup as her shoulders heave with snorts and giggles. Neither seems to have heard my question.

I rise to my feet, which gets their attention. "I'm leaving."

"No, my lovely," Foxglove says. "You must stay until the end."

I put my hands on my hips. "Why? Does it have anything to do with sealing the treaty? If not, I'm done here."

Lorelei's eyelids are heavy as she regards me. "It's important you stay until the end," she says, words slow and slurring together.

"But why?"

"For the treaty," Foxglove says, not nearly as intoxicated as Lorelei. "The ambassadors should see you retire with the king so they know you'll be mating."

I feel the blood leave my face. "But we aren't married yet. Humans don't mate until after marriage."

Foxglove throws his head back in bellowing laughter. "That's funny, dear."

"I'm serious."

"Honey, you are the king's mate now. That's all the permission you need to take him to bed. Besides, you'll be married in a couple weeks. There's no need to feel guilty about it."

It's not guilt I feel, but I don't say so. Propriety has never been my main concern in life, but I'd hoped the excuse would keep Aspen away for at least a while longer. My eyes flash to him at the other end of the table. The pixie in the pink dress leans over the table, lashes fluttering as she says something to him. His eyes lock on mine as he grunts his reply, his expression bored. She's clearly flirting with him, which is oddly irritating. Does she not realize she's at a mate ceremony? *His* mate ceremony? Then again, why do I care? She says something else, then pouts. He keeps his gaze on me as she flutters away.

Lorelei lifts my barely touched wine cup from the table, stealing my attention to her. "Come on, Evelyn, celebrate with us."

Anger roars through me. My words come out in a furious whisper. "This is not a time to celebrate. My sister is dead. Do you have no concept of grieving?"

The two fae seem to sober a little at my words. Lorelei sets down both cups of wine, while Foxglove's lips turn down in a frown.

Tears threaten to spill from my eyes, and I can feel the lump returning to my throat. Around me, the beautiful ambassadors laugh and chat and dance. A few have taken servants to the velvet pillows to kiss—perhaps more than kiss, if I dare look hard enough. The pixie is flitting in front of a guard, finger trailing over his bronze chest plate. The Sea Court ambassador has a servant—a female fae with a dainty pink bunny nose—giggling in her lap. It all seems garish against the landscape of my loss. Even if I wasn't wholeheartedly against this stupid ceremony to begin with, I wouldn't be able to celebrate. Not without Amelie.

I hold my breath, willing the pain to recede. I can't break down. Not now. Not in front of all these fae.

"May I have a word?" a quiet male voice asks.

I find the vicar at my side. His complexion has paled, likely from the excessive lust and frivolity around us. I can't imagine he feels anything close to comfortable here. With a deep breath, I don a shaky smile. "Of course."

He takes a few steps away from the table, and I follow.

Once we're out of earshot of the others, he says, "I thank you for your greatest sacrifice for the good of Eisleigh. You have brought peace for another hundred years."

I'm not sure what to say, considering my sacrifice was forced upon me. "It is my duty."

"And how have you been treated since you've been here?"

I open my mouth, but no words come. What do I even say? *I was attacked by a kelpie, my sister is dead, and now I'm forced to marry a beastly fae. Oh, and did I mention, the monster I'm marrying may have murdered my sister?* I want to tell him this, but I don't, suddenly aware that everything I say could be taken back to the council and used as grounds to invalidate the treaty. "I've been treated...as expected," I finally say.

"Very good. I'll be sure to tell the council that you have taken the first step in securing the alliance. I'll be back to oversee your wedding." He pauses and looks around the room. "Where is your sister? I know her marriage alliance was forgone, which surprised the council, but at least yours will continue as planned. Still, I'm surprised she isn't here at all."

My mouth falls open. How does he not know? "My sister is—"

"There you are, my mate." Aspen steps between me and the vicar. "It's time for us to retire."

"But—"

He raises his voice over mine, addressing the room at large. "Thank you for attending our celebration and witnessing this first step in securing the treaty. You may stay or you may return to your courts, I don't care."

The ambassadors burst into laughter, although based

on Aspen's disinterested tone, his words hadn't been made in jest.

He continues. "My mate and I will retire now." With that, he takes my arm and pulls me toward the hall. Before we reach it, I catch Cobalt's eyes flashing me a warning. I give him a subtle nod. *Don't worry, Cobalt. I know what happens next.*

In the hall, a pair of guards flank us, and I pull free from Aspen's grasp. "How does the vicar not know what happened to Amelie?"

He lets out an irritated grumble. "Come."

"No, not until you tell me."

His face transforms into a smile, but the effect is more devious than kind. "Our room is this way, mate," he says too loud, eyes flashing over my head.

I turn, finding a fae figure—the one from the Sea Court—hovering in the doorway of the dining room, her bunny-fae companion kissing her ear. Then another fae, the glittering one, peeks into the hall.

Now that I know we have an audience, I understand Aspen's forced smile. He extends his hand to me. I grit my teeth and take it.

I remain quiet as we continue down the halls, flanked by the two guards. The eerie feeling I'm being watched follows me. We ascend a staircase, and I wonder if he's taking me to the balcony where we had our ceremony. Instead, he stops before the final staircase that would lead there and turns to an ornate pair of doors protected by another set of guards who open them for us. Aspen all but pushes me inside before slamming the doors shut behind us.

"Do you want war?" he shouts, rounding on me.

"Excuse me?"

"Because that's what will happen if your people think your sister is dead."

My hands clench into fists. "Are you saying no one knows the truth? Not even our mother?"

"No one can know a thing until I am certain what happened."

My voice rises to a shout as I close the distance between us. "So you haven't taken her body to Mother to be buried? What are you doing with it then? Where is she?"

"Lower your voice," he hisses. "I am taking care of it."

My stomach churns. What does that mean? What does any of this mean?

He turns his back on me and storms over to a small table. There he pours wine from a decanter and swallows the glassful in a single gulp. As he stands there, eyes closed, I take in my surroundings.

We're inside an immense bedroom, lit by a fire roaring in a hearth as well as several of the orb-like lights above the sconces on the walls. The bed sits in the center of the room, the base consisting of elegant roots that seem to be growing straight from the floor, its posts of slender, white birch. Branches tangle overhead with red-orange leaves to form a canopy, and the blankets are bronze silk brocade.

I turn in a circle, taking in the rest of the room—furnishings of deep, dark wood, plush rugs, a turreted ceiling painted like an autumn sky. I've never seen such elegance, such autumn incarnate indoors. When I finish my circle, I'm again facing Aspen. I must have caught him off guard, because he watches me with the same curious look I saw on his face after our kiss.

I watch him right back, eyes narrowing to slits.

He sets down his glass. "We should perform the Bonding ritual."

The Bonding ritual. So that's what it's called. I cross my arms over my chest. "We most certainly will not."

His expression darkens. "Why did I expect anything else?" he mutters.

"Yes, why did you? We may have done a ridiculous dance and called it a ceremony, but I am not your mate. When we marry, it will be for alliance purposes only. Nothing more, and you know it. Do you really think I'm going to participate in a ritual where I give you my name?"

"You know."

I turn up my chin. "I should have been told sooner. Giving you my name—"

He takes a step toward me, and something like panic crosses his face. "Did it ever occur to you that I don't want to do this either? Especially when it means I have to give you my name in return?"

I'm surprised by this. He has to give me his name too? Cobalt only mentioned my part in the ritual. Still, what good will having his name do me? It's not like humans have access to whatever makes fae overpower us.

"I've been thwarted by your kind time and time again," he says. "Now I'm supposed to trust you with the one thing that could be my undoing."

"Well, it seems like forgoing the ritual will be mutually beneficial then."

He presses his fingers to his temples, grumbling

something unintelligible. "Fine," he finally says. "We've both had a long day. We'll postpone the Bonding."

"We'll cancel it," I correct.

Aspen's jaw shifts back and forth. "We'll get some sleep and reassess in the morning."

"Then I'll be going." I spin on my heel toward the door.

Aspen strides toward me, blocking the door. "What do you think you're doing?"

"I already told you," I say with a sneer. "I will never allow you to bed me, not even for the sake of sleep. I'm returning to my room."

"How do you think that will look to the ambassadors? The vicar? I don't know who's a spy, who's plotting against me."

I let out a sharp laugh. "I know exactly who."

He tilts his head back, surprised. "Who?"

I cup my hand over the side of my mouth and motion him closer. My voice starts as a whisper and ends in a roar. "No one, you arrogant, self-obsessed, paranoid fool. No one is plotting against you. You're the one murdering humans and endangering the treaty, no one else!"

His chest heaves with rage, and I realize I've gone too far.

I try to keep my composure as I take a step away from him. "I should leave."

"No," he growls. "I will." With that, he storms to the doors and out of the room, leaving me in stunned silence.

24

For minutes on end, I just stand there, unable to move. But can you blame me? Aspen left me in what is obviously his personal bedroom. I'm both too afraid to leave and too afraid he'll return at any moment.

When I finally get the nerve to further investigate my surroundings, I find my belongings have already been transferred here. One side of the wardrobe holds most of the fae dresses that used to be in my old room. The dressing table and screen have been brought over as well, taking up a corner of the room next to an enormous carnelian tub. My bag, my surgery kit, and all my stray items have been neatly arranged behind the dressing screen.

The only things missing are Amelie's. I blink back tears at the thought.

I find a nightdress in the wardrobe and change behind the screen, even though the room is empty. Then I take my dagger and wander the room again, investigating every crack, looking under every table and within every shadow. Once I've surmised no threat has been left for me, I make my way to the bed. My fingers tremble as I turn down the covers, peel back the spider silk sheets. This is Aspen's bed. *His bed*. The thought is equal parts disturbing and thrilling.

I allow the latter sensation to prevail, finding satisfaction in the fact that I've momentarily won. He forfeited his bedroom to *me*. And if he's going to be so difficult, I certainly won't suffer for it. Let him wander the halls or sleep in a closet, or whatever it is brooding fae do when their pride is wounded. Let me get a good night's sleep for once.

And I do.

I DON'T SEE ASPEN THE NEXT DAY. OR THE NEXT. I HARDLY see anyone at all, for that matter, save for Foxglove and Lorelei. Since the king has yet to return to his bedroom since our argument, I begin to grow more and more comfortable, taking meals in there, snooping through Aspen's things. Yet I've found nothing to occupy me for long and spend most of my time alternating between grief and boredom.

By the third day, my curiosity is too strong. "Where are King Aspen and Prince Cobalt?" I ask Foxglove, meeting his eyes in the mirror as he twists a lock of my hair. "During the day, that is," I quickly add, in case I'm supposed to be keeping up the ruse that Aspen and I have been spending the night together.

"Hasn't your mate told you?" He places a jeweled pin

in my hair. "The king has been inundated with correspondences regarding some issue with the humans."

"What kind of an issue?"

He shrugs. "It's not my place to know or say. I'm his
ambassador, not his confidante. When I'm needed to go
smooth things over, I'm sure he'll let me in on all the
details."

I chew my bottom lip, wondering what this could be
about. Is it about Amelie? Has Aspen finally decided to
tell my people the truth? Or could he be trying to invalidate our alliance and break the treaty? The blood leaves
my face at the thought.

"He must know you're restless with him so preoccu-
pied," Foxglove continues. "Which is why he's brought a
guest to visit."

"A guest? Who?"

His expression brightens. "I went out of my way to
make it a quaint little human ritual. What do you call it...
sitting for tea? I made up a room like a parlor and
imported tea from your village. Isn't that too cute?"

"But who is my guest, Foxglove?"

He rolls his eyes. "It doesn't matter if I tell you. You
don't know her. Not personally, at least, but once I'm
finished with your hair...there!" He steps back and evalu-
ates my auburn tresses. "Now I can take you to meet her."

I follow Foxglove out of Aspen's room and down the
hall, eager to discover who my mysterious visitor will be.
We stop at an open door, and I freeze when I see what's
inside.

"You're impressed, right?"

I press my lips tight together, the strain of suppressing
my laughter almost too much to bear. Inside the little

room is a fine couch, a tea table, and an elegant chair. Surrounding these furnishings is an eyesore of human junk, from a grandfather clock to a coat stand dangling with numerous umbrellas, coats, and—oddly—a pair of boots. Everything is coated in doilies and frilly shawls, the floor sprawled with overlapping rugs of unfashionable design.

"Does it remind you of home?"

I'm not sure if I should be offended by that, considering he saw my home and should know this tacky room looks nothing like the parlor at the apothecary. "Yes," I manage to say. "Just with more...stuff."

"More character, you mean," he says. "I love human knickknacks. Some of these were left as offerings at the wall."

"Is this where our offerings end up?" I ask, lifting a corner of a yellowing doily. "In unused rooms at all the palaces?"

"Of course not." Foxglove says. "This just so happens to be my personal collection. When the king asked me to make you a private room to take guests, I figured I'd put these things to use. They didn't come cheap, you know. That rug itself cost me six garnets."

My eyes widen. "Are you saying our offerings are taken from the wall...and sold?"

"Only the most curious things. The rest is discarded. I'm sure hundreds of years ago, seelie fae were eager to get their hands on anything human. A new emotion to taste from a bite of pastry. A new human-like characteristic to learn from a pair of kid gloves. By now, Faerwyvae has enough human influence to keep the seelie quite satisfied."

"If our offerings are sold or discarded, how in the name of iron do the fae decide which girls to select for the Reaping?"

Foxglove shoots me an odd look. "The fae don't choose. Your human council does. The hosting court can override that decision with a choice of their own, of course, but that's a rare thing."

My head swims as I ponder the implications of everything he's saying. All those times Mother brought Amelie and me to the wall with our offering of bread and milk. All that time we thought the gesture would keep me and my sister safe from the Reaping. All that time we were wrong. It was my own people who were in charge all along.

"They're so precious, don't you think?" Foxglove says with a sigh, oblivious to my agitation. "Such silly, useless things. Yet, they have an irresistible charm."

"They sure do," I mutter.

Foxglove beams. "I'm glad you approve. Aspen will be pleased, and I'm sure your guest will be equally so."

"Where is my guest, anyhow?"

"She's waiting below. I wanted you to see your parlor before I brought her in. I can fetch her now if you're ready." He takes a step toward the door, then pauses, furrowing his brow. "You *do* like it right?"

I pull my lips into what I think is a warm smile. I'm sorely out of practice, but Foxglove deserves to see my gratitude. As gaudy as the room is, and as disappointed as I am to learn the futility of our offerings, I know his heart was in the right place. "Of course, Foxglove. I love it."

I take a seat on the couch as I wait for my guest. A few minutes later, Lorelei brings in a tray of tea, cookies, and salt. She freezes when she enters, looking around the room in terror. "What in all the rotting oak and ivy is this awful mess?"

I hush her. "Foxglove worked really hard on this."

"I can see that. The question is why?"

"He thinks it's what a human parlor looks like. Which is beyond me, considering he's the ambassador to the human lands."

She sets the tray on the table, nose wrinkled in disgust as she eyes her surroundings. "So you're saying every parlor doesn't look like this?"

"No, but don't tell Foxglove."

Noise sounds down the hall, and I rise to my feet. A moment later, Foxglove enters with a woman. A human woman. Her eyes widen as she enters the room, but other than that, her expression remains blank.

"Miss Fairfield, I'd like for you to meet Doris Mason," Foxglove says.

The woman curtsies, then takes a seat in the chair across from me. I return to my seat on the couch, pondering the familiar name. *Doris Mason.* Where have I heard that? Then it dawns on me. "You're the Chosen from the last Reaping."

"Yes," she says, her voice light and breathy.

"We'll give you some privacy," Foxglove says. Then he and Lorelei leave the room.

I'm left staring at Doris, a mingle of shock and confusion running through me. Doris was one of the Chosen from one hundred years ago. Yet she looks no older than Mother. Her eyes are distant and watery, their shade a dull gray, her hair is brittle wisps of dirty blonde, and she wears a thin green dress that barely reaches her calves.

"Is that tea?" she asks, eyes falling on the tray between us.

I shake my head to clear it. "Yes. So sorry. Where are my manners?" I pour two cups, then offer her a plate with a cookie.

As she sips her tea, a hint of clarity seems to focus in her eyes. "I haven't had tea in ages. Not like this, at least."

"It's a nice change from wine, isn't it?"

She nods.

I feel a flush of anxiety building as I search for what to say next. These situations have never been my forte, considering I'm not one for small talk. An intellectual debate with a magister would be more in my comfort zone. "Might I ask what village you were from?"

"Marchvale," she says. "I barely remember what it was like anymore. I'm sure it's changed since I last saw it."

"And you were sent to Faerwyvae with your cousin, right? To the Summer Court, if I remember correctly?"

"Yes, but Nadia passed away many years ago. It's been over sixty years that I've lived without her. It gets harder every day to remember her face."

Finally, a topic that piques my interest. I can think of no other way to pose my question but to be blunt. "How are you still alive when your cousin is not?"

She ponders my question, eyes wandering the cluttered walls. "You won't age the same way you used to," she says. "Being in Faerwyvae will change you a little. You'll be open to a very small amount of its magic. You can live longer than you would in Eisleigh, age less quickly. And so long as you live, your family and their descendants will be compensated back home. So, at least there's one motivation not to take your own life."

She says the last part so casually, it takes me a moment to realize she wasn't being sardonic. I make the firm decision not to laugh, then consider everything else she said. *Faerwyvae will change you. You'll be open to its magic.* I want to tell her I don't believe in magic, but the statement seems childish in this circumstance. Here sits a woman who wouldn't be alive, were she still in Eisleigh. Yet she hardly looks a day over forty. I know there's a scientific reason for this, but I haven't the slightest idea what it could be. "What about your cousin? Did she not age as slowly as you did?"

Doris shakes her head. "Nadia didn't fare so well. Probably because she had no children to live for, nor was she well-loved."

"Was her husband unkind to her?"

"I don't know if one could call a fae kind or unkind," she says. "They simply are what they are, despite the clothes they wear or the food they eat. Nadia and I were married to the Summer Queen's cousins, neither of whom wanted us. Neither kept us well, but I doubt either of our husbands thought they were doing anything but their utmost duties. Nadia's husband never visited her bed and chose to live with his favored lover instead. My husband visited my bed many times. But just as many times, he visited the beds of his numerous mates. I was breeding stock to him, a conduit to provide him heirs. And heirs I gave him. Many. I think that's the only thing the fae like about humans. We conceive well."

My stomach churns at that. "How are the children treated, being half-fae?"

"They are well," she says. "You'd hardly know they are half-fae at all, aside from their appearance. The magic here seems to favor them as if they were fully fae. My sons and daughters will far outlive me. Many of the children of the Chosen who preceded me are still alive today."

It had never occurred to me what became of any offspring between the fae and humans. If I'd given it any thought, I would have assumed the fae ate their half-human children. At least that assumption has been proven wrong. "Are any of the previous Chosen still alive in the other courts?"

She shakes her head. "I'm the last. No—I suppose there are two of us now. Three of us? Where is your sister?"

I can't bring myself to talk about Amelie, even though Doris might be the one person who could understand. "She isn't here," I say, then take a sip of my tea.

"I see." I'm not sure if I imagine it, but she seems to shoot me a knowing look. She then reaches across the table and gives my hand a squeeze. "Persevere, Miss Fairfield. If I can do it, so can you."

I look into her worn eyes, her empty expression, the lips that can barely form a smile. A morbid thought crosses my mind. *If this is what perseverance looks like... perhaps Amelie was the lucky one.*

25

I can't shake my meeting with Doris, even long after she leaves. I'd always imagined the Chosen were unhappy with their predicaments—miserable, even —but seeing the evidence before me is more than I can handle. And hearing how she and her cousin were treated by their husbands...how did my people never hear of this?

My mood sours further when I open the bedroom door and find Aspen waiting inside, pouring a glass of wine from the bedside table.

"Come to steal your room back?"

He ignores me. "Did you enjoy your guest?"

I cross my arms over my chest. "You mean, did I enjoy that glimpse into my future? Did you arrange our meeting as some sort of threat?"

He sips his wine, not looking at me. "I thought you might be lonely for human company."

"So you sent me an abused old woman?"

He pinches the bridge of his nose and closes his eyes. "Ungrateful human."

"Have all the Chosen been treated so poorly? Used as breeding stock? Neglected until they died of loneliness?"

He sets down his glass and storms over to me. "I didn't wait here the past hour so you could return and gripe about Doris Mason. I came to tell you I'm leaving."

"Leaving?"

"I have to deal with a skirmish near the wall. Cobalt will be coming too, along with some of my guards and soldiers. That leaves you in charge of the palace. Try not to burn it down." He turns to leave.

I'm flummoxed as I process his words. "Wait," I call after him before he reaches the door. "What's the skirmish about? And how long will you be gone?"

He considers me a while before answering. His posture relaxes. "It's the Holstrom father. He wants my blood. I'll likely be gone no longer than three days."

I want to make a cutting retort, to tell him three days is far too short. But there's a fatigue in Aspen's bearing that I hadn't noticed until now, making me hold my tongue.

Aspen continues. "Mr. Holstrom won't leave the wall until I face him in person. His recklessness is putting both humans and fae alike in danger. So I'll go put an end to this stupidity."

"What are you going to do to him?"

He shrugs. "Give him what he wants."

I raise a brow. "What is that supposed to mean?"

"I'll offer him a bargain. Let him choose his weapon and draw blood from me in any way he likes without fear of reproach. Then we will call a truce and return to our lands."

"You're going to *let* him attack you?"

"Just once. If he continues to fight me after he draws blood, the truce is off."

It seems like an odd way to settle a dispute. Then again, it makes sense for the fae. Of course they would end conflict with a bargain. But will it be enough for Mr. Holstrom? Would the blood of an immortal king be enough to compensate for losing two daughters? *It will if it kills Aspen.*

He seems to read my mind, lips pulling into a smirk. "Perhaps you'll get your dearest wish and the Holstrom father will deal me a fatal blow."

"Perhaps."

He takes a step toward me, eyes locked on mine. "Maybe you should give me a kiss for luck. I am your mate, after all, about to go off to battle. You might never get the chance again."

I lift my chin, deepening my glare. "I'm counting on it."

With a laugh, Aspen turns and leaves the room.

THE NEXT MORNING, I WATCH FROM MY WINDOW AS A retinue gathers on the palace grounds, preparing to leave. They look so small from this high up in the palace, but I'm certain I see Aspen riding at the head of the group on a black puca, his antlers clear even from this distance. Even if he had no antlers, I'd be able to recognize his haughty posture anywhere.

Cobalt must be down there too, and Foxglove. My heart sinks a little at the realization I'll no longer have Foxglove's company to entertain me for the next few days, just Lorelei.

The retinue files into a line, then departs the grounds. With a wide false smile, I pin Aspen's figure in my sight and give him a gracious wave. Never mind the fact he isn't looking. "Good riddance," I say in a singsong voice.

Relief washes over me when I see the last figure disappear into the trees of the forest at the edge of the palace grounds. Freedom. For three days I'll have no one to answer to but myself. I throw open the doors of my room, my joy fading as I see a pair of guards posted outside. Of course Aspen left guards. Or more likely *spies*.

No matter. I won't let it interfere with my plans. "Will one of you be a dear and have wine brought to me at once?" Then I close the door.

I dress quickly, not bothering to wait for Lorelei, then take a seat on the couch at the far end of the room, next to a round stump-like table.

When the knock comes, I sit upright. "Come in."

A servant enters bearing a tray. His slender legs end in dainty hooves, but disappointment flutters through me when I see his face. He's beautiful and youthful, like most of the fae living in the palace, but he's not the one I was hoping for. Still, I wave him forward, and he sets the tray on the table next to me.

"Will that be all?" he asks.

I look from him to the open door. The guards remain on each side, but their backs are to me. Not that it matters; for all I know, fae have superior hearing. I lower my voice anyway. "There is something else. First, tell me your name."

"My name is Ocher."

"Ocher, I hope you don't mind me asking...did you ever serve my sister?"

His brows knit together. "Yes," he says, hesitantly.

"Did you ever serve her while she was meeting privately with the king?"

"A time or two."

"Were you the one who served the wine the night she went missing?" I can't bring myself to say the truth. *The night she died.*

"No. That was Vane, I believe."

"Vane," I echo. My voice is still just above a whisper. "Do you think you could do something for me? Could you send him here?"

"I suppose so," he says, then blushes. "I mean, yes, of course."

"Very good." I smile, then raise my voice. "This is not the wine I wanted. I want the red wine that was served with breakfast yesterday morning. Why would I want this violet wine so early in the day?"

Ocher shifts from foot to foot. "Violet and red are merely different in flavor. Either can be consumed morning or—"

I turn my nose to the air, summoning the snobbery of Maddie Coleman, cringing at how uncomfortable it feels. "I can tell a difference. Now get on with it, or I'll tell the king you didn't listen to me."

He looks perplexed.

"And for your insolence, be sure you send another

servant in your stead. I can't abide by this." I give him an exaggerated wink.

"Ah." He flashes me a knowing smile. "Understood. I'm so sorry. My mistake." He bows low, then backs out of the room, tray in hand.

I pace the room until my doors open once again. This time, I recognize the face of the fae. It's the handsome male, the one who thanked me for my mercy. As he approaches, I ask, "Are you Vane?"

"I am," he says in a whisper as he sets down the tray. "Ocher said you asked for me."

"I did, and I thank you for coming." One of the guards shifts outside my door but remains facing away from me. "I'll make this fast. Was anything amiss when you served my sister the night she disappeared?"

Color rises to his beautifully pale cheeks, and a flash of guilt crosses his face. "I brought honey pyrus wine. King Aspen was furious. But it was an accident, I swear—"

"Never mind that," I say. "What was she like when you saw her? Did she seem...troubled?"

He looks taken aback for a moment. "No, she looked serene. Smiling. Laughing. She seemed to think me bringing the wrong kind of wine was nothing more than a silly joke."

I chew my bottom lip. "Did anything else happen? You said Aspen was furious. What exactly did he do?"

"The king realized what kind of wine I'd brought almost as soon as I'd set it down. He stopped Amelie just before she went to pour herself a glass. Then he took the tray and said he'd get the wine himself. Made me take him to the kitchen and show him our wine stores, explain the mishap. He scolded me but nothing more. Then he left with a bottle of Bloodberry wine."

"Is that a...normal kind of wine?"

He shrugs, then points at the tray. "It's what I brought you here. It's served at most common meals. And it doesn't cause dangerous hallucinations in humans, if that's what you mean."

"What about when Aspen left you? Did he seem angry still? In any kind of rage?"

"No," Vane says. "I apologized so many times, he had to order me to stop. Once he left, he seemed perfectly forgiving, which is why I was so surprised when he ordered our execution the next day."

I press my lips tight together, wondering how much he knows about my responsibility for that predicament. "There's nothing else you can think of? Nothing that seemed strange?"

"After what you did to make the king find mercy, I wish there was something I could say to help you, but there isn't."

I sigh, all my hopes for potential answers dashed like waves upon jagged rocks. Then one more question comes to mind. "Were any of the servants overly friendly with Amelie? Was she *intimate* with any of them?" At another blush from Vane, I add, "That includes you."

"We all found her to be fair, for a human," he says, "but no one dared take her to bed or do more than look at her. No one would be so stupid to court the king's betrothed. In fact," he casts an anxious glance behind him at the guards outside the door, "I've likely overstayed my welcome."

I want to drill him with more questions, but he's probably right. Besides, I'm not sure what else to ask. All further questions I'd prepared hinged on him having something of value to tell me. "Very well. Thank you for speaking with me."

Once he's gone, I'm left alone to ponder the conversation. It leaves me just as frustrated as I was before. Speaking to Vane had been my one great idea, my one way to possibly gain some sense of control over the questions that continue to plague me. I should have known better than to get my hopes up. The longer I've been in Faerwyvae, the less control I seem to have. Nothing makes any more sense than it did when I arrived. There's no explanation for much of the fae's supposed magic, no clues to what happened the night Amelie died, and no evidence anything will ever make sense again.

There's only one thing left to do. I pour myself a glass of wine and sprinkle a pinch of salt into it. With a raise of my glass to no one, I mutter, "Might as well enjoy my freedom."

26

Dread settles over me as the third day dawns since Aspen left, and I realize he'll be returning any time now. My days without him have been peaceful and uneventful. Then again, I suppose that's what they were like the few days leading up to his departure as well. Still, I can't help but think all that will eventually change. He'll hassle me to join his bed. Or try and get me to submit to the fae Bonding ritual. He'll stir my anger and I'll stir his, I just know it.

I freeze, noticing my inexplicable flush of excitement at the thought.

Well, I must be more bored than I thought.

The day comes and goes. Then another.

A new dread begins to emerge, one that has me pacing the open expanse in the dining room after breakfast while Lorelei watches with concern.

"What if something happened?" I mutter.

"The king will be fine, I'm sure of it," Lorelei says.

I roll my eyes. "Not to him. To the treaty or something."

"Give Foxglove some credit. He spins truces even better than he spins that pretty hair of yours. If they aren't back yet, it's likely only because they are negotiating the finer details."

"What if Mr. Holstrom refuses? I mean, *anything* could happen." In fact, I've spent the best part of two days analyzing every possible logical outcome. Most end in war. "Blazing iron, if my marriage to Aspen ends up being for nothing, I'll be livid. And if it turns out he's to blame for breaking the treaty, I'll kill him my—"

Shouts ring out somewhere inside the palace.

Lorelei rises to her feet. "What the bloody oak and ivy?"

I dart out of the dining room, then pause, listening for more sound. Another shout comes, then muffled, frantic voices.

Lorelei puts a hand on my arm to keep me from pursuing the source. "Don't. It might not be safe."

She's probably right, but I have to know what's going on. My eyes flash to the guards in the hall, the same two who guard my room. They've been following me at a distance everywhere I go since Aspen left, and I've given up trying to persuade them not to. Finally, they might be useful for once. "You," I point to one, a female with bright blue eyes and a distinctly feline face, "see what's going on and report back to me at once."

She stands at attention but doesn't move. Her expression is querulous as she ponders my request.

I square my shoulders, summoning the snobbery I

feigned with the wine servant the other day. "As the king's mate and lady of Bircharbor Palace, I demand it."

The guard finally moves to obey, and Lorelei nudges her shoulder into mine. "Look at you, acting like a queen," she whispers.

We remain in the hall, waiting anxious minutes on end for the guard to return. When she does, she brings Foxglove as well. The ambassador's face is pale, expression troubled. Lorelei and I run to meet him.

"What's going on?" I ask.

"The king has been injured." Foxglove says. "Gravely so."

A surge of emotion rushes through me, but I can't identify what it is. Relief? Worry? Satisfaction? "What happened?"

Foxglove wrings his hands. "I finally convinced the Holstrom father to agree to a bargain. The king would be unarmored and allow Mr. Holstrom to draw blood using a weapon of his choice. The man chose a bow as his weapon and aimed for the king's heart."

At the look on Foxglove's face, Lorelei gasps, bringing her hands to cover her mouth. "Tell me he isn't dead."

"He isn't, but...the arrowhead was iron, of course. It got lodged between his ribs just below his heart. Prince Cobalt tried to free it, but the shaft was ash and burned his hands. He was only able to snap the shaft and potentially drove the arrowhead deeper."

Lorelei spins toward me and takes me by the shoulders. "You can help him."

My eyes go wide. "What?"

"You're a—whatever you call it—a surger."

"A surgeon," I correct, "and I, well, don't you have a fae healer? Gildmar?"

"Gildmar was summoned immediately," Foxglove says. "She met us on our way back to the palace and has already done what she can, but she can't get the arrowhead from between his ribs, especially with his blood becoming more and more poisoned with every minute the iron remains inside him. She can hardly go near the wound at this point, much less tend it."

A sense of purpose settles over me. This is exactly what I'm trained for. "I suppose I could help. Where is he?"

"He's in the east wing on the bottom floor."

"Let me get my things," I say. "Then take me there."

I can hear the king well before I see him. As we approach the east wing, moaning echoes from wall to wall, a guttural sound like a wounded animal. We reach the door at the end of the main hall and pause just inside. Aspen lies on a stone table and Cobalt paces the length of it, face twisted with worry. Next to the table stands a short fae with bark-like skin and branches of leafy hair, hand covering her mouth as if protecting herself from a foul smell.

I take a step inside, drawing Cobalt's attention. "Evelyn, what are you doing here?"

"I think I can help him."

Cobalt's brow furrows, either with concern or confusion. His voice comes out small. "You think you...can?"

I wonder if he meant to say *want to*. With a nod, I

approach the table, Foxglove and Lorelei hovering just behind me. I note the smell of blood filling the air, something I am intimately familiar with. But another pungent odor assaults my senses as well. Tangy. Sharp. Dangerous.

"I can almost taste the iron in the air," Lorelei says with a cough. "Oak and ivy, that's strong."

Foxglove covers his mouth with his sleeve and takes a step back. With a deep breath, I look over the king. His face is covered in a sheen of sweat, teeth gritted, head lolling side to side as he moans in agony. His golden skin has faded so pale it's almost white, with an unhealthy blue tinge beneath it. His lips are chapped and peeling, and his eyes look sunken, a bruise-like purple surrounding them.

Cobalt faces the tiny fae. "Gildmar, show her the wound."

She eyes me for a moment, then reaches for the silk sheet covering Aspen's body and pulls it away from his neck. With a gasp, she springs away and drops the sheet as if it burned her.

"I'll do it." I take a cautious step forward, training my expression beneath my surgeon's calm despite my racing heart. With quick, deliberate movements, I set down my surgery kit and pull the sheet down, exposing Aspen's chest. The tang of blood and iron increase, and the fae step farther away. My hands tremble as I tuck the sheet around his waist and take in his damaged chest.

A poultice covers the wound, which is on his left side, not far from his heart. If he has a heart, that is. The skin around it is every shade of black, purple, and blue, with blue-black streaks spreading out in every direction across his torso. His breathing is shallow, labored. I don't need to know much about fae physiology to know Aspen is dying.

"What can I use as antiseptic?" I call out.

"Anti-what?" Gildmar asks, her voice like the creak of an old door.

I close my eyes, realizing—*of course*—they don't have antiseptic. Or know what it is. "Wine then. Someone get me wine. Now."

"I'll get some," I hear Cobalt say, followed by the sound of his feet tearing from the room.

I reach for the poultice, lifting a corner. "Has this helped at all?"

"It is slowing the iron poisoning his blood," Gildmar says, "but with the arrowhead stuck inside him, there's nothing I can use to stop it completely."

"I need clean cloth." Gildmar hands me strips of red spider silk. I've never used silk for dressing wounds, so I can only hope it will suffice. I set the cloth next to Aspen, then open my surgery kit.

Scalpel in hand, I return to Aspen.

His eyes fly open, a roar escaping his lips. "No!"

I look from his maniacal expression to the scalpel in my hand. Understanding dawns on me as I remember what Lorelei said about human metals—even weak ones —being unbearable to a fae with a current iron injury.

As Aspen's body begins to convulse, the scalpel slips from my shaking hands and clatters to the floor.

"Close it!" I hear Lorelei shout behind me. "Close that box!"

I sink to my knees, fumbling to replace the scalpel and shut the kit. Only when I secure the clasp does Aspen settle back down. I stand, finding the king once again listless. Fresh blood streaked with black oozes from his side beneath the poultice.

I'm frozen in place, at a loss for both words and actions.

"You can treat him," Gildmar says. "He's calm now."

"I can't use my tools," I whisper.

"No, but you can use mine." The little fae indicates a table strewn with herbs, poultices, shells, sticks, and sharp, white bones.

"I was trained to use tools. *These* tools." I point to my kit, lying useless on the floor.

"Your hands will work too."

I shake my head, backing toward the door. My breaths grow faster, shallower. "No. I can't do this."

Lorelei takes hold of my arm. "What's wrong?"

I meet her eyes, frantic. "I'm not trained for this. I have no idea what to do if I can't use my tools."

"You don't need your tools," she says. "Just do what you did for me."

I sigh. It's time to admit the truth. "I didn't do anything for you, Lorelei. I merely inspected your wound, helped you stretch. The fact that you felt better afterward was negligible. A placebo, if anything."

"Then how do you explain this?" She lifts the hem of her skirt, revealing her leg. Her smooth, unmarred leg with its perfect brown skin. I look to the other, thinking there must be some mistake, but both look exactly alike.

"It's a coincidence," I manage to say. "You were already on the mend."

She crosses her arms and lifts a brow. "Seriously? That's your best explanation."

I admit, I have no way to explain how she could have

healed that much in a matter of days. "All I know is that it wasn't because of me."

Her eyes go steely, lips pressing into a tight line. "Don't you dare let my king die. Don't you dare give up right now, no matter how much you think his death might suit you."

Her words send a shock through me. The option of letting him die had yet to cross my mind, but now that I'm forced to consider it...would it be better if I simply did nothing? I look over at Aspen, watching the tendrils of black crawling over his torso. If I leave him be, the iron will poison his blood. He'll be dead before long.

I could let it happen. He did let my sister die, after all. And he may have been directly responsible for her death in the first place, not to mention the deaths of the Holstrom girls and who knows who else.

He deserves to die.

The thought makes my stomach churn. That's not how I was trained. Mr. Meeks taught me that a surgeon treats anyone, regardless of station or history. Some surgeons are even sent to treat convicted criminals sentenced to hang.

I may never become the medical professional I wanted to be, but that doesn't mean I'll stop being the apprentice I was trained to be.

My heart rate begins to slow, breaths growing deeper. I return to Aspen's side, meet Gildmar's eyes. "Hand me that shard of seashell, then fetch me strands of spider silk and a splinter-thin bone. And where in the blazing iron is that wine?"

27

Cobalt brings the wine. I remove the poultice and pour the deep red liquid over the wound. Gildmar uses a dropper—much like the ones my mother uses for her tinctures—and drips honey pyrus extract into Aspen's lips, explaining it will help manage the pain. I wish we had laudanum, but the extract seems to work nearly as well. The king's body goes limp and his moaning ceases. Then, with deft fingers, I take the sharpest shard of seashell and make the incision, widening the opening on either side of the arrow shaft.

I ignore the blood that pours forth, ignore how much blacker it is than red. When I finally see the head of the arrow, I understand the problem. Its head is edged with four barbs. Removing it isn't simply a matter of turning the arrow to let it escape between two ribs. I'll need to twist it, angle it, pull it to the side. All without puncturing his internal organs.

For one moment, I freeze, unsure how to proceed.

Gildmar has no forceps, no tweezers. I will have to use my hands through all of this. Without a second thought, I pour wine over my hands to clean them and reach inside the cut.

Time slows. I close my eyes, forgetting how far off protocol I've gotten, ignore the feeling of Aspen's blood and tissues on my skin. A calm certainty floods through me, and I follow it, find the tip of the arrow. I slide it to the side and Aspen groans.

"More honey pyrus," I say to Gildmar.

She moves to obey, and I shift the arrowhead again. One of the barbs is free. Then another. I rotate it slightly, turn it to the side.

Free.

The arrow comes away, and I toss it to the floor, knowing none of the fae can take it from me. I cleanse the wound again, check for internal damage. It's hard to tell considering everything is discolored with the tendrils of black, but he appears without further injury. I call for spider silk and bone, which Gildmar hands me. As quickly and as neatly as I can with the makeshift tools, I stitch him back together.

I tie the last stitch, then step back. Time seems to shift back to normal, and I release a heavy sigh. Only now do I realize the sweat on my brow and back of my neck. Only now does it dawn on me what I did.

I performed a surgery without normal tools. Unguided. And mostly with my hands.

I'm not sure whether I should be proud or horrified. More than anything, I'm exhausted. The surgery took mere minutes, but every part of me was in the task, focused like never before. Now I can feel the energy draining from me.

"You did it," Lorelei says, coming to my side.

Foxglove gives me an appreciative nod. "You saved the king."

"That you did," Gildmar says from the other side of the table. "Something not even I could do. If you hadn't been here...well, I suppose Cobalt would have had me executed for being the death of his brother."

"I wouldn't do that, Gildmar," Cobalt says.

"Well, you should," she says. "Luckily, you don't have to. Apparently, your brother won the golden lot when the Reaping brought this human girl to be his mate."

Cobalt's face falls, and my eyes snap away from him.

"I'm going to clean up," I say. "I'll return to check on the king after."

I make my way back to Aspen's room, wanting nothing more than to be rid of stairs. Why did he have to place his bedroom nearly at the top of the palace? By the time I reach it, I find a bath of steaming water waiting for me. I probably have Lorelei to thank for that, although I can't imagine how it was filled in the time it took me to get here. Without delay, I peel off my blood-stained dress and toss it in a heap in the corner of the room. If the fae don't have any powerful detergents to clean blood from silk, the dress is ruined. I hadn't considered asking for an apron before the surgery began.

A moan escapes my lips as I sink into the tub. I feel like I could fall asleep, but as soon as I try to relax, my mind wanders to dark thoughts, making my muscles tense yet again.

I saved the king when I could have killed him. Should I have let him die? My heart sinks at the thought.

No. I did what I was trained to do. What I've always wanted to do. I saved someone.

I just hope his life was worth saving.

HOURS LATER I MAKE MY WAY BACK TO THE ROOM WHERE I performed the surgery, only to find Aspen's body being lifted by several guards. A wave of terror goes through me. Did something happen? Had my surgery failed to save him?

"What's going on?" I ask.

A hand falls on my shoulder, and I find Gildmar at my side. "Worry not," she says in her ancient voice. "He's recovering."

"Then where are they taking him?"

She looks at me, aghast. "To your rooms, of course. The king should recover in comfort and privacy, where his mate can tend to him with ease."

I hate the way she says *tend to him*, as if I'm Aspen's subservient woman, eager to fulfill his every need. But I understand the sentiment. I was responsible for healing him, after all. I can think of him more like my patient rather than my mate. Wouldn't I want my patient to heal in comfort?

"Of course," I say, trying to hide my irritation.

I follow the guards back to the bedroom, cursing the stairs twice over now that I've had to ascend them for the second time today, then watch as they lay Aspen on the bed. When they depart, Gildmar remains. "I brought you more extract of honey pyrus." She hands me a vial. "Give him more when he seems to be in pain."

"Thank you," I say, then set the vial on the bedside table.

"I'm still astonished you managed to save him when I could not." Gildmar's voice comes out small, heavy with remorse. Then her eyes meet mine. "I never knew humans had such powers. Where did you learn such healing?"

"My mo—" I stop short, realizing I was about to say *my mother* when I'd meant to say Mr. Meeks. The mistake unsettles me, unearthing a flood of memories from my childhood. Memories of me and Mother "treating" her patrons. She'd stand at their heads, burning herbs over them, administering tinctures, while I'd place my hands over their bodies. Mother would praise me for clearing their energy and aiding in healing, and I would swell with pride. It wasn't until Amelie nearly died that I understood my folly. That's when Mr. Meeks showed me what true medicine was. When I realized Mother wasn't a healer but a fraud at worst and an herbalist at best. When I stopped believing in magic.

I shake the memories from my mind. "Surgery is a miraculous thing," I say instead.

She gives me a wide smile, making the corner of her eyes crinkle on her brown, bark-like face. Then she takes her leave.

I'm left alone with Aspen dozing on the bed. With slow steps, I approach him and look him over. Outfitted in nothing but a clean, elegant robe of bronze silk, his chest rises and falls in an even rhythm, face slack, lips slightly parted. He looks nothing like the fierce, dangerous king I've come to know.

My eyes rove across his torso. His skin still looks pale, but a hint of gold has replaced the ghostly blue. At least the tendrils of black seem to have receded a bit, showing only a few thin veins peeking above the collar of his robe. I reach a hand toward the collar, slowly peeling it away to reveal the bandaged wound. The skin is still angry around it, red, black, and purple with plenty of black tendrils branching away, streaking in every direction.

I return the collar to cover his torso, but as I pull my fingers away, Aspen's hand covers mine, heavy and warm. My eyes flash to his face, but his eyes remain closed. His face contorts, head rolling slowly from one side to the other. He mutters something I can't understand.

I retract my hand from under his and rush to the bedside table. "You need more honey pyrus," I say, then pour a dropperful between his lips.

His face relaxes and his muttering fades.

I watch him for a few moments, wondering what exactly I've gotten myself into. How long will I have to play nursemaid to him?

"Evie." The word comes from Aspen's lips, slow and heavy.

I try to ignore the irritation that lights a fire in my chest at the sound of my nickname—the nickname only Amelie ever used for me. "Yes, it's me."

"Are you...going...to kill me?" Each word comes out with great effort, but a smile tugs at the corner of his lips, eyes remaining closed.

"No, I saved you. Only iron knows why."

He winces. "Don't say iron."

I say nothing, hoping the honey pyrus will return him to his slumber.

He lifts his hand, an action that seems to pain him, and motions me forward.

I take a hesitant step toward him, then another.

"Evie," he repeats.

"What?"

"I wanted it to be you."

My brows furrow. "You wanted it to be me for what? To save you? If you're telling me you got wounded on purpose just so I'd have to—"

"No. At the wall."

"The wall," I echo.

"When you told me your name. I wanted it to be you. To be my Chosen."

I clench my teeth, heat rising to my cheeks. "So, what? You killed the Holstrom girls so you could punish me instead?"

He shakes his head. "No. And I didn't want to punish you. I wanted you."

I roll my eyes. "You're clearly drunk on honey pyrus, Your Majesty."

"Don't call me that." His tone deepens, darkens, though his words still sound slurred and strained. "It's Aspen when we're alone."

"Fine, *Aspen*. I'll do you a favor and forget this conversation ever happened."

Aspen goes quiet for a few moments. "I didn't know you weren't eldest," he whispers, "until you arrived at the palace. I wanted to ask you if you'd be with me instead. Remember that night? The dining room?"

Heat rises to my cheeks, recalling the glamour he placed over himself. "How could I forget."

"I was going to ask you then. But you hated me so much."

A cold suspicion crawls up my spine. "Did you kill my sister? Did you kill her so you could have me instead?"

"No." I'm surprised at the certainty in his tone. "She was sweet. Kind. I would never have hurt her."

I shake my head. "Well, this is all coming a little too late. My sister is dead, perhaps because of you."

His expression flickers. With pain? Sorrow? "It wasn't her body."

Ice chills my blood. "What?"

"The body. On the shore. Not your sister." His face goes slack as he loses consciousness.

I move closer, putting my hands on each side of his face, lightly slapping his cheek. "What do you mean it wasn't her body? Wake up! Explain, damn you!"

He remains silent, motionless.

My mind spins with questions, anxiety building and building higher and higher until I think I will explode. Is what he said true? Or was he simply hallucinating and speaking nonsense? Was he playing with me, trying to get into my head?

All I know is I'll get those answers. I'll nurse this son-of-a-harpy back to health if it's the last thing I do. And if I find out he lied...well, that will be the last thing *he* will live to do.

28

I continue to monitor Aspen, seeking any sign that he's returning to consciousness. The evening fades to night, and I alternate between dozing on the couch and checking Aspen for signs of life. I give him honey pyrus on occasion, but only partial doses. This means I have to administer it more often, but it also gives me the hope that I can catch him lucid.

So far, no luck. All he does is mutter and moan, face twisting in agony, each time he wakes. By morning, his skin is burning with fever.

I call for Gildmar and have her fetch me fresh spider silk cloth so I can change the dressing of his wound. She brings me more honey pyrus too, wine steeped with fae herbs, and an aromatic broth to try and feed Aspen. Each time I examine him, my stomach sinks. The tendrils of black have stopped receding. They aren't growing, but they no longer seem to be fading away. His skin grows hotter and hotter.

"Is there anything else we can do?" I ask Gildmar. A

full day has passed since the surgery, and I'm beginning to lose hope he'll recover. "Are there any fae methods for reversing iron poisoning?"

She shakes her head. "A wound as bad as his could take months—years even—to fully recover from. It was too close to his heart, and the poisoning spread too fast."

"How long do you think he'll be like this? When will he wake?"

"Weeks, possibly."

My hands clench into fists. I can't wait weeks. Not after what he told me yesterday. I'll go out of my mind wondering if what he said about my sister is true.

"At least he has your care," she says. "I never thought much about human-fae pairings, aside from being a necessary function to maintain the treaty. But seeing you care for him like this...it makes me think I've been wrong about humans. Perhaps you aren't all greedy invaders. Perhaps this peace we have is worth keeping."

Guilt fills my stomach with lead. She has no idea I'm only caring for him in a purely professional manner. Has no idea my main motivation for bringing him back to health is to bleed answers from him. But if perpetuating the lie is what keeps humans and fae at peace...

"He's very important to me," I say with a pleasant smile.

She pats me on the shoulder. "I'm sure he feels the same about you. Now, I'll leave you to rest. I'm sure you haven't slept much."

I watch her shuffle out the doors, suddenly curious how old she is. She seems ancient compared to Aspen, and Aspen is a thousand years old. It's possible her age is unrelated to her appearance. Other Earthen fae might be like her, for all I know, considering the only other I've seen was the Earthen Court ambassador.

I return to Aspen's side, then press the back of my hand to his forehead. Still burning. I push his robe aside and check the black veins, trying to find evidence that they are fading. His torso is hot to the touch, even warmer than his forehead. I take a seat on the bed next to him, my fingers skating across his skin until they reach his wound. I lay my palm over the bandages.

"Come out of this, Aspen." My whisper sounds more like a hiss. "I'm not done with you yet. If you dare die on me, I will decimate your corpse and cut it into a thousand pieces, then feed you to a kelpie."

Heat radiates from his skin, warming my palm through the cloth dressing. I grit my teeth, anger seething toward the wound. Even after everything I did to accomplish a successful operation, it still wasn't enough. He's still suffering, fighting against a poison I don't understand. A poison no human antibiotic or fae remedy can help.

I hate feeling this helpless. Useless. Powerless.

I close my eyes, breathing away my anger. "Heal, damn you."

Aspen makes a noise and my eyes fly open. His face is contorted, twisted with pain, breaths labored. He tries to speak, but his open mouth pulls into a grimace.

I reach for the vial next to the bed and give him half a dropperful of honey pyrus. He doesn't immediately relax, but the furrows between his brow begin to lessen. After a few minutes, his breathing evens out. His expression still looks pained, but his jaw has unclenched.

My hand moves to his forehead, and I'm startled to

find a sheen of sweat over the skin. The fever has broken. That is, if fae process illness like humans do.

He tries to speak again, and I realize he's asking for something to drink. I reach for the herbed wine. Despite my many protestations in favor of water, Gildmar insisted fae heal better with wine. I put the shallow bowl to his lips, help him incline his head to drink it. After a few swallows, he sighs, then lays back on the pillow.

"Aspen," I say, "can you hear me?" *Please be lucid. Please be lucid.*

"Yes." The word comes out like a croak.

"How do you feel?"

He grimaces. "Awful. Am I dead yet?"

"Not yet."

His eyelids flutter. "I can't...open my eyes. The light. It hurts."

I reach for a clean cloth and immerse it in a bowl of cool water. After I wring it out, I drape it over his eyes. "Better?"

"No. I need more honey pyrus. The pain. It's too much."

I return to my seat on the bed, leaning in close. "I'll give you more honey pyrus, but only after you answer my questions."

A corner of his lips twitches into a half smile. "Cruel human."

"Monstrous fae."

"What do you want to know?" His words are still thick and heavy, barely above a whisper, but at least they're coherent.

My pulse begins to race. "Yesterday you said the body you found on the shore wasn't my sister's. Was that true?"

He winces, but I can't tell if it's from pain or from the realization of what he said. "Yes," he finally confesses.

"What happened to Amelie?"

"I don't know. She was never found."

"Whose body was it, then? Who was the girl I saw being pulled from the caves?" The memory seizes me. Pale skin, face obscured by hair dark with water and tangled with kelp. There was no part of me that doubted it was my sister, but the truth is, I never saw the body close enough to know for certain.

"A selkie," Aspen whispers.

My eyes go wide. "A selkie? How did she die?"

"She must have lost her sealskin. Without it, a selkie can only live on land in seelie form until sunrise unless she dons human clothing."

"Was she the one your guards saw running into the caves?" I ask. "Or was that my sister?"

"Impossible to say."

My heart sinks. I thought I'd feel relief knowing there was a possibility Amelie was still alive, but now I'm just as disheartened as ever. If she really did run to the caves, then she could have been devoured by the sea or some fae monster, leaving no trace of her remains. Or she could be...anywhere. "You truly don't know where Amelie is? Why she disappeared?"

"I don't."

"Promise me."

His head moves, facing me, despite his vision obscured by the cloth. "I promise. I know nothing about her disappearance or her current whereabouts." After a moment, he adds, "Can you promise me the same? That you had nothing to do with it? That you have no part in any plot against the fae, my throne, or my life?"

"How can you ask me that? Of course I don't."

"The promise of a human means nothing when they can lie, but I want to hear you say it."

I swallow hard. "I promise. I had nothing to do with Amelie's disappearance, nor am I part of any plot against you, your throne, or faekind."

He sighs, face relaxing. "Is that all?"

I could leave him to rest, pour a dropper of honey pyrus between his lips now that he's answered my most pressing questions. But why waste the opportunity? "No. There's more I need from you. What really happened to the Holstrom girls? What treasonous act did they perform? I want you to tell me everything."

He lets out an irritated grumble. "At least give me more honey pyrus and wine first. If you're going to make me talk, I want to have a voice at the end of it. And sweet oblivion to slip into once it's over."

"Fine." I grab the vial. "I'll give you a few drops now, and a half-dropper after."

He parts his lips and I drop in the extract, followed by a few hearty sips of wine and broth.

Once he settles back down, I say, "Go on."

"Impatient human." His voice is gravelly, but somewhat stronger than before. "Very well. It was days before the mate ceremonies were to take place. The girls hadn't been here a week, even. They'd been cold, distant. Worse than you."

"I doubt that."

He continues. "Theresa came to me in the night. She'd barely said a word to me before this, but there she was, slipping into bed next to me, whispering, telling me she was eager to start living as mates now. I was perplexed but too intrigued to dismiss her. Not when she seemed to want it so badly."

My stomach churns, and an unexpected fury moves through me. "Spare me the details."

He smirks. "Are you judging me?"

"No."

"You are. I know humans hold mating as a sacred act, but most fae don't. However, it was that very realization that sparked my suspicion. I was on alert after that and grew even more concerned when she said she wanted her sister to join, that Maryanne couldn't bear the thought of becoming my brother's mate without having experienced a man before. The girl stepped out of the shadows and into the bed with us. Said I seemed like a lover who could provide the instruction she needed."

"I told you to spare me the details," I say through my teeth.

"You also said you wanted to know everything."

"Then get on with it."

I can tell he's amused by my discomfort. He continues. "After that, my suspicion only grew. I wasn't falling for their false passions, not even as Theresa climbed in my lap, trying to lull me with her words. Kissing me."

I hate the visions that swirl inside my imagination. Theresa and Maryanne Holstrom, Sableton's perfect little sweethearts, crawling all over Aspen, caressing him. Tasting him. My fingers dig into my palms as I try to quell my fury. Why do these visions infuriate me so?

"I knew they were up to something," Aspen says, "and I wanted to know what it was. I didn't close my eyes. Not when Maryanne turned my lips to hers. Not when Theresa lifted the iron blade, bared her teeth as she brought it down. My mind cleared at once, and I understood their true intentions. I blocked the thrust of the blade and turned it on her, then her sister. They were dead before their bodies struck the ground."

My fury extinguishes to horror. "You killed them. Without question. Without trial."

"They never had a chance." I'm surprised at the sorrow in his tone. "I was so enraged when I realized what was happening, I never stopped to think I could have overpowered them, could have kept them alive for questioning. Not even their bodies at my feet halted my anger. I was blinded by it. Swallowed by it. I shifted to my unseelie form and tore through Faerwyvae, past the wall, into your village. There I slaughtered every animal I'd gifted the Holstroms, my antlers tearing into flesh and bone, dooming the treaty, damning all of the Fair Isle to war."

Bile rises in my throat as my eyes flash to his twisting antlers. I shudder. "You really did it. You murdered the Holstrom girls and killed their animals."

"They were defenseless." His voice is a sorrowful whisper. "I can still smell the blood of the cows, the pigs, the sheep. Feel the resistance of their flesh as it met my antlers. I can still see the bodies of the girls, littering the floor. I've had that bedroom scoured and sealed off. Made a new one here."

I try to ignore how shaken he seems by relaying the tale. Try, instead, to see the monster he is. "You told my people it was treason."

"It was. They made an attempt on my life, and I delivered my cruel justice."

"And you expect me to believe you had nothing to do with my sister going missing?"

"I already promised you I don't," he says, his tone darkening. "I am not kind and I am not a hero, but I don't kill unprovoked. Your sister never did a thing to anger me. I may not have loved her, but I would never have wished her harm. And I never would have hurt the Holstrom girls if they hadn't come to kill me first."

I don't know what to think, what to believe. Could he be crazy? Could he have imagined the dagger in Theresa's hands? Misunderstood some unintentional gesture? Then again, their behavior in the first place is unimaginable. If they had the gall to seduce him in the night, days before their weddings, then it could be I never really knew them at all.

"Take me away, Evie," Aspen mutters. "Send me to oblivion. Let me forget."

With trembling fingers, I grab the extract and give him half a dropperful. He slips into unconsciousness before the vial returns to the table. I stare at him, pondering the duality between the vicious beast that kills defenseless girls, and the vulnerable king who mourns their deaths.

With every answer I get, my world shifts further upside-down.

Too shaken by the story to do anything else, I slide to the floor and cry into my hands.

29

The next morning, I leave Aspen alone in his room so I can get some air. He managed to sleep through the night, and last time I checked his wound, the black tendrils were finally beginning to fade in earnest.

I find myself standing at the open expanse in the formal dining room, leaning against the rail as I breathe in fresh, salty air. It's so much better than the tension of the bedroom. The sea crashes at the shore then recedes, revealing entrances to the coral caves between each wave. I can't help but ponder what Aspen said.

Somewhere out there, Amelie could be alive.

"I hope you don't take offense, but you look terrible."

I turn to find Foxglove and flash him a smile. "I do take offense, but I think you must be right. Lorelei said the same thing earlier."

"Come," he says, "you should bathe. Dress. Let me brush out your hair."

I shake my head. "I don't want to disturb the king. He's been sleeping soundly all morning."

"We won't need to. Lorelei fetched some clothes from your room and brought them to your parlor. We've had a tub brought in as well."

I raise my brows. "Do I smell that awful?"

Foxglove does his best to hide his distaste, but it isn't working. "Humans do have rather...*odd* aromas that fae don't have. Besides, you could use the relaxation of a bath after everything you've done for His Majesty."

"Fine," I say with a sigh. "Take me to the bath."

He leads me to the garish parlor where I'd met with Doris Mason. Inside, I'm greeted by Lorelei and a steaming bathtub. Foxglove takes his leave and Lorelei helps me undress. She asks if I'd like privacy, but I make her stay with me. I've had enough alone time with my thoughts. Now I just need some company that isn't an unconscious Aspen.

She perches at the edge of one of the horrid chairs while I soak in the tub. We chat about mindless matters, sharing a few shallow laughs, but my worries aren't kept at bay for long. I need to tell someone about what I've learned. Perhaps I can trust Lorelei. Amelie seemed to.

"Aspen told me some things when he was awake," I say, trying to keep my tone nonchalant. I toy with my rowan berry necklace, keeping it from soaking too long in the water.

"Like what?"

I take a deep breath. "About Amelie."

She sits forward eagerly. "Does he know what happened to her?"

"No, but she might be alive." I watch her face for any indication that she already knows.

Her brows furrow. "Alive? But the body—"

"It wasn't Amelie's. It belonged to a selkie woman who lost her sealskin."

Lorelei is clearly perplexed. So she didn't know after all. "A selkie woman doesn't simply lose her skin. What happened to her? And what happened to Amelie?"

"He didn't have answers to either. I've been puzzling over it ever since. Why didn't he tell me? Why did he allow me and everyone else in the castle to believe Amelie died? Yet, he allowed the vicar to assume she's still alive and well."

Lorelei leaves the chair to crouch beside the tub, expression grave. She keeps her voice low. "Those questions are best saved for Aspen and asked in private. If he kept this information from us, it's for a reason. Don't tell anyone else."

"Why? What reason could he have for hiding it? He could be sending guards out looking for my sister. Instead, everyone thinks she's dead."

"I'm sure his most trusted guards know," Lorelei says. "There were many who witnessed the body they found. They will know the truth. He could have trackers seeking Amelie right now. If someone means him or her harm, it's best our efforts to find Amelie are made with discretion."

I nod. "Perhaps you're right. I just hate not knowing what's going on."

"I'm sure the king feels the same."

I chew my bottom lip. "He also told me about the Holstrom girls. He confessed to killing them, saying they came to assassinate him with a dagger. How do I know it's true?"

She lifts a shoulder in a shrug. "Guards found a blade in his room. It was of human design and was traced back to your village smith."

"But how do I know his account of things isn't skewed? I know he can't lie, but how do I trust his perspective is accurate?"

"You either trust him or you don't. I can't tell you how to feel. All I can say is I trust Aspen with my life."

A feeble smile tugs at my lips. "Even though he punished you by appointing you my lady's maid?"

"Meh," she says. "I've had worse company."

"Speaking of worse company." I jump at Foxglove's voice. He stands in the doorway looking flustered. He closes the door behind him, then lays out a sheer, spider silk dress in a deep plum color on top of the clothes Lorelei had brought. "We're going to need to speed up our plans. Forget just getting you clean. We need to make you look like a queen."

"What? Why?"

Foxglove gives me an apologetic smile and adjusts his spectacles. "It's time to meet your future mother-in-law."

I'm trembling by the time I'm dressed and ready to meet my guest, unsure what to expect. Foxglove has been cryptic at best, hushing every question with an admonition that I'll ruin my makeup if I keep talking. He painted my lips with rouge, powdered my cheeks with crystalline dust, and lined my eyes with black and gold kohl. My hair has been brushed out in long waves, something he insisted on doing instead of his usual updo. My dress is so sheer, I blushed when I first saw myself in the mirror.

Now, as I walk down the halls, I can feel each breeze as if I were naked. All the fae dresses have been light and gauzy, but this one is unlike any I've worn so far. The plum spider silk is tight around my torso, then flows outward at the waist, trailing past my ankles. Its plunging neckline reveals a generous portion of my curving breasts, and the silk barely covers the rest.

At least Foxglove let me keep my dagger strapped to my thigh, the only argument I won. I blanched when he muttered that I might end up needing it.

I tug at one of my long bronze earrings, fashioned into a strand of maple leaves. "Is all this really necessary?" I ask Foxglove.

He and Lorelei exchange a glance. "You'll see," he says.

I hold my breath as we enter the formal dining room. There at the other end, standing at the rail I left not long ago, is Queen Melusine. She's facing away from us, so all I see is a cascade of silky, indigo hair, pale blue arms, and a long, sinuous serpent's tail. As she turns, we sink into bows and curtsies. I'm grateful for the moment to compose myself before I face her, but the time to rise comes too soon, and I find myself straightening with Foxglove and Lorelei, pulse racing.

Now I can see Melusine fully, and my state of dress makes sense. The Queen of the Sea Court has a human-like upper body, both slim and seductively curving, breasts barely hidden beneath strands of her glossy, blue hair. Her face holds an unprecedented beauty with angled eyes the color of a stormy sea, high blushing cheekbones, a perfect nose, and full coral-red lips. Strands of pink coral hang from her ears and around her slim neck. The planes of her flat stomach disappear into scales that end in her shimmering blue-green tail.

I feel overdressed and hideous in her presence.

"Your Majesty," Foxglove says, taking a step forward. "Queen Melusine, I would like to introduce Miss Evelyn Fairfield."

Melusine smiles, showing rows of pointed teeth. *Fangs*. I resist the urge to back away from her. Fangs don't mean anything, I remind myself. Foxglove has fangs, and he's harmless. Pleasant, even. But the more I've gotten to know Foxglove, the more his pointed teeth seem dainty and fashionable. Melusine's, on the other hand, look anything but, with their sharp, serrated edges and elongated tips. Oddly, they do nothing to take from her beauty. Somehow, the danger they present makes her more breathtaking.

"Your Majesty." I curtsy again, doing my best to keep my composure.

She eyes me, nose turned up as if she's assessing an unusual speck of dirt. "Where is that son of mine?" Her voice is light, flowing. Like a melody. Every word carries the roar of the ocean, the song of the siren.

"Resting," Foxglove says. His voice sounds like shattering glass after the lilting tune of hers. "He's recovering from his injury."

Melusine looks displeased, though not surprised. She must already know what happened to Aspen. "And where is my other son? Where is dear Cobalt?"

"Here." Cobalt enters the room and bows before his

mother, his moves flustered as if he'd rushed to make it here.

She wrinkles her nose at him as she eyes him from head to toe. "You dare greet me like that?"

He straightens, jaw shifting back and forth. "I take seelie form on land, Mother. You know this."

"I thought you'd have the decency to humor me, at least. Never mind, then. Take me to see Aspen."

"He's resting," Foxglove says again. "With his recovery so recently begun, we don't want to wake him."

Melusine throws her hands in the air. "Why did I come all this way if not to see my son?"

"Good question," Cobalt says. "Why did you come?"

She seems to ignore the ice in his tone. "This was my castle, once," she says. "I wanted to make sure it's in good hands."

"I'm more than capable of ruling in my brother's stead while he's incapacitated."

"You mistake me," she says. "I'm not curious about your hands, but hers." Her eyes slide to mine.

Cobalt follows her gaze, eyes going wide when they take in my appearance. He'd been so distracted by his mother, it's the first time he's looked at me since entering the room.

I resist the urge to cross my arms over my chest, and instead, put on my most convincing smile. "I am pleased to meet the mother of my mate," I say.

She slithers toward me on her serpent's tail while her upper body remains upright, bearing regal. Once she stops, I have to tilt my head to meet her eyes as she towers over me. "Are you?" she asks, tone mocking. "Are you truly pleased to meet me?"

"I am. I've heard so much about you."

She barks a musical laugh. "Not from Aspen, I'm sure. He barely considers me his mother anymore. He treats me as a fellow royal of the Council of Eleven Courts, nothing more."

"Still, I'm pleased to be in your presence just the same."

"Such human politeness," she says with disgust. "Fake."

"Mother," Cobalt says, a warning in his tone. "Aspen plans on making her his queen, which will make her nearly your equal."

She scoffs at that, eyes never leaving mine. "Nearly my equal. Ha! I see no crown on her head, nor have I gotten an invitation to her coronation. I've hardly heard more than whispers about this supposed upcoming wedding."

"There have yet to be any plans made for her coronation," Foxglove says, "all things considered. When Aspen recovers, I'm sure he'll—"

"Yes, I'm curious what he'll do with her." She slithers even closer, and I'm certain she sniffs at the air around me. "What are you to him?"

I swallow hard, hoping she can't hear my racing heart. "I'm his mate."

A corner of her lips pulls into a smile. "Are you though?"

"We performed the ceremony last week."

"Nothing more than a pretty show," she hisses. "Something tells me you have yet to become his true mate. You don't have the right...smell about you."

I want to argue that Foxglove and Lorelei had me

bathed and cleansed until my skin was pink before I came to meet her, but I stop myself. First of all, my bathing habits are none of her business. And second, I have the feeling she isn't talking about *that* kind of smell. She's referring to something I don't understand. Something fae.

I realize another thing. Foxglove and Lorelei didn't have me dressed in silk and painted with rouge just to look pretty for the queen. They did it to give me an advantage. To place me as her equal. They wanted her to see me as someone to respect. And here I am cowering before her like a wounded dog.

I square my shoulders and stand at my full height. My voice takes on the same bored quality I've heard Aspen use so many times. Every word I'm about to say is a gamble, but I take it. "Well, this has been pleasant, hasn't it? Now, if we're done parsing words and smelling each other, I think I'll go check on my mate." I turn away from her, keeping my chin held high, then pause before I reach the hall. "I'll have someone fetch you when he wakes. If he wants to see you."

I enter the hall, and Foxglove and Lorelei follow. Only when I'm out of earshot, do I let out the breath I was holding. I don't dare look behind me, terrified I'll see a raging sea serpent charging after me, but we continue on, and my head remains attached to my shoulders.

Lorelei finally breaks the silence with a laugh. "Learning how to play the game, are we?"

"I'm playing it," I say. "Let's just hope I don't lose."

30

I'm still seething over my encounter with Melusine as I pace my room. Who does she think she is, coming here to look me over and try to make me feel inferior? How does she benefit from such actions, aside from potentially scaring me away? From what Cobalt told me, Melusine is politically unseelie, meaning she can't be too pleased her son's marriage is keeping the peace. Or perhaps she thinks I'm not good enough for her son, feeble human that I am.

"I'll show her who's feeble," I mutter as I pull the bronze earrings from my ears and toss them on the bedside table. I catch sight of Aspen and turn to face him, amazed at the color that has returned to his cheeks. With a sigh, I sit on the bed next to him to check his vitals. "No wonder you're so awful. I know where you get it now."

He says nothing, of course, sleeping peacefully while I touch his forehead. His temperature has gone down, and even the sheen of sweat has disappeared. I move my hand to his chest, intending to change the dressing over the wound.

Aspen's eyes fly open, and his hand circles my wrist. I lose my balance, toppling toward him. He catches my other wrist, then shifts his weight. Before I know it, I'm pinned to the bed, Aspen straddled over me. His lips peel back from his teeth, chest heaving as his eyes bore into me.

"You're clearly feeling better," I say with a sneer as I try to twist from his grasp.

"What are you doing here?"

"What do you think I'm doing? Tending your wounds, like I've done every nauseating hour since you were injured."

"Injured." He says the word as if it's foreign to him.

I freeze. "You don't remember?"

He searches my eyes, brows knitting together. "I was wounded."

"Yes. In your idiotic attempt to satiate Mr. Holstrom's bloodlust, you nearly got yourself killed."

"You...did something to me."

"It's called saving your pathetic life, and you're welcome."

He seems to relax and releases my wrists but doesn't move from over me. My body is still pinned between his legs and thighs.

I push at his chest, but he doesn't budge. "Will you get off me?"

His eyes widen as he looks at me as if seeing me for the first time. He takes in the sheer plum dress, eyes roving over the lowcut neckline. His lips twist into a mischievous smirk, making him look more like himself than he has in days. "Why, are you scared?"

I roll my eyes. "I'm scared you'll pull your stitches and all my hard work will be for nothing."

"No, you are scared of me," he says, voice low. "I can feel it."

I push at his chest again, tempted to punch him in his wound. It's then I realize the trails of black have all but disappeared from his torso. "I'm not scared. This is just highly inappropriate." But now that he mentions it, perhaps I should be afraid. He clearly isn't in his right mind, considering he woke up without memory of what happened. And even if he were in his right mind...my eyes involuntarily flash toward his antlers. If he wanted to, he could gut me here and now. I wouldn't have time to scream.

"You're thinking about what I did on the farm."

I shoot him a scowl. "So, you do remember."

A pained look crosses his face. "I won't hurt you, Evie."

I can't help but stare at his antlers again, imagining them covered in blood and gore.

Aspen seems amused. "Curious? You keep looking."

"Yes, I keep looking. There's a pair of razor-sharp antlers just inches from my face. I'm trying not to get stabbed in the eye." My words come out more breathless than I intend.

"I'm more than capable of handling my antlers. And how do you know they are razor sharp if you've never felt their cut?"

Part of me wants to push him away, make him stop his teasing, but another part of me is morbidly fascinated with his antlers, now that I know what they are capable of. There's something enticing about facing the danger of them. I want to touch them, admire them, the same way I want to admire a well-crafted blade or scalpel. Do they feel like bone? Rock?

He rolls his eyes as if he can hear my thoughts. "You can touch them. You're probably the first human in my presence who hasn't tried."

The first human who hasn't tried. This makes me think of my sister. Did *she* try to touch them? Were they ever close enough for her to do so? Or did she simply ask in her charmingly naive way? Without realizing it, my hand moves toward them, pulled by an invisible force.

Aspen leans closer, bracing himself on his forearms.

My fingers find the tip of one of the tines. It's sharp, but not enough to pierce skin without pressure. I'm surprised to find how smooth the surface is, covered in soft velvet. I run my fingertips down the length of the main beam, then trace one of the lower tines that branch off it. I'm mesmerized. Thrilled to be touching such a delicate yet powerful weapon.

Aspen shudders.

I pause, my sense of self-awareness returning. "What was that for?"

"My antlers are very sensitive," he says. His voice is quiet, breathy. "Every touch is both pleasure and pain."

I pull my hand away, heat flooding my cheeks. I had no idea antlers held sensation. "Why in the bloody name of iron didn't you tell me you could feel that?" I say through my teeth.

"Because I didn't want you to stop."

His words pull the breath from my lungs, and the

intensity of his gaze holds me in place. This close, I can see his eyes like I never have before. They aren't brown like I originally thought, but every color of autumn. Golds, bronze, emerald, and ruby swirl in his irises. I can't stop myself from thinking it—*he's beautiful.* The most beautiful creature I've ever seen. And he's looking at me like I'm beautiful too. A luxurious feast for a starving man. His full lips are so close to mine, I can feel his breath, smell the rosemary on his skin. I can't help but remember our kiss during the mate ceremony, and that same strange fire roars in my chest.

As if he can feel it too, he closes the distance between us, lips crushing into mine. I don't think to stop him, to fight him. I give in to the kiss, let it deepen. My body hums with a hungry desire, eager to consume more of him.

With his knees, he pushes one of my legs aside, then the other. As a reflex, I wrap them around his waist, drawing him closer. My lips part for his tongue, and a soft moan escapes his mouth. I bring one hand to his lower back, and the other explores the firm muscles of his chest, careful not to skate too close to his wound.

One of his hands leaves the bed to do some exploring of its own. I feel his fingers caress my neck, then turn my head to the side so his lips can trail over the skin where his fingers just were. His kisses move down my neck and across my collar bone, then trace lower along the neck-line of my dress.

When his lips return to mine, I claim them eagerly. His hand slides from my neck and over the curve of my breast. I gasp, feeling the trail of his fingers through the spider silk, sensations multiplied as if his fingers were flames. His thumb makes lazy circles over the crest of my breast, and a shock of pleasure runs through me, so intense I arch my back to meet it. A fire ignites at the apex of my thighs, and I think I will die if it isn't quelled.

His other hand finds my knee, traces up my thigh. I know where it's going and I don't care. I want it to go higher. Want him everywhere all at once. I have no control, no awareness but him. His fingers reach my dagger belt. He winces, then jolts upright. It's enough to shatter the moment, bringing clarity to my mind.

My breaths come out heavy as I recover from the spell of passion. The spell that had me powerless. Vulnerable. Completely unlike myself. I pull away from him, straightening my dress. "What in the name of iron was that?"

Aspen puts the tip of his thumb to his mouth, as if soothing a burn. He winces again, shaking out his hand. "Why are you wearing that damn thing?"

I ignore the question, scooting farther away from him. "You did it again, didn't you? You glamoured yourself to make me want you."

His expression darkens. "Is that the only way you can imagine kissing me? Under the pretense of a glamour? Am I really so disgusting to you?"

"Yes, you're disgusting." I slide from the bed and to my feet, eyes locked on him, ready for any sign that he'll pounce. "Only a disgusting creature would use a glamour to seduce a woman."

He shakes his head. "If that's what helps you sleep at night."

"Speaking of sleeping at night," I say, moving to the wardrobe. I grab a nightdress, a robe, and a heavy blue gown. "The bedroom is yours again. I'll sleep in my parlor."

"You liked your parlor, then?" He grins, eyes alight with mischief.

I don't rise to the bait. With my head held high, I stride to the doors, ignoring the attention of the guards waiting outside. "Oh, and by the way," I call out behind me, "your mother's here."

The last thing I see before I slam the doors is Aspen's look of utter horror.

31

T he couch in my parlor isn't nearly as comfortable as Aspen's bed, nor the couch in his room that I'd been sleeping on while he'd been recovering. I don't know how much of that is due to a discrepancy in quality or from the weight of my humiliation.

Every time I close my eyes, I see Aspen's face, feel Aspen's lips, hear his breath in my ear. I see myself pulling him closer, hips writhing against his. The fire ignites all over again, and I hate it. I cover my eyes with my hands, as if that could banish the visions in my mind. As if it could make me forget the taste of his lips.

My humiliation turns to fury when I wake the next morning. I go over my list of reasons why I hate Aspen, King of the Autumn Court.

I hate that he glamoured himself.

I hate that he tried to seduce me.

I hate that he made me feel out of control.

I hate his lack of apology.

Hate the way he looked at me.

Hate the way he kissed.

The way he breathed.

The way his hands felt on my—

A knock sounds on the parlor door.

Snap out of it, Evie. I steady my ragged breathing just in time to greet Lorelei.

"You're requested on the balcony," she says, looking both flustered and pleased. "The king has fully recovered and will be holding audience with Queen Melusine."

I furrow my brow. "The balcony?"

"That's where you had the mate ceremony."

"Yes, but why are we going there?"

"Aspen holds court there. It's his throne room of sorts."

"I see." I twist my fingers together, anxiety building in my chest. "Must I go?"

"I think it's wise. You'll be sitting at the king's side where his queen would be. It's a bit of a power move, hosting his mother before his throne as opposed to over breakfast."

"I suppose that does sound important." My heart sinks. I think of all the pruning and prodding Foxglove did yesterday to make me a suitable match for the Sea Queen. Am I ready to face her so soon? Better yet, am I ready to face Aspen so soon?

Lorelei's mouth quirks at the corner. "You've clearly got a lot on your mind. Care to share?"

"No," I say in a rush. There's no way I'm telling her or anyone about what happened last night. Not that most in the palace don't already assume such behavior exists between me and the king. Does Lorelei know the truth? That we aren't true mates?

"Fine then. Let's get you dressed."

"On one condition." I hold up a finger. "Put me in a more modest dress today. No exceptions."

BY THE TIME WE REACH THE BALCONY, THE TWO BROTHERS are already there. Aspen sits on one of the ornate thrones on the raised dais, the one to his right remaining empty. I hadn't paid much attention to the thrones during our mate ceremony, but now that I'm less distracted, I notice their beauty. Both are identical, constructed of twining roots and branches, gold leaves sprouting from the sides. Cobalt stands at Aspen's left, a step down from the dais. Several guards wait on each side of the balcony.

Cobalt offers me a kind smile, while Aspen lounges in his throne, barely looking at me. The king reminds me of a jungle cat, lazing in his tree. Beautiful and dangerous, even at rest.

I keep my gaze on the empty throne as I make my way forward. Today I'm dressed in a pale blue gown. The cut of the neckline is still low, but the top is a heavy silk brocade, the skirt layers of frothy blue chiffon. An elegant necklace of bronze and sapphire circles my neck.

I take my seat in the empty throne, trying to ignore the tension rising between me and Aspen. Or am I imagining it? I glance at the king from the corner of my eye, but he's paying me no heed. His chin rests on his fist, elbow propped on the arm of the throne. His other hand sprawls across the armrest. Too close to mine. He taps his fingers in a bored way, and all I can think about is how they felt on my skin.

"Sleep well?" Aspen's voice is a cold whisper, and he doesn't face me to say it.

My eyes dart away from his fingers, straight ahead. "Yes," I say through my teeth. It's a lie, of course.

"You didn't check my bandages this morning." This time he turns his head toward me. "Do you neglect all your patients like that?"

"You were obviously feeling well enough to manage on your own."

"Oh, but I much prefer to be managed by you."

Heat flushes my cheeks, and I refuse to meet the smirk I know is waiting for me.

I'm saved from coming up with a clever reply when I catch sight of movement on the stairs leading to the balcony. Indigo hair. Dazzling blue eyes. Queen Melusine seems somehow more beautiful than she was yesterday as she slithers up the remaining steps to the balcony floor. She smiles indulgently as she approaches. "Aspen, my dear son. So wonderful it is to see you well. How is it you recovered so quickly?"

He covers my hand with his, and I resist the urge to flinch. "I had a good healer. Evelyn has many talents."

She looks down her nose at me, then returns her attention to Aspen. "Many talents, indeed. Although I heard quite the rumor yesterday. Though you recovered, you and your mate spent the night apart. Trouble in the bedroom?"

Aspen gives her a smile that doesn't reach his eyes. "No trouble, Mother, though I do appreciate your concern. Dear Evie was keeping me awake and thought it best to leave me in peace. She moans in her sleep, you see."

The way he says *moans* makes my breath catch. There was a hint of jest in his tone, and I know it was meant for me. Teasing. Tempting. I keep my breathing steady, trying not to over-think it.

Melusine's eyes dart toward me, as if she caught the jest as well. For a moment, her expression turns from haughty to worry. In the blink of an eye, her composure returns. "What a generous mate you have. In fact, I'd like to get to know her a little better. Evelyn, will you walk the shore with me tonight? See me off before I return home?"

I open my mouth, not sure what to say. I almost wish Aspen would answer for me, but he doesn't. What does she want with me? Is it safe to speak with her in private? And by the coral caves, no less. Then another thought comes to mind. *The coral caves.* Melusine is the Sea Queen. If Amelie really did run to the caves the night she disappeared, Melusine might know something. It's a long shot, but it's all I have.

"I'd be honored, Your Majesty," I say.

"You'll be leaving tonight, then?" Cobalt asks, speaking for the first time.

"Yes, dear son, but don't look so sad. If you miss me, you'll have to visit more often." With that, she turns and slithers back the way she came.

"Adjourned," Aspen says, even though Cobalt and I are the only ones in attendance aside from the guards.

Cobalt looks from Aspen to me, hesitating, then leaves the balcony. I'm tempted to do the same, but there's something I need from Aspen.

He remains seated on his throne, scowling after his mother. I shift in my seat to face him. "We need to talk."

His scowl disappears, turning to mischief as he eyes the length of the gown. "I can think of something better we can do. It doesn't involve talking at all."

I blush. "No, thank you. You are never taking advantage of me like that again."

He scoffs. "Take advantage? I'm not the one who forced secrets from my lips in a vulnerable state."

"I never imagined you could admit to being vulnerable."

"I never imagined you could kiss the way you did."

My heart races at his words. The truth is, I never imagined I could kiss like that either. Honestly, I think he did most of the kissing. I just opened to it, followed his lead. Moved the way he moved, breathed the way he breathed—I shake my head, squeezing my thighs together.

"Stop trying to change the subject. I need you to explain some things. First of all, why didn't you tell me my sister was alive? You let me believe she was dead."

His expression darkens, looking from his guards to the other end of the balcony. "Keep your voice down."

"Then answer the question."

He lets out an irritated grumble. "I never planned on lying to you, but you seemed so convinced the body you saw was hers. I figured it might be safer that way, for everyone involved. At least until I discovered the truth."

"How in the bloody name of iron did you figure that was safer?"

"I don't know who's behind this," he says, rubbing his

brow. "If the person responsible thinks we assume your sister is dead, they won't expect us to be looking for her."

"Does that mean you *are* looking for her?"

He nods. "Not that it's doing any good. There are no trails. No clues. Every day I await the ransom note, the bargain. Every day nothing comes of it. I hate dealing with assassins I can't see. They should at least have the decency to face me head on."

"Who would hold Amelie against you like that?"

"It could be anyone. Any of the unseelie who want war. Any of the humans who want the same. Any of the seelie council fae who'd prefer to see my brother on the throne. The hosting court of the Chosen is always at risk during the month following a Reaping. What I do or don't do with you could turn the tide. If I treat you badly, refuse a marriage alliance, halt compensation to your mother, any of that could forfeit the treaty. It makes me a target from all sides."

My heart does a flip at the mention of my mother. "How are you compensating her, anyway? I imagine it isn't with farm animals."

"She refused all talk of compensation. There was no bargain Foxglove could tempt her with. So I purchased her apothecary and put it under her name, in addition to leaving a heavy fund to maintain it. She will never have to worry about rent or repair. Even if she refuses to spend a coin from the fund, it will be done on her behalf."

A lump rises in my throat. My mother. She's being taken care of. Her life's passion—the apothecary—is secured. Was that Aspen's doing? Foxglove's? The council? I can't bring myself to ask.

"Regardless," Aspen says, interrupting my thoughts,

"even before the Reaping, I tended to attract the disdain of seelie and unseelie alike. I have many potential enemies. Many who would like to see me lose my throne."

I remember what Cobalt had said about Aspen. How he constantly shifts sides. "Why do you do it?" I ask. "Why do you attract the rage of the council? If you just chose a side and stuck with it, they wouldn't resent you the way they do."

He lets out a cold laugh. "No, I'm sure you're right, but that's not something I'm willing to do."

"Why? You talk about maintaining the safety of the isle. Isn't that more important than childish games?"

"What I do isn't a game," he says, meeting my eyes with his steely gaze. "What I do creates balance. A balance that—if upended—could create chaos for my people."

"I don't understand."

"No, you don't."

I lean toward him. "Then tell me. I need to know what's going on."

He lets out a heavy sigh. "There's something you should understand. The seelie, the unseelie, it isn't a matter of good or bad. The seelie want the experiences the humans opened for them. To love. To feel. To hate. The power of choice and consequence. Luxury. Lack. Poverty. They want all of it. The unseelie want the old ways. They want solitude. Connection to nature. Instinct."

"That makes sense," I say.

"Since the war ended, we've maintained balance. The seelie live how they want to live, and the unseelie follow their own ways. There is give and take. Each court and ruler and citizen has the right to choose. For most of us, it's enough, but for others..."

I lean closer, entranced by his candid words, his serious tone. He's never spoken this way before, not even when he was recovering from his wound. "Go on."

"Some of the seelie see the unseelie as barbaric. Lesser. Vile, dangerous creatures that shouldn't be allowed the level of freedom they get. You've met the kelpie. Would you say he should be allowed to torment stray travelers the way he does?"

I shake my head, the memory of nearly drowning still fresh in my mind.

"But it is the kelpie's nature. Lost travelers are his prey, the same way a rabbit is prey to a wolf. The radical seelie want the unseelie ways to end. To force them seelie or destroy them. The radical unseelie feel the same way, but in reverse. They want the human influence off the isle, to free their kind from the shackles of the seelie way. Without human influence, clothes, food, the seelie would cease to exist. We would revert to our unseelie forms and the isle would return to what it was long ago. Can you see the conflict?"

"Yes, but what does that have to do with you shifting sides on the council?"

"What do you think would happen if the council shifted too heavily one side or another?"

I lift my shoulder in a shrug, even though I think I know where he's going with this.

"If one side or the other got total control, the other side would be eliminated. If the seelie ruled the council, the unseelie would be outlawed, banished, executed.

Strapped into clothing, human food forced into their mouths. On the other hand, if the unseelie took control, they would exterminate the humans in their sleep, not bothering with the formalities of war. They would force the seelie to abandon all that they have come to hold dear."

My eyes widen with realization. "You're trying to prevent that from happening."

"I believe every fae has a right to choose. For that, we must maintain balance."

I sit back in my throne, feeling drained. Everything I thought I knew about Aspen is crashing around me. He may be arrogant and irritating and possibly paranoid, but he's fighting for something I can understand. For not the first time in my life, I wonder just how wrong I've been about faekind. "This is indeed complicated."

"It is," Aspen says. "Sometimes I feel like the unseelie are right. That it would be better not to feel pain or pleasure. To take my stag form forever and live on instinct in the pure radiance of my true nature. But other times," he meets my eyes, "I feel like I couldn't possibly give all this up."

"Why did you choose me?" I find myself asking, voice barely above a whisper.

"I told you the first time you asked," he said. "My words were true. I chose you because you put a knife to me."

I narrow my eyes. "When you were recovering, you said you hadn't wanted to punish me."

"No, you're right, but my words are true just the same. After the assassination attempt by the Holstrom girls, I nearly agreed to wage war on your kind. The seelie on the council talked me out of it, encouraged me to choose another for the Reaping. I could have left it to random choice, but there was a name I couldn't get out of my head. The name of the woman who could have tried to kill me but held back, even when I feigned an attack on her at the wall."

"Why was such a thing so unforgettable to you?"

He shrugs. "If you'd been an assassin, you'd have tried to kill me then. Your ferocity paired with restraint made me think you'd be strong enough to stand at my side, yet not so full of hate that you'd try to kill me."

"Oh," I say. That wasn't the answer I was expecting. "But I didn't know who you were at the wall. I didn't even see your antlers. If I'd been an assassin sent to kill you, I wouldn't have known you were my target."

"I may have glamoured my antlers and dressed in the colors of the night, but if you were an assassin, you'd have known me anyway. You'd have been expecting me."

I chew my lip, processing the information.

"Was I right about you?" he asks. "Or are you still thinking of turning that blade on me?"

I look down at my thigh and the blue chiffon hiding the dagger beneath it. I'm not ready to answer that question, so I stand. "I should take my leave, Your Majesty."

He takes hold of my hand, gently. "I meant it, Evie. It's Aspen when we're alone."

I turn to go, but he doesn't release me. I'm about to throw him a scowl, but his expression is serious. "Come back to our room," he says.

"Why, so you can take advantage of me again?"

"I'll sleep elsewhere tonight. You claim the bed." Finally, he lets my hand slip from his fingers.

"I'll consider it." I feel his eyes on me as I make my way across the floor.

It's no surprise when I hear him say my name. I turn. "I never glamoured myself in your presence but once."

I tilt my head. "Excuse me?"

"At the wall. That was the only time I've worn a glamour in front of you."

"But the day I arrived at the palace...in the dining room...you said—"

"I was teasing you, allowing you to believe I'd donned a glamour. But I hadn't."

I put my hands on my hips. "I thought you said you couldn't lie."

His eyes sparkle with mischief. "I told you no direct lie. Deception, on the other hand, is what we fae excel at."

I bristle. He just admitted to being able to deceive me without lying. A dangerous confession. But even more dangerous is the truth—that all those times I was drawn to Aspen, pulled by his strange beauty, powerless before it, I had no glamour to blame. It leaves me with a confession of my own. There is a very strong part of me that wants him.

32

That night I meet Melusine on the shore. She stands near the edge of water, waves lapping over the end of her tail. The sun is setting in brilliant shades of pink and gold, and a gentle breeze catches my hair, sending stray tendrils blowing behind me. With slow, confident steps, feet bare in the cool sand, I close the distance between us and stand before her.

"Your Majesty," I say with a curtsy.

She gives me a deep nod. "Come, Evelyn, let us stroll." She turns and slithers down the shore, away from the palace.

I follow, silence falling between us. The only sound is the crashing of waves and the occasional splash of something breaking the surface of the water. I catch sight of a whale's tail in the distance, then the leaping of a fish. Then another. Moving closer and closer to the shore.

Melusine smiles upon each visitor, each crab that scuttles from behind its rock to watch its queen.

I catch movement up ahead; seals leap upon the large

rocks at the far end of the shore, then beautiful women with long, opalescent tails climb upon the higher rocks. Are they naturally drawn to their queen and simply want to see her? Or is she trying to demonstrate her power? I swallow my unease, wishing I hadn't left Aspen's guards at the other end of the shore.

"How gracious of you to meet with me tonight," she says in her melodious voice, waving a greeting at a siren with emerald green hair.

"Yes," I say, "and so gracious of you to want to get to know me better."

"That I do. You are my eldest son's mate. Soon-to-be queen of the palace that once was mine."

"I...am determined to take great care of the palace," I say, careful to avoid words like *vow* and *promise*. "And to serve the interests of human and fae alike."

"Yes, but your interests will always lie more with humans, will they not?"

I think about everything Aspen said about balance. About freedom and choice. "I'm certain I can learn to hold both my kind and yours in equal affection."

"Even the unseelie?"

I swallow hard and don a pleasant smile. "You mean like you?"

She tenses, lips peeling back from her sharp teeth.

I pretend it doesn't frighten me. "If I can walk peacefully at your side, I'm sure I can advocate for others. My mate, as I'm sure you know, often shifts his alliance to unseelie. I will have to learn to appreciate both parties."

"Spoken like an ambassador."

"Like a queen," I correct her, before I realize the boldness of my words.

"You aren't quite what I expected. Not after everything I heard about you. And your sister."

The blood leaves my face. It's a struggle to keep my voice neutral as I ask, "What exactly *have* you heard about my sister?"

"Oh, that a terrible tragedy took place here. Word has it the poor girl died. Yet, my son has said nothing of this to the humans. Could it be he fears their wrath?"

We've stopped, coming to the end of the shore where a large cliff extends over the water, giving way to the enormous rocks the selkies and sirens are so fond of. I face her, searching her eyes for truth. "You wouldn't have anything to do with my sister's disappearance, would you?"

She laughs. "What use would I have for a filthy human girl?"

"You didn't answer the question."

"I didn't take her, nor did I kill her, if that's what you're asking."

I study her words, seeking every crack she's left unfilled, every hole she's left unburied. There's a lot of room for deception.

"Now let me ask you a question," she says. "And I'll ask it directly. Will you or won't you perform the Bonding ritual with Aspen?"

This surprises me. "What?"

"A simple yes or no. Will you or won't you?"

"How do you know we haven't already?"

She slithers closer to me, sniffing the air like she did the day before. When she pulls away, she laughs, amusement dancing in her eyes. "No, you haven't. There's a distinct smell about a human who has been Bonded with a fae. You don't have it."

"What kind of smell would that be?" I ask, out of defensiveness more than anything.

"It is nothing a fae can explain to a human. Just know it's obvious to all of us that you aren't his true mate, no matter how well you lie."

"On the contrary, I am his mate. Your ambassador was here to witness the ceremony. We—"

"You and I both know that ceremony meant nothing to you." She flicks her wrist in a dismissive gesture. "To be honest, it hardly means much to the fae. Aspen could have a hundred mates if he wished. It is but the first of three steps required to fulfill the treaty, and even if you were to perform the human wedding next, you'd still be missing a vital piece."

"I don't understand." I regret the admission as soon as the words are out of my mouth.

Melusine lets out an exaggerated gasp. "You mean he hasn't told you?"

"Told me what?"

Her lips pull into a sympathetic smile, making my blood boil. "What a devious boy he's been. You see, if you fail to Bond before the timeframe given by the treaty, the pact will be considered void."

My pulse quickens at her words. "You mean we'll revert to war?"

"It's obvious that's what Aspen wants, otherwise he would have told you."

My mind is reeling for the second time today.

"Now, Evelyn, I can see you are hurt by this. I can almost promise you, my son will only hurt you more the longer you are together. End this farce and return home to your people."

"So we can go to war?"

Her tone darkens. "So we have a chance at securing the isle for who it rightfully belongs to."

"Which you think means the fae. The unseelie. You want this war."

She shrugs a delicate shoulder.

"Whatever happened to the mercy you felt after giving birth to Aspen?"

"That wasn't mercy," she says. "That was weakness. A symptom of birthing a seelie son. I made a bargain to end the war in exchange for his life. Once the human I'd made the bargain with died, my mind became clearer little by little. I was a fool to give up the isle. And I will never be that fool again."

"Why are you telling me this?"

"Because our interests are aligned. I know you don't want to do the ritual. I don't want you to either. Promise me you won't."

"I can't make that promise," I whisper.

"You can and you will. I know you don't love my son. Set him free. Otherwise, the ritual will Bond the two of you by the power of your names. It is a terrifying thing to give one's name to another, and a curse to have another's name within your control. That's just the Bond itself I'm talking about. Think of the other heartaches you could avoid by forgoing a relationship with him. Love between a human and a fae is a tenuous thing. It's intoxicating but devastating. If he leaves you for another, mistreats you, your heart will break, cutting deeper than any normal heartache. If you stay together, he will resent you for standing in the way of his true nature."

I think of Doris Mason, her lifeless eyes. Of her cousin who passed away from neglect. Is that the dark side of all human-fae pairings? And what about what Aspen said? How sometimes he thinks it would be better to give up the seelie way? Could I trust he won't eventually turn unseelie in earnest? *We'll only be allies, not lovers,* I tell myself, but it doesn't give me comfort.

She smiles knowingly. "That is no life for you. Take the mercy I am offering you. It's only a matter of time before the treaty breaks some other way. Promise me you won't do the ritual, and you will be allowed to live and return to your village. Warn your people. Take your mother to the mainland and escape the burden you now bear. Take as many of your people off this isle with you as you can."

Anxiety crushes my lungs as I consider. I could take this bargain. I could take my people to safety, free them from the responsibility of upholding the treaty century after century. Let them live in freedom, no longer in the shadow of the faewall. No longer fearing fae retribution. But in turn, everyone who escapes to the mainland would lose their homes, their land, the day-to-day lives they cherish. And it would all be my fault. I feel like my legs will give out from the weight of the burden riding on my shoulders.

"Promise me."

I breathe away the anxiety, seeking control, logic. With a deep breath, I close my eyes, focusing on the feel of my dagger against my thigh, hidden beneath my skirts. I pat it once, and my mind begins to steady. One thing becomes clear. I cannot make any kind of bargain with Melusine. "I won't."

Her fangs flash, lips peeling into a snarl. "Promise me or I will make you regret the day you denied my mercy."

"No."

She lets out an angry roar. The ocean responds, sending its waves to echo her, rising from the sea toward the sky. Shark fins break the surface, jaws snapping from the waves. The sirens begin to wail a harrowing tune.

I hold my ground, ready to meet it. As powerless as I am against the sea, I refuse to run.

Melusine's gaze locks on me, eyes like a swirling tempest as she slithers forward, arms outstretched, monstrous waves at her back ready to crash over my head.

"Mother."

Melusine freezes, head darting to the side. The waves are thrown backward, dousing me in a cold spray. I gasp, the chilling water drenching me from head to toe. In the blink of an eye, the sea is calm again.

"Aspen, dear," she hisses through her teeth.

He strolls towards us at a leisurely pace. "Didn't you know it's considered treason to attack the mate of a king?"

Her composure relaxes and her lips pull into a smile. Her tail is the only thing that betrays her, swishing wildly, erratically, in the sand. "You mistake me, my son. We had an argument that got out of hand. Nothing more. You do know how my temper can be."

"I do," he says. "Regardless, you've overstayed your welcome."

She lifts her chin. "I wouldn't call anything I received a welcome. You'll have to try harder tomorrow."

"Tomorrow?" A look of surprise interrupts his stoic expression.

"The council meeting," she says. "You didn't forget, did you?"

The calm returns to his features. "Of course not. I'm simply surprised you aren't sending an ambassador in your stead."

"Not for such an important meeting. Until then." She smiles, then dives into the sea, sinuous tail snaking across the sand until it disappears beneath the waves.

Aspen puts his hands on my shoulders and turns me to face him. "Are you all right?"

My hands ball into fists, fury roaring inside me. "*You.*"

33

"Me?" Aspen smirks. "What did I do to spark your displeasure this time?"

"Was she right? Did you keep the truth about the Bonding ritual from me?"

His smile fades.

I take a step away, pulling from his grasp. "She was right, wasn't she? You were going to let me break the treaty without realizing it."

"Yes."

"Why? After everything you told me about protecting the balance. How could you do this?"

"You said you wouldn't do the ritual. I wasn't going to force you."

I throw my hands in the air. "I may have reconsidered if I'd known the truth. You should have told me. You should have told me everything from the start."

His lips press into a tight line. "You weren't the easiest to talk to."

"Neither were you."

"You seemed so set in your opinion of me. I wouldn't grovel at your feet just to give you an explanation."

"Because of your pride?"

He shrugs. "Perhaps. It didn't seem worth my time when you wouldn't have believed me anyway."

"So you were just going to let me unwittingly break the pact?"

"Better you than me."

My fingers clench into fists. "How can you say that so casually when it would have meant war?"

"Because if *I* were to break the treaty, there's a good chance I'd lose my throne as well. Besides, what were my other options? I could let you make your choices based on human prejudice, resulting in war with a people who might not deserve my protection in the first place. Or I could tell you the truth and make you feel forced to perform the ritual, resulting in a Bond with a woman who hates me, a woman who could use my name against me, use it to dethrone me."

"I wouldn't have." My voice comes out small, uncertain.

He barks a cold laugh. "Not even you believe that."

"I *couldn't* have," I correct. "A human can't use a fae's true name against them. Giving me your name will do nothing. I don't have any special hormones to secrete that mess with your brain. You'd be the one with all the power."

His expression twists into a look of bewilderment. "*Hormone*? What are you talking about?"

"It's what gives you the power to glamour others. It overrides parts of our brain."

He shakes his head. "It's our magic that allows us to

use a glamour. The power of giving another your true name uses a strong enough magic for even a human to use on the Fair Isle. Haven't you heard about the end of the war? The exile of the Fire King? The head of Eisleigh's council exchanged names with the Fire King and banished him. The Fire King, in turn used the councilman's name to promise he would never set foot on the Fair Isle again and would live on the mainland until his death. That's what the Bond is about. The ultimate sign of mutual fear and respect. It can be forged between friends, enemies, allies, and—yes—humans and fae."

I'm surprised to hear this part of the story, but it still doesn't mean anything. There's no proof the councilman had any power over the Fire King when he used his name. Still, I'm too exhausted to argue. "Aspen, I just want the truth. What happens next?"

"Nothing has changed on my side. I still won't force you to do the ritual. The choice is yours. If we must go to war, so be it. If you choose to give me your name, I will give you mine in return."

"I thought you were afraid I'll betray you."

He sighs. "If you were ever going to hurt me, you would have let me succumb to iron poisoning."

I feel a flash of guilt, remembering the moment I considered doing just that. "Your mother said there is a timeframe determined by the treaty. When must the Bonding ritual be performed by?"

His expression falters, almost apologetic. "The treaty states the ritual must take place no later than a week before the human wedding ceremony."

I do the math in my head. My mouth falls open, and

the breath flies from my lungs. "Tomorrow is a week before the wedding."

He nods. "That's why the council is coming. I am to present you as my Bonded by midnight. If not, the treaty is broken, and the council will determine next steps."

I close my eyes and turn away from him. All I want to do is scream, to pound his chest and berate him for letting things go so long without telling me the truth. But I'm still too drained to fight or argue. Instead, I feel like I'm going to be sick.

After a stretch of silence, I hear Aspen's footfall behind me, then to the side of me. I can't bring myself to look at him. "What did you argue with my mother about?" he asks.

"She...she wanted me to promise I wouldn't perform the ritual."

He curses under his breath. "Of course she did." He goes still, studying me. "What did you say?"

I chew my bottom lip, eyes darting toward his face then away again. "I refused to give her my promise."

"Because you detest bargaining with the fae, or because you're actually considering it?"

"Both."

"For your people?" he asks.

"Of course," I say. "I'll do anything to keep the isle free from war. That's why I'm here. Why I've persevered this long."

"But you hate it here, don't you?"

"I don't *hate* it." My stomach sinks when I say it, but it's the truth. The fae may terrify me at times, and more than one has directly tried to kill me. But others— Lorelei, Foxglove, Cobalt, Gildmar, even Aspen—are showing me there's more to Faerwyvae than I grew up believing. I may not love it yet, but I'd rather not see it destroyed by war.

"What about me?" Aspen's voice comes out soft, hesitant. "Do you still hate me?"

My pulse quickens. "Not entirely."

"Is there any part of you that wants to do the ritual for...us?"

My eyes widen and find his, but I say nothing.

His expression darkens, and he turns away, shaking his head. I watch as he stalks down the beach. For an unfathomable moment, I feel cold at the sight, at the distance growing between us. Without a second thought, I march after him. "Aspen, don't you dare walk away from me."

He pauses, then turns to face me. His expression flickers between cool stoicism and the vulnerability I've rarely gotten to see.

I close the distance between us. "I said I wanted the truth."

"I never promised to give it."

"Yet you did anyway," I say. "Don't walk away from me when there's clearly more to say."

He lets out a grumble. "You really want the truth?"

I nod.

"The truth is, I've wanted you from the start. From the day I met you at the wall. I wanted you when I first laid eyes on you in the dining room, when Foxglove crushed me with the news that you would be my brother's bride. I wanted you later that night when I met you at the rail. I wanted to offer you a change of plans, to offer myself to you instead. I wanted you even after you burned me with your scorn, rejected every flirtation I threw your way. I wanted you every time we were together in a room, regardless of who else was there. I wanted you then and I want you now, and it infuriates me that you feel nothing in return."

My breaths are quick, shallow, pulse racing. He gave me the truth; I could leave it at that. I could walk away. I could tell him he's right, that I feel nothing in return. I could ignore all those times I felt drawn to him, like a fire was burning every part of me at once. For so long, I'd mistaken it for the fire of rage, and it was there. But there was another fire coexisting alongside it, something I've never given credit to. It's that thing that makes me feel breathless, out of control, and completely unlike myself. It's passion. There's no logic about it, no textbook to tell me how to cut it apart or navigate it. It's something I always swore I lacked, something only girls like Amelie have.

But if we're talking about truth, let me admit mine. I am no stranger to passion. I simply choose to ignore it, lock it up, and keep it at bay. It's something I've never let myself explore. Who would I be if I did?

I see Aspen beginning to grow tense again, his vulnerability fading behind his stony mask of pride. I could let this end here. Now. Let him walk away, allow the tension to grow between us until it solidifies into a wall.

"You're wrong," I finally say, the words flying from my throat before I can swallow them down. "I don't feel nothing."

His eyes widen, the mask slipping. "What *do* you feel?"

I can't bring myself to use words, so I reach a tentative

hand toward his cheek. He closes his eyes, trembling with restraint at my touch. I run my fingers along his jaw, his sculpted cheekbone, the lobe of his ear.

When he opens his eyes, I have but a moment to bask in their color, in the desire radiating from them. After that, his lips are on mine. My arms wrap around his neck, pulling him closer, fingers tangling in his hair. His hands move down my back, and his lips trail my neck, my collarbone. I tilt my head back, gasping as he kisses behind my ear.

"I want to pick up where we left off." His voice is a low rumble, sending a shiver up my spine.

"Yes," is all I can manage to say.

"But not here." He pulls away from me. Disappointment sinks my gut, but before it can take root, he links his fingers with mine. We run down the shore, back toward the palace. At the base of the rock wall just beneath the palace, there's a cave that leads to a tunnel, a tunnel that leads to stairs, and stairs that lead to the lower levels of the palace. I'd come this way to meet Melusine.

At the mouth of the cave stand the guards I left behind. Aspen dismisses them, ordering them to wait farther down the tunnel. They obey, leaving us alone in the cool darkness of the cave, lit only by sparse orbs of light. When we can no longer hear the footsteps of the guards, Aspen turns to me, lips crushing against mine as he presses my back against the smooth, dark stone. Warmth spreads through me from head to toe, and I feel the flames of passion return. I run my hands up his chest, up the silk of his waistcoat, then to the collar of his shirt. From there, I touch his neck, his cheek, his brow. Slowly, my fingers crawl into his hair until I reach the base of an antler. Aspen inhales a sharp breath as I slide my fingers over the length of the branch.

He pulls away slightly, eyes closed. Worried I've done something wrong, I remove my hand. When he opens his eyes, his lips pull into a smirk. "You really are the most desirable being I've ever encountered," he says. "I was willing to let you go time and time again, thinking that's what you wanted. To marry my brother. To forfeit the ritual. To break the treaty."

"And now?" I whisper.

He kisses me lightly on the lips. "I can still let you go, if that's what you want. If you're going to leave, do it now. Leave before my heart realizes what's happened."

The vulnerability has returned to his eyes, more transparent than ever before. There's a sorrow in his voice that shatters me. I remember what Aspen's mother had said, that her mercy had been a weakness. She regretted ending the war to save Aspen's life. She left him when he was likely still a child in fae years. Abandoned him to raise his baby brother on his own in an enormous palace.

Aspen's aloofness, his cold demeanor, his hard edges and sharp words—it all seems so fragile now. I put my hand to Aspen's cheek, run my thumb over his lower lip.

He shudders. "Leave me now or I won't be able to stop."

I inch toward him until our lips almost touch. "I don't want you to stop."

Our kisses return, deeper, heavier. My lips part for more of him, and I feel his tongue brush against mine. His hands move up my back, my arms, my shoulders. His fingers trail the neckline of my dress. I regret my modest clothing now, wishing my dress were thinner. Or better yet, gone altogether.

As if he can read my mind, his fingers move to the shoulder of my dress, then slide it down, revealing my naked flesh. I shiver as the cold air snakes across my skin, but his lips trace a line of fire between my breasts, then over my exposed mound of curving flesh. I shudder as his tongue lingers over the summit. He tugs the other shoulder of the dress, pulling it down until my entire top hangs around my waist. It's still not enough. I want to be closer.

My fingers find the collar of his shirt again. This time, I seek to loosen his cravat, throwing it to the ground once freed. Then I find the buttons of his shirt, his waistcoat, undoing each one with trembling fingers. He helps me with what remains, shrugging off his jacket, the open shirt, his trousers. I look him over, eyes lighting upon every muscle, every inch of golden skin. All that remains of his wound is dark bruising and several small tendrils of black. My eyes go lower, and I can't help but blush when I finally understand the truth of Foxglove's *kingdom* innuendo.

He grins when he catches the look on my face, then returns his efforts to freeing me from my dress. Hands on my hips, he spins me around to untie the sashes that secure the skirt around my waist. It falls to the stone floor in a puddle of chiffon, leaving me bare in the cold autumn air with nothing but Aspen's roving hands to warm me. Only one thing remains.

I step away from him and reach toward my thigh to undo my belted dagger, tossing it to the side where Aspen won't accidentally touch it. When I return to face him, his eyes are drinking me in.

"Beautiful Evie," he says.

"Dangerous Aspen," I whisper.

He kisses me softly this time as he reaches for my thighs. With little effort he lifts me, and my legs go around his waist. The fiery yearning pulses at my core and I feel that sense of losing control growing stronger and stronger. This time I don't fight it. I welcome it. Welcome his kisses, his hands, his fingers. All of him.

In this moment, there is no looming war, no ritual, no pact, no separation of our kind. In this moment, things are simple—he is mine and I am his. I'm teetering on the edge of passion, tasting all it has to offer me, sampling its joys and pains and moments of euphoria. But I want more than an edge, a sample, a taste.

I let myself fall completely.

34

The morning dawns on us, sending streams of light into the mouth of the cave. I open my eyes, lifting my head from Aspen's warm chest. Salty air tickles my senses, blending with Aspen's rosemary and cinnamon. He wakes, and his eyes meet mine. For a moment, the silence between us feels tense, awkward.

A wave of fear runs through me. Does he regret this? Do *I* regret this?

His lips pull into the wicked smile I know so well, and he kisses me. Memories of last night rush through me in a wave of pleasure, and my body responds in turn. His hands rove my skin, slip beneath the discarded dress I'd used as a makeshift blanket to caress my back, my hips, my thighs.

"You kept your promise," he whispers between kisses.

"What promise?"

"That I'd never bed you. Luckily, you never said I couldn't *cave* you."

I smile against his lips. "I'm pretty sure I never used

the words *I promise*. Nevertheless, I should have given you more credit. Turns out, any place will do."

"It will," he says. "However, bed sounds nice. Do you think you'll reconsider?"

I pull away from him and pretend to ponder. "Hmm. I suppose I can do that."

"What do you say we return to the palace, get in bed, do this all over again, and have a proper sleep on a surface that doesn't feel like cold knives?"

I want to say yes, but a more serious thought comes to mind. "What about the ritual?"

His vulnerability returns, but only for a flash. "Have you decided?"

I lay my head back on his chest, bringing my fingers to trail over his golden skin and the hard muscles of his torso. "Tell me about it."

He's silent for a moment. "At its simplest, the Bonding ritual requires only one thing—an exchange of names. I'm sure you are already familiar with the act of giving one's true name."

"Yes," I say, suppressing a shudder. I don't mention that it's something human children are taught never to do. Always be careful of your wording when introducing yourself to a fae, we're told. Never say anything like, *I give you my name.*

"Well, the Bonding ritual is nothing more than that," he says. "One party states that they give their true name to the other, and the other party states the same. That's all it takes for the Bond to take hold."

"What exactly is *the Bond*?" The way he explains it sounds so simple. If it truly is that way, why is it so taboo to talk about?

"It's just the name given for two people who've exchanged names."

"Do all mates perform the Bonding ritual?"

"No. Mate relationships are common, but Bonding rituals are rare. The ritual is performed as often by mates as it is by friends, enemies, and allies, but never without great cause. In any case, it's uncommon. It's always a component of sealing the treaty with a Chosen after a Reaping though."

"Is there really nothing more to it? No candles or flowers or oaths?"

"These extravagances can be included in the ritual," Aspen says, "but they aren't a requirement. We could do it right now, if you wanted."

My breath hitches. Am I ready for that? "Can I have a few hours first?"

He lifts my chin with his fingertips, bringing our eyes to meet. "I meant it when I said I wouldn't force you. That's a promise I'm still willing to keep."

I nod. "I just need a little more time to wrap my head around it."

"I can give you time," he says. "And I can give you another promise. I will never use the Bond to hurt you. I'll never use your true name against you."

His words send a wash of relief through me.

A flicker of worry crosses his face. "Can you promise me the same?"

My lips pull into a smile. I must admit, I like this vulnerability he's been showing me. "Yes, Aspen, I promise you the same."

He rolls, shifting me beneath him. "Then how about this." He grins and kisses my neck. "We go to bed."

Another kiss, beneath my collarbone. "We get naked again." Another kiss between my breasts. "We sleep." Another. "Then we perform the ritual *if* you choose to. I'll give you candles, flowers, a sunset view, and all the oaths you could want while we exchange our names." His fingers stroke the inside of my thigh, creeping higher and higher.

Fire blazes at my core, and part of me wishes we could skip the returning to the palace part, but a comfortable bed is not something I can deny. "I can agree to that."

Getting dressed is slow going, with every move thwarted by breathless kisses and roving hands. It's a miracle we don't reenact our entire night here and now. Eventually, we dress and make our way down the tunnel, Aspen's fingers laced in mine. Farther down, we meet his guards. I'm glad they don't react to our giddy mood as they follow us down the tunnel toward the palace.

My legs feel like water as we emerge from the tunnel and begin climbing the stairs, each flight taking us higher in the palace. We're still several floors away from reaching our bedroom when I can no longer pretend I'm not out of breath. My fatigue is a combination of the endless stairs and all the energy spent over the course of our passion. I can't help but wonder how much more fatigued I'll feel an hour or two from now. The thought is oddly thrilling, although it doesn't help me walk any faster.

Aspen must see me lagging, because next thing I know, he lifts behind my knees, sweeping me off my feet and into his arms. I secure my arms around his neck, laying my head on his shoulder. I'm reveling in his seemingly effortless strength when Aspen comes to a sudden halt.

"What happened?" calls a voice nearby. Cobalt is running toward us. "Is she all right?"

Aspen's voice comes out cold. "She's fine."

"Then why—"

"My mate grew tired while climbing the stairs."

"Well, where have you been?"

"With *my mate*." Aspen's tone holds an edge that makes the prince blanch.

Cobalt looks from me to Aspen, and I feel a pinch of sympathy for him.

"If you don't mind, dear brother," Aspen says, "we'll be on our way."

"Where are you going now?" Cobalt asks.

"You sure are full of questions."

Cobalt narrows his eyes. "We're supposed to be preparing for the council meeting."

"We have time."

"The preparations have already begun, since you couldn't be found," Cobalt says, tone darkening. "Besides, there are stacks of correspondences that have been piling on your desk since before you were injured. If you'd like me to attend to them in your stead, I'd be more than happy to, *my king*." He says this last part with a hint of malice in his tone.

Aspen lets out an irritated grumble and sets me on my feet. He rubs his brow, then faces me, bringing his hands to my cheeks. "Change of plans."

"It's all right," I say. Disappointment sinks my gut, but seeing Cobalt stripped me of all desire, anyway. "Do what you need to do."

"Give me a few hours," he says. "We'll still have time to do everything we spoke of. *Everything*."

At first, I think his emphasis is meant for the ritual. However, the mischief in his eyes says something else. I grin. "I'll be waiting."

He lights a kiss on my lips, a silent promise, then joins Cobalt.

With a sigh, I make my way back to our room alone.

After the warmth of Aspen's arms, the bedroom feels cold, empty. Still, after a night on a stone floor, the bed looks inviting. I'm not sure how much time we spent sleeping in the cave, but my body tells me it wasn't long. We were...preoccupied...most of the night.

With slow steps, I make my way to the wardrobe, exchanging my gown for a nightdress and placing my dagger on the dressing table. I stare longingly at the empty tub, wondering if I should find Lorelei and ask her to have it filled. No, there will be time for that later. Right now, sleep is calling.

I climb into bed and nestle beneath the covers. My mind spins with the realization that so much has changed in a matter of days. The man who I thought was my enemy is now my lover. The land I once despised will soon be a place I help rule. And the heart I thought would never open to any man, any king, any fae, is warm with contentment. Hungry with desire. Open for new forms of passion to emerge.

With a satisfied smile, I close my eyes and drift into a peaceful sleep. It might be hours that pass, or it might be minutes, but I become subtly aware of a sound in the room, footsteps crossing the floor toward the bed. My heart flutters with anticipation, but I'm too tired to open my eyes. "Aspen?" The word comes out small and breathless.

A hand presses down hard on my mouth.

My eyes fly open, and I fight the hand that grasps me, but when my vision clears, the face overhead comes into focus. The fight leaves me. My heart leaps into my throat.

It's Amelie.

35

I struggle to say Amelie's name, but she keeps her hand clamped over my mouth. With her other hand, she brings a finger to her lips. I nod, and she releases me. I spring from the bed and wrap my arms around my sister's neck, fighting the sobs that tear through me. "Amelie! For the love of iron, you're alive."

She hushes me. "Keep your voice down."

I pull away from her. Her expression is panicked, something I've never seen on her normally serene, beautiful face. "What happened to you?"

She takes my hands in hers, an urgency in her tone. "We need to go."

"Go where? Why?"

"You're in danger. We need to leave now."

"What kind of danger?"

Her voice is a furious whisper. "I can't explain now, but you must come with me. Get dressed at once."

I hurry to obey, my fear propelling my legs to the wardrobe. The thick fur cloak Amelie wears makes me think I should be dressing warm. Instead of one of the fae dresses, I unbury my old trousers and blouse from the back of the wardrobe and pull the pants over my legs. I don't bother looking for my corset, and button the blouse over my bare chest. Next, I fetch a cloak and shove my feet into a pair of beaded slippers. Then I reach for my dagger.

"We don't have time." Amelie pulls my other arm. "Come on. Hurry."

"I need my dagger," I say as I shake from her grip. My fingers close over the sheath before she can pull at me again. I tuck it into the waist of my trousers as Amelie shoves me toward one of the crystalline walls. "Ami, what—"

Just then, she presses her hand to the wall, and a previously unseen door opens outward into darkness. Amelie pushes me through it, then closes the door behind us. I feel Amelie's hand on my arm as she tugs me forward. "Hurry," she whispers.

"Where are we going?"

"You aren't safe."

"But where are you taking us?"

Amelie doesn't answer, just leads me down endless blackness with nothing but stairs beneath my feet. It's a struggle not to trip on my slippers as she drags me down, down, farther down.

I'm reeling from the suddenness of it all. The strangeness. All I can think is that Aspen was right. There really has been a threat all along. And somehow, Amelie is saving me from it. But what about the king?

I continue to follow her, fighting the barrage of questions that rise inside me. Every word I say gets hushed by

Amelie as she insists we must hurry. Danger. I'm not safe.

Finally, the stairs turn to the flat surface of a black tunnel floor, and a subtle light glows up ahead. It's a pinkish light, and with it comes the smell of salt, a rumbling echo of sound. We draw nearer to the light, and the black cave walls melt into coral. Coral all around, knitted tightly together to form walls. A spray of water seeps through now and then, and I swear the roar of waves is coming from overhead.

A chill crawls up my spine as Amelie darts into the coral cave. "Ami, where's Aspen?"

She turns around, eyes wide with terror. "Come on, Evie. Hurry."

Now that she's in the light, I can see my sister fully. Strands of kelp tangle in her copper hair, and a thin dress of seafoam silk covers her body. I look at what I'd first mistaken for a heavy fur cloak, realizing it's something else entirely. The gray-brown mass of fur isn't a cloak but a skin. A sealskin. The head is pulled back like a hood and the flippers are tied together like a clasp.

"What's going on, Amelie?"

"You aren't safe."

My shoulders tremble as I look at her, look at the panic in her eyes, the pain on her face. "You keep saying that, but I need more. What am I in danger from? Where is Aspen?"

Her face crumples. "I can't tell you."

I take a few steps closer. "I'm your sister. You can tell me anything. Whatever is happening, I'll listen. If you've gotten into any kind of trouble—"

"Just come with me."

I look from her face to the head of the sealskin. "You took the skin from the selkie woman."

Her eyes glaze with tears. "Nothing was supposed to turn out this way. I never meant for her to die. I left her my dress. She was supposed to wear it."

I take a step away from her. "Why?"

"Evie, we don't have time. Come."

I shake my head, taking another step back.

Her chest heaves with a sob. "Don't make me do this."

"Do what?"

She lets out a wail of sorrow, then takes something from her side—a pink branch of coral set above a hilt of driftwood. That's all I see before she lunges at me, swinging her blade while tears pour down her cheeks.

I dodge the coral blade, retreat from her, backing into the black cave until I slip on a pool of water. My feet fly out from under me and I sprawl on my back. "Ami, stop!"

My shout doesn't deter her. She darts at me with her blade.

I roll to my side, letting my sister crash to the floor next to me. With one hand, I push myself to my feet. With the other, I retrieve my dagger.

Amelie stumbles to stand, then faces me. We circle each other, weapons between us. Neither of us know much about hand-to-hand combat, my sister less than anyone. Her distress shows on her face, wet with tears and contorted with endless sobbing.

"You don't have to do this," I say.

"I do."

"Why? What happened?" But the answer is clear. "You've been glamoured."

"I made a bargain."

"With who?"

Her lips remain pressed tight.

Still, it isn't hard to guess. "Melusine. But why? What could she possibly offer you?"

"Just come with me," she begs. "Come with me willingly and I won't have to hurt you."

I take in her trembling limbs, her agonized expression. "I'm more worried about hurting you."

"It will hurt me more if you don't come with me. It's the only way I can save you."

I furrow my brow. "What did you bargain away?"

"My ability to lie. And my name."

My eyes go wide. "What did you get in return?"

"Love." With that, she runs at me with her coral blade.

I hardly have time to think. I spin to the side, feeling something sharp graze my ribs. She surges forward again, swinging her blade wildly. My dagger remains in hand, but I can't bring myself to use it against her. Instead, I dart and dodge, crying out when the coral meets its mark again and again. Her attack is relentless, but her skill is weak. The best she can do is cut my flesh. She has no idea how to disarm me, much less land a killing blow. But even without skill, she could get lucky. If I don't defend myself, it's only a matter of time before my strength fades, before my ability to dodge becomes compromised.

I have to fight her.

I block the next blow with my dagger, knocking her hand to the side. She comes at me again. Again. I stumble back, dodge left, swipe at her arm. She shouts as my blade makes a cut, but she isn't deterred. Perhaps it's the glamour fueling her, but she's tireless, unconcerned with every cut I land on her. I, on the other hand, feel my arms growing weaker, my side a searing ache where her blade had grazed.

This must end.

Amelie rushes at me again. I dodge, sending her reeling forward. Before she can recover her momentum, I step behind her. Raising my elbow, I meet the back of her head with a sharp jab.

Her body goes limp and she slides to the floor. I cry out as I help catch her fall, wincing as I strain the side of my body that was cut. Without bothering to check my own injuries, I hover over Amelie, testing her pulse, her breathing.

She's alive.

I let out a sigh and close my eyes, pondering the best way to bring her back to the palace. There's no way I can carry her up all those steps. Panic rises in my chest.

"Amelie."

I turn my head and find Cobalt emerging from the black cave, eyes locked on my sister. "Thank the Great Mother you're here," I say, tears pouring down my cheeks. "Help me carry her. Please."

His eyes slide to mine. "I'm so sorry Evelyn."

I'm taken aback, not sure what he's apologizing for. Does he not realize Amelie is alive?

Then he leaps forward and grabs me.

36

I wake gasping for breath, coughing water onto a small, sodden cot. My throat feels raw, and all I can taste is salt. I remember Cobalt charging me, the clasp of his hands around me. Then all I saw was water, felt it pouring into my throat and lungs. I cough again and drag my aching body to sit. All around me are coral bars, sharp and pink, woven together at the top to create a cage.

My hands fly to my waist, my thigh, searching for my dagger and finding it nowhere.

"I'm sorry I had to do this, Evelyn," Cobalt says from the other side of the bars. I know it's him even though he hardly looks like the Cobalt I've known. His skin is covered in shimmering blue scales, making his body look lithe and sinuous. A crown of red coral sits over his brow while delicate webs stretch between each finger and toe. Gone are his boyish good looks, replaced with the terrifying beauty of the sea.

This must be his nix form.

The realization startles me. When the fae talked about shifting their physical forms from seelie to unseelie, I thought it could be nothing more than a mental shift, adapting the behavior of lesser creatures. The greatest physical change I imagined was subtle, like a chameleon altering its color. At most, I thought perhaps the fae underwent animalistic metamorphoses over time, like a caterpillar turning into a butterfly. But this...this is something else. He actually *changed*. Where the bloody iron is my logic for that?

I press my lips tight and fix Cobalt with a glare. Behind him and all around my cage is a cave of coral, its walls tightly knitted. I hear rolling waves rumble overhead, feel the salt spray through minuscule fissures within the walls.

With a jolt, I recall Amelie, lying unconscious after I knocked her out. "Where's my sister?"

I see motion at the far end of the cave, stirring in the darkness. Amelie stands, looking at me through tearstained eyes, the head of the sealskin resting over her scalp. She pulls the rest of the skin tight around her body, but not before I recognize the dress she's wearing. It's the one I slipped out of this morning.

Cobalt turns to her. "Go," he says, voice surprisingly gentle. "Wait for me. We must prepare for the council meeting."

She meets my eyes, lower lip quivering, then stalks away and out of sight.

I burn Cobalt with my scowl. It wasn't Melusine that Amelie had made the bargain with, but Cobalt. "What have you done to her?"

"She won't always feel this way," he says. "She's upset

that you forced her hand. Hurting you was the last thing she wanted to do."

"Because you made her do it. Didn't you? You glamoured her, ordered her to take me from the palace. To kill me if I refused."

He gives me a sad smile. "Sometimes we have to make difficult choices to do the right thing. Before now, she was happy with me. She will be happy again."

"I don't understand why you're doing this. Why capture me after everything that happened? You saved me from the kelpie, you, you..." I don't want to say what I'm thinking. *You were kind to me. You were caring. You...kissed me.*

"I thought you would trust me if I saved you from the kelpie, thought you'd ally with me if you understood the dangers of the unseelie."

My eyes go wide with realization. "You arranged the kelpie attack."

He nods, eyes full of regret.

"You told me not to do the ritual with Aspen."

He takes a few steps closer to the bars of the cage. "And you refused to promise me you wouldn't. Refused my help. Refused to heed my warnings about my brother."

"Your warnings were lies."

"No, my brother is dangerous," Cobalt says. "I tried to tell you, but you didn't believe me. You *still* don't believe me."

"No, I don't."

His brow furrows. "Why? I offered you my protection, my affection. You rejected me time and time again. Yet, I see you had no issue accepting my brother."

I deepen my glare. "Is that why you took my sister?"

His expression softens. "Your sister was much more eager to listen. All she wanted was love and I gave it to her. When she realized we could be together if only you'd marry Aspen instead, she was willing to do what was required. She came to me willingly, left the palace on her own accord, all without even a glamour. It wasn't until today that she realized things weren't going quite as she'd expected, and I was forced to use the power of her name."

"You did this before, didn't you?" I ask. Everything makes so much sense now. "You bargained with the Holstrom girls and glamoured them to try and assassinate the king. What did you take from them?"

"The same thing Amelie gave me in return for my love," he admits. "The ability to lie. All the Holstrom girls wanted was protection from the king. Unlike you, they heeded my warnings. I offered my protection in exchange for their lies. They agreed, as long as I promised to put my lies to good use against the king. Then I promised I'd have Aspen dethroned if they gave me their names. Again, they agreed. I knew sending them to assassinate Aspen would serve well whether it failed or succeeded. If they managed to kill him, he'd no longer be a problem. If he killed them, he'd show his instability as a ruler and bring the council one step closer to forcing him to step down"

"If the Holstrom girls already gave you the ability to lie, why take it from Amelie too?"

"The power of the bargain wears off after a while if the bargainer dies. I needed that power, either from you or Amelie. Like I said, Amelie was more than willing."

"Is that why you're keeping Amelie alive, to keep your

ability to lie? Is that why you didn't send her on some foolish errand to kill Aspen this time?"

He opens his mouth, flustered. "There's more between Amelie and me than there ever was with the other girls. I'm keeping her alive because she's my mate and soon-to-be wife. We are Bonded."

A chill runs through me, and nausea churns my gut. They performed the ritual.

Cobalt continues. "I can't let you and Aspen Bond. That's why I sent Amelie for you this morning after I realized you and my brother had seemingly grown close. I can't have you and Aspen bringing the treaty any closer to being fulfilled."

"Why? Is it war you want?"

"No, not war. I want Aspen off the throne."

I consider his words. "If Aspen and I don't perform the ritual by midnight, we'll break the treaty."

He nods. "He'll do worse than break the treaty. I've made sure of it."

"What have you done?"

"It's not what I've done, but what Aspen is about to do. Now that he thinks you changed your mind about him and sided with our mother instead, he'll show his true nature."

"He couldn't possibly think I'd do such a thing," I say.

"He thinks you're on your way home right now to fulfill your end of the bargain with Melusine. You left him a letter, after all, saying exactly that."

"He'll see through it. He'll never believe the letter was mine."

"My brother?" Cobalt lets out a cold laugh. "The most paranoid king that ever lived? The boy who was abandoned by his own mother after she came to regret saving his life? Of course he'll believe it. He's always looking for proof that others are out to get him. That no one could ever love him."

A lump rises in my throat, but I keep my breathing steady. "He's smarter than you think. He knew something happened to Amelie. Knew the body on the beach wasn't hers."

"He may have known that," he says, "but only because the proof wasn't convincing enough."

I'm about to argue that a letter isn't strong enough proof, when a chilling realization strikes me. Cobalt is confident. Prepared. There's more to this than I know. "What other proof did you give him?"

"I put a glamour over Amelie to make her look more like you." His words are nonchalant, free of malice, as if we were talking about nothing more than the weather. "After she brought you from the palace, I sent her to steal one of your dresses. Then she snuck into the stables and stole a puca. I made sure Aspen's most trusted few saw it happen. Foxglove. Lorelei. Several of his guards. It took him a few accounts before he believed it, but it was clear when he finally did."

"No."

"He was crushed. Heartbroken. So enraged, he shifted into his stag form and tore from the palace grounds."

I blink to fight the tears, clenching my jaw. "Where is he now?"

"He's probably looking for you. Once he realizes you're nowhere to be found, the rage will consume him. He'll attack your village and draw first blood. Perhaps much of it. He'll make the slaughter at the Holstrom farm look like a picnic." He shakes his head with disgust, as if he has no hand in any of it.

"How can you say it isn't war you want, when that's exactly what will happen after this?"

He shakes his head. "We won't go to war. The treaty will not be broken, because I will be there to save it. Aspen will perform this final act of recklessness, revealing the unstable maniac he is. It will give the council the fuel they need to be rid of him once and for all and put me in his place. Aspen has been keeping Faer-wyvae from the peace it deserves, and I am but one of many who feels that way."

It all makes sense now. Of course Cobalt wants to be king. All the times he talked about Aspen's faults, how he has no shortage of allies that would stand against the king...he's been planning this all along. "What about the unseelie? They couldn't possibly support you. You're seelie, aren't you?"

"I have my mother to sway them. The unseelie trust her word."

"Your mother supports all this?"

A corner of his mouth quirks. "She knows some of my plans, although she thinks I'm under her thumb. She'd always promised to support my claim to the throne if I could get Aspen out of the way. Little does she know, I won't be furthering the unseelie cause like she expects."

"No, you'll further the seelie cause," I say. "Fight for a radical seelie council. Eradicate the unseelie."

"Can you blame me? The unseelie are uncivilized. You know about my mother, how she abandoned her children. That's not rare for unseelie. They're hardly better than animals, eating their young, leaving the lame to die. And what about creatures like the kelpies and vampires and goblins? Do they deserve to terrorize their victims?"

His words make my stomach sink, but I remember what Aspen told me. About fair choice and the balance necessary to preserve it. Was he right? Or would the world be better if the unseelie were gone?

"I'm ready to make you a bargain," Cobalt says. "Go home. Return to your people. Take the ones you love most and get them out of the village tonight. I'll get you there at once, before Aspen can unleash his wrath. Hide from my brother until his dark deeds are done. I'll have guards waiting. They'll stop him before he can draw too much blood. That will be enough to lose Aspen his throne without starting a war. Then I will be made king and the treaty will remain intact. Don't you see? Amelie and I are mates. We're Bonded. She and I will marry in your and Aspen's stead, securing the treaty."

"And then what? You'll let Aspen go on his jolly way?" I let out a bark of laughter. "I doubt that. Your first order as king will be to have him executed."

"Don't let your emotions cloud your good sense, Evelyn," he says. "Aspen's removal is necessary, and yes, he will need to be disposed of entirely. But don't you understand? Your relationship with him is tenuous, even if my brother remained in power. He might marry you, and he might even make you his queen, but what about when he grows tired of you? What about when your fragile human body slowly begins to age? What then?"

I think of Doris Mason and her cousin, anxiety rising in my chest.

Cobalt shakes his head. "This is the only logical solution. Take my bargain and save your people. The seelie way will keep the Fair Isle safe. Reject my bargain and I will leave you here to die.

My heart leaps into my throat. "You're going to kill me?"

"I can't directly hurt you, Evelyn. I promised as much on our picnic. I may be able to lie, but that doesn't mean I'm immune to vows and promises. Instead, I'll leave you here. It won't be long before the tide comes in."

Panic seizes me, the taste of salt still fresh on my tongue, my lungs still raw from being filled with seawater.

Cobalt frowns. "Don't make me do this, Evelyn. It will break your sister's heart. Think of her. Think of everything she sacrificed to save you."

My heart sinks, and I do think of her. Amelie, with her fickle heart and reckless ways. Did she know what she was getting herself into when she made her bargain with Cobalt? I know he deceived her, made her believe everything was going to work out perfectly for all of us, but did she stop to think what her actions could do to me? No. When she made the bargain, she didn't do it for me. She did it for herself. For Cobalt. *For love.*

"Make the logical choice, Evelyn."

The logical choice. I could accept Cobalt's bargain and save my people from war, but in doing so, Aspen loses his throne and his life. I lose the heart of the lover I was just beginning to know and care for. And Faerwyvae will take one step closer to a radical seelie reign. The only other choice is my own death. With that, I alleviate nothing. All else will likely still come to pass, but the blood

Aspen spills in my village could belong to someone I care about.

"Live or die?" Cobalt says. "Those are your only choices."

I take a deep breath and close my eyes, running through the options in my mind, piecing logic with logic, trying to formulate an answer that doesn't make me feel like my heart is being ripped in two. The options twist and blur, fueling my anxiety until it rages inside me. My head is pounding, lungs heaving. There's no way out of this. No way out.

Then something tugs at me. Not at my mind, but at something else. Something calm and quiet. My heart? I breathe away my thoughts, let my swirling deliberations cool to a simmer as I focus on the calm inside me. A surgeon's calm, the kind I felt when treating Aspen's injury. It's a strange certainty that no logic can explain. I open myself to it, let it wrap around me like a blanket.

"Do the right thing, Evelyn."

"Get out of my sight," I say through my teeth.

His expression darkens. "You're making a mistake."

I burn him with my glare. "Get. Out."

37

The tide comes in fast, as does my panic. I pull my cloak around my arm and throw my weight against the bars of the cage. The coral shards go straight through the fabric, spearing my skin. I wince, then double the fabric, triple it. Throw myself at the bars again. Again. They don't budge.

I may have refused Cobalt's bargain, but that doesn't mean I've accepted the fate he left me with.

If only I had my dagger. If only I had *anything* to get me out of here.

I aim a kick at the bars, but my beaded slippers are no match for their strength, especially with the water rising higher and higher, slowing my momentum. Before long it's around my waist.

I grit my teeth as another surge of water floods in. The echo of waves overhead is louder than before. Terror seizes me, sending memories to the surface, reminding me what it felt like to nearly drown, twice now. I remember the kelpie dragging me under the water with me powerless and stuck on his back. My fingers clench into fists. I'm even more furious now that I know Cobalt had been to blame. He likely distracted me on purpose while I ate the honey pyrus, laughed as I tumbled away from our picnic to wander alone. The forest had been silent, empty until the kelpie found me. A kelpie—*a water fae*—the only creature in the woods. There's no mistaking every moment had been Cobalt's design.

Something sparks in my mind. An idea. A dangerous idea.

The kelpie.

I remember what Amelie had said about them. They seek out lost travelers and take them to their deaths. My idea is so foolish, so reckless, it sends my pulse racing.

"Help!" I shout at the top of my searing lungs. "Help! I'm lost!"

All that answers is more water, more waves. The flood reaches my chest now.

"Help! I'm lost and I can't find my way. Please come help me. Anyone." I repeat my plea over and over, trying to ignore the water that laps into my mouth as the tide rises to my neck. I have to brace myself on the bars of the cage to maintain my footing, and its sharp edges cut into my palms. I shout again. Screaming. Begging. "I'm lost! Help!"

A dark mass enters the cave, slithering beneath the surface of the water. I swallow my shouts, terrified I've called in something worse. As the shape draws near, a horse-like head breaches the water, its mane of black swirling around it. I remember the other kelpie, how its mane seemed to flow in a wind I didn't feel. Now I know it was an invisible current it was flowing in.

"Will you help me?" I ask, coughing water as a wave douses my face.

"Come with me," it says. Its voice sounds the same as the first kelpie—ethereal and chilling.

"First, will you break me out of this cage?"

It watches me with its glowing red eyes. "Break you out?"

The words turn my stomach. I should probably be more literal. "Will you kick the bars of the cage with your hooves, but be careful not to kick me? When the bars break and I am free from the cage, will you carry me somewhere—to someone—specific?"

"Who would you have me take you to?"

"Take me to King Aspen directly, as fast as you can. Go only routes that are safe for a human to travel. If we must travel by water, keep my head above it at all times. If we travel by land, move as fast as you can."

"I could take you to King Aspen." He says it more like he's considering it than agreeing to it. He studies me, likely poring over my words. Now that I know better, I expect the part of the bargain he doesn't say. He will take me to King Aspen. Then he'll continue on to the nearest body of water to drown me. With his mane wrapped around my hands, I won't be able to stop it.

To hurry his resolve, I add, "After that, you can go anywhere you like."

"I will," he finally says. He turns around, rear facing me. I move to the far end of the cage and shield my face with my arms. The kelpie sends a sharp hoof into the coral bars, then another. After a third kick, the coral splinters and shatters, leaving a large opening near the bottom of the floor. I take a deep breath and swim through it. A shard of coral scrapes against my arm. Another grazes my ankle as I push myself off the floor. Broken bars from the cage float by, drifting in the current. My fingers clasp around one, and I don't let it go, not even as I mount the kelpie.

With my free hand, I grab his mane, and the kelpie swims forward with a speed his heavily muscled body shouldn't be capable of. True to his word, the kelpie keeps my head above water as we navigate the twisting, turning caves. Waves still crash over my face as water funnels inside, but I manage to keep my lungs clear. Finally, the tunnel floors incline slightly, and light shines up ahead. The kelpie gallops toward it. To freedom. To fresh air and open sky.

Freed from the coral caves, I'm faced with a familiar sight. The shore beneath the palace stretches before us, nearly swallowed by the tide. The last blush of sunset peeks over the horizon, sending the beach under a pink-orange glow. With a jolt, the kelpie takes off along the shore, away from the palace toward the jagged rocks. My heart leaps into my throat as it seems like the creature intends to dash us directly into them, but in a single leap, he crests the top of the nearest rock, then leaps to another, then another, more like a goat than a horse-creature.

Once clear of the rocks, another stretch of shore spreads before us. But the kelpie veers away from it and into the water instead. With a splash, he goes under, but the water only reaches my chin. If I thought the kelpie was fast on land, he is a streak of lightning in the open sea. In mere minutes the shore and the palace are nowhere to be seen.

The water is colder the farther we get from the shore, making my teeth chatter. Anxiety fights to overwhelm me, and I wonder if I left too much room in my bargain with the kelpie. Surely, taking us this far out to sea can't be the fastest way to reach Aspen. All I can do is breathe, persist. Trust the fae creature is taking me where I need to go and try not to die in the process.

THE SKY IS DARK BY THE TIME I NEXT SEE LAND. IT'S nothing but a black shape on the horizon, growing larger as the kelpie speeds toward it. Cool night air greets me as we emerge from the sea and into the dark forest beyond the shore. I lost my cloak sometime during the swim, leaving my sodden blouse clinging to my skin, uncomfortably cold and heavy. My breaths grow shallow, coming out in ragged gasps. *Hang on, Evie,* I tell myself. *You just have to find Aspen.*

My head begins to spin, blood leaving my face as my eyes grow heavy. I bite the inside of my cheek to maintain consciousness. *Not now. Not now. Just keep going.*

Painful minutes drag on. Based on our surroundings, we still appear to be in Faerwyvae, although I swear numerous seasons have passed us by. A sprinkle of snow, bathing the night in blinding white. Autumn leaves and a reddish glow. A dense heat I've never felt before. To the left, a blanket of fog covers everything, but I think I can make out a few towering stones of the faewall here and there. Finally, the warm air cools. Flowers grow in clusters, their petals taking to the wind in the kelpie's wake.

"Your king," comes the ethereal voice.

This snaps me to attention. I lean forward, seeking any sign of Aspen. There, coming toward us in the distance is an enormous silhouette. A stag. *Aspen.* Like Cobalt, Aspen's appearance has shifted drastically. However, there's nothing human about the king as his stag hooves tear the earth beneath him. It's a chilling sight.

The distance is closing between him and the kelpie too fast, but my limbs won't move. The kelpie's mane has grown so tight over my hand, I've lost all feeling in the arm. The other hand feels dull and heavy from the cold.

We're close enough now, I can see Aspen's breath puffing in clouds from his stag nostrils.

"I brought you to your king," the kelpie says. I know what will happen next. He'll veer away, back toward the ocean or some nearby lake.

With a grunt, I lift my arm, fingers still wrapped around the branch of coral I stole from the cave. I swing it into the kelpie's mane, severing the black strands until my hand is released. No longer tethered to the creature, the kelpie's speed knocks me backward. I tumble to the ground, rolling. The kelpie speeds off into the night. I turn the opposite direction, seeking the stag. He's growing dangerously closer.

I stumble to my feet, every muscle screaming in protest. "Aspen!"

He continues forward, showing no sign of slowing.

I hold out my hand, palm streaked shades of purple and red where the kelpie's mane strangled my flesh. "Aspen, stop!"

He closes the distance, eyes wild with fury.

"It's me. Evie."

The stag snorts, mouth lathering. He'll be upon me in a matter of seconds, and I'm too weak to move. Tears pour down my cheeks. I'm too late. He doesn't know me. He's become the monster I always thought him to be.

"Aspen, I give you my true name!"

His hooves dig into the earth, and dirt sprays over me as he skids to a halt.

My shoulders are racked with tremors. The stag has stopped mere feet away, teeth bared, muscles quivering. He stomps and paws the earth, head down, antlers pointed toward me.

"Aspen," I whisper. "Did you hear me? I'm here. I came for you."

His stag eyes are locked on mine, so unlike the ones belonging to the fae I kissed this morning. Only his antlers look the same, yet much larger. I've never seen a stag so large or so majestic, so undeniably beautiful. His coat is a russet gold, hooves a glimmering onyx.

With a deep breath, I release the bar of coral, a searing pain shooting through my palm as the jagged shards release from my flesh. Keeping my other hand outstretched toward him, I take one trembling step, then another, each move almost unbearable.

Aspen remains in place watching me warily, but as I move closer, his breathing begins to even, and his lips close over his teeth.

"That's it. I'm here now." Finally, he's close enough to touch. I let my hand fall on the side of his stag face.

"You gave me your name." It's Aspen's voice, but it sounds distant, weak, as if coming from far away.

"Yes."

"You left me."

I shake my head. "No, Aspen. You were deceived by Cobalt."

"Cobalt," he echoes softly.

"He took me and locked me in the coral caves so I couldn't come to you, so we couldn't perform the ritual. He's the one who took Amelie too. It's she everyone saw riding away on the puca. She's under his control."

"You didn't leave?"

"No."

Silence falls between us. Then Aspen says, "It hurt when you left." His words remind me of those of a child. There's no wit, no banter, none of his sharp personality. I wonder if that's part of being in his unseelie form.

"I'm sorry it hurt."

"I don't like feeling like that." His tone carries a hint of anger. "I don't like to feel at all."

"I don't like feeling like that either," I say. "It hurt to be trapped in a cage, unable to tell you the truth. But I had to persevere. I had to come find you, even if it hurt."

"You humans have no choice but to feel. I don't have to."

"You mean, if you remain in this form?"

"Yes. I could stay unseelie. I could forget your face. Forget what it means to hurt or love or rage."

I bring my forehead to the side of his face, nestling into his soft coat. "Is that what you want? To forget me?"

A shudder runs through him. Then another. "No."

I stumble back as the stag pulls away, his massive shape shifting and undulating. Another shudder seizes him, and suddenly the stag is gone, replaced by a familiar figure crouching in the dirt. He wears nothing but trousers and a linen shirt, open at the neck. I kneel next to him, take his face in my hands. "Aspen."

He slowly meets my eyes. "Evie."

I bring his lips to mine, reveling in their softness, the feel of them already so familiar to me.

He pulls away. "You're crying."

I realize he's right. Sobs tear through me while tears stream over my face. "Of course I am. I thought I was going to lose you to the stag forever. I thought you would forget me and destroy my village."

"Why would I destroy your village?"

"Isn't that where you were going? To exact revenge upon me and my people?"

He shakes his head. "I...I don't remember. The rage consumed me."

"But you're free of it now?"

He nods, but his expression darkens. "Cobalt did this."

"Yes, and he's going to try to take your throne. It's been his plan to trick you into breaking the treaty all along. All these attacks, these betrayals, these mysteries. Cobalt has been behind all of them."

"Where is he now?"

"Probably taking your place on the council," I say.

He rises to his feet, helping me up with him. "I have to stop him. We need to get back to the council by midnight and prove we've done the ritual."

"Do you think we can make it?"

"It's possible if we hurry. You'll have to ride me."

"Under other circumstances, that would sound like a highly enticing invitation." I give him a weak smile, but my muscles protest at the thought of mounting another galloping creature.

Aspen must sense my resistance because he puts a hand on my cheek. "Don't worry. I'll be gentle."

"Are we still talking in innuendo?"

"I'm serious."

I let out a sigh. "All right."

"Oh, and Evie?"

"Yes?"

He smiles, thumb brushing my cheekbone. "I know it isn't candles and kisses like I told you it would be, but I give you my true name too."

We bring our lips together. Despite my exhaustion, I bask in the feel of him against me and wrap my arms around his neck. It feels like the energy is humming between us, strong and dangerous. Perhaps it's simply desire, but I can't help wondering if it's the result of being Bonded. Is this what it feels like to exchange names with another? To give another your power while making them vulnerable at the same time? Logic tells me it's impossible. The act of giving one's name is only significant to the fae. Yet, there's this odd pull between us. Like a bridge. A bridge between two cliffs with nothing but jagged shards of rock below.

Before I can explore the strange sensation more, an ethereal voice calls out behind us, "The human is mine."

38

A spen and I pull away, finding the black kelpie before us, head lowered as he stomps his front hoof in challenge. The king leaps in front of me, hiding my body behind his. "She is not yours," he says.

"Twice she has escaped me without a taste," the kelpie says. "First, she was saved by the pretty prince. Second time, she escaped through trickery. We had a bargain."

"I only promised you could go wherever you wanted after you took me to Aspen." My voice comes out with a tremor. "I never said you could take me with you."

"Human trickery. That is why I hate your kind. You come to my home, invade my land, swim in my waters. The stupid ones have the gall to get lost, polluting everything with their stench, their recklessness. The menacing ones come with iron shackles, with traps and blades and tricks."

"She is neither stupid nor menacing," Aspen says, "but she is my mate. She is under my protection. If you try to harm her, you face my wrath."

"Wrath," the kelpie hisses, taking a step closer. "Such a human reaction."

"It will be my reaction nonetheless."

The kelpie's eyes blaze brighter, the red growing deeper. "Why should I care about your wrath? We aren't in Autumn but Spring. You don't rule here."

"I am still a king."

"I am unseelie. I bow to no king."

Aspen squares his shoulders. "The water in you is the water in me. If you won't respect me as king, respect me as one of your kind."

"Water," the kelpie hisses. "You're Autumn through and through."

"Yet water swims in my blood."

The creature cranes his neck to peek at me behind Aspen. "What about her blood?"

"Her blood is not up for discussion. She made you a bargain that you accepted, and she bested you. It is not her fault you agreed to it. Now you will let us go without further argument."

The kelpie stomps its hoof, creating a furrow in the ground beneath him, teeth peeling back. Aspen's posture grows defensive. He leans forward, hands clenched into fists as a snarl escapes his lips.

The kelpie paws the earth again, then freezes. His head swivels on his sinuous neck toward the fog in the distance and the faewall I know is behind it. I follow his line of vision and see figures moving in the mist. When I look back at the kelpie, it's gone.

I remember what Cobalt had said about sending guards to stop Aspen from killing too many humans during his rage. "We need to leave. Now."

Aspen doesn't utter a word as he shudders from head to toe and shifts back into a stag. He lowers himself for me to climb on his back, then we take off. I don't dare look behind me, terrified of what I'll see. I can only hope Aspen is fast enough to outrun Cobalt's guards. To my horror, Aspen doesn't run away from the faewall, but parallel to it. The dense fog remains in my periphery as we speed through the forest.

"How will we get back in time?" I ask him, arms wrapped around his neck as I lean into him. "In fact, how did the kelpie get me here so fast? It took nearly a full day to get from Sableton to Bircharbor by carriage. How will we get there by midnight?"

"We'll get there." His words sound far away again, but his tone is more alert, more aware. "Each section of the wall falls on a different axis. Each axis belongs to a different court. Sableton is near the Spring axis."

"What exactly does an axis mean in this instance? Is that just where a court's lands touch the wall?"

"Perhaps a better word for a human would be *portal*. These portals run along the length of the wall and allow us to travel quickly to and from courts that, without them, wouldn't be anywhere close to the wall. When you first came here, Foxglove had the carriage bypass the axis line to take you to Bircharbor by traditional means in what's considered the long way to Autumn."

"Why?"

"To give you time to adjust," he says. "I didn't want you bombarded with interaxis travel on your first day.

That's what we're doing now. We'll travel along the wall until we reach the Autumn axis."

"That must be what the kelpie did as well," I say, trying not to dwell on the missing logic and just be grateful instead. If this strange method of travel hadn't been available to me, Aspen would have crossed the faewall into my village.

"I don't think I would have hurt your people," he says as if he can read my thoughts. "I was looking for you. That's all I remember."

I stroke his neck but say nothing. There's no use wondering what might have happened if I hadn't stopped him, and there's no use holding any *maybes* against him. Cobalt is to blame for this. I'll save my anger for him.

We fall into silence, and my eyes begin to grow heavy.

"Sleep," Aspen says. "I'll make sure you stay righted on my back."

I close my eyes and let nightmares of blood and waves take me.

"I CAN SEE THE PALACE JUST AHEAD."

I jolt awake, craning my neck to look around Aspen. Soon I can see the palace too. It glows gold in the moonlight, bright against the black sky. You'd never know by looking at it that a dangerous coup is taking place inside. Once we reach the front steps of the palace, Aspen lowers himself to the ground so I can dismount, then shifts into his seelie form. I grimace as I shake out my aching limbs.

Aspen takes my hand and we dart inside. Guards

stand at attention as we enter, expressions concerned. "Is the council in session?" he barks at them.

"Yes, Your Majesty," one says, brow furrowed.

"Should I carry you?" Aspen asks under his breath.

I remember how good it felt to be in his arms, head against his chest. Was that just this morning? Part of me wants to say yes. "No," I say with a sigh. "I want to stand on my own two feet when we confront Cobalt."

"And I want to tear his head off," he grumbles.

I shiver at his tone. It occurs to me I have no idea what to expect of the confrontation. How do fae handle situations like this? I've seen Aspen send his servants to the dungeon and order their execution, but will that be punishment enough for his brother? I can only imagine this ending in blood and teeth.

"Where is the meeting held?" I ask as we move higher in the palace.

"The balcony," he says.

We climb higher and higher until we reach the staircase that leads to the balcony. Before we take a step, we pause. Two figures are seated at the middle of the staircase, huddled close together in whispered conversation.

"Your Majesty!" Foxglove exclaims when he sees us. He and Lorelei all but run down the stairs. Their expressions are horrified as they look from Aspen's furious face to my bruised hands and torn clothing.

"Pardon me saying this, Your Majesty," Lorelei says, "but what in all the rotting oak and ivy is going on?"

Aspen ignores her question. "Is Cobalt sitting with the council right now?"

"Yes," Foxglove says. "He seemed most certain you wouldn't be returning for the meeting."

"And you!" Lorelei narrows her eyes at me. "You ran away."

I shake my head. "It's a long story."

"One we don't have time for right now," Aspen growls, pushing past them and ascending the steps two at a time. I follow behind at a much slower pace, with Foxglove and Lorelei at my side.

"You need a bath," Lorelei hisses in my ear. I can tell she's angry with me. I understand her feelings, considering she was one of the few who saw me—Amelie— riding away on the puca.

"I need more than a bath," I say.

I hear chattering voices up ahead, followed by Aspen's roar as he crests the stairs to the balcony. Picking up my pace, I enter behind him.

Aspen's chest heaves as he stares at the far end of the balcony where Cobalt sits in Aspen's throne, the throne at his right remaining empty. In a semicircle around him sit ten other fae in elegant chairs, including Melusine. I recognize none of them as the ambassadors I saw at the mate ceremony, which tells me these are the court rulers. Their appearances are even more unique and varied than their ambassadors had been, some wearing gowns, others in suits. A few wear nothing, their forms more animal than human. The council fae turn, and Melusine's eyes widen when she sees us. A wolf with snowy white fur and red eyes snarls, while a female fae with pale blue skin and flowing hair hisses, the sound like the wind through the trees. Cobalt, however, keeps his expression neutral.

"Brother, how good of you to return," Cobalt says. "You're late."

Aspen's eyes blaze with fury. "And you are on my throne."

Cobalt gives him an apologetic smile. "This isn't your throne anymore. The council has accepted me as king in your stead. You have proven unfit to rule time and time again. Now you have forfeited your crown."

"For what reason?"

"How much time do you have?" Cobalt says with a laugh. "First of all, how about you explain where you've been?"

"I don't owe you an explanation."

"But you owe them one." Cobalt extends his hand toward the council. A large, stout fae with curling horns, brown skin, and thick, yellow hooves nods in agreement. "You were supposed to be here, doing your duty. Instead, you were...where, exactly?"

"Yes, King Aspen," Melusine says, her tone full of musical sweetness. "I too want an explanation for why you thought it appropriate to neglect your duties."

Aspen's jaw shifts back and forth, but he says nothing. What could he possibly say to satisfy them, when all he can do is tell the truth? If there was ever a time for clever deception, it would be now. "I was misled," he finally says. "My actions were the result of—"

"Your actions were the result of instability and a volatile temper," Cobalt says. "Several witnesses saw you react to the news that your human mate had fled the palace to return to her people. Instead of handling the situation with the grace of a king, you shifted into a stag to destroy her village in retribution."

An androgynous-looking fae wearing a slim black suit

lets out a low chuckle. "Tasty." The voice is smooth and feminine. Her skin is pale, hair slick, blonde, and cropped at the base of her neck. When she smiles, I see elongated canines. I've never seen her kind of fae before, but I've heard of them. *Vampire.*

"I didn't destroy her village, nor did I make it past the wall," Aspen says.

Cobalt shrugs. "But that's where you were headed. My guards reported that they saw you near the wall. If it weren't for Miss Fairfield, you'd have drawn human blood."

I can feel Aspen's rage as if it were my own. It burns every part of me, so hot I can keep it inside no longer. "He went there because of you. *You* captured me. *You* sent my sister—disguised as me—to run away and make Aspen think I left. *You* kept me in a cage and left me to drown."

The prince rolls his eyes. "The human has clearly had second thoughts about running away. Don't listen to her lies."

"You're the one who's lying." The council erupts with laughter at my words. "It's true. He can lie. He's been able to lie since the Holstrom girls arrived, took the ability from them in exchange for feigned protection. He orchestrated their attack on Aspen." More laughter at this, making my cheeks burn crimson.

"We all know humans weave fantastical tales," Cobalt says. "But let's not get off topic. Aspen left the palace at a critical time. He failed his duties as a royal on the Council of Eleven Courts. Not only that, but he failed to secure the pact by neglecting to perform the Bonding ritual with his Chosen."

"We performed it," Aspen says. "You know we did. Each of you can sense it."

Cobalt seems unconcerned. "It's past midnight, Brother."

"It was well before midnight when we performed it."

"Then you should have been here to prove it. Regardless, let us go back. Before your reckless actions tonight, you managed to lose one of the Chosen. Amelie disappeared from Bircharbor, and witnesses say she fled from you."

"You have her!" I shout.

He continues as if I said nothing. "Before that, you executed the previous Chosen without trial. Only your word is testimony to their supposed crimes. Before that, you have constantly wavered your political stance, for no other reason than to make trouble."

Some of the other fae are nodding, eyes glistening with malice as they stare at Aspen with open hostility. A fae with bright orange skin covered in delicate scales flicks his forked tongue at him, then snaps his teeth.

"You don't care about your duties as king," Cobalt says. "You are erratic, unreliable, and a danger to human and fae alike."

Aspen begins to shudder, hands clenched into fists. "Get off my throne."

"I, on the other hand, have done everything you could not. I am firm in my political standing. I am constant in my motivations. I went so far as to secure the second step in the treaty before you even made Evelyn your mate."

Melusine shoots Cobalt a surprised look.

"Come greet the council, Amelie." Cobalt waves, and a figure emerges from the staircase behind us.

Amelie is outfitted in a resplendent gown of copper and red, bringing out the fire in her hair. She still wears the sealskin like a cloak over her shoulders, yet gone are the tears I last saw on her face. Her expression is stoic, posture regal and serene as she brushes past us and makes her way to the other side of the balcony. "Greetings," she says, taking a seat in the empty throne at Cobalt's side.

My body goes cold. I'd forgotten to expect her here. The sight of her done up like a queen, all smiles and sweet grace, sends bile rising to my throat. How much of her demeanor is controlled by Cobalt's glamour over her? I refuse to believe she would stand by any of this, refuse to believe she could look at me, covered in blood and bruises and hold an unwavering smile. How much has she given away for love?

"You see," says Cobalt, "Amelie ran away from my brother, terrified of his temper, but I found her. Protected her. Kept her from my brother's rage. I made her my mate weeks ago and performed the Bonding ritual."

"Cobalt," Melusine sings, a dangerous lilt to her melody. "You told me she gave you her name, but I wasn't aware that you gave her yours in return."

Cobalt holds his mother's eyes without a hint of regret. "Ah, well, now you know."

She leans toward her son, teeth bared. "But you saved the treaty."

He smiles at her. "And you helped make me king."

A storm darkens her blue eyes as her tail swishes angrily on the floor, but Cobalt pays her no heed.

"You are no king," Aspen says. His gaze falls on each

council fae in turn, burning them with his glare. "He is not my heir. You cannot give him my throne."

"They can if the king is indisposed without naming an heir," Cobalt argues. "I, as your brother, can take your place."

"You have no Autumn blood."

"Yet, this is my home. I have lived here my entire life. And when it mattered most, I stepped in where you could not."

Aspen shudders head to toe, and I think I know what happens next. "You have five seconds to get out of my seat before I rip you to shreds."

"Take one step, and you'll be committing treason," Cobalt says. "The council has already agreed. I am King of Autumn."

With a roar, Aspen's body is torn apart in a mass of fur and hooves. A flash of shock crosses Cobalt's face as the enormous stag charges him. The council fae leap from their seats, backing out of the fray. Some of the fae watch with terror, while others—like the wolf and vampire— look delighted at the spectacle. Cobalt tosses himself to the ground, and Aspen's hooves crush the arm of his throne to splinters.

Cobalt rises to his feet just as Aspen charges again. The force knocks Cobalt backward and sends him skid- ding into the rail at the edge of the balcony. Cobalt shud- ders, his princely demeanor gone. In the blink of an eye, his unseelie form takes over. His fingers come to dangerous points, webs between them like serrated knives. He stands his ground as Aspen charges again, lips peeled back to reveal his fangs.

Aspen doesn't falter, just tears across the floor at great speed.

The two collide in a tangle of scales and teeth and antlers.

"Guards!" Cobalt's shout echoes across the balcony. I whirl, wondering where the guards are, but the fae in bronze armor are nowhere to be seen. Come to think of it, I haven't seen any other guards since we arrived, aside from the two at the front of the palace. When I look back at the two royals, my breath catches in my throat.

Over the rail climb slithering bodies, dripping seawater. Most resemble Cobalt with slim physiques, webbed fingers, and gills. They wear armor of pink coral, their weapons similar to the one Amelie attacked me with. Several of them leap upon Aspen, then several more.

Footsteps sound on the floor behind me, and I feel a rush of hope. Aspen's guards—dozens of them—surge forward from the stairwell, followed by Foxglove and Lorelei. "Found them in the dungeon," Foxglove mutters to me when he reaches my side.

Aspen's guards charge the sea fae, but more of Cobalt's guards leap over the rail to face them, baring teeth, shattering armor with their coral swords and knives.

Aspen still struggles against his assailants, trying to throw them off, but all it does is allow Cobalt to dart away from his brother's reach. The sea fae pull at Aspen's ears, wrench his antlers, slick the ground beneath his hooves until he's scrambling to maintain purchase.

Finally, Aspen stops struggling. The sea fae tug him down, down, until he's sprawled on the floor.

I'm frozen in horror as I watch Aspen shift back into

his seelie form, chest heaving as Cobalt's guards pull his arms behind his back. He keeps his eyes trained on his brother, fury emblazoned on his features.

"Cobalt," Aspen says through his teeth, "I challenge your claim to the throne."

39

Silence falls over the balcony.

Cobalt's lips pull into a devious grin. "Are you sure that's wise, brother?"

"The throne doesn't belong to you," Aspen growls.

"That's your opinion, and if you're offering me a challenge, that choice won't be yours to make."

"The challenge has been made," Aspen says. "Do you accept?"

Cobalt shudders and shifts back to his seelie form. "I do."

I hear a sharp intake of breath from Foxglove. "This isn't good," he mutters.

"What's going on?"

He wrings his hands. "If the council has already agreed to accept Cobalt as king, a challenge for the throne was King Aspen's last hope. But, oh, I can already see this going badly."

The sea fae release Aspen and allow him to rise to his

feet, yet they maintain a tight circle around him. The council erupts in chatter.

"What does a challenge for the throne entail?" I whisper to Foxglove.

"They will have three options," he explains. "Either a battle of strength, a presentation of factual debate, or a decision of fate."

I look from Aspen to Cobalt, a spark of hope igniting within me. "Aspen will win a battle of strength."

He nods, but his expression is grave. "There's no doubt about that. But as the challenged, it's Cobalt's right to select which option they take. He'll know better than to select a battle of strength, even if he were to name a champion to fight in his stead."

"He can do that?"

"Yes. Either royal can name another to fight for them. Their champion can secure the win in their patron's name."

Cobalt walks to the other side of the balcony, then leans against the rail. He watches Aspen, a pleased smile on his lips.

My blood goes cold. "Why does he look so confident?"

"Because he's going to choose the option he knows he can win," whispers Foxglove. "A presentation of factual debate. He clearly believes his motives were just, and he already received the support of the council once. There's no doubt he can do it again."

"The council decides the winner of the debate?"

He nods.

"Then Aspen will have to stand up for himself. He'll tell them the truth." My words come out weak, and I can feel their folly before they leave my mouth. It was hard enough for Aspen to get past his pride and tell me the truth. How will he fare when facing a council that is already set against him, not to mention a brother who can lie? I feel the blood drain from my face. "Oh no. This isn't good."

"You understand now."

Aspen's eyes continue to burn into his brother as Cobalt grins back at him. "We must select the mediator," Aspen says.

"Queen Melusine," Cobalt proposes.

Aspen lets out a cold laugh. "I think not, brother. I agree the mediator should be unseelie, since we are both seelie, but our mother is not a neutral party."

Cobalt's expression falters for only a moment. "Queen Nyxia."

The vampire in the black suit steps forward with a feigned gasp as she brings her slim white fingers to her lips. "Me? I'd be honored. I'll need ink and paper, of course."

Aspen's eyes lock on one of his guards. "Go." The guard leaves, and the council fae return to their seats.

I can't help but shudder as I watch the vampire stroll to the middle of the balcony, stopping in front of the two thrones. Leaning toward Foxglove, I ask, "Should I be worried?"

He ponders before answering. "I think the Queen of the Lunar Court will serve well as a neutral party. She's never had love for either of the siblings."

"Yet she must have agreed to Cobalt taking Aspen's throne."

Foxglove adjusts his spectacles, grimacing. "That she did."

The guard returns moments later with ink, quill, and two pieces of parchment. He marches between the seats of the council and hands his materials to Nyxia. The vampire then makes her way to Cobalt's side of the balcony, where he and Amelie stand. My sister dabs at a cut above Cobalt's brow, a worried frown tugging her lips.

"She has some nerve," Lorelei says with a glower, coming up next to Foxglove and me. Hurt and rage mingle in her eyes as she watches my sister.

"Come," I say, swallowing my own hurt, "let's go to Aspen." We make our way to his side of the balcony, and I try to ignore the stares of the council watching every step I take. The guards sneer and hiss as I draw near but don't stop me as I approach Aspen. His expression softens when he meets my eyes. I want to reach for his hand, but the sharp looks the sea fae give me make me hesitate.

The council erupts in whispers, and I turn to see Cobalt taking one of the papers from Nyxia, then writing something with ink and quill. Once finished, she waves the parchment in the air to dry the ink and then folds it into a neat square. Then she turns on her heel and comes our way.

"The battle has been set in ink," Nyxia whispers as she approaches, holding Cobalt's folded sheet of parchment. She then hands Aspen a blank sheet of paper. "Write the name of your champion, if you are to use one, then sign your name."

"Think hard, brother," Cobalt calls from the other side of the balcony, tone mocking. "Are you strong enough to fight your own battles? Or will you need a champion?"

Aspen grumbles and turns toward the balcony rail.

He spreads the parchment over the top of the rail, then extends his hand toward Nyxia for the ink and quill. I look from Aspen to Cobalt and back again. Cobalt looks so certain, so confident. There isn't a doubt in his mind that he's going to win. He knows Aspen would never name a champion. He knows he'll easily win over the council with a presentation of factual debate.

Ignoring the hisses of the sea fae guards, I race to Aspen's side before he can press the quill to the paper. "Choose me," I say. "Choose me as your champion."

He pauses and meets my eyes. His expression shifts from worry to resolution. "No. I won't have you involved in this. This is between me and my brother."

"But you know he's going to choose debate." My voice is a furious whisper. "The council has already accepted his word. What can you say to change their minds?"

"I have no need to change their minds," he mutters. "If they fail to see reason after I've said my piece, then the council can be damned, with all of Faerwyvae with it."

My hands ball into fists. "I can help you. You know I'm good with words. Name me your champion and we can wipe that grin off Cobalt's face."

He reaches a hand to my cheek, brushing his thumb along my jaw. "No, Evie. This is my mess. I'm going to clean it up on my own."

"But you're not alone anymore. You have me. I can do this."

He leans forward and brushes his lips to mine. "No."

I tense, and my lips don't respond to his. Anger flushes my cheeks as I glare at him. He can't just kiss me and tell me no. He can't just make this choice as if it has only to do with him. This isn't just his throne to lose. It's mine now too, and we will both suffer if this goes badly.

If Cobalt wins, Aspen dies.

I won't lose him. Not after we've come this far, fought this hard. Not when we were finally becoming something *more*.

"Aspen." The word escapes my lips, cold and powerful. Energy hums around us, as if the air between me and the king is sizzling, charged with lightning. It startles me, reminding me of the way I felt after we exchanged names. Again, I imagine a bridge, and we are the two cliffs it connects. In my mind, I cross that bridge, aware of the jagged rocks waiting hundreds of yards below. I don't know how I know to do this, but I do. "By the power of your true name, I order you to name me your champion."

His eyes widen, and it feels like an eternity that we stand locked beneath each other's gaze. Then he blinks. It's clear when he discovers what I've done, when the power of his name being used against him dawns on his realization. His face flashes with hurt, something close to fear dancing in his eyes. The expression remains for only a moment before he steels it behind a mask of indignation. "Is this what your vow is worth?" he says through his teeth. "When you promised you wouldn't use my name against me?"

"I had to," I say, trying to hide the tremors that seize me beneath his angry stare. My breath feels like it's been pulled from my lungs. *I'm doing this for both of us. Please understand.*

"Then you leave me no choice," he says with a snarl. He returns to the parchment and scrawls my name on it. He presses so hard, he pierces the paper in places. Then, below it, he signs his name. He doesn't meet my eyes when he gives the parchment to Nyxia, who folds it with her slender fingers.

With slow, elegant steps, she makes her way to the middle of the balcony and faces the council. She unfolds one sheet of parchment, then the other, reading each before holding them out for the council to see. "King Aspen has named Evelyn Fairfield his champion. Cobalt, on the other hand, will represent himself and has chosen a decision of fate."

I blink a few times, staring dumbfounded at the vampire. "A decision of fate? Not a presentation of factual debate?"

"You heard her correctly," Cobalt says, chin raised. "It's set in ink; you can see for yourself."

I round on Foxglove. "What in the name of iron is a decision of fate?"

He returns to wringing his hands, face pale. "I never thought he would choose it."

"What. Is. It?"

Foxglove's expression turns apologetic. "It's a matter of magic."

"Come, Evelyn," Cobalt says. "It's time to journey to the Twelfth Court."

40

"Twelfth Court," I echo, but no one seems to hear me. Cobalt makes his way to Aspen's throne, ignoring the shattered arm as he settles in. The council fae exchange excited whispers.

I turn to Aspen, but he doesn't meet my eyes. "Aspen, I—"

"Time to fight for my throne," he growls.

My throat feels tight at the ice in his tone. I turn to Foxglove. "What's happening? What is the Twelfth Court?"

"I told you," he says. "It's a matter of magic. The Twelfth Court isn't a true court, but a realm of magic that connects all courts. Going there is a rare thing, a sacred and dangerous excursion. Cobalt must trust his personal cause greatly to resort to such radical action."

"Don't worry," Lorelei says. "There's a chance you can win." However, the doubt on her face betrays her words.

"How?" I look from her to Foxglove. "I don't even believe in magic."

The two fae exchange an amused glance as if I've said something foolish. "You don't have to believe in a thing for it to be real," Foxglove says. "It can exist with or without your blessing, you know."

"Perhaps, but how am I supposed to win a battle using something I don't believe in?"

Lorelei shrugs. "How do you breathe every day? How do you sleep when you're tired? How do you perform surgery with your hands?"

I want to argue with her, to tell her the first two are controlled by the autonomic nervous system, and the latter is only done after years of training. But I hold my tongue, remembering the way time slowed down when I tended Aspen's wound. The way my hands knew what to do, what to feel for. There was something chilling and instinctual about it. Something I still don't understand.

"We're waiting," Cobalt calls.

I blanch, finding all eyes on me.

Foxglove gives me a gentle push toward the thrones. "Go. You can do this."

If only I knew what *this* was. With trembling steps, I make my way to the empty throne and lower myself into my seat. Foxglove and Lorelei stand next to me, a comforting presence at my side.

I take in the stares of my audience, unnerved beneath their scrutiny. Nyxia watches me with a curious expression, hands steepled at her waist. Behind her, the blue fae with the flowing hair lets out a windy hiss, while the white wolf pants, tongue lolling from between his teeth. The fae with horns and hooves scowls, and the orange fae with scales flicks his tongue at me several times. Melusine, on the other hand, refuses to look my way at all.

I shift my gaze to Cobalt's side of the balcony, where Amelie stands at the rail, looking as serene as ever. Even when she meets my eyes, her features remain unchanged. My gaze then roves to Aspen, still surrounded by Cobalt's guards. His eyes lock on mine. I try not to read too much into his expression, not sure I'll like what I find.

Silence falls over the balcony. I lean toward Foxglove. "What happens now?"

He bends toward me. "Next you and Cobalt travel to the Twelfth Court and petition the All of All."

I furrow my brow. "The All of All? Is that some god? Some deity?"

"The All of All is a culmination of all that is and all that is not."

"But what exactly is it? And how do I get to the Twelfth Court? I take it I won't find a door here on the balcony."

Foxglove shakes his head. "The Twelfth Court exists on its own axis, separate from the other courts, yet within them all at once. You can reach it from anywhere."

"How?"

"Enough chatter," Cobalt says. "Let's go."

"But I don't know—"

"If you can't figure it out, then you don't deserve to petition the All of All." With that, he faces forward and closes his eyes.

My pulse races, mind spinning as sweat beads at my brow. I can't do this. I was wrong when I made Aspen choose me as his champion. I don't know how to access an invisible court, how to petition some magical deity. I don't know what I'm doing, and I don't know how to get out of this. I messed up. Big time.

I feel a squeeze on my shoulder, Lorelei's fingers. I remember her words. *How do you breathe every day? How do you sleep when you're tired? How do you perform surgery with your hands?*

With a deep breath, I close my eyes, trying to shut out my fears, my worries, my regrets. I focus on the feel of my breath rushing through my nostrils, the sound of my blood pounding through my ears, the feel of my heart hammering in my chest. I summon my surgeon's calm, of hands that remain steady in crisis. I summon my fiery passion, the part of me that chose to open my heart to Aspen, to explore unknown parts of myself. I summon the mysteries I've yet to unfold, the instinct I felt when performing Aspen's surgery, the magic of a little girl putting her hands on the sick. I summon my mother's strength, her care, and my sister's reckless love.

My eyes flutter open, a calm warmth spreading over me. I'm not surprised by what I see, even though the vision before me looks unlike anything I've ever seen before. The balcony remains intact, but its shape is more liquid than solid, like particles of light weaving together to create a floor, bright glowing orbs of multi-hued radiance to represent the bodies in the audience. I turn my eyes to the sky, finding dark shades of violet and indigo swirling with other colors I can't put a name to.

Time isn't quite frozen, but it isn't what it was before. It's slow and fast, gentle and violent. This world is everywhere and nowhere at once. Oddly, the thought doesn't worry me. It makes perfect sense and no sense at all. I accept it.

A warm yellow light beckons me forward, and I leave my throne to follow it. I'm subtly aware that my body feels weightless, like I'm nothing more than one of the glowing orbs the council fae have become. I follow the light as it flutters away from me, down what used to be stairs, into a tunnel of swirling particles. The particles give way to darkness, with nothing to see but the light that leads me on and on.

The light stops just ahead and disappears, pitching me into a black void. My mind begins to sharpen, growing clearer. A violet speck of light begins to pulse in front of me, growing larger and larger, providing subtle illumination. I glance at my hands, aware that my body has returned to its familiar shape and density.

The speck of light becomes a violet sun. It rises overhead, beaming rays of warmth onto me. As it sets, a crescent moon takes its place and stars shoot across the sky. Violet clouds cover the moon and the sun returns, but my attention snags on something near my feet. Narrow stalks shoot from the ground and open into dazzling violet buds. The petals unfurl into flowers, then tower higher and higher. I walk through the enormous flowers, mesmerized, watching them sway in a warm breeze. The sun shines high overhead, warming my face.

When the sun sets, the flowers shiver and shake, petals dropping at my feet, each one as large as I am. I run forward, dodging the falling petals, spinning to avoid being pinned beneath them. Once the petals cease falling, the stalks begin to wrinkle and sag, then shrivel back down toward the ground. In the blink of an eye, there's nothing. Everything is smothered in a blanket of violet. Silence. Death.

A flash of panic rises inside me, and all I can think is to run. Escape the nothingness. Then suddenly, something sprouts from the nothingness. Then another. New blooms, born from death. Calm returns to me as I continue on, watching the cycle repeat around me, again and again. After a while, it no longer terrifies me when the nothingness returns.

As the petals unfurl yet again, I'm starting to wonder if this is all I'll see, if the Twelfth Court is nothing more than this endless cycle where seasons change and the sky shifts high above. Then a violent breeze sweeps by, blowing away the petals, the stalks, the ground beneath my feet, until only darkness remains. The wind swirls around me, pushing me on all sides, making me lose my balance. As I right myself, a figure stands before me. Like everything else here, she's composed of violet particles of light. Her long hair flows behind her, like the blue fae on the council. This fae, however, has the wings of a pixie.

"We get along well," she says with a mischievous grin.

"What do you mean?" My voice sounds strange in this place, like a version of me I've never heard before.

She taps the side of her head. "Thought. Intellect. You live your life in your head much of the time, yes?"

"I do, but...what does that mean?"

"It means the air in you is the air in me." With that, she disappears.

I'm left in darkness again. I take a few steps forward and see something up ahead. It's small, round. A rock? As I reach it, the rock seems to come to life. It rises on gnarled legs, then turns to face me.

A *goblin*. I leap back.

"I know you," he says with a snarl.

My breath hitches. Can it be? This goblin may be

violet, but he looks uncannily like the one that chased Amelie and me. "You!"

"Ah, you remember," he says. "Vile beasty, you are. Why are you here? Did my claws teach you nothing?"

"They taught me to fear your kind."

"Fear. Pah! You think you know fear? You scared my children. Nearly crushed their toes with your giant beasty boots when you came to *my* land."

"Your children?"

"Did you not see them playing near the rock? No, your beasty eyes were fixed elsewhere. No respect. No caution."

I think back to our excursion to the faewall that day. When we crossed the wall to the other side, I remember seeing nothing but fog. We were hardly on the fae side for more than a few seconds, but I admit, I hadn't considered our surroundings. I was so fueled with terrified excitement at the time. "I'm sorry if I scared your children, but you scared me and my sister. You glamoured her. You nearly bit her."

"Just a nibble," the goblin says. "A price for making my babies cry."

I furrow my brow. I don't know if I can forgive the goblin for the havoc he wreaked on me and Amelie, but I can understand his motivations, in a twisted sort of way. "I know what it's like to want to protect the ones you love. To fight for them."

"Safety. Security. Family," he says with a nod. "The earth in you is the earth in me."

The goblin disappears and darkness returns. I remain motionless, puzzling over the odd encounter. What is this place? Is any of this real? I continue on through the black nothing.

I take only a few steps before warmth envelops me. A ball of violet flame emerges from the black and floats around my head. I follow it with my eyes, watching as it undulates and grows, then takes the shape of a beautiful woman. Her hips sway as she dances around me, eying me with scrutiny.

"You think you're better than me," she says, voice light and sultry. "But we know each other well."

"Passion," I say with a shudder.

She nods, then lunges forward, feminine face shifting into a beastly snarl. "And rage." I pull back, but her snarl dissipates into a trilling laugh. "That, you know well. The other, you are just getting to know."

"Yes." This time, I know what to say. "The fire in you is the fire in me."

She winks, then disappears.

I take off into the darkness again, eager to finish this strange quest. I need to find the All of All, not these mischievous fae. How do I find this deity? The thought is barely finished before something emerges from the ground. It begins as a bead of violet water and grows, rippling into the form of a hulking horse-creature.

Kelpie. Of course.

The creature bares its teeth at me. "Twice you have gotten away. You won't escape three times."

"I won't bargain with you this time."

"No? Isn't there somewhere you are meaning to go?"

I try my best to steady my nerves. None of the previous three fae were anywhere near as terrifying as the kelpie. "I am looking for the All of All."

"You are lost," he says. "Stupid human, invading places that are not your own and getting lost on the way."

"I'm not lost," I say. "Looking isn't necessarily lost. I'm simply on my way somewhere that I have yet to find."

"Sounds like lost."

I take a deep breath, remembering what the kelpie said when he confronted me and Aspen. "I'm sorry my kind have invaded your land, and I'm sorry humans infuriate you. You love your land, your water."

"Fury and love are human emotions."

"Yet you have them just the same," I say. "Admit it. You're angry that I've escaped you twice. Anger is an emotion."

The kelpie's violet eyes burn brighter.

"You are more than just an animal. You feel emotion."

"I don't."

"You do, and I understand wanting to deny that. I too have denied emotions before." I think about how I suppressed my tears after I thought Amelie had died, how I refused to recognize my attraction to Aspen.

"Humans can deny them?" His tone is curious.

"Yes, but it doesn't make them go away." I take another deep breath. "The water in you is the water in me."

I expect the violet kelpie to disappear like the others, but it doesn't. He just stands there, considering me. Perhaps I wasn't convincing enough. Finally, he lets out a slow hiss like a sigh. "I will take you to the All of All."

I hesitate. "I told you, I won't bargain with you again."

"If you are not lost, I will not require a bargain."

I watch him for a few moments, seeking hints of deception. Logic is telling me not to trust the kelpie, but my heart feels calm. "Fine," I say and climb upon the kelpie's back. Steadying my hands on the creature's neck, we take off into the darkness. Time swirls around us, racing and reversing. Hours pass. Seconds pass. No time at all has passed.

Before I know it, I am on my feet, and the kelpie is nowhere to be seen. I'm again in the black void. A voice speaks into my mind, but it sounds like no voice I've ever heard before. It's quiet and loud, powerful and meek. "You seek us."

"Are you the All of All?" My voice sounds harsh against the emptiness, returning no echo, no resonance.

"We are the All of All," the voice says. "What are you?"

"Human," is all I can think to say. "I am petitioning on behalf of King Aspen for the Autumn Court throne."

"What is it you offer us?"

My mind goes blank. No one said anything about an offering. Besides, what could I possibly have to offer all that is and all that is not? I'm nothing special, have nothing special. Cobalt has lies, words, conviction, passion. I have those things too, but how could mine compare to his? What do I have that he has not? "I...I don't know."

Silence.

I begin to tremble.

"You can offer us a look at your heart," the All of All says. "If your heart is true, we will allow your petition to pass. Do you agree?"

I swallow hard. "Yes." With a jolt, a ball of violet light escapes my chest to hover in the air before me. Images swirl inside it, memories. I see myself, Amelie, Mother. I watch myself giggle and laugh, then scream and cry. I watch as I hug Mother, then shout hurtful words at her. I see myself turn my nose at the sight of Maddie Coleman, watch as I help Mr. Meeks perform an amputation. The violet ball goes still, then shifts. It's Aspen's face I see now. I see myself shouting at him, ignoring his smiles, his jests, his flirtations. Then I watch as I fold myself into his arms, lips pressing into his. I watch as I face him as a stag, hand outstretched as I give him my name. Then I see myself on the balcony, using that very name against him.

The violet light goes still again, then lurches back into my chest. Panic seizes me. There's no way the All of All will allow my petition to pass after seeing all of that.

"Your heart has darkness," the All of All says. "It also holds light. It is smooth and rough, holds hate and love. It is both a wild beast and a tame creature."

There's no use denying it. "Yes."

"This is a true heart."

Surprise ripples through me. "It is?"

"There is magic inside it. Things you don't yet understand. Things you will explore."

I nod.

"We have made our decision." Before I can respond, the darkness explodes into thousands of particles of violet light. It surges around me, pushing me back. The breath is stripped from my lungs as I lurch through the void, feeling it rushing past me as I'm tossed backward.

With a lurch, I slam into the back of my throne. I open my eyes, meeting the astonished faces of the council. A collective gasp roars through them. I feel a hand on my shoulder and meet the wide eyes of Lorelei. Foxglove covers his mouth with his hand, gaze sliding to my brow.

That's when I feel the weight on my forehead. I reach a hand, finding something firm surrounding my skull like a...a crown.

I lift it from my head and find a gold circlet decorated with strange, swaying feathers. Or perhaps leaves. It's delicate and exquisite and breathtaking all at once. My eyes find Aspen's. His expression is equally as awed as everyone else's.

"No," Cobalt says with a gasp as he rises to his feet from the throne. "How?"

I ignore him, brushing past him and Nyxia and the dumbfounded sea fae guards toward Aspen. When I reach the king, I bow and hand him the crown. "The All of All has chosen."

He takes the crown from me, turns it over in his hands as he inspects it. I expect him to place it on himself, and for a moment, it looks like he expects the same. But he freezes, then places the crown back on my head. "I think this belongs to you," he whispers.

I rise from my bow, puzzling over his actions. His furrowed brow tells me he isn't quite sure about them himself.

Aspen turns and faces the council, raising his voice for all to hear. "The All of All has chosen my champion as the winner of the decision of fate. My challenge to the throne has been heard, judged, and decided. I am King of Autumn." He turns his gaze on Cobalt. "And you, dear brother, are charged with treason."

41

"No!" Cobalt shouts. He points at the crown on my head. "That crown means nothing. It's no gift from the All of All."

Aspen nods at Queen Nyxia. "As mediator, the ruling is yours."

The vampire looks caught off guard for a moment, gaze moving from Aspen to Cobalt. Finally, her eyes settle on me. "The All of All have spoken. The crown is their answer."

"She could have stolen the crown," Cobalt argues. "The All of All would never choose her over me."

Aspen lifts his hand, signaling toward his brother. "Guards, seize him."

The armored fae race toward Cobalt, swords and spears drawn as they charge him. With a hiss, Cobalt shudders and shifts into his nix form, blue scales glistening in the moonlight. He points at his sea fae. "Take them down."

The sea fae tear across the floor to meet the guards,

while a few anxious council fae dart to the perimeter of the balcony, Melusine among them. Others roar to join the battle against the sea fae. With a shudder, Queen Nyxia shifts into a towering shadow with red eyes and sharp teeth. The blue wind fae floats off the floor and turns into a puff of mist as she swirls around the sea fae, lifting Cobalt's guards from the floor and tossing them off the side of the balcony. The white wolf sinks his teeth into a scaly blue leg, eliciting a shout of pain. The fae with curling horns slams his fist into a sea fae's head. The orange fae with scales stands close to the battle but doesn't join, merely watching with mild curiosity.

I hear the sound of crashing waves and turn to look over the balcony. The water is rising from the sea to impossible heights, leaping against the side of the palace, lapping over the balcony rail, catching those who've fallen.

I return my attention to the chaos of the balcony as a flash of blue darts toward the rail. Aspen follows, taking Cobalt by the shoulder and forcing his brother to face him. I see them lock in battle before the spray of a wave hits me in the face. When I open my eyes, Aspen is leaning over the rail, looking down. A flicker of movement catches my attention to the left, a mass of gray-brown fur.

"Amelie!" I run toward her, and she freezes. Her selkie skin has enveloped her body from the neck down. All that remains is her face. The head of the seal rests on her brow, and she seems seconds away from pulling it down. I close the distance between us, putting my arms where her shoulders should be. "Amelie, don't you dare leave me."

Her green eyes glaze with tears. "I have to go."

"No you don't. Shed the skin. We'll keep you safe from Cobalt."

Her expression hardens. "I don't want to be kept safe from him. He's mine and I am his."

I stumble to find my words. "That's just the glamour talking. Stay with me. Please."

"I can't." She pulls the seal's face over hers, then drops to her belly, hobbling toward the rail. I reach for her, feel my arms close around her slick fur as another crashing wave pummels me.

When I open my eyes, Amelie is gone.

I run to the rail, staring over it, but all I see is the raging ocean. Waves spray up the side of the palace, into the open windows. There's no sign of my sister. Still, I continue to watch, seeking any sign of her. I don't leave the rail, not even when the waves calm and subside. Not even when the water levels recede to normal, as if nothing had happened at all.

"They're gone," Aspen says, coming up beside me. "Cobalt, your sister, my brother's guards. All his sea fae leapt over the rail."

I continue watching the sea, not sure what I'm hoping for. Amelie left. She chose Cobalt. All I've ever wanted was to protect her. Keep her safe. Even now, I want nothing more than to save her from Cobalt's clutches. But what do I do if she doesn't want saving?

Aspen puts a hand on my lower back. "Let's go," he says. "You're shaking."

He's right. I'm racked with tremors, partially from the cold water dripping from my body, partially from my suppressed sobs. Finally, I pull away from the rail and let him guide me back inside the palace. Once we reach the hall, it's no surprise how much is flooded. I imagine the entire west portion of the palace will be a sodden mess, not to mention broken windows and damaged furnishings.

Aspen's guards flank us, the council fae walking just ahead. A few seem dazed, while others are chatting animatedly, as if they'd just returned from a fascinating play. The white wolf pads down the hall, blood dripping from his muzzle. Nyxia strolls at a leisurely pace, chin lifted as if without a care. Melusine, of course, slithers down the slick hall with ease, shoulders squared. Another fae, a female with golden-brown skin, honey-colored hair, and enormous yellow butterfly wings turns to face us. She pauses until we reach her side.

"King Aspen," she says with a bow of her head. "I will lend you my weather until Bircharbor can dry out."

Aspen nods. "Thank you, Queen Dahlia. We will accept your generosity."

She hesitates before moving on, eyes resting on the crown above my brow. Then, with an exaggerated smile, she flits away.

"Who is she?" I ask, once she's out of earshot.

"The Queen of the Summer Court," he says, a growl in his voice. "It's going to be an effort to speak to any of them like they didn't nearly strip me from my throne."

Nearly. They had, in fact, stripped him *completely* from his throne. It was only his challenge to Cobalt that won it back, and even that had nearly been thwarted. How would it have gone if I hadn't forced Aspen to name me his champion? Would Aspen have succeeded in petitioning the All of All? It's impossible to know.

Only one thing is clear. I betrayed Aspen when I used his true name like that, regardless of how things turned out. I'll never forget the look on his face when he realized I'd shattered his trust. It showed me something else too; I still don't trust Aspen. Not fully, at least. If I had, I would have let him make his own decision. I would have believed he had what it took to defeat Cobalt.

"King Aspen," says a sultry male voice, stealing my attention.

The orange fae with scales stands before us. His body is long and lean, dressed in a modern black suit, neck slightly longer and slimmer than a human neck would be. He has no hair, just more iridescent orange scales. His face is mostly flat with a lipless mouth, slits where his nose should be, and beady black eyes.

"King Ustrin." Aspen gives the fae a short bow.

The scaly king returns it, bending at the waist. "Congratulations on winning back your throne. It seems your mate here is quite accomplished."

"I'm very grateful for her," Aspen says, although the edge in his tone isn't lost on me.

King Ustrin's eyes move to me. "Might I have a word, Miss Fairfield?"

I look from Aspen to the orange fae. Would it be rude of me to say no? There's something unsettling about the lizard-like king that has to do with more than just his odd appearance. I summon my calm. "Of course, Your Majesty."

Aspen hesitates before pointing at two of his guards then at me. The guards break off from the rest and stand behind me. "We'll speak later," he whispers, but I can't read his tone. "I need to see the council fae off." Then, without so much as looking at me, he moves on, following the flock of fae.

King Ustrin regards me through slitted lids but says nothing.

Perhaps he's waiting for me to bow, so I do. After I rise, he remains silent. "Might I ask what court you rule, King Ustrin?"

"Fire," he says. His eyes slide to the crown on my brow. "A curious crown the All of All gave you. Why did the king gift it to you instead of keeping it for himself?"

Not even I know that answer. Still, I refuse to admit it. "I will be his queen once we're married, and he already has a crown of his own. He must have wanted to show his appreciation for me winning him back the throne."

"Yes, yes, that does make sense." He takes a step forward and sniffs the air, much like Melusine had done. His tongue darts in and out of his mouth. "You're familiar."

I recall the fae I encountered in the Twelfth Court, how they sought similar elements between us. "The fire in you is the fire in me."

He laughs, a low hissing sound, tongue flicking. "I suppose that's true. But there's something else. A certain...feel about you. Like that of an old enemy."

I bristle. This isn't going anywhere like I hoped. Then again, what else was I expecting? I still know very little about the fae, about their politics and biases. I'm only just now getting to understand the Autumn Court. Other courts are far beyond my familiarity.

Time to take control.

I square my shoulders and adopt Aspen's bored tone. "King Ustrin, I do thank you for introducing yourself to me, and it's been a pleasant chat. However, I've had a long day. Forgive me for cutting our acquaintance short, but I must get some rest."

He smirks, narrowing his eyes, but makes no argument. "Of course. How careless of me. You did just win a battle, after all. We'll speak again, I'm sure." With a bow, he lowers himself, then turns away.

I let out a heavy breath once he's at the far end of the hall.

A hand falls on my shoulder, making me jump, but it's just Lorelei. "Come on. You should clean up and get some sleep."

I nod, and Lorelei leads the way. The guards follow closely behind. It isn't far until we reach the door to Aspen's bedroom, and I can't help but fear it's been destroyed. The floor beneath my feet is slick with water, but at least it isn't flooded. The room itself is on the east side of the palace, so there's a good chance it might be salvageable.

The guards push open the door, and Lorelei and I step inside. The orb lights burn low in their sconces, but from what I can tell, the room has remained mostly unscathed. Water seems to reach only a quarter of the way across the floor, soaking a few rugs. But the bed, the wardrobe, and everything on the far wall appears dry.

I turn to the guards. "I'll bathe now."

"We should leave the doors open," says one of the guards.

I'm about to argue when I remember the hidden door Amelie had opened. The secret tunnels could very well connect to many other rooms like this one and were likely how Cobalt was able to get to the Holstrom girls, how he was able to sneak Amelie out of the palace the night she disappeared. For all I know, he could be lurking in those tunnels now. Watching. Waiting. I shudder. "Very well."

"We'll set up the tub behind the dressing screen," Lorelei says. I follow her to the tub, help her drag the dressing screen in front of it to hide it from the view of the hall. The tub is empty, and just looking at it makes my muscles hunger for relief. Lorelei takes a step away. "I'll put in the order—"

Before she can finish, the tub suddenly fills with hot, steaming water. Herbs and flower buds float over the top, the scent of rosemary wafting upward. My mouth falls open. All I can do is stare.

Lorelei laughs. "Your mate must have great foresight regarding you."

"You think he did this?" I look beneath the tub, trying to find the pipes and drains I've never been able to locate. "How? It came out of nowhere."

"As king, Aspen can perform minor manipulations over all the elements. But he gets earth and water from his parents. This," she waves her hand over the tub, "is easy for him. I mean, it's easy for any of the water fae employed here too, but I have a feeling he had a hand in this one."

I still can't piece it together. Aspen isn't anywhere close to this bedroom right now, nor is there any source for the water. It makes my temples throb to consider that maybe, just *maybe*, magic is real.

I think of everything I experienced today. The journey to the Twelfth Court. The crown I brought back. The way I was able to use Aspen's name. There could be a scientific explanation. The Twelfth Court could have been the result of a hallucination. Aspen's response to me using his name could have been from superstition and cultural conditioning.

Yesterday's magic is today's science.

Perhaps decades from now it will all make logical sense. Perhaps one day I'll understand what happened. Someday I'll understand how I healed Lorelei's leg, how I performed a surgery on instinct alone. Maybe someday I'll be able to explain how a crystalline tub with no plumbing can fill instantaneously with water. But today... today there's only one thing I can say about it.

It's magic.

42

I jolt awake, sitting upright in bed. What woke me? Aside from the nightmares, of course. Night after night I dream my lungs are filling with water, that sea monsters are hunting me, nipping my heels as I try to swim away.

But I don't think that's what it was this time.

My heart races, body trembling from its pulse. Or is it the room that's shaking? I look at the space next to me on the bed. I'm not surprised to find it empty. It's been three days since Aspen won back his throne, and I've hardly seen him since. Every move I make to try and talk to him is brushed aside with excuses. He's too busy. He has to oversee the repairs of the palace. He has correspondences to send. He certainly hasn't stepped foot in his bedroom. Still, my heart plummets with disappointment.

Will he ever stop avoiding me?

Another tremor rattles through me, and this time I know the room is shaking. I fling myself out of bed, run to the wardrobe, and extract a robe. Pulling the robe around my nightdress, I tear from the bedroom. Aspen's guards stand at attention when they see me. "What's going on?"

One of the guards steps forward. "The king is sealing off the coral caves that connect to the palace," she says.

"How? With explosives?"

"Yes."

My eyes widen. "Take me to him."

She hesitates. "It's not safe—"

I put my hands on my hips. "Take me to him now. Please."

She leads me down the hall and stairs, then stops outside the entrance to the dining room. I round the corner and step inside. Aspen stands at the far end, looking out the open expanse, hands on the rail. He's dressed in cream and gold, but his waistcoat is wrinkled, blue-black hair tousled between his antlers. Warm summer air— thanks to Queen Dahlia—wafts through the opening, making the room stifling hot. I wish I'd brought a lighter robe.

As I approach the king, another rumble rocks the palace, and I see a spray of water shoot into the sky. "Aspen, what in the name of iron is going on."

"Destroying the caves." He doesn't turn to face me, just keeps his gaze fixed on the scene outside. I follow his line of vision and see numerous guards on the beach. The tide is out, exposing several entrances to the coral caves. Half of them appear collapsed, filled with shards of coral. The guards are filling an open cave with what looks like kegs of gunpowder.

"Isn't there a safer way to do this?"

He shakes his head. "I must be sure Cobalt has no way of sneaking into the palace. When he returns, he'll have to face me head on."

When he returns. There's no doubt in his voice that it will come to pass, and I can't say I disagree with him. The prince already went so far as to manipulate my sister, me, the Holstrom girls, the council...why would he stop now? Besides, we don't know how many council fae are his loyal allies.

Another explosion has me gripping the rail for stability, and I grit my teeth until it passes. "Aspen, we need to talk."

"I have work to do."

I cross my arms over my chest, angling my body toward him. He still won't meet my eyes. "No, we need to talk. Now. I'm tired of this wall between us. Our wedding is supposed to be in three days. *Three days,* Aspen."

"Everything has already been prepared," he says. "It will continue without issue."

"Not if you blow up the palace before then."

"I'm not going to blow up the palace."

"Are you going to use explosives to seal the tunnels between the rooms too? Blow open the walls? Put my life in danger without saying a word to me?"

He rounds on me, eyes blazing. "I'm trying to protect you."

"Protect me? You've hardly looked at me in days. Is this what it's going to be like when we're married? Are you going to hold what I did against me forever?"

He holds my gaze, and his mask of fury begins to slip. Vulnerability peeks through, a shadow of the hurt I caused him. "You broke a promise," he whispers.

I try not to tremble beneath that look in his eyes. I've been preparing for this conversation for days, but it doesn't make it any easier. With a deep breath, I steel myself. "I'm sorry that I used your name against you. I should have trusted you to win against Cobalt."

His posture begins to relax. "Yes, you should have."

"But *you* should have considered my request."

He grumbles and turns away from me. "Some apology."

I pull his sleeve, but he won't look at me. "This is what I mean. If we are going to be married, I want you to listen to me. Consider the things I say."

He faces me again. "I did consider what you said when you asked me to name you my champion, and the answer was no. Is that what life is going to be like together? Are you going to use my name against me every time you don't get your way?"

I feel a wave of fury rising inside me, but I breathe it away, finding my calm. "That's not going to happen all the time," I say. "I can promise you that. But I can't promise I'll never use your name again. Not if I think it will save you."

Aspen's expression shifts between steely and soft, eyes locked on mine.

I reach for his hands, holding them tight as another explosion rocks the ground beneath us. "I'm not going to lose you, Aspen. I thought you were going to die if I didn't force your hand. Perhaps I was being brash to make you name me your champion, but I don't regret doing it. I'll do it again if I think it will save your life. All I can do now is ask for your forgiveness."

He closes his eyes and lowers his head. "I've never

been terrified of anyone the way I'm terrified of you. You have the power to use my name. The power to control me. The power to break my heart."

I let go of one of his hands to touch his face, fingers trailing his jaw. "So do you. But didn't you say that's what the Bond is about? Mutual fear and respect?"

He opens his eyes. "Yes, but I want more than that."

My breath hitches at the intensity of his stare. "What is it you want?"

He says nothing, just lowers his lips to mine in a soft kiss. I lean into him and wrap my arms around his waist. I think I know what the kiss is telling me, words we've yet to exchange. These words may not hold the power that the Bond holds, but they mean more than our names. I pull my lips away from his, but our bodies remain pressed together. "Aspen, I—"

"Your Majesty."

With a startle, Aspen and I separate and face Foxglove. His hands tremble, making the envelope he holds within them quiver as well.

Aspen darts toward him. "What is it?"

Foxglove hands Aspen the envelope. I can see the seal has already been broken. But what snags my attention more is the seal itself—an elegant scrolling *E* etched in the wax. *Eisleigh's crest.* Foxglove wrings his hands. "The human council has invalidated your pairing. You are no longer eligible to secure the pact."

Aspen tears the letter from the envelope, scans it with wide eyes. He lowers the paper and slowly meets my gaze. "The treaty is broken."

Another blast from outside shakes the ground

beneath us, matched only by the pounding of my heart. My lungs feel tight, breaths shallow as I try to comprehend Aspen's words. If the treaty is broken...

I swallow hard. "We're going to war."

ABOUT THE AUTHOR

Tessonja Odette is fantasy author living in Seattle with her family, her pets, and ample amounts of chocolate. When she isn't writing, she's watching cat videos, petting dogs, having dance parties in the kitchen with her daughter, or pursuing her many creative hobbies. Read more about Tessonja at www.tessonjaodette.com

ALSO BY TESSONJA ODETTE

CPSIA information can be obtained
at www.ICGtesting.com
Printed in the USA
LVHW030106281021
701775LV00001B/26

9 780578 688046